# WEEKEND WARRIORS
# &
# PAYBACK

**Also by Fern Michaels . . .**

# FERN MICHAELS

## WEEKEND WARRIORS & PAYBACK

ZEBRA BOOKS
KENSINGTON PUBLISHING CORP.
http://www.kensingtonbooks.com

ZEBRA BOOKS are published by

Kensington Publishing Corp.
850 Third Avenue
New York, NY 10022

Printed in the United States of America

ISBN: 0-7394-5720-9

# CONTENTS

# WEEKEND
# WARRIORS

# Prologue

The traffic was horrendous on Massachusetts Avenue, but then it was always horrendous at this time of day. Rush hour. God, how she hated those words. Especially today. She slapped the palm of her hand on the horn and muttered under her breath, "C'mon you jerk, move!"

"Take it easy, Nik," Barbara Rutledge said, her eyes on the slow moving traffic. "One more block and we're there. Mom won't mind if we're a few minutes late. She hates it that she turned sixty today so the longer she has to wait for the celebration, the better she'll feel. I don't think she looks sixty, do you Nik?"

"Are you kidding! She looks better than we do and we're only thirty-six." She leaned on the horn again even though it was an exercise in futility. "Just tell me one thing, why did your mother pick the Jockey Club for dinner?"

"The first crab cakes of the season, that's why. President Reagan made this restaurant famous and all her political friends come here. If you want my opinion, thirty bucks for two crab cakes is obscene. I can eat lunch all week on thirty bucks if I'm careful. Mom pitched a fit last week when I took her to Taco Bell for lunch. We both ate for five bucks. She was a good sport about it but she can't understand why I don't tap into the trust fund. I keep telling her I want to make it on my own. Some days she understands, some days she doesn't. I know she's proud of me, you, too, Nik. She tells everyone about her two crime fighting girls who are lawyers."

"I love her as much as you do, Barb. I can't imagine growing up without a mother. I would have if she hadn't stepped in and taken over when my parents died. Okay, we're here and we're only thirty minutes late. This isn't the best parking spot in the world but it will have to do and we're under a streetlight. In this city it doesn't get any better than that."

"We really should hit the powder room before we head for the table. Mom does like spit and polish, not to mention perfume and lipstick," Barbara said, trying to smooth the wrinkles out of her suit. Nik did the same thing.

"I spent the day in court and so did you. We're supposed to look wrinkled, messy and harried. Myra will understand. Ooops, almost forgot my present," Nik said, reaching into the backseat for a small silver-wrapped package. She handed Barbara a long cylinder tied with a bright red ribbon. "Your brain must be as tired as mine. You almost forgot yours, too. What about this pile of books, Barb?"

"They're for Mom. I picked them up today at lunchtime. You know how she loves reading about murder and mayhem. I'll give them to her when we leave."

Myra Rutledge was waiting, a beautiful woman whose smile and open arms welcomed them. "My girls are here. We're ready to be seated now, Franklin," Myra said.

"Certainly, madam. Your usual table, or would you prefer the smoking section with a window view?"

"The window, Franklin," Barbara said. "I think tonight in honor of my mother's birthday you two can have a cigarette. Just one cigarette after dinner for both of you. I will of course abstain. Yes, yes, yes, I know we all quit but this is Mom's birthday and I say why not."

Myra smiled as she reached for her daughter's hand. "Why not indeed."

"This is so wonderful," Myra said, sitting down and leaning across the table. "My two favorite girls. I couldn't ask for a better finale to my birthday."

"Finale, Mom! Does that mean when you go home, you and Charles won't celebrate?"

"Well . . . I . . . perhaps a glass of sherry. I did ask Charles to come but he said this was a mother daughter dinner and he would feel out of place. No comments, girls."

"Mom, when are you going to marry the guy? You've been together for twenty years. Nik and I know all about the birds and the bees so stop blushing," Barbara teased.

"Yes and it was Charles who told you two about the birds and the bees," Myra smiled.

Charles Emery was Myra's companion slash houseman. When his cover was blown as an MI 6 agent his government had relocated him to the United States where he'd signed on as head of security for Myra's Fortune 500 candy business. His sole goal in life was to take care of Myra, a job he took seriously and did well. Both girls were grateful to his attention to Myra, lessening her loneliness when they went off on their own.

Myra's eyes sparkled. "Now, tell me everything. Your latest cases, who you're dating at the moment, how our softball team is doing. Don't leave anything out. Will I be planning a wedding any time soon?"

It was what Nikki loved about Myra the most, her genuine interest in their lives. She'd never invaded their privacy, always content to stand on the sidelines, offer motherly support and aid when needed but she never interfered, or gave advice unless asked. Nikki knew Myra enjoyed the times the three of them spent together, loved the twice-monthly dinners in town and the occasional lunches with her daughter or perhaps a short stroll along the Tidal Basin.

Yes, Myra had a life, a busy life, a life of her own beyond her girls. She sat on various charitable boards, worked tirelessly for both political parties, did numerous good deeds every day, was active in the Historical Society and still managed to have time for Charles, Barbara and herself.

"You staying in town tonight, Mom?"

A rosy hue marched across Myra's face. "No, Barbara, I'm going home. No, I didn't drive myself. I took a car service so don't fret about the trip to McLean. Charles is waiting for me. I told you, we'll have a glass of sherry together."

"No birthday cake!" Nik said.

The rosy hue crept down Myra's neck. "We had the cake at lunchtime. Charles needed a blowtorch to light all the candles. All sixty of them. It was very . . . festive."

"How does it feel to be sixty, Mom?" Barbara asked reaching for her mother's hand across the table. "You told me you were dreading the day."

"It's just a number, just a day. I don't feel any different than I did yesterday. People always talk about 'the moments' in their lives. The special times they never forget. I guess this day is one of those moments. The day I married your father was a special moment. The day you were born was an extra special moment, the day Nikki came to us was another special moment and then of course when the candy company went 500. Don't laugh at me now when I tell you the other special moment was when Charles said he would take care of me for the rest of my life. All wonderful moments. I hope I have years and years of special moments. If you would get married and give me a grandchild I would run up the flag, Barbara. I don't want to be so old I dodder when you give birth."

Nikki poked Barbara's arm, a huge smile on her face. "Go on, tell her. Make your mother happy on her sixtieth birthday."

"I'm pregnant, Mom. You can start planning the wedding, but you better make it quick or I'll be showing before you know it."

Myra looked first at Nikki to see if they were teasing her or not. Nikki's head bobbed up and down. "I'm going to be the maid of honor and the godmother! She's not teasing, Myra."

"Oh, honey. Are you happy? Of course you are. All I have to do is look at you. Oh, there is so much to do. You want the reception at home in the garden, right?"

"Absolutely, Mom. I want to be married in the living room. I want to slide down the bannister in my wedding gown. I'm going to do that, Mom. Nik will be right behind me. If I can't do that, the wedding is off."

"Anything you want, honey. Anything. You have made me the happiest woman in the whole world. Promise that you will allow Charles and me to babysit."

"She promised me first," Nikki grinned.

"This is definitely 'a moment.' Do either of you have a camera?"

"Mom, a camera is not something I carry around in my purse. However, all is not lost. Nik has one in her car. I'll scoot over there and get it."

Nikki fished in her pocket and tossed her the keys.

"I'm going to be a mother. Me! Do you believe it? You'll be Auntie Nik," Barbara said, bending over to tweak Nikki's cheek. I'll ask Franklin to take our picture when I get back. See ya," she said flashing them both an ear-to-ear grin.

"I hope you had a good day, today, Myra. Birthdays are always special," Nikki said, her gaze on the window opposite her chair. "Knowing you're going to be a grandmother has to be the most wonderful thing in the world. I'm pretty excited myself." She could see Barbara running across the street, her jacket flapping in the spring breeze. "Do you remember the time Barbara and I made you a birthday cake out of cornflakes, crackers and pancake syrup?"

"I'll never forget it. I don't think the cook ever forgot it either. I did eat it, though."

Nikki laughed. "Yes, you did." She was glad now she had parked under the streetlight. She could see several couples walking down the street, saw Barbara open the back door of the car, saw her reach for the camera, saw her sling it over her shoulder, saw her lock the door. She turned her attention to Myra, who was also staring out the window. Nikki's gaze swiveled back to the window to see Barbara look both ways for oncoming traffic, ready to sprint across the street at the first break. The three couples were almost upon her when she stepped off the curb.

Nikki was aware of the dark car that came out of nowhere, the sound of horns blowing and the sudden screech of brakes. Myra was moving off her seat almost in slow motion, her face a mask of disbelief as they both ran out of the restaurant. The scream when it came was so tortured, so animal-like, Nikki stopped in her tracks to reach for Myra's arm.

The awkward position of her friend's body was a picture that would stay with Nikki forever. She bent down, afraid to touch her friend, the friend she called sister. "Did anyone call an ambulance?" she shouted. She heard a loud, jittery response. "Yes."

"No! No! No!" Myra screamed over and over as she dropped to the ground to cradle her daughter's body in her arms. From somewhere off in the distance, a siren could be heard. Nikki's trembling fingers fumbled for a pulse. Her whole body started to shake when she couldn't find even a faint beat. Maybe she wasn't doing it right. She pressed harder with her third and fourth fingers the way she'd seen nurses do. A wave of dizziness riveted through her just as the ambulance crew hit the ground running. Tears burned her eyes as she watched the paramedics check Barbara's vital signs.

Time lost all meaning as the medical crew did what they were trained to do. A young woman with long curly hair raised her head to look straight at Nikki. Her eyes were sad when she shook her head.

It couldn't be. She wanted to shout, to scream, to stamp her feet. Instead, she knuckled her eyes and stifled her sobs.

"She'll be all right, won't she Nikki? Broken bones heal. She was just knocked unconscious. Tell me she'll be all right. Please, tell me that. Please, Nikki."

The lump in Nikki's throat was so large she thought she would choke. She tried not to look at the still body, tried not to see them straighten out Barbara's arms and legs. When they lifted her onto the stretcher, she closed her eyes. She thought she would lose it when the young woman with the long curly hair pulled a sheet up over her best friend's face. Not Barbara. Not her best friend in the whole world. Not the girl she played with in a sandbox, gone to kindergarten with. Not the girl she'd gone through high school, college and law school with. She was going to be her maid of honor, babysit her baby. How could she be dead? "I saw her look both ways before she stepped onto the curb. She had a clear path to cross the street," she mumbled.

"Nikki, should we ride in the ambulance with Barbara? Will they let us?" Myra asked tearfully.

*She doesn't know. She doesn't know what the sheet means.* How was she going to tell Myra her daughter was dead?

The ambulance doors closed. It drove off. The siren silent.

"It's too late. They left. You'll have to drive, Nikki. They'll need all sorts of information when they admit her to the hospital. I want to be there. Barbara needs to know I'm there. She needs to know her mother is there. Can we go now, Nikki?" Myra pleaded.

"Ma'am?"

"Yes, officer," Nikki said. She loosened her hold on Myra's shoulders.

His voice was not unkind. He was too young to be this kind. She could see the compassion on his face.

"I need to take a statement. You are . . ."

"Nicole Quinn. This is Myra Rutledge. She's the mother . . ." She almost said, "of the deceased," but bit her tongue in time.

"Officer, can we do this later?" Myra interjected. "I have to get to the hospital. There will be so much paperwork to take care of. Do you know which hospital they took my daughter to? Was it George Washington or Georgetown Hospital?" Myra begged. Tears rolled down her wrinkled cheeks.

Nikki looked away. She knew she was being cowardly, but there was just no way she could get the words past her lips to tell Myra her only daughter was dead. She watched as police officers dispersed the crowd of onlookers until only the three couples remained. Where was the car that hit Barbara? Did they take it away already? Where was the driver? She wanted to voice the questions aloud but remained silent because of Myra.

Nikki watched as the young officer steeled himself for what he had to do. He worked his thin neck around the starched collar of his shirt, cleared his throat once, and then again. "Ma'am, your daughter was taken to the morgue at George Washington Hospital. There's no hurry on the paperwork. I can have one of the officers take you to the hospital if you like. I'm . . . I'm sorry for your loss, ma'am."

Myra's scream was primal as she slipped to the ground. The

young cop dropped to his knees. "I thought she knew. I didn't . . . Jesus . . ."

"We need to get her to a doctor right away. Will you stay with her for a minute, officer? I need to get my cell phone out of the car to make some calls." Her first call was to Myra's doctor and then she called Charles. Both promised to meet her at the emergency entrance to GW Hospital.

When she returned, Myra was sitting up, supported by the young officer. She looked dazed and her speech was incoherent. "She doesn't weigh much. I can easily carry her to the cruiser," the officer said. Nikki nodded gratefully.

"Can you tell me what happened, officer? Did you get the car that hit Barbara? Those couples standing over there must have seen everything. We even saw it from the restaurant window. Did they get the license plate number? I saw a dark car, but it came out of nowhere. She had a clear path to cross the street. He must have peeled away from the curb at ninety miles an hour."

"I ran the license plate one of the couples gave us, but it isn't going to do any good."

"Why is that?" Nikki rubbed at her temples as a hammer pounded away inside her head.

"Because it was a diplomat's car. That means the driver has diplomatic immunity, ma'am."

Nikki's knees buckled. The young cop reached out to steady her.

"That means he can't be prosecuted," Nikki said in a choked voice.

"Yes, ma'am, that's exactly what it means."

# Chapter One

*Sixteen months later*

It was dusk when Nikki Quinn stopped her cobalt-blue BMW in front of the massive iron gates of Myra Rutledge's McLean estate. She pressed the remote control attached to the visor and waited for the lumbering gates to slide open. She knew Charles was watching her on the closed-circuit television screen. The security here at the estate was sophisticated, high-tech, impregnable. The only thing missing was concertina wire along the top of the electrified fence.

Nikki sailed up the half mile of cobblestones to the driveway that led around to the back of the McLean mansion. When she was younger, she and Barbara referred to the house as Myra's Fortress. She'd loved growing up here, loved riding across the fields on Barbara's horse Starlite, loved playing with Barbara in the tunnels underneath the old house that had once been used to aid runaway slaves.

The engine idling, Nikki made no move to get out of the car. She hated coming here these days, hated seeing the empty shell her beloved Myra had turned into. All the life, all the spark had gone out of her. According to Charles, Myra sat in the living room, drinking tea, staring at old photo albums, the television tuned to CNN twenty-four hours a day. She hadn't left the house once since Barbara's funeral.

She finally turned off the engine, gathered her briefcase, weekend bag and purse. Should she put the top up or leave it down? The sky was clear. She shrugged. If it looked like rain, Charles would put the top up.

"Any change?" she asked walking into the kitchen.

Charles shook his head before he hugged her. "She's gone downhill even more these last two weeks. I hate saying this, but I don't think she even noticed you weren't here, Nikki."

Nikki flinched. "I couldn't get here, Charles. I had to wait for a court verdict. I must have called a hundred times," Nikki said, tossing her gear on the countertop. Her eyes pleaded with Myra's houseman for understanding.

Charles Martin was a tall man with clear crystal blue eyes and a shock of white hair that was thick and full. Once he'd been heavier but this past year had taken a toll on him, too. She noticed the tremor in his hand when he handed her a cup of coffee.

"Is she at least talking, Charles?"

"She responds if I ask her a direct question. Earlier in the week she fired me. She said she didn't need me anymore."

"My God!" Nikki sat down at the old oak table with the claw feet. Myra said the table was over three hundred years old and hand-hewn. As a child, she'd loved eating in the kitchen. Loved sitting at the table drinking cold milk and eating fat sugar cookies. She looked around. There didn't seem to be much life in the kitchen these days. The plants didn't seem as green, the summer dishes were still in the pantry, the winter placemats were still on the table. Even the braided winter rugs were still on the old pine floors. In the spring, Myra always changed them. She blinked. "This kitchen looks like an institution kitchen, Charles. The house is too quiet. Doesn't Myra play her music anymore?"

"No. She doesn't do anything anymore. I tried to get her to go for a walk today. She told me to get out of her face. I have to fight with her to take a shower. I'm at my wit's end. I don't know what to do anymore. This is no way to live, Nikki."

"Maybe it's time for some tough love. Let me see if she responds to me this evening. By the way, what's for dinner?"

"Rack of lamb. Those little red potatoes you like, and fresh garden peas. I made a blackberry cobbler just for you. But when you're not here, I end up throwing it all away. Myra nibbled on a piece of toast today." Charles threw his hands in the air and stomped over to the stove to open the oven door.

Nikki sighed. She straightened her shoulders before she marched into the living room where Myra was sitting on the sofa. She bent down to kiss the wrinkled cheek. "Did you miss me, Myra?"

"Nikki! It's nice to see you. Of course, I missed you. Sit down, dear. Tell me how you are. Is the law firm doing nicely? How's our softball team doing? Are you still seeing that assistant district attorney?" Her voice trailed off to nothing as she stared at the television set whose sound was on mute.

Nikki sat down and reached for the remote control. "I hope you don't mind if I switch to the local station. I want to see the news." She turned the volume up slightly.

"Let's see. Yes, I'm still seeing Jack, and the firm is doing wonderfully. We have more cases than we can handle. The team is in fourth place. I'm fine but I worry about you, Myra. Charles is worried about you, too."

"I fired Charles."

"I know, but he's still here. He has nowhere to go, Myra. You have to snap out of this depression. I can arrange some grief counseling sessions for you. You need a medical checkup. You have to let it go, Myra. You can't bring Barbara back. I can't stand seeing you like this. Barbara wouldn't approve of the way you're grieving. She always said life is for the living."

"I never heard her say any such thing. I can't let it go. She's with me every minute of every day. There's nothing to live for. The bastard who killed my daughter robbed my life as well. He's out there somewhere living a good life. If I could just get my hands on him for five minutes, I would . . ."

"Myra, he's back in his own country. Shhh, listen. That man," Nikki said pointing to the screen, "was set free today because of a technicality. He killed a young girl and he's walking away a free man. Jack prosecuted the case and lost."

"He must not be a very good district attorney if he lost the case," Myra snapped. Nikki's eyebrows shot upward. Was that a spark of interest? Childishly, she crossed her fingers.

"He's an excellent district attorney, Myra but the law is the law. The judge let things go because they weren't legal. Oh, look, there's the mother of the girl. God, I feel so sorry for her. She was in court every single day. The papers said she never took her eyes off the accused, not even for a minute. The reporters marveled at the woman's steadfast intensity. Every day they did an article about her. Jack said she fainted when the verdict came in."

"I know just how she feels," Myra said leaning forward to see the screen better. "What's she doing, Nikki? Look, there's Jack! He's very photogenic."

Nikki watched as the scene played out in front of her. She saw Jack's lips move, knew he was saying something but she couldn't hear over the voices of the excited news reporters. She saw his arm reach out but he was too late. Marie Lewellen fired the gun in her hand point-blank at the man who killed her daughter.

The television screen turned black and then came to life again.

Barnes looked directly into the camera, his eyes wide with shocked disbelief. Blood bubbled from his mouth. "I . . . should have . . . killed . . . you, too . . . you bitch!"

"You killed my little girl. You don't deserve to live. I'm glad I killed you. Glad!" Marie Lewellen screamed.

Barnes fell face forward onto the concrete steps of the courthouse.

Chaos erupted but the camera stayed positioned, capturing the ensuing panic.

"Oh my God!" was all Nikki could say.

Myra reared back against the cushions. "Did you see that! That's what I should have done! I hope she killed the son of a bitch! Is he moving? I can't see. Is he dead, Nikki? Charles, come see this. Why didn't I have the guts to do what that woman just did?" Myra shouted, her skinny arms flailing up and down. "If she killed him, I want you to defend her, Nikki. I'll pay for everything. Use your whole firm. Every expert, every specialist in the world. She killed him. She got in his face and killed him. Tell me he's dead. I want to know if he's dead!"

Nikki looked at Charles, who was busy staring at the ceiling. "He's dead, Myra."

"Look, look! They're handcuffing her. They're going to take her to jail. I want you to leave right now. Post her bail, do something. Don't let them keep her in jail. Say you'll take her home with you. Tell them she won't be a menace to society. Charles, get my checkbook."

"Myra, for God's sake, simmer down. It's not that easy."

"The hell it isn't. She was crazed. Temporary insanity. Are you going to do it or not, Nikki?"

"Yes, but . . ."

"Don't give me buts. You're still sitting here. I never asked you to do a thing for me, Nikki. Never once. I'm asking you now."

"I didn't say I wouldn't do it, Myra. I need to think. I need to talk to Jack. I can have my paralegal go down to the station. Tomorrow morning will be time enough. There is no way in hell she's getting out of jail tonight. She has to be arraigned. Can you wait for morning, Myra?"

"Yes, I can wait for morning." Myra swung around. "Charles, did you see what that woman just did? I would cheerfully rot in prison if

I had the guts to do that. First thing in the morning, Nikki. I want you to call me with a full report."

"You don't answer the phone, Myra," Nikki said sourly.

"I'll answer it tomorrow. Isn't it time for dinner? Let's eat off trays this evening. I want to see what happens to that poor woman. They'll be reporting on this for hours. Does she have other children? A husband? Isn't anyone going to answer me?"

Nikki's jaw dropped. Charles spun around on his heel, a smirk on his face.

"I can tell you what Jack told me. She has two other children, and yes, she has a husband. She's a homemaker. She works at a Hallmark shop on weekends for extra money that goes for all the little extras young kids need. Her husband is a lineman for AT&T. Her two boys are nine and eleven. Jenny, the daughter that was killed, worked after school till closing at the same Hallmark shop. She had a flat tire the night she was killed. She was fixing it herself when that creep offered to help and then he snatched her and dumped her body out near Manassas. Jack said they're a very nice family. Marie went to PTA meetings and they went to church as a family on Sunday."

"They'll need someone to take care of the boys, to cook and do all the things a mother does in case they don't let her out right away. Charles, find someone for the family. Use that employment agency we use when we do our spring cleaning. I hope they give her a medal. Someone should."

"Myra, for God's sake, she killed a man in cold blood. She took the law into her own hands. Civilized people don't do things like that. That's why we have laws."

"Where was the law when that bastard killed my daughter? Did Barbara get justice? No, she did not! My daughter is dead and no one paid for that crime. My unborn grandchild is dead and no one paid for that crime either. I'll go to my grave never having seen my grandchild. Don't talk to me about justice. Don't talk to me about the law because I don't want to hear it. Those laws, the justice that freed that man . . . *suck*."

Nikki looked up to see Charles standing in the doorway. She watched as both his clenched fists shot upward. In spite of herself, she grinned. Myra was alive and belching fire. All she had to do was get her to calm down and maybe, just maybe, she would return to the land of the living.

\* \* \*

It was midnight when Jack Emery finally returned Nikki's call. She crawled into bed, her head buzzing with the evening's events.

"Did you see it, Nikki?"

"Of course I saw it. Myra and Charles saw it, too. I'll say one thing, it snapped Myra out of her fugue. At least for now. She wants me to defend Marie Lewellen. I said I would."

"You can't defend her. It's open and shut. Insanity isn't going to hold up. She admitted to buying the gun at lunchtime from some punk on the street. That goes to premeditation. They've charged her with first degree murder. I'll be prosecuting, Nikki."

"Pass on it, Jack. You did enough to that woman."

"What the hell is that supposed to mean, Nikki?"

"It means that asshole got off. That's exactly what it means, Jack. Myra was right when she said it sucked. You didn't fight hard enough. He was guilty as sin and you damn well know it."

"The judge threw out . . . why am I defending myself? I did the best job I could under the circumstances. I tried to stop her at the courthouse. I was seconds too late. Don't go sour on me now. Turn it over to someone else in your firm, Nikki."

"I can't do that, Jack. I promised Myra. She's never, ever, asked anything of me. I have to do what she wants. I'm going to give you the fight of your life, too."

"If you take this case on that means we aren't going to be able to see one another until it's over, at which point we'll probably hate each other's guts. Is that what you want?"

Nikki's mind raced. No, it wasn't what she wanted but she knew where her loyalties lay. She loved Jack Emery. "Beg off, Jack. Let some other A.D.A. take the case."

"I guess I'll see you in court, Counselor," Jack said coldly.

It was his tone, not his words, that sparked her reply. "You bet your sweet ass you'll see me in court." Nikki snapped her cell phone shut and threw it across the room.

Nikki punched at the thick downy pillows. She knew she wasn't going to be able to sleep now. She felt like crying. A second later she bounded out of the twin bed and ripped down the covers from the bed that once belonged to Barbara. If she wanted to, she could stick her hand under the pillow and pull out Barb's old beat-up teddy bear and hug it to her chest the way Barb had done every night she slept in the bed. It almost seemed sacrilegious to touch it. Instead she picked up the pillow and looked down at the tattered bear named Willie. She almost stuck her finger in the hole under Willie's chin but changed her mind. She lowered the pillow and went back to her own bed. Tears rolled down her cheeks. "God, I miss you, Barb. I think about you every day. I just had a fight with Jack. At least I think it was a fight. I wish you were here so I could call you up and tell you all about it." She punched at the down pillows again. Maybe she needed to read herself to sleep. Her gaze traveled to the built-in bookshelves across the room. The three top shelves were hers because she was taller than Barbara. The three bottom shelves belonged to Barbara and were loaded with everything *but* books. No, she was too wired-up to read.

The first month she'd come here to live, Myra had knocked out two walls and turned this room into a two-girl bedroom. They'd spent so many hours in here, huddled in their beds, giggling, telling secrets, talking about boys and sharing all their hopes and dreams. Even the bathroom had twin vanities and twin showers. Myra didn't stint and she didn't favor one over the other. She simply had enough love for both of them. She looked now at the twin desks, the colorful swivel chairs, the bright red rocking chairs. It seemed so long ago, almost like a lifetime. She stared at the colorful rockers and at the cushions they'd made at camp one year. Barbara's was perfect, her stitches small and neat. Her own was sloppy, the seams loose. But it wasn't the cushions that held her gaze. The chair was rocking, moving slowly back and forth. She looked up to see if the fan was on. A chill washed down her spine. She shuddered as she reached for her robe. Maybe Charles had left some coffee in the pot. If not, she could make some more.

Nikki walked down the long hallway to the back staircase that led to the kitchen. She blinked when she saw Myra and Charles sitting at the table, highball glasses in their hands. She blinked again. "I couldn't sleep," she mumbled.

"We couldn't either," Myra said.

"After what we saw on television this evening, I can understand why. I'm going to make some coffee."

"Nikki, Charles and I want to talk to you about something."

Nikki reached for the coffee canister. There was an edge to Myra's voice. A combative edge. Something she'd never heard before. "About what, Myra? I said I would take Marie Lewellen's case."

"I know. That's just a small part of it. Do you remember a while back when you told Charles and myself about two young women who came to see you? Kathryn Lucas and Alexis Thorne, only that wasn't Alexis Thorne's real name at the time?"

"I remember," Nikki said, measuring coffee into the stainless steel basket.

"You helped Alexis by going outside the law. You couldn't help Kathryn because the statute of limitations had run out but if there was a way to help her, would you do it?"

Nikki felt herself freeze. "Are you talking about inside the law or outside the law, Myra?"

"Don't answer my question with a question. Would you help her?"

"I can't, Myra. There's nothing I can do for her. I looked at everything. Time ran out. Yes, I feel sorry for her. I understand how it all went down. She waited too long, that's the bottom line."

"You looked the other way for Alexis. You knew someone who was on the other side of the law and you got her a new identity, you helped her start a small home business as a personal shopper and you made it happen for her. You believed in her when she told you her story. She was a victim, she didn't deserve to go to prison for a whole year. She can never get that year of her life back. The men and women who turned her into a scapegoat walked free and are living the good life and her life is ruined. Kathryn is a victim and no one is helping her. Marie Lewellen could spend the rest of her life in jail unless you can get her off. Legally."

Nikki sat down across from Myra and Charles. "I think this would be a real good time for you to tell me *exactly* what you two are talking about."

"The system you work under doesn't always work," Charles said.

"Sometimes that's true," Nikki said carefully. "For the most part, it works."

Myra looked at Nikki over the rim of her glass. "What if we take the part that doesn't work and make it work? What if I told you I was willing to use my entire fortune, and you know, Nikki, that it is sizeable, and use it to . . . make that system work. For us. For all the Maries, the Kathryns and the Alexis Thornes who got lost in the system."

"Are you talking about going outside the law to . . . to . . . avenge these women? Are you talking about taking the law into your own hands and . . . and . . ."

Myra's head bobbed up and down. "Charles can help. He dealt with criminals and terrorists during his stint at MI 6. You're an attorney, a law professor. With your brains, Charles's expertise and my money, we could right quite a few wrongs. It would have to be secret, of course."

"And you just now came up with all this?" Nikki said in awe. "No!"

"Yes," Myra and Charles said in unison.

Nikki looked at her watch. "Just eight hours ago, give or take a few minutes, you were practically comatose, Myra. You didn't want to live. You were so deep in your misery and your depression I wanted to cry for you. Now you're all set to take on the judicial system and dispense your own brand of justice. You'll get caught, Myra. You're too old to go to jail. They aren't kind to old people in jail. NO!"

Myra took a long pull from the highball glass. "If I can't satisfy my own vengeance, maybe I can do something for others where the system failed." She spoke in a low, even monotone. "Kathryn Lucas, age thirty-eight. Married to Alan Lucas, the love of her life. Alan had multiple sclerosis as well as Parkinson's disease and lived in a wheelchair. They owned an eighteen-wheeler, Alan's dream. In order to keep his dream alive for him, Kathryn drove the rig and Alan rode alongside her. One night when they stopped for food and gas, Kathryn was raped at a truck stop by three bikers. Alan was forced to watch and could not help his wife. Rather than report the rape and destroy what was left of her husband's manhood, she remained silent. She did nothing. She carried it with her day and night for the next seven years until Alan died. Needless to say, whatever was left of the marriage after the rape, died right then and there. The day after she buried her husband she went to you, gave you all the information she had on the case and you turned her away because the stupid statute of limitations had run out. You told me she had a partial license plate, her husband took pictures, and she said one of the bikers was riding an old Indian motorcycle. You said she told you they belonged to the Weekend Warriors club, probably white-collar professionals out for a fling. Charles said there aren't many Indians in existence and they're on every biker's wish list. It shouldn't be hard to track it down. You just sit there, Nikki, and think about three men raping you while Jack is forced to watch. You think about that."

"Myra, I don't have to think about it. I feel terrible for Kathryn Lucas. Yes, she deserves to have something done but she waited too long. The law is the law. I'm a goddamn lawyer. I can't break the law I swore to uphold."

"The circumstances have to be brought into consideration. I need you to help us, Nikki."

"What is it you want me to do?"

"We could form this little club. You certainly know plenty of women who have slipped through the cracks. Like Alexis, Kathryn, and many others. We'll invite them to join and then we'll do whatever has to be done."

Nikki stood up and threw her hands in the air. "You want us to be *vigilantes!*"

"Yes, dear. Thank you. I couldn't think of the right word. Don't you remember those movies with Charles Bronson?"

"He got caught, Myra."

"But they let him go in the end."

"It was a damn movie, Myra. Make-believe. You want us to do the same thing for real. Just out of curiosity, supposing we were able to find the men that raped Kathryn Lucas, what would we do to them?"

Myra smiled. "That would be up to Kathryn now, wouldn't it?"

"I don't believe I'm sitting here listening to you two hatch this . . . this . . . what the hell is it, Myra?"

"A secret society of women who do what has to be done to make things right," Myra said solemnly.

"It could work, Nikki, as long as we hold to the secrecy part," Charles said quietly. "There is that room in the tunnels where you and Barbara used to play. You could hold your meetings there. No one would ever know. I know exactly how to set it all up."

Nikki struggled for a comeback that would make sense. In the end, she said, "Jack Emery will be prosecuting Marie Lewellen. We'll be adversaries."

"I see," Myra said. She slapped her palms on the old, scarred tabletop. "Then you have to get her out on bail and we'll find a way to whisk her and her family away to safety. I have the money to do that. It will be like the Witness Protection Program. Charles can handle all that."

Nikki sat down with a thump. "If I don't agree to . . . go along with this, what will you do?"

Myra borrowed a line from her favorite comedian. "Then we'll have to kill you," she said cheerfully. "So, are you in?"

"God help me, I'm in."

# Chapter Two

*Eight months later*

Lightning ripped through the darkness, a crazy-quilt of fireworks in the sky. Thunder sounded like a sonic boom as the worst storm in five decades slaughtered the state of Virginia. Vicious waterfalls of rain reduced visibility, forcing the procession of vehicles to a halt.

The lead car's brake lights came to life as the driver waited for the electronic gates to swing open. In mid-swing, an arthritic limb from one of the three-hundred-year-old oaks crashed downward to land on top of the electrified fence of Myra Rutledge's McLean, Virginia, estate.

The occupants of the cars shivered as the limb sizzled and crackled, flames shooting upward to meet the savage lightning attacking the night.

One by one, the cars proceeded to inch forward only to stop when the lead car sounded its horn and ground to a stop because the opening wasn't large enough to drive through. Doors swung open, rain-clad figures huddled, arms waving, their shouts carried away on the gusty, hurricane-like winds.

A piercing whistle, the kind heard at ball games, shrilled in the stormy air. "Back up one at a time. Give me enough room and I'll take down the gates," a voice ordered with authority.

With visibility at zero minus, the occupants of the cars did their best to follow the order. Bumpers and front ends collided as a blast from the last vehicle in the procession of cars came to life with a savage bellow.

The eighteen-wheeler driven by Kathryn Lucas skirted the cars with long years of expertise. With a mighty roar that matched the rolling thunder overhead, she crashed through the massive iron gates. "God, I always wanted to do something like that," she chortled gleefully. "Oh, Alan, I wish you could see what I just did. If it wasn't for this big rig, we'd all still be sitting outside those monster gates. Can you just see that ancient Rolls or the Benz tapping those gates! I swear those gates are made of something besides iron. I wouldn't be surprised if I did some serious damage to this fine vehicle. I love you, will always love you. Remember that, Alan. This is Big Sis signing off." Talking to her late husband always made her feel better. Believing her husband was still with her in spirit gave her great comfort. It didn't mean she was nuts, or that she was losing it. All it meant was she felt better and she was sharing with the only man she ever loved or would love in the future.

The portico as well as the old farmhouse was awash with light, beckoning warmth and safety to the drivers of the vehicles. The Honda Civic, the customized Jag, the BMW and the Benz lined up in formation and parked two across. The ancient Bentley parked behind the eighteen-wheeler.

Umbrellas were raised only to sail upward in the sixty-mile-an-hour winds. The five women sprinted toward the light spilling from the main doorway that was being held open by a tall, stately looking woman: Myra Rutledge. Rain poured through the open doorway, soaking the beautiful heart of pine floor. "Welcome to Pinewood," she said.

Charles Emery used all his shoulder power to shove the monster bolt into the lock position on the solid oak door. The bolt, the lock and the door itself dated back to the days when the slaves were routed through Pinewood to the underground railroad.

"Come, come. We have dry clothes for you all," Myra said as she handed out thick, luxurious towels that were as large as bath sheets along with a flat, white box containing candles.

"The power will probably go off soon and there seems to be something wrong with the generator that lights this part of the house, so we're going to be using candlelight until we can get the power working. Take any room at the top of the steps. Follow me, please," Charles said.

The moment the women were out of sight, Myra lowered her body to the third step from the bottom of the breathtaking circular staircase. Her gnarled hand reached out to touch one of the polished oak spindles. She remembered all the times her daughter had whooped her way down the bannister, Nikki right behind her. They had both continued to do it in the years to come. It was all so long ago. Two years since that fateful day when her daughter had been killed. An eternity. Tears gathered in her eyes. She wiped at them angrily.

Now, it was payback time.

Myra looked around the foyer that was half as large as the church she worshipped in.

There was no life here, no indication anyone truly lived here. Suddenly, she wished for flowers, huge bouquets of colorful Shasta daisies, green plants, cacti, anything to take away the museum-like look of the house. Flowers these past two years hadn't been a priority.

The chandelier overhead flickered, thanks to the rickety old generator. A moment later the only light to be seen came from the candle in Myra's hand. She wished now she had listened to Charles and replaced the generator, but in the scheme of things, generators hadn't been a top priority in her life these past two years either. She'd been too busy grieving, living in a cocoon of pure hell.

"We're coming down, Myra," Nikki shouted from the top of the stairs. "Hold the candle high!"

Myra thought she heard a giggle from one of the women and then, in the blink of an eye, Kathryn Lucas was whooping her pleasure as she slid down the polished bannister, her candle straight in front of her, Nikki behind her. Long years of practice allowed Myra to reach out one long arm to break the younger woman's fall. Nikki slid expertly to the floor and was on her feet a second later, a wide smile on her face.

"Now that was fun! If I had a staircase like this, I'd be sliding down it morning, noon and night. Did you ever slide down, Mrs. Rutledge?" Kathryn asked.

"Call me Myra. I did it once on the day of my fiftieth birthday. I wanted to do something outrageous, something silly. I was sore for a week, since there was no one at the bottom to catch me."

"You know what I always say . . . I say whatever turns you on. Maybe someday I'll tell you about some of the way-out things Alan and . . . never mind. That's a whole other story and a lifetime ago."

Myra smiled. She liked this rambunctious young woman.

"Ladies, if you're dry and comfortable, I would like you to follow me," Charles said.

When the tight procession reached a solid wall of bookshelves, Myra stepped in front of Charles. With a trembling hand, she counted down the various carvings on the intricate molding that ran the length of the bookshelves. At the same moment her fingers touched the lowest carving, the wall moved slowly and silently to reveal a large room with wall-to-wall computers that blinked and flashed as well as a mind-boggling, eye-level, closed-circuit television screen showing Kathryn's rig crashing through the electronic gates. Each wall seemed to be made up of television screens. MSNBC was playing on the south wall, CNN on the north wall. From somewhere, fans whirred softly and there wasn't a window to be seen.

"This," Myra said waving her arms about, "Is our command center and we have Charles to thank for insisting on putting in a cutting-edge, solar-powered electrical system. In spite of our current weather, there's enough stored power to last a month.

"We installed a modern-day ventilation system years ago when my girls used to play here. It's been updated recently. At one time this was just a storage area with a trap door. This is where my ancestors took the slaves and routed them to safety. Beneath the house is a maze of tunnels. Charles and I hung bells at each entrance and exit so the girls wouldn't get lost. The tunnels have all been shored up by Charles in case . . . in case . . . we ever need to use them. Please, take your seats," Myra said, indicating a large round table surrounded by deep comfortable chairs. On the table in front of each chair lay a bright blue folder.

Kathryn Lucas whirled and twirled around as she looked at everything, the engineer in her appreciating what she was seeing. "It looks like a war room," she said, excitement ringing in her voice.

Myra smiled. "That's exactly what it is. When you go to war you need a war room. Please, take your seats."

Myra stood up, the palms of her hands flat on the tabletop. She looked at each woman in turn. She'd rehearsed a pat little speech but suddenly she couldn't remember the words. Barbara had always said, "cut to the chase, Mom, spit it out." "You all know why you were invited here," she began, her voice shaky. "You all agreed to the rules as Nikki outlined them to you. All of you here this evening are victims of a justice system that doesn't always work. We can't save the world and we can't right the wrongs done to us, but we can avenge ourselves. I see us as sisters under the skin, a sort of sisterhood if you will."

"I like the way that sounds," Kathryn said, settling back in her chair.

Myra paused to take a deep breath, to marshal her courage, to pray to God she was doing the right thing. "Two years ago my daughter Barbara was struck down and killed by a hit and run driver, who had diplomatic immunity." Tears welled in her eyes as her gaze swept the room. "I want the man who killed her to pay for what he did." She swallowed hard and then continued. "I know each of you here tonight has suffered a loss that also went unpunished. We'll go over each case momentarily. Afterwards we will vote to see which case needs the most immediate attention. As I point to you, please give us your name and your profession."

"Isabelle Flanders, architect."

"Alexis Thorne, securities broker. Actually, I'm an ex-securities broker and a felon. I am also a personal shopper."

"Julia Webster, plastic surgeon."

"Kathryn Lucas. I'm a cross-country truck driver. I'm also an engineer."

"Yoko Akia. My husband and I own a flower shop."

"Of course you all know Nikki Quinn," Myra said. "Nikki spent several years with the FBI before opening her own law firm. She also teaches law at Georgetown University."

Myra held out her hands to Charles. "Last but certainly not least, Charles Martin, my right hand and my left hand. Charles has many special talents, as you will find out. To protect ourselves from each other, should any of you decide to expose our accomplishments, Charles will videotape each of our meetings." She squeezed Charles's hand. "If you will open your folders, we can get started."

*And God help us all,* she thought.

"Inside each of your folders you will find your own case history and the case history of your sisters. We felt it necessary for each of you to get to know one another. However, reading about someone doesn't quite give you the same feel as seeing that person go about their daily routine. The stills and videos you are about to see were taken to help your sisters know you better. Please refrain from commenting until Charles turns off the screen. I'm sure you're all going to be a little surprised at what you see," she said as the first picture appeared on the screen . . . Nikki in a courtroom standing before a jury. "We've been working on this presentation for some time now, so there is quite a bit of footage even though it has been carefully edited." The picture switched to Yoko working in her flower shop.

Hearing Yoko gasp, Myra said, "Yes, we've been spying on all of you. We wanted to make an impression on you here tonight, to show how technologically capable we are and to show you that we mean to ensure the secrecy of this organization."

The women stared, transfixed as their images flashed across the screen. When the screen turned dark, twenty-seven minutes later,

Kathryn Lucas was the first to speak. "I don't see how videotaping me in my flowered underwear will help anyone get to know me better or ensure the secrecy of the Sisterhood."

"How did you get in my house?" Julia Webster demanded.

"You filmed me buying *Tampax*," Alexis Thorne grumbled.

"You actually watched me buying groceries and saw that humiliating moment when I didn't have enough money to pay for them at the checkout?" Isabelle Flanders said angrily.

"It is no one's business but mine that I mix manure with peat moss for my plants," Yoko Akia said quietly, her eyes lowered.

Nikki Quinn's eyes apologized and accused at the same time. "I can't believe you videotaped me, Myra. Me, Myra. Christ, I'm the one who agreed to help you form the group! So what if I cried and kicked the door and threw the whole damn case file down the courthouse steps. So what, Myra. I hate to lose. I hate it when scumbags win and the good guys have no other recourse but to cry. I didn't see you or Charles on that damn film, Myra." Her tone was so vehement, the other women sat up straighter in their chairs.

"It was done to remind you of why you're here, Nikki." There was no apology in Myra's voice. It's to show you what we can do, what we're going to be doing from here on out. Think of it as your security blanket."

Nikki wasn't about to give up. "There's more, isn't there?"

"Miles and miles of tape. It's all safe and secure. None of you have a thing to worry about, since it's for your own protection. Yes, we were intrusive and yes, we were thorough. The reason Charles and myself aren't on the tape is because we're old and we're boring. And . . . we're paying for this party. End of discussion."

The women looked at one another but no one offered up a comment.

Myra picked up a bright red folder. Her movements were slow and deliberate. The women leaned forward expectantly.

"Alexis Thorne, you're here because the brokerage firm you worked for pinned a crime on you that they themselves committed. You did a year in prison for *their* crime. They ruined your life and you are now a felon with a new identity, thanks to Nikki Quinn.

"Isabelle Flanders, you're here because one of your trusted employees, while driving you to a construction site, had a car accident that killed a family of three. Because you were unconscious when they pulled you out of the wreckage, she accused you of driving the vehicle. You lost your business in the lawsuits that followed and you were wiped out financially. You are virtually living hand to mouth working at whatever you can find to support yourself while your employee will never have to work another day in her life, thanks to generous court settlements.

"Julia Webster, you're here because you thought you were married to a man who took his marriage vows seriously. He infected you with the HIV virus and made it impossible for you to continue your career as a plastic surgeon. A death sentence looms on your horizon because of those infidelities.

"Yoko Akia, you are here because your father brought your mother to this country under false pretenses. Unable to speak English at the time, she thought she was coming to the golden world. Instead of the golden world she expected, her world turned into a life of corruption and prostitution. She died at the age of thirty-three.

"Nikki Quinn, you are here as our legal counsel. It's important for all of you to know that Nikki has put her career on the line to join us."

Charles took that moment to press a button on the remote in his hand. Nikki's picture flashed on the monitor. The same picture that had appeared a short while ago. She flinched at the memory.

"Last but not least, sisters. I'm here because my daughter was killed by a hit and run motorist who had diplomatic immunity. At the moment there is nothing I can do, but the day will come, I'm sure, when the man will find his way back to this country. When that happens, I want to be ready to exact my vengeance. Until that happens, I'm here to help you in whatever way I can.

"What we're going to do now is this. Each of you write your name on the slip of paper that Charles will give you and drop it into the shoebox in the middle of the table. Charles will pick a name and that's the first case we'll work on."

Myra watched the play of emotion on the women's faces as they wrote their names on the small squares of paper Charles handed out. She saw misery, despair, hope and hatred. She couldn't help but wonder whose name would come out of the box.

Charles clicked the remote and a statue of the scales of justice flashed on the monitor. This was Myra's cue to end her speech. "Unlike her," she said, pointing to the screen, "we are not blind, nor do we care about the scales of justice because those scales favor the criminal more than the victim."

"Kathryn Lucas," Charles said clearly, reading from the slip of paper he'd drawn from the Keds shoebox.

"Kathryn swallowed hard as the others stared at her. She felt

light-headed. She turned to look around the room. She saw everything as if in slow motion. It was all so surreal. "I have to get my dog
out of the truck. I didn't think we'd be here this long. I don't know
why I left him in the truck. I shouldn't have done that. It's like . . .
like when I left Alan in the truck that . . . that time. I want my dog. I
*need* my dog. I need him right now." She was off her chair a second
later, the panic on her face obvious to everyone in the room.

"I'll go with you," Charles said calmly. "I didn't know you had
your dog with you or I would have insisted you bring him in with
you."

"If you know I wear flowered underwear and gargle with Lister-
ine, how could you not know about my dog?" Kathryn snapped as
she followed Charles out of the secret room.

"We know about your dog, Kathryn, we just didn't think you
would bring him with you this evening. I apologize. Let me get you
a slicker."

"We don't have to go outside. All I have to do is whistle and click
this remote," she said, pressing a small black box in her hand. The
door to the cab will open and close on its own. I didn't know about
gadgets like this until after . . . until after Alan died and I got my
dog. He's been K-9 trained. Open the door. He'll find me."

And he did. Charles stepped backward until his back was pressed
against the newel post on the stairway. In his life he'd never seen a
more magnificent dog. He said so in a shaky voice.

"Charles, this is Murphy. I named him after the man who taught
me how to drive that rig out there. He was one sorry son of a bitch.
Shake hands, Murph." The Belgian Malinois held out his paw.
Charles shook it manfully. "Now, Murph, show him those beautiful
teeth of yours." The dog obliged and growled as he did it, his lips
peeling back as his ears went flat against his head.

"How much does he weigh?" Charles asked nervously.

"One hundred and ten pounds," Kathryn said smartly. "I got him
the day after Alan's funeral. I needed someone in . . . in . . . in his
seat. Murph was fully trained at the time. He's three years old. He's
been trained to kill, if necessary." Charles blinked at her flat, emo-
tionless voice.

"Are you ready to return to the others?"

"*We're* ready," Kathryn said.

The panel in the wall moved quietly and closed just as quietly.

"This is Murphy," Kathryn said by way of introduction. The col-
lective gasp pleased her.

"I'm afraid of dogs," Yoko said, drawing her legs up under her so they wouldn't dangle on the floor.

"Get over it, because this dog goes where I go." Her voice was not unkind, just cooly matter-of-fact.

Yoko's feet stayed under her rump.

"*Seitz.*" The Malinois dropped to his haunches and then stretched out at Kathryn's feet. "He understands German, as I do," Kathryn explained.

"Tell us how you came to us and then tell us your story, Kathryn," Myra said gently.

Kathryn ran her hands through her hair as she struggled for the words she needed and wanted to say. "I've only ever talked about this once and that was to Nikki Quinn, the day after Alan's funeral. It wasn't easy then and it isn't easy now. I was walking down the street and there was this walk-in legal clinic where lawyers do pro bono work. I walked around the block a few times before I got up the courage to go inside. I waited seven years to tell my story and when I finally told it to Nikki Quinn she told me the statute of limitations had run out and there was nothing I could do legally.

"I'm very nervous talking about this. It's still as painful as the day it happened. It's like a beacon in the forefront of my mind. I've lived with it every hour of every day for seven long years."

"You have to tell us everything, Kathryn. It's the only way we're going to be able to help you," Myra said gently. "Start at the beginning and tell us everything you can remember. We'll ask questions when you're finished. What kind of a day was it? Where were you headed? What were you hauling?"

Kathryn took a deep breath. "It was a nice day. The sun was out. It was one of Alan's better days. He loved riding shotgun, as he called it. Listen, I need to tell you, right now, right up front, how much I loved that man. He was my white knight. He was the wind beneath my wings. He was the reason and the only reason I wanted to get up in the morning. He was my one true love. You need to know all this so you don't misjudge me or Alan when I finish my story.

"We were both orphans, both of us working our way through school. We met in one of our engineering classes. Back then we thought we were going to build a whole new world. In our third year, Alan was diagnosed with multiple sclerosis. He was one of the unfortunate ones because it attacked him quickly and viciously. By the time we graduated he was using a cane to get around. Suddenly, building new worlds didn't seem important to either one of us. We both worked for a year and the money we saved during that year was used to put me through truck driving school. I made enough money the first couple of years to put a down payment on that rig out front.

"There were no remissions for Alan. He just got steadily worse. The day came when he couldn't walk anymore so I took on extra jobs to get the truck outfitted with a hydraulic lift so he could get in and out of it and then into a wheelchair. In addition to the multiple sclerosis he was also diagnosed as having Parkinson's disease. He loved being on the road. It was what he lived for. He used to sing as we tooled along. He'd talk on the CB to other truckers. They all knew us. When we'd pull into a truck stop they'd always help so I could shower and they'd help Alan. He hated that part of it but the other truckers were good to him. After a while it didn't matter. It was so hard for him in the beginning to let others see how incapacitated he was.

"We didn't have a house or a home base of any kind. We lived out of our truck. Sometimes if there was a long layover, we'd camp out in a cheap motel. His medical bills bled me dry. He . . . loved me so much. Sometimes late at night I'd hear him cry. In the daytime, he kept this tight control. You know what I mean. I used to cry in the bathroom at the different truck stops and then wear my dark glasses so he wouldn't know. He always knew, though.

"That afternoon we drove into Bakersfield, California, to pick up a load of computers to be delivered up to Mojave and from there we were going on to Vegas with some repaired slot machines. We headed up Highway fifty-eight through the Tehachapi Pass, delivered the computers to the military base and then stopped at the Starlite Cafe for fuel and to get something to eat. It wasn't one of my regular truck stops. I was starving, so we stopped. I think I was there once before, but it was years and years ago. I was ahead of schedule by forty-five minutes that day.

"I got out of the truck, walked around to the passenger side and was getting Alan's wheelchair out of the special motorized compartment I had built behind the cab when I heard . . ."

. . . . *a loud roar that shook the ground. She swung around to admire the cycles. She and Alan had ridden during their first two years in college. In fact, they'd belonged to a motorcycle club. It had always been Alan's secret desire to own one of the 1930 Indians. She waved and smiled, knowing Alan was probably admiring the Indians from his perch in the cab. Some of her fondest memories were of the little back road trips they used to take during those first two years of college.*

*"Hey, Red,"* someone called out.

Kathryn whipped around, her hand going to her heart. *"You scared me there for a minute. How's it going?"*

*"Sorry. I didn't mean to frighten you. I was wondering if you needed any help."*

*"Thanks, but no. I do this all the time."*

*"Is it for him?"* the biker asked, pointing to Alan who was staring at them through the window.

She stared up at Alan and smiled. He looked so anxious. *"I was admiring your motorcycles. Alan and I used to ride Indians. No other bike like them in the world."*

*"You got that right, Red,"* the biker said referring to Kathryn's mane of auburn curls.

*"So what's wrong with him?"* the biker asked bluntly.

*"My husband has multiple sclerosis and Parkinson's disease."*

*"Damn shame. Must be hard on you, Red."*

A chill washed up her spine. *"I manage,"* she said curtly as she stepped away. She pulled the wheelchair closer. Out of the corner of her eye she saw two men in cycle garb step out from behind the back of the truck. Her heart took on extra beats as she tried to figure a way to outrun the men if need be. Why in the damn hell had she parked so far away from the main parking area? Because there had been no other spots available when she'd pulled in. Now the lot was practically deserted.

*"I really have to get moving. Nice talking to you,"* she said, stepping closer to the cab door.

They came behind her, yanking her arms backward. The man she'd been talking to kicked the wheelchair away. She watched it skid across the parking lot. They ripped at her boots, at her clothes until she was naked, and then they dragged her across the shallow ditch at the end of the parking area and into the undergrowth.

She tried to scream, but they chopped at her throat as she fought them with every ounce of strength in her body until she couldn't fight any longer. She closed her eyes and tried to put her mind and body in another place, a place that was warm and gentle, a place where Alan protected her. She felt them change position, felt them roll her over, felt their hands, smelled their bodies. She knew she was crying, whimpering as they raped and sodomized her over and over again. *"If I ever find you, I'll kill you . . .*

*". . . .* but I never went after them." She wiped at the tears streaming down her cheeks. "I have all this evidence and it doesn't do me one little bit of good. All because of a stupid law. A damn stupid law that doesn't care about me or about Alan," Kathryn said bitterly.

"Are you up to some questions, Kathryn?" Nikki asked.

"Sure. Nothing could be worse than saying all that out loud."

"Why didn't your husband get on the CB or roll down the window and call for help? Why didn't he blow the horn? Why didn't you call for help?" Julia asked.

"I took the ignition key with me. The CB is powered. So are the windows and horn. I needed the key to open the compartment."

"Maybe if he had opened his door . . ."

"No," Kathryn interrupted. "It wouldn't have helped. He couldn't get out and down without my help. I tried to call for help but they chopped my neck. I could only make croaking sounds. He did everything he could under the circumstances. He took their damn picture. We have a partial license plate. They were wearing jackets that said Weekend Warriors. That's a motorcycle club with a thousand different chapters all across the country. It's made up mostly of white-collar professionals."

"Did you report the rape to the police?" Alexis asked.

Kathryn hung her head and mumbled, "No. No, I didn't. The reason I didn't was Alan. He had a seizure and I had to think of him. I crawled back to the truck, found my clothes and the key that was in my shirt pocket. I was like a zombie, okay? I shifted into neutral and got dressed and went inside to get help for Alan. The paramedics came and revived him. I was *alive*. I wasn't sure about Alan. He was my primary concern. If you want to think that was stupid, go ahead and think it. There was no way in hell Alan could hold up to police questioning and a trial. Absolutely no way. Alan was never the same after that night. Neither was I, but I tried. Alan didn't seem to have a choice. He kept having more and more seizures. Then he had his last paralyzing stroke. He lost his will to live. I know that. I tried to keep him alive as long as I could. I did everything. Everything. If only you had known him when he was young. If only you had known the Alan I fell in love with. If you had known him, you would understand. I survived and he didn't. It's that simple.

"Here's my evidence," Kathryn said tossing a packet on the table. "You people sitting here make me remember why I didn't go to the police. They would have been just like you, questioning me, asking me questions like I was the one who did something wrong. I told you what happened. There's my proof. The partial license plate number. The picture Alan took. There's some definition to it. It needs to be enhanced. One of the bikers was named Lee. They belonged to the Weekend Warriors. I know what they looked like. I know how they smelled and I damn well know how they felt. Because of Alan, I waited too long. If I had to do it all over again, I wouldn't do anything different. If you people hadn't come along when you did, I would have started on my own search. Just because the eyes of the law are closed doesn't mean my eyes are closed. Alan's gone now. I don't care what happens to me."

"You say that like you mean it," Nikki said quietly.

"I do mean it," Kathryn said coldly.

And what would be your revenge against the men who did this to you, Kathryn?" Myra asked quietly.

Kathryn didn't blink or miss a beat. Head high, her shoulders back, the words shot out of her mouth like bullets. "I want to slice off their goddamn balls with a dull knife."

# Chapter Three

The silence in the room was deafening. Kathryn raised her eyes and stared around at the group of women. "You look shocked!" she said, wondering if it was what she'd said or the way she'd said it. "I'm serious here. It's better than they deserve. You asked me a question and I gave you my answer. I didn't need to think about my answer because I've thought about nothing else for the past seven years." Bitterness rang in her voice as she let her gaze sweep from one woman to the other, finally coming to rest on Charles, who was staring at her intently, a look of compassion on his face.

"Obviously, none of you care for my answer. You know what, that's just too damn bad. I think I want to know a little more about how this is all going to work or I'm outta here with my dog. I don't have to prove anything to any of you. I came here because I thought you would help. You certainly led me to believe that was the case. I didn't come here to be judged."

"Of course you've thought about it. You would have to be inhuman not to have dwelled on it almost to the exclusion of all else. I'm sure we've all thought about how we want to be avenged. I know I have. You aren't being judged, dear. We're simply asking questions to better understand so we can finally get you the justice you deserve," Myra said.

They all started to talk at once. Myra picked up her gavel and banged it three times on top of the polished table. "One at a time, sisters. It's important for all of us to understand right now that each person's idea of vengeance and retribution is different from someone else's. I want each of you to tell me what you think would be a fitting punishment for the men who attacked and raped Kathryn. In the end, it has to be Kathryn's decision and we will all abide by that decision. Let's be clear on that. Isabelle, tell us what you think."

Isabella cleared her throat nervously as she fiddled with the long braid hanging down her back. "I'm real big on an eye for an eye. I agree with Kathryn. I have to admit, I cheered that Bobbit woman." She looked at Kathryn. "I think your punishment is just."

Yoko clapped her hands against her cheeks. "What about their families? What if they have wives? Maybe the wives don't know their husbands . . . do . . . things like that. It will be like you are punishing them also for something they did not do."

Nikki responded in Kathryn's defense. "Obviously they weren't thinking of their wives when they attacked Kathryn. We have to stay focused and remember that our issue is with the criminals, not their families."

"Alexis, what's your opinion?" Myra asked.

"You play, you pay. Kathryn is right. They didn't think about their families or their wives. They were out for a good time and the hell with everything else.They goddamn well violated her and they should be made to pay for what they did. I agree with Kathryn. Let's slice their balls off and pickle them. We can send them their balls anonymously. Yeah, yeah, I like that," Alexis said vehemently.

Charles straightened his tie as his gaze swept across the ceiling. A smile tugged at the corners of his mouth and did not go unnoticed by Kathryn.

"Julia, what do you think?" Myra asked.

Kathryn jerked upright at the doctor's cold, deadly voice. "I'll do the operation. I'll use my dullest surgical knife. I will place all testicles in formaldehyde and will label each. However, I think we should use Ziploc bags. They'll be easier to mail. I will even volunteer to mail them. Does that answer your question?"

"Yes," Myra said. "Yoko?"

Yoko looked first at one woman and then another as she struggled to find the words she wanted. She stared at the shoebox in the middle of the table.

Kathryn leaned over and pinched Murphy's ear. The huge dog reared back and stood up. "What's your damn problem, Yoko?" Kathryn said as her foot pressed against the dog's foot to make him turn around until he was facing Yoko. "You should be champing at the bit to go after these guys. Wasn't your father just like them? Your history says he was."

"Well . . . I . . ." Yoko's eyes filled with tears.

Kathryn jabbed her finger in Yoko's direction. "You'd better not turn out to be a weak link, sister. I'm not putting my ass on the line and I don't think these other women will either if you have to sit and ponder everything and then weasel out when the going gets tough. I think you're too wishy-washy for my taste. I'm going to keep my eye on you. This dog of mine is going to do the same thing. Now, what the hell is your answer?"

"I apologize if I don't think fast enough for you, Kathryn. I feel you are justified in wanting revenge. What you propose is drastic. You said yourself you are alive and well. Perhaps not mentally well, but well just the same. I am most sorry about your husband's death. Your grief is palpable. I understand this. I will vote no this time because I do not know these men."

"You know Kathryn. By coming here tonight you pledged to be her sister. It's not important for you to know the men," Julia hissed between her teeth. "You had better not turn into a weak link because if you do, I'll go after you myself."

Myra nodded. "Your decision is recorded, Yoko. Nikki?"

Nikki thought about all the rape cases she'd taken to court and lost. Cases where the victim was raped twice, once by a man and then again by the courts. "I agree," she said, her voice ringing out loud and clear.

"I vote yes also," Myra said.

"Your revenge is approved by the majority of the sisters, Kathryn."

"Now we need to set up an airtight, working plan. I think this is the time when we need Charles's input. Charles worked for the Queen of England at MI 6 and he was an excellent operative until his cover was blown. The Queen herself made sure he was led to safety here in the United States. We can trust him and we can rely on him."

Charles stood up, every inch the stiff-upper-lipped Brit. "What we have here," he said waving his arm about, is a multimillion-dollar command center. There is absolutely nothing we can't find out about anybody. I know many people who will help us just for the joy of helping to right old wrongs. There are no codes that can't be broken. I was taught to do this early on in my career and I've stayed up on the latest developments. I'm only telling you this in case we come up against some coded messages or the like. I believe I know just about everything there is to know about encryption. These sophisticated computers and their memory banks rival those at the CIA. I personally built them. Any questions so far?"

The women all shook their heads.

"Good. Then I'll continue. This is how I see it. Obviously the men who attacked Kathryn live somewhere in the state of California. I feel confident in saying somewhere within a five hundred mile radius of where Kathryn was attacked. I see this as a four-man—excuse me, woman—job." Charles's gaze raked the room as he tried to decide which three women would work best with Kathryn in the lead.

Isabelle tugged at her braid, her hands shaking. "I have a question. Maybe it's more of a statement. If this means going to California, I'm afraid I can't go. If I don't work, I won't be able to pay my rent. I can't afford to take off any time. If there's something I can do from this end, I'll be more than happy to comply."

"Isabelle, your bank account is quite robust these days. Your next statement will reflect a transfer of money. You have nothing to worry about, dear. We also paid up your rent and your health insurance a year in advance. Your time is now your sisters' time. This was just a little down payment in advance until we can right your cause," Myra said.

Isabelle nodded gratefully.

"Is anyone else worried about time away?" Charles asked.

"I do not think I can leave the nursery and my husband. He would not understand," Yoko said.

Kathryn stood up, her arms flying upward. Murphy reared up, his ears going flat against his head. "That's it! That's it! Just tell me what the hell you're doing here? Did you think this was going to be some kind of tea party? Don't give me any of that Asian different culture crap either. For starters, I don't want you on my case. All I have to do is look at you to know you're about as dependable as shit."

The picture of serenity, Yoko replied, "You are a hothead, Kathryn."

Taken aback, Kathryn responded bluntly, the way she did everything. "That's true, I am. I'm also kind, considerate, thoughtful and I'm damn loyal to those near and dear to me. When I give my word, I keep it. What's your *shtick?*"

"I am all those things myself, Kathryn. I did not know what to expect when I came here this evening. Now that I know what is expected, I will make arrangements so that I can fulfill my duties to this organization. I wish only to be helpful to all of you. If you have difficulty with my ways, you must tell me. I have no wish to be like you. I want only to be able to understand and act within my own boundaries. You need have no fear of me being, what you called, the weak link. I am very strong, mentally and physically. I had to be, to survive. I just want to help so that when it is my turn you will want to help me."

Kathryn grimaced. "Okay, okay, but I'm still going to keep my eye on you."

"And mine will be on you, also, Kathryn."

"What's next?" Nikki asked, looking at Myra.

The room grew still. Even Charles looked up from the computer he was working on.

"I think we should go into the house and have some food while Charles works on the computers. It is late and we have all day tomorrow to finalize our plans. Is that agreeable to everyone?"

"I must go home," Yoko said.

"No. You will stay," Myra said cooly. "Nikki explained all this to you in advance. Please don't bring this to a test, Yoko. If you do, you will not like the outcome. My arms are long and they stretch quite far."

Yoko bowed. "I will stay, then. I wish to see in writing the next time what the rules are for me."

"The same rules apply to each of us. You aren't special so don't pretend to be something you aren't. You speak fluent English and you graduated college. You were born in this country so don't give us that Asian stuff. I read your dossier," Kathryn snapped irritably.

"We'll see you in the morning, Charles. Would you like some coffee or a sandwich?"

"There can't be food or drink in here, Myra. I'll get something later. We'll meet in the dining room at eight if that's all right with everyone. Good night, ladies."

Everyone except Nikki passed on the offer of food and headed for the staircase that would take them to the second floor. Kathryn walked to the door and let Murphy out. She waited until he returned and then slammed and locked the heavy door.

The storm continued to rage as Nikki followed Myra into the kitchen. "I'm starved. Did Charles make anything good for us?"

"There's a ham and a breast of turkey. Would you like me to make some coffee?"

"Myra, what I would really like is a good triple shot of your best scotch. I think I'll have a ham and turkey sandwich. That's a no on the coffee."

Myra measured coffee into the stainless steel basket. At Nikki's questioning look, she said, "It's for me. Charles will be in later and I know he'll want coffee. How do you think it went, Nikki?"

"I'm not sure, Myra. It got a little tense there for a minute. For the first shot out of the gate, I guess it went okay. This was our first meeting. No one really knew what to expect. I think things will fall into place in the morning when Charles shows us what he retrieved from all those computers. Once we set up a plan, things will level off. The women have to get to know one another. It's the unknown that is throwing everyone into a flap. As much as I hate to admit it, I think it's all going to work out." She leaned her elbows on the table and stared at the sugar bowl.

Myra nodded. She knew this beautiful girl sitting across from her as well as she knew herself. There's something bothering you, Nikki. Do you want to talk about it or is it something personal between you and Jack?"

"I do need to talk, Myra. One of my paralegals told me she saw Jack having dinner with a beautiful redhead the other night. It bothers me. I'm feeling kind of betrayed right now. Marie Lewellen's case goes to court next month. I've used up my last postponement. I can't win it, Myra. Jack knows I'm just going through the motions. He's taking the whole thing personally. I hate it when he does that. You should have heard him the day you posted Marie's bail. He was like a rooster in a duck pond. Did you . . . ah . . . decide when you're going to spirit her and her family away?"

"It's better if you don't know, Nikki. Just go about your daily business the same way you always do."

"Myra, that's goddamn near impossible. I don't have a normal life anymore. I'm up to my eyeballs in illegalities. I could lose my license to practice law. I've lost my boyfriend who was supposed to put a ring on my finger this year. I damn near cheered when those women voted to castrate those creeps that attacked Kathryn. What does that make me, Myra? Tell me. I need to know what I'm turning into here."

"Jack will come back, dear. I'm sure the dinner with the redhead was a witness or a friend. Jack loves you. If you lose your license, we'll have Charles get you a new identity. You know, Nikki, it really isn't all that hard to do if you have the right contacts. You aren't turning into anything. You are still the bright, intelligent girl I love and admire. You haven't changed. Circumstances changed."

Nikki bit into her sandwich. She chewed thoughtfully. "I can't be on Kathryn's team this time around. I have to be here for Marie. After that, I'm all yours. I will take some of that coffee, Myra. By the way, that was a nice thing you did for Isabelle. She's been having a terrible time."

"We'll get her life back for her. If she's the kind of person I think she is, she'll pay me back as soon as possible. I like Kathryn. I wanted to cry for her. I like all the women. It's all so unjust, so unfair. But then that's why we formed the Sisterhood, isn't it?

"Nikki, how will you handle it when Marie Lewellen . . . disappears?"

"Very carefully, Myra. Have you been in touch with her lately?"

"Goodness, no. I've stayed away just the way you said I should. She sent me a note thanking me for posting her bail. I haven't called either. Have you seen her?"

Nikki pushed her plate to the center of the table. "No. I do talk to her on the phone. She told me her husband took his vacation. She said he had something like forty-five days coming to him and was going to do some things to the house. Their pictures are going to be all over the news and in the newspapers. Where are you going to relocate them?"

"It's better if you don't know, Nikki. Julia Webster is going to do some plastic surgery on both Marie and her husband once they're settled in their new home. Children change on a day-to-day basis. We'll have them home-schooled for a year or so until we feel they've changed enough not to warrant scrutiny. We have it under control, dear."

"Okay, I'm off to bed." She looked around. "I always loved this kitchen. I mean, I really loved it."

Myra nodded. "I'll clean up here and make some sandwiches for Charles for later. I know, Nikki, that you still have mixed feelings about what we're doing. I'm hoping in time you will grow as comfortable with it as I have. If not, you'll just have to suck it up," Myra said cheerfully.

In spite of herself, Nikki burst out laughing. She hugged Myra good night before she headed up the kitchen staircase that would take her to her old room at the end of the long hall that ran the length of the house.

"Screw you, Jack," she muttered as she pulled off her sweatpants. As she tugged at the bottom of the pant legs she saw the dark red X on the hem. Barbara always made a red X on her jeans and sweats so they wouldn't mix them up in the laundry. Tears burned her eyes and trickled down her cheeks as her index finger traced the X. "We're doing it for you, Barb. Wherever you are, I hope you understand. I miss you, Barb. I'd give anything if I could talk to you about Jack. Watch over us, okay." She didn't feel the least bit silly or self-conscious talking to someone who wasn't there. Barbara's spirit would always live in this room. The faint scent of her perfume still lingered in the air after all this time. She knew in her heart it would stay in the room forever, just like the furniture would stay as well as her clothes and her skis. She looked over at the rocker that was moving slowly back and forth.

Nikki walked over to the old rocker and placed her hand on the armrest to stop the chair from moving. It continued to rock.

*"What's your problem. Nik?"*

Nikki yelped and ran back to the bed. "Barb?"

*"Yes."*

"Is it really you?"

*"In spirit. Do you want to give me a quiz?"*

Nikki shook her head. Was she dreaming? "I'm glad you're here. At least I think I'm glad you're here. I need to talk to you about Jack. I need to talk to you about a lot of things. You know what's going on, don't you?"

*"Every single thing. I have one kick-ass mother, don't I? If you're asking me if I approve, I do. Get them all, Nik. Make them pay for what they did to those women. I hope you can continue to do it forever. It's about time someone took matters into their own hands. I wish I was there to help you. Just promise me you won't get caught."*

Nikki laughed. I'll do my best not to get caught. Can you just picture me in the slammer?"

*"No, I can't picture that at all. Promise me you'll be careful. I wish I was there to help you and Mom and all those women."*

"God, I wish that so much, Barb. I miss you. It's always worse here in this room. It's like you're still here. I can smell your perfume. I can see your skis leaning up in the corner and your mom gave me your sweatpants tonight. I started to cry when I saw the red X on the bottom of the pants leg. Jack had dinner with some good-looking redhead. My paralegal saw them."

*"They look good on you. Let's get back to Jack. He's just trying to tick you off, Nik. Guys do that, as you and I both found out along the way. He knew your paralegal would tell you she saw him with some good-looking chick. You aren't going to fall for that, are you, Nik?"*

"It doesn't matter. It still hurts. So, how . . . how is it on the . . . other side?"

*"Peaceful. Quiet. Beautiful. We were talking about Jack . . ."*

"He's so competitive. I can't win the case with Marie Lewellen. We all knew that going in. You know the drill, open mouth, insert foot. He took me on. My name is going to be mud when Marie disappears. I'm not calling him, so don't even suggest it."

*"I wasn't going to suggest any such thing. Why don't you call up Mike*

*Deverone and ask him out to dinner. He always had the hots for you. And he has a brain, plus he's an excellent lawyer as you well know."*

"That's a thought."

*"How come I always have to do your thinking for you. Where's Willie? Toss him over here, okay. I miss the little guy.*

Nikki walked over to the twin bed Barbara had always slept in. She pulled down the spread and raised the pillow. She hugged the little bear before she tossed it in the direction of the rocking chair. She almost fainted when she saw the little bear swirl in mid-air and then stop as though someone had reached for it. She plopped down on the edge of her own bed, her emotions running wild as she stared across the room at the rocking chair.

"Listen, are you going to . . . you know, hang around or do you have to . . . go . . . back. I'm dead on my . . . sorry, I'm out on my feet and I have to get up early."

*"I thought I would sit here and rock with Willie for a while. You don't mind, do you? I'll watch over you while you sleep, Nik."*

"No, I don't mind. Barb, do you come here . . . often? If I need you, what should I do?"

*"Just call my name. Hey, isn't there a song by that name?"*

"Probably. There's a song for everything, just like there's a book for everything in the world. There's even a song for pantyhose. You should hear that one. Someone with red hair named Corinda Carford sings it. You'd get a kick out of it, Barb, because you always hated pantyhose. I have the CD in my apartment if you ever want to hear it."

*"Okay. Good night, Nik. Sweet dreams. Don't forget to blow out the candle."*

" 'Night, Barb." Nikki cupped her hands around the flame and blew it out as instructed.

*"Good girl. Now, go to sleep."*

Nikki crunched her pillow into a ball under her head. One eye open, one eye closed, she listened as the rocker moved back and forth on the pine floor, the sound finally lulling her into a deep, dreamless sleep.

# Chapter Four

Murphy nosed open the swinging door that led to the dining room where a buffet was set up on the sideboard. Charles, wearing a pristine white chef's coat, presided over the wide array of food. Myra was already seated at the head of the table, her napkin spread on her lap. She looked regal as always. She motioned for the women to take their seats.

"Good morning, ladies. I trust you slept well," Charles said. The women nodded as he poured orange juice from a crystal pitcher into elegant goblets. Myra poured the coffee from an antique, silver pot that had once belonged to her great grandmother.

"For breakfast we have ham, bacon, sausage, kippers, scones, Eggs Benedict, waffles, pancakes and a banana-pear compote. Tell me what you would like and it will be my pleasure to serve you," Charles said.

Kathryn giggled. "I'll have one of everything and Murphy gets the same. He eats what I eat. Who cooked all this? No offense, Myra, but you don't look like the type who cooks."

Myra smiled. "I told you Charles was a man of many talents. He prepared breakfast. He graciously allowed me to do the place setting. I apologize for the lack of flowers on the table."

"Are the telephones working yet?" Yoko queried.

"Unfortunately, no."

Yoko dropped her gaze to stare at her lap.

Kathryn bristled as the others all started to talk at once.

"Is the power on?" Julia asked.

"Yes, the power came on around six this morning just as Charles was finishing up his work. I really don't like to talk about business at mealtime, so let's speak of pleasantries," Myra said as she buttered a scone, Charles's specialty.

"Tell us about this old house," Alexis said. "It's beautiful. I just love old houses that are steeped in charm and character. I bought a little house before . . . you know, *before*. It was a cozy little bungalow with a garden bathroom and a real fireplace. I had window boxes jam-packed with flowers and I had these clay pots of flowers on each side of the steps. I just loved that little house."

"Past tense, Alexis?" Isabelle said.

"I had to sell it to help pay my legal fees. I have a small apartment now with a shower and no bathtub."

"That's all going to change, dear. I promise," Myra said. "You asked about this house. It's over three hundred years old. The property spreads out over three hundred acres. My neighbors are a mile away in each direction. We really are secluded, which works to our advantage. My family was always interested in preserving the rights of others and preserving justice. My great-grandfather was a judge and so was my grandfather. My parents and grandparents never *owned* slaves. They had paid workers and after so many years of service, each family was given a generous plot of land. Pinewood originally consisted of over a thousand acres. All but the remaining three hundred acres that I own were given away to the people who worked for our family. My grandparents, along with several other families, aided the runaway slaves through the tunnels under the house.

"I feel like I'm now in a position to do my part by carrying out my ancestors' tradition of helping others."

"This looks absolutely delicious," Nikki said, digging into her Eggs Benedict.

"If there's nothing else I can serve you ladies, I'll leave you and meet up with you again in our command center, in, let's say, ninety minutes. Enjoy your breakfast."

"Wherever did you find that jewel of a man?" Julia asked.

"I knew Charles in my youth. My parents at the time didn't think his lifestyle was befitting a Southern lady like myself, so after three months in Europe, they dragged me back home," Myra drawled. "I married later on and took over the candy company. It was just a short time later when our offices got a call from the Queen herself asking if Charles could be relocated here to us in the United States because Charles's life was in danger. We said yes and he took over the security of the firm. It was the best decision I ever made. We both retired at the same time. And now, we've all arrived at this place in time. With Charles's expertise, we're going to make the Sisterhood work for all of us."

Nikki stood up and patted her stomach. "That was a wonderful breakfast and I ate way too much. Would anyone like more coffee?" she asked.

"Fill it up," Kathryn said, holding up her cup.

"I've had my limit," Isabelle said.

Alexis and Julia shook their heads.

"I would prefer tea," Yoko said.

Kathryn rolled her eyes. "Now, why did I know you were going to say that? When in Rome . . ."

Myra stood up in the hope of warding off another verbal confrontation between Yoko and Kathryn. "I'd like you to meet my ancestors," she said, pointing to the various old-fashioned sepia-toned pictures in heavy gilt frames "This is my mother and father. On the far wall are my grandparents and next to them, their parents. The other family members, and there are many, are on the wall going up the staircase. This is my daughter Barbara when she was six. It was her first pony," Myra said, pointing to a modern painting over the sideboard. You might not recognize her, but the picture next to Barbara on her first pony is our Nikki. They were both such sturdy little girls," she said with a catch in her voice.

"Our ninety minutes are about up, Myra. We both know Charles doesn't like to be kept waiting. I can clear up things here and join you when I'm finished if that's all right with you," Nikki said in an effort to drive away the stricken look on Myra's face.

"Of course, dear. We can fill you in when you join us," Myra said, leading the parade out of the dining room and down the hall to the living room. Within minutes they were all seated at the round table, their faces expectant as Charles waved a sheaf of papers.

Charles walked around the table much the way a teacher does when giving a test.

"This is what I was able to retrieve. The computers are still working and these things take time. There are motorcycle groups and organizations in every one of our fifty states. There are as many as ninety such organizations in some states while others may only have three or four. I have here eight thousand clubs. I was able to whittle that number down to forty-seven when I asked the computer to flush out just Indian motorbikes. In addition to the forty-seven organizations, there are splinter groups that I was able to track down. Sometimes they spring up overnight, so the count is not as accurate as I would like. I further condensed the number when I asked for just Weekend Warriors. The computer tells me there are twenty-nine Weekend Warrior groups. From those twenty-nine

groups, nine cells have splintered off and are now calling themselves Road Warriors. A total of eleven groups that meet our criteria
are located in California.

"I filled out an application to join both the Weekend Warriors as
well as the Road Warriors. My application arrived while we were
having breakfast. I faxed it back moments ago. When you're accepted, you're given a handbook with the rules and regulations,
dates and times of meetings, proposed road trips, a calendar of
events as well as a list of all the members along with their addresses
and phone numbers. This only happens after you pay your dues,
which is quite hefty: $900 a year. You have to send them a scanned
picture of yourself, which I did. I gave them my credit card number.
As soon as it clears, I have the choice of having them overnight the
materials or I will be given a password and I can download said
material. I'm electing to download. The faxes should be coming
through any minute now and Kathryn can see if her attackers still
belong to either group."

"Way to go, Charles," Kathryn chortled. He preened for her benefit. The others clapped their hands in glee.

"What'd I miss, What'd I miss?" Nikki said, taking her seat at the
table. "By the way, the power went out again."

Myra shrugged. "We'll fill you in later, dear. Just listen to Charles
for now. He is absolutely amazing."

"I then checked the Department of Motor Vehicles and managed
to secure the license plates for the Indian motorcycles in those nine
groups." Charles took a deep breath and stared straight at Kathryn.
"I found one plate with the same three numbers you gave us. I now
have the full license plate number. It belongs to Dr. Clark Wagstaff.
He's an oral surgeon in Los Angeles. I ran a D&B on him and the
report just came back. Dr. Wagstaff owns the medical building he
practices in. His net worth, excluding the medical building, is
around nine million. He takes in over a million dollars a year after
taxes. I'm checking his income tax records. That might take a little
longer but I will have answers for you by the end of the day. Possibly
sooner."

Kathryn's clenched fists shot upward. "Yessss. What about the
one they called Lee? Were you able to pull up anything on him?"

"I won't know about Lee until the rest of the faxes come
through. I tend to think he's a colleague or possibly a business partner. I think it's safe to say the third man is either a relative or another colleague."

The phone on the fax machine rang. Charles smiled. The women sat back, their eyes glued to the machine next to Charles.

Twenty minutes later Charles stacked the faxed sheets into the printer and made copies for each woman. He handed them out. "My job for the moment is done. What you have to do now is come up with a plan to bring these three men together. I'm going to see if I can catch an hour or so of sleep. Which one of you really knows your way around a computer? Nikki?"

"I'm pretty good at it. Why?"

"Let me show you. When Kathryn identifies the three men, I want you to log on to this particular computer and type in the name. Send it as an e-mail to this address," he said pointing to an e-mail address on a yellow pad next to the computer bank. "In an hour's time you will have a report on each man from the day they were born. Can you handle it, Nikki?"

"Yes. Charles, who does this e-mail address belong to?" Nikki hissed as a vision of the FBI, the CIA and Washington D.C.'s District Attorney, Jack Emery, pounding on Myra's front door flashed in front of her eyes.

"Why, the Queen of course. Ask a silly question and you get a silly answer. I'll see you all in a bit."

Myra picked up her pen and yellow pad. "You need a plan, Kathryn. Something that will entice these men to want to participate. You said you and your husband used to ride. What was it you liked? What kind of invitation would you consider accepting? Just how enthusiastic are bikers?"

Kathryn talked as she flipped through the faxes. "Bikers are a breed unto themselves. Alan and I weren't bikers in the true sense of the word. We used to do back road trails just for fun on weekends. It's the speed, the wind in your face, your hair flying behind you. That part isn't the same anymore because the laws changed and now you have to wear helmets. It's that free spirit thing everyone aspires to. Then there's the camaraderie, the stories. You know, like fishermen when they say they caught a *really* big one. Maybe a contest. All expenses paid. Perhaps a prize that would be impossible to turn down. The prize could be a mint-condition Indian if you could manage to get your hands on one. I have to tell you they are almost impossible to find. A mint-condition Indian would definitely raise the stakes."

Myra scribbled on her pad. "I think Charles will be able to find us one."

"No, Myra, you don't understand. We don't need an actual bike.

We're just going to say that on the invitation to whet their appetite. To make them want to do whatever it is we come up with. We're only inviting the three of them, right?" Kathryn asked. She flipped more pages and finally let out a whoop. This one!" she said, waving the paper high in the air. "Dr. Sidney Lee!"

"Two down and one to go. Keep looking, Kathryn," Nikki said.

Isabelle interrupted. "No, no, no. You have to invite a select group and you really do need to have the bike as a prize. Invite maybe a dozen or so besides the three in question. It will make it look more real. You will have to award the bike to one of the others to avoid questions later on. When the trip is over, we spirit the three away and no one will be the wiser."

"This is not going to be the piece of cake you think it is. If these men have wives, we have to set something up for them so they don't go yapping to the cops. Maybe we could tell them they all won a trip to the Golden Door or something. Or a package deal, the wives get the spa and the guys get the road trip. Then you have to allow for the time we snatch them. How many days? And what about their offices? Are they going to be closed, open, what?" Alexis said as she doodled on the pad in front of her. "We have to get them back here so Julia can slice and dice. Then we have to get them back to California. It could get hairy."

"We can use my rig for transport. Cycles and all. Five days driving cross country. Five days back. Maybe four if we push it. That's eight or nine days just driving time. And that's not allowing for sleep. We need time for Julia to hack off their balls. Unless she does it in back of the truck. We can spray some Lysol or something. What kind of time are we looking at, Julia?" Kathryn stopped turning the pages of the faxes. "This is the third one," she said, her voice filled with venom. "Dr. Samuel La Fond." She handed the sheet to Nikki.

"Sixteen hours at least. They'll be sedated. I don't have a problem doing it in back of the truck," Julia said.

"Okay. We'll drop them off at some place close to the area where the ride is to take place. I think it's definitely a plan. What do you think, Yoko?" Kathryn asked.

"I think it will work. I would like to offer a suggestion. After . . . after the surgery you will want to stay to see their reaction. That will not be a good thing, Kathryn. I think you should go to their offices first so you can look at them in the bright light. You have waited many years for this. Do not deprive yourself of seeing them in their own environment. It is unlikely they will recognize you. Although, you might have to dye your hair or Alexis can change your appearance some way. I think it will help you to see them before . . . before they have their respective surgeries. That is all I have to say."

"Yoko, I think you're absolutely right. What do the rest of you think? Is it a good idea or not?" Kathryn asked.

"Very good," Nikki said. "Yoko is right, once you dump them you have to get far away. It's a rough plan, but doable. Now we need to give some thought to what they'll do when they pull their pants down for the first time. Are they going to go to the police? Will they call the other guys who were on the trip to find out if they're minus any of their body parts? They're going to be together so that means they're going to discover their . . . respective surgeries around the same time. If you were the only one they attacked, Kathryn, they're going to put two and two together. If attacking women is a pastime with them, they won't know who to blame. The police will have to ask a lot of questions. They aren't going to admit they raped any-one. We need to think about this a minute. What would be the charge if they reported it? In all the years of practicing law, this . . . this type of . . . case never came up."

"Grand theft of the genitalia," Alexis volunteered. She did her best not to laugh out loud.

"Police reports are a matter of public record. They could print the report in the newspaper. How's that going to look? They'll have to leave the country," Isabelle smirked.

"They won't tell their friends because part of the biker psyche is that testosterone thing. They'll be like wild animals till they figure it out. They could come after you, Kathryn. Bikers are like truckers. They take care of their own. I saw that on a documentary once," Myra said. "What do you think, Nikki?"

"I think you're right. I think you were their one shot, Kathryn. The time was right for them. The situation felt right, where you parked, your incapacitated husband, the whole thing. If they're pil-lars of their community and they probably are, they wouldn't risk doing something that terrible again and again. What you're going to need, Kathryn, is an airtight alibi for the time in question. Is-abelle is about your height. Alexis can make her look enough like you to pass muster. We can have her go to a resort or something, register under your name, use your credit card. She'll make herself scarce so people don't get a good look at her. A good red wig, a lit-tle patching here and there with some spirit gum and voilà, she's you. Can you deal with that, Kathryn?"

"Absolutely."

Almost to the minute of Charles's prediction, the e-mail pinged.

"Oh, excuse me, incoming mail," Nikki said, getting up from the table.

Nikki pressed download and waited for the sent material to complete the transition. She then clicked Print and waited. Page after page shot out of the printer with amazing speed. She scooped up the pages before she transferred them to the copy machine and printed out nine copies. One copy for everyone plus one extra. She was about to hit the Delete button a second later when the e-mail disappeared in front of her eyes. She felt a chill wash up her spine. She added the extra set of papers to the bottom of her own report.

"My goodness," Myra said. "This is so thorough. I suggest we read them in silence and then discuss each man. Do you all approve?" The women nodded as they lowered their heads to read the reports in front of them.

A long time later, Myra removed her glasses and looked around at the women.

"This is the most amazing thing I've ever read. These men are such upstanding citizens it boggles my mind. They sit on various charitable boards. They donate handsomely to many worthy causes. All three are incredibly wealthy. Their children go to Ivy League colleges. Their wives do volunteer work. They all donate one day a week at a free clinic. They go to church on Sunday with their wives. They play golf one day a month. Two weekends a month they take road trips with the Weekend Warriors. They've never been caught in an uncompromising position and there is no hint of scandal attached to them in any way. The three of them have been friends since college days. They're well thought of with their patients and have a thriving, lucrative practice. They do not falsify insurance records and they don't cheat on their income taxes.

"Each of them has an Indian and something called a Harley Hog. That about sums it up, sisters."

"That's a pretty impressive report," Kathryn said quietly. She looked at the faces staring at her. "I'm not saying they aren't all those things. They raped me and the one named Lee sodomized me. That should be added to the report." Her voice turned desperate-sounding when she said, "They stripped me naked and knew my husband was watching when they did all those things to me. That makes them no better than wild animals in my eyes."

"I think your gums just started to recede, Kathryn. I'll call and make an appointment for you. In the meantime, we have the rest of the day to fine-tune our plan. Choose your partners for this project and tell me when you feel you'll be ready to leave. You have a month to complete this project. You must be back here by the first Monday of the month, at which time we'll pick our second case."

"I need to take Murphy outside. He needs some exercise. Is it okay?" Kathryn asked.

"Of course. Come along, dear. I think we could all use a break about now. I can make some coffee and some tea for Yoko. The phone lines might be repaired and hopefully, the power is on. Charles said he was going to gas up the kitchen generator so let's hope he did or we'll be drinking soda pop."

Kathryn headed for the front door, Isabelle and Alexis headed for the stairs and the upstairs bathroom while Myra, Nikki, Yoko and Julia walked toward the kitchen.

Outside in the bright sunshine, Kathryn walked alongside her dog. She raised her eyes once to look upward. She muttered under her breath, words she'd said thousands of times, always under her breath. Except that one time when Alan had his last seizure and she'd screamed at the top of her lungs because she couldn't take it one day longer. Her husband had just stared at her and then closed his eyes. She knew in that one split second that he'd finally given up. Two hours later she held him in her arms and kissed him for the last time.

"I hope you can hear me, Alan. It's payback time!"

Murphy nudged her leg.

"I'm okay, Murphy. I'm okay now."

# Chapter Five

The TV wall monitor blossomed to light with a *zzzzzing* sound. The figure of the scales of justice consumed the entire screen within seconds. Kathryn felt like she should stand up and voice a loud cheer. She thought about it a second longer and then she did it, a look of pure joy on her face. "Hey, she's my kind of lady! I'm taking that blindfold to mean she's looking the other way because the other way sucks. Okay, that's it, that's all I have to say." Her voice was sheepish-sounding. The others smiled.

Charles hit the computer keys, the clicking sound loud in the quiet room. A map of the state of California appeared. He clicked again and again, localizing different areas, talking and explaining as map after map took over the screen. "You need to decide on a specific area for your proposed road trip. Once you've settled on a route, we can fine-tune it so we don't have any glitches. I took the liberty of making a list of twelve possible candidates for the trip. I selected four Road Warriors and eight Weekend Warriors plus the three 'special guests.' We'll have a total of fifteen cycles on the trip. Since our three nefarious cyclists live in the Los Angeles area, it would seem logical to start the trip there.

"I would like to make a suggestion here. Lone Pine is about six hours from Los Angeles and about four hours north from where you were attacked, Kathryn. It's remote but there is a little town. The overnight camp stay, if that's what you're considering, could take place in the Alabama Hills. If you're planning on taking your truck, Kathryn, it would have to be parked on a dedicated road so as not to leave tire marks." He clicked the keys and a map of Lone Pine appeared. "I'll print these out for you and an alternative route if you decide this doesn't fit your needs."

"How are we going to decide who wins the Indian?" Kathryn asked.

Myra smiled and reached to the middle of the table for the shoebox. "The same way we chose your case to be first. It's called the luck of the draw. Very apropos, don't you think?"

"I like it," Yoko smiled. The others beamed their approval.

"Then what?" Julia asked.

"Then they make camp, build a fire, have a few drinks followed by dinner at the restaurant in town. Assuming there is a restaurant in Lone Pine. Where, as luck would have it, we are sitting there in our biker duds, you know, tight black leather pants, our tits half hanging out of our vests, lots of silver stud jewelry, our Harleys parked out front, courtesy of my truck and Myra. The wealthy philanthropist, Charles in disguise, will appear with the shoebox and a certificate of ownership for the Indian that will be shipped to the lucky person in a fortnight. How's that, Charles? A fortnight is two weeks, right?"

Charles allowed himself a small smile. "Correct."

"We party hearty, make sure the others get back to camp while one of us keeps our three busy. We then load them and their bikes into my truck and split. When the others wake in the morning, they'll have mega hangovers and just assume our three got lucky with us three and head off home. I think it will work as soon as we—as Charles puts it—fine-tune the whole scenario. What do you all think? Will it fly?"

The women's heads bobbed up and down.

"Okay, this is what we need in the way of material things. Sisters, get your pencils ready. We need three Harley Hogs. That's so they'll take us seriously. Women on Hogs are special. Trust me on that. They'll be brand new, Myra, so you can resell them to get your money back afterward." Myra waved her hand in dismissal to show she wasn't concerned about the cost.

"We have my truck. Julia knows what we'll need for her list and will write everything down or bring it from her office. Whatever works for her. Alexis will need to replenish her disguise trunk or whatever she uses to change our appearances. We'll need biker duds, the leather. Secondhand would be best, so they look worn in. Push-up bras. Our tits have to be up and almost out of the vests. Lots of silver junk stud jewelry. Worn boots in our size so we don't get blisters."

"Why do our tits have to hang out?" Yoko asked, her face miserable. "My breasts are small."

"Because they do," Julia said. "Alexis can build you up with that putty stuff. You can be a thirty-six B if you want. You might be a little top-heavy but you won't be bending over so it shouldn't be a problem."

Yoko's almond-shaped eyes literally turned round. "You can do this?" she said, directing her question to Alexis.

"Honey, I can give you a set of knockers that will blow any man's socks off," Alexis grinned.

Myra laughed aloud while Charles turned about, his ears and neck bright red.

"I accept," Yoko said smartly.

"Done," Kathryn said, smacking the tabletop. "What's next?"

"What's next are the wives," Nikki said. "I think it should be a separate entity and not part of the bike deal. We'll send them two weeks ahead of the bike trip and then they have two weeks afterward. That will also make it easier for the men to accept the road trip without harping wives. Their kids are all in college so that won't pose any problems. Myra, you will be the wealthy female philanthropic person like Charles who donates these three free months to their wives. All three of them do volunteer charity work, according to the dossier Charles printed out. Just pick out an organization they help out, make it your pet charity, and award the certificates. How does that sound?"

"I love it," Myra said. "Thank you for giving me a job to do. I was afraid I would have to sit here and wait for details." She looked so pleased, so grateful, Nikki found herself smiling.

"You are the CIC, Myra. You need to keep your hand in all this," Kathryn laughed.

"CIC?" Myra said, looking perplexed.

"Yeah. You know, Cat *In* Charge!"

"Oh, I see. Yes. Cat *In* Charge. So I am, dear. Did you hear that, Charles?"

"Meow!" Charles said.

"Doncha love it when a plan starts to come together?" Kathryn said. "What does that leave us yet to do?"

"The invitations. I'm sure Charles has a program for that. We have to cover our butts in our private lives and then we have to make arrangements to get to California," Isabelle said.

"I have to pick up a load of toilet seats, four thousand to be exact, and they have to be in San Francisco by next week. I was supposed to dead head back with a load of carrots but I can cancel that and pick up a load of lettuce when we're done. You're welcome to drive with me or you can fly and we'll meet up. If Isabelle is staying here, and Nikki has to be here for her court case, that means Julia, Alexis and Yoko have to partner with me."

"I will drive with you, Kathryn. We can get to know one another. Perhaps I can learn not to be afraid of your dog. Will you have me as your navigator?"

"No!" The single word shot out of Kathryn's mouth so fast her tongue felt like it had been scorched. "Wait! I didn't mean no you can't go with me. What I meant was . . . Alan always said he was my navigator. That means you can't be my navigator. You can be . . . you can be . . ."

". . . your lookout?" Yoko said.

"Yeah. Yeah, lookout is good. No offense, Yoko."

"None taken, Kathryn. I understand. It is possible we might become friends."

*Anything is possible,* Kathryn thought. "I suppose." Yoko smiled warmly.

"We need to make reservations if Kathryn's stand-in is to go on vacation. It's still Isabelle, isn't it?"

Myra looked at Isabelle, who nodded. "Isabelle can make the reservations and work with Alexis on her disguise. I see a possible problem."

Nikki stopped writing long enough to look up and say, "What do you see?"

"Kathryn's truck. Earlier we said when the men try to figure out what happened to them, they would start looking at possibilities and eventually Kathryn's name will come up. If her truck isn't here, and she makes a delivery to San Francisco, that puts her and her truck in California. Even though she is making a legitimate delivery and picking up a legitimate delivery on the way back, it's still going to be a problem."

Julia jumped in. "Unless, after the delivery of the . . . ah toilet seats, she offhandedly tells the people at the delivery site that she's taking two weeks off and going to a resort for a few weeks. Isabelle will make her reservation from San Francisco so she has a ticket to prove that she, a.k.a. Kathryn, did indeed leave there, registered at a resort and then flew back to San Francisco and from there back to here under her own name."

"You need to tell us, Kathryn, how you're going to get fuel on your way to Lone Pine or whatever destination you choose. If you stop along the way, someone is going to remember a woman truck driver. This is all based on the men honing in on you, Kathryn. It may never happen. But, if it does, we need to protect you," Nikki said.

Kathryn looked up at the platform where Charles was standing next to the computer bank. He nodded. "I think I can make arrangements for fuel along the way." He scribbled something on the pad he was holding in his hands.

"Any other questions or details you think we need to discuss?" Nikki asked, looking around the table.

Myra stood up. "I'm going to make us some lunch. Kathryn, you might want to take your dog for a walk. Nikki will assign each of you to a computer where you will order whatever you need shipped to this box number in Washington, D.C. Overnight everything. We have a special Visa for things like this. She'll give you the number. Charles will work on getting the motorcycles. He'll arrange for you to pick them up in San Francisco for your trip north. Talk among yourselves, make it as easy as possible. Pay attention to all the little details people tend to ignore. The little details that can trip you up. I'll come for you when lunch is ready."

In the foyer, Myra looked up at the chandelier. "Ah, the power is on again. Light always makes things so much better, don't you think, dear?"

Kathryn held the door open for the dog. He bounded outside. "I don't know. Myra. It seems I've lived in darkness for so long I can't tell the difference anymore. I don't know what to do. I'm lost. It was like Alan was an extension of myself. I took care of him for so long I don't know what to do with myself. When he was lying there in that . . . that box . . . I got so angry. I screamed and yelled at him for leaving me. He didn't give a good rat's ass about me. He was so ready to die it was pathetic.

"You know what else, Myra. There was only one other person at Alan's funeral beside myself. A trucker who just happened to be in the area. I wanted to kick him out of the funeral home but I didn't. The damn funeral director kept coming into the room that was bare of flowers because I didn't even have enough money left to buy a bunch of daisies to put on his casket. I have to deliver those toilet seats and I have to bring back a load of lettuce or I won't be able to pay for his funeral. I had to charge his funeral. Alan must be spinning in his grave. That damn undertaker wanted me to cremate him, said it was cheaper. I couldn't do that because I need to have him in a place where I can . . . I can go. I didn't want him blowing away in the wind. What does that make me, Myra?"

"A grieving widow who loved her husband. I paid for your husband's funeral, Kathryn. You can pay me back someday or not pay me back. It really doesn't matter. I'm so sorry for your loss because I know *exactly* how you feel. When my daughter died, I wanted to die with her. It wasn't until Nikki and I saw Marie Lewellen shoot the man on the courthouse steps that I came to life. That's what I should have done but I was so grief-stricken, all I could do was think about my own misery. She had the guts to shoot and kill the man who took her child's life. I can't wait till my case comes up," Myra said vehemently.

"I'll personally kill the son of a bitch for you, Myra. No parent should have to bury a child. I do thank you for paying for Alan's funeral. I didn't know you had done that. I swear, I'll pay you back." She opened the door for Murphy.

"Kathryn, you may not be able to go back to trucking if you stay in the Sisterhood. Your time will be required on the cases we have to deal with. Perhaps not every one, but on most of them. Charles and I have taken the liberty of fattening up your bank account as well as the other sisters'. If we want this project to be successful, we can't have you worrying about food and bills, now can we?"

"Just how rich are you, Myra?" Kathryn asked bluntly. "If I had a hundred bucks in my bank account, I'd feel rich. Dog food and diesel fuel are expensive."

"I'm sure they are, but you don't have to worry about that anymore. As to how rich I am, I'm not sure. My accountants tell me I'm a billionaire. And all that money comes from making candy. The first batch was made right here in this kitchen on this very table. The old wood-burning stove is gone, but I'm sure they poured the candy into trays on this table. Is your dog hungry?"

"He's always hungry. The day I got him I forgot to feed him. He didn't whine or cry or anything. He just waited. I have so many regrets, Myra. I need to know something. I don't know if you have the answer or not but I have to ask. When my case is over, what if I don't feel vindicated? What if . . . I'm not doing this for me. I'm doing it for Alan."

Myra whirled around. "Stop right there. You are not doing this for Alan. You are doing it for yourself. You have to admit that to yourself. You cannot hide behind your husband. Make no mistake about that. I think there are many things you need to come to terms with, Kathryn. In your off time, dear, I'll make arrangements for you to talk to a psychiatrist and a grief counselor. I should have done that but I didn't. You're much too young to let all of what went on before destroy your life. Don't even think about saying no. Mothers always know best."

"Then I won't say no. Do you have any scraps or leftovers I can feed Murphy?"

"I thought you said he ate what you ate. We have turkey, ham and I think there's some roast beef. Fix him a plate and then you can set the table while I make sandwiches and coffee."

"Myra, do you mind if I ask you something?"

"No, dear, ask me anything you like."

"Do you think we'll get caught? Do you think there's anyone out there smart enough to figure out what we're doing?"

Myra looked down at the ham platter she was holding. "I look at it this way, Kathryn. No one's luck holds forever. I'm sure at least one of us will make a mistake along the way. Will it be a serious mistake we can correct or will it be so serious we get caught? I don't know the answer to that. I'm sure there are many smart people out there who, if they had all the facts, would put two and two together. If we're careful, if we stick to our plan, I think we can have a good run. Charles and I have had two years to put all this together. There are many safeguards in place. I don't want you to worry about a thing. Charles and I will do the worrying. Besides, that's what you're supposed to do when you get old. Please don't deprive us of this pleasure."

"Okay, Myra."

"What's wrong with your dog, Kathryn?" Myra asked as the fur on the huge dog's head and back stood on end. He growled, a low menacing sound.

Kathryn whirled around. "Someone's coming. What should I do?"

Myra ran to the kitchen window. "It's Jack Emery. He's Nikki's beau. Boyfriend, significant other, or whatever you call them these days. Quick, Kathryn, take Murphy and go up the kitchen stairs. Don't let him bark. I'll get rid of Jack. Hurry." She put her hands to her head as though that would help her to think as she grappled with the knowledge that Jack Emery was going to be knocking on her door any second.

She looked down at the plate on the floor and quickly set it in the sink. She jerked at the refrigerator door handle and jammed the ham platter onto the shelf just as the kitchen doorbell rang.

He was so good-looking, Myra wished she was thirty years younger. "My goodness, Jack, what *are* you doing out here at this time of day? Nikki isn't here. Her car wouldn't start so Charles

drove her into town. They're coming to tow it any minute now. *Please, please, don't let Nikki or Charles come out here. Please.*
"I called her apartment but there was no answer. She's not in the office, either." His tone was so cold, Myra frowned.
"Maybe she went shopping. I am not her keeper, Jack." *Now he's going to ask about the gate, the cars and Kathryn's truck.* "Is something wrong?"
Of course there was something wrong. She steeled herself for the words she knew were coming.
"You caught me just as I was leaving. I'm playing bridge this afternoon. If I hear from Nikki, I'll tell her you drove all the way out here to see her. You should have called and I could have saved you the trip, Jack."
"Marie Lewellen split. She's gone and she took her family with her. That means you lose the bail money you posted."
Myra allowed a shocked look to spread across her face as she asked in a horrified voice, "All of it? The whole million dollars! I refuse to believe that. Are you saying she . . . moved? She wouldn't do that. Where could she possibly go? Maybe the family went on an outing. Disney World is a possibility. Distraction, one last family vacation before the trial, that kind of thing." *That sounded real good, Myra. Keep your wits about you.*
"She split, all right. I'm sure she had some help. No, no one saw anything. She must have left during the heart of the storm. No one was out and about. This is Nik's fault. You never should have posted her bail, Myra. I know Nik talked you into it. This trial was nothing but a farce using the taxpayer's money. It's cut and dried. We could have saved a lot of money by her pleading guilty and cutting a deal."
"I don't much care for your tone of voice, young man. This is between you and Nikki. It's my million dollars to lose, not yours, so don't get huffy and righteous with me. And while we're in this talk mode, why did you cheat on my Nikki?"
"What are you talking about? I didn't cheat on Nik!"
"Then who was that redhead you were seen having dinner with?"
"My sister-in-law. Are you sure you don't know where Nik is, Myra?"
"I don't have a clue."
"Who do all those cars belong to out there?"
"Why are you asking me all these questions, Jack? The cars belong to the canasta girls. It's so weird. None of them would start.

Charles had to ferry everyone home. The garages are going to make a fortune today."

"Who does the rig belong to?"

Myra put her hands on her hips. "Now why are you asking me all these questions, Jack? Not that it's any of your business, but they delivered some fixtures for the bathrooms upstairs. I'm going to do some remodeling. You know, sinks, tubs, toilets, *toilet seats,* that kind of thing. The driver asked if he could sleep for a few hours, since he had to go back on the road. I thought he had left. I wouldn't go near that truck if I were you. The driver has a mean, vicious dog with him. Dogs are better than guns. I saw that on a documentary not too long ago. I don't mean to rush you, Jack, but I have to get ready for my pinochle game."

"I thought you said you were playing bridge."

"Did I? Well, we never really decide until we sit down. Maybe it's poker today. Then again, it might be canasta. Is it important for you to know what kind of game I'm playing?"

"No. I was making conversation, Myra. Was Nik jealous?"

"No. She was . . . pissed off. She has a date with someone named Deverone. Do you know him? She said he has a brain. I really have to go, Jack. I hope you find Marie and her family. I really don't want to lose my million dollars. You people aren't very sharp, are you?"

"Oh we're sharp, all right. That woman had some help. Don't you worry, I'll find her. And the people who helped her. Aiding and abetting a murderer is a serious offense."

"It certainly is," Myra said, properly horrified.

"Be sure to tell Nik to call me if you hear from her."

"I'll do that. It was nice seeing you again, Jack. I wish the circumstances weren't so dire. Please let me know if you find Mrs. Lewellen. I would like to get my bond back." Jack nodded.

Myra scooted over to the kitchen window and crossed her fingers. "Don't let him go near the truck. Please don't let him go near the truck," she muttered. He didn't. She didn't realize she was holding her breath until it exploded from her mouth in a loud *swoosh.*

"You can come down now, Kathryn. Hurry. I have to warn Nikki that Jack was here."

Myra threw the dead bolt on the kitchen door before she headed for the living room and the secret panel. The moment the panel was back in place, she rushed to Nikki.

"Jack was just here. He said Marie Lewellen split during the night. He wanted you. I couldn't come to get you, so I said Charles had taken you back to town. He's pretty upset, Nikki. He wants you to call him. The redhead was his sister-in-law."

Myra plopped down onto her chair, breathless with what had just transpired.

"He questioned all the cars and the truck, Nikki."

"Did he, now?"

"Yes, and he didn't believe a word I said. I could see it in his face."

# Chapter Six

Nikki gathered up her papers and jammed them into a bright yellow folder she removed from her briefcase. She looked around, honing in on Myra. "Just for the record, Jack doesn't have a brother. He has a sister who lives in Canada. She comes here quite often. As a matter of fact, I saw her a few weeks ago at the hairdressers.

"I have to go back to town. The judge probably has a warrant out for me by now. Charles, you're going to have to drive me in keeping with Myra's little . . . fib. I have to CYA. It won't hurt to call a garage to come out and look at *all* the cars. Just shrug and keep saying they wouldn't start. It's called covering your ass, Myra. Jack isn't just sharp, he's razor sharp. Are you getting my point?"

Myra made a mental note to call to have the gate repaired. "Yes, dear. We'll carry on here. Call me and let me know how things are going. Tell the judge I'm very distraught over Mrs. Lewellen and ask him what recourse, if any, I might have. Tell him I send my regards and to say hello to Mavis."

Nikki snapped the lock on her briefcase. "Let's hit the road, Charles." At Myra's inquiring look, she said, "The Sisterhood stuff is in this file." She pointed to a bright yellow folder with a sticker on the top that said, *Quinn Law.* "I'll call you after I speak with the judge . . . and Jack."

Nikki followed Charles through the secret opening and then waited until she was certain it was closed tightly before she said, "Did Myra tell the others about Marie Lewellen? I know Julia knows, but what about the others?"

"She's going to tell them now," Charles said, reaching for his keys on the hook by the kitchen door.

Ninety minutes later Nikki marched down the corridor that led to Judge Olsen's office. She gave her name to his secretary and took a seat, her heart fluttering in her chest. She did her best to steel herself for what she knew was coming.

Ruth McIntyre looked over her granny glasses to stare at Nikki. "The judge has been trying to reach you for hours, Miss Quinn." The statement clearly said her routine, as well as Judge Olsen's routine, had been upset with their inability to get in touch with her.

"I was in McLean, Mrs. McIntyre. It was impossible to leave, with the storm and all. The power went out. The phones went down. The battery on my cell phone went dead. I apologize."

"Mr. Emery was here bright and early. The judge and myself were both here at seven." The glasses on the end of her pointy nose jiggled with indignation.

Nikki eyeballed the cranky secretary and didn't flinch. *I'm really sick of this crap,* she thought. A tiny smile played around the corners of her mouth. It was downright amazing what a group of women hell-bent on securing justice could do to one's psyche. "Jack Emery can walk from his apartment to the courthouse while I, on the other hand, was over an hour away. I'm here now," she said tightly.

Nikki continued to stare at the judge's secretary. She absolutely would not allow this woman to intimidate her. *She's got to be ninety if she's a day,* she thought. She still wore her hair in the style of the 1920s, with its side part and tight finger waves. Pressed powder covered her face and filled the deep trenches alongside her mouth and under her chin. Perfect quarter-sized circles of rouge were painted dead center on her cheeks. Waxy, salmon colored lipstick crept up to and filled in the deep lines over and under her lips. Even from this distance, she could smell her Evening in Paris perfume.

Today the indomitable old bat was wearing a high-necked blouse with a flounce curled around her stringy neck. Nikki knew it was a flounce because Ruth McIntyre said it was a flounce. Myra said she never heard of such a thing, but then Myra was a fashion plate and didn't hark to the olden days like Ruth McIntyre did. She was in a time warp, bottom line.

"I have a call in to Mr. Emery. I believe he's somewhere in the courthouse. I had him paged. You'll just have to wait till he gets here. The judge isn't going to want to go through this mess twice."

"That's fine. After all, it's not like I have anything else to do, Mrs. McIntyre," Nikki responded, her reply courteous but sarcastic. She reached over for a battered and tattered copy of *National Geographic.* She flipped through the curled-back pages and was about to replace the magazine on the table when Jack Emery entered the office.

"It's nice to see you finally made it, Counselor," he said. His tone was velvet, edged with steel.

"It's nice to see your cheery face, too, Counselor," Nikki said, taking her cue from his tone of voice. She ached to have him reach for her, to put his arms around her shoulders. It wasn't going to happen. He was pissed, and when Jack was pissed you ran as far as you could to get away from him.

"The judge will see you now," Ruth McIntyre said. "Remember to be respectful," she said, wagging a long, bony finger at Jack.

"Yes, ma'am," Jack said.

Nikki ignored the comment and walked through the door ahead of Jack. Her stomach rumbled and she could feel her left eye start to twitch.

She hated this judge. Hated his narrow-minded, sanctimonious attitude toward people and the law. Everything was either black or white. He refused to acknowledge the color gray existed. He went strictly by the book. He should have stood down years ago, but for some unfathomable reason he was still sitting on the bench. She longed for the day when she would see him nodding off in the middle of a trial so she could start a movement to have him retire. Anything. *Anything.*

"Sit down," he barked. He reminded her of a bulldog. *He's Ruth's twin,* Nikki thought crazily. The only difference was, where she smelled like Evening in Paris, he smelled like Lava soap and vinegar.

They sat. And they waited while the judge eyeballed them over the rim of his glasses. He fixed his beady, watery eyes on Nikki. He jabbed at the air with his index finger. "You told me Mrs. Lewellen was not a flight risk, that she had deep ties to the community. You managed to get her bail. You lied to me, Miss Quinn."

Determined to maintain her composure, Nikki resisted the urge to stiffen her shoulders. "No, Your Honor, I did not lie to you. That was what I believed at the time. I had no reason to believe otherwise. These past months as we prepared for trial gave me no indication she would take flight. Furthermore, Your Honor, I only have Mr. Emery's word that she absconded. She might have gone to visit someone. It is getting close to the trial date. She might have felt the need to get some space around her."

Jack turned sideways in his chair. "She's gone. And they didn't take anything with them, either. We went through the house. Their suitcases are still in the closets. Their toothbrushes are still in the bathroom. There's food in the refrigerator. They just walked away. That tells me they had to have help."

"I hope you had a search warrant," Nikki snapped.

"I had probable cause. That's all I needed," Jack snapped in return.

"Did you put out an all-points, Mr. Emery?" the judge asked.

"Yes, Your Honor, we did."

The judge jammed his finger in Nikki's direction a second time. "That means Ms. Rutledge forfeits the bond she posted. You tell me now, young lady, did you have anything to do with your client's disappearance?"

Nikki's eyes popped wide. Now her shoulders did stiffen. "Your *Honor,* I did not lift one finger to help my client leave. I didn't even know she was gone until Mr. Emery notified Mrs. Rutledge, who by the way asked me to ask you if she has any recourse to regain her money. She also said to give her regards to your wife Mavis."

"Hrumpf," the judge puffed. He leaned back in his old, cracked, leather chair that fit his lean, bony body like a glove. "I'm leaving the case on my calendar. I want weekly reports on my desk every Monday morning by seven thirty. File the necessary papers as the occasion arises. I'm not happy with this situation, Counselors. Not happy at all."

"Nor am I," Nikki said.

"It's appalling," Jack Emery said.

"It's appalling because you want your face splashed all over the news, Jack. I want to know what your probable cause was. You went out there in the middle of the worst storm ever to hit this state *knowing* Marie was going to take off." She jabbed her finger at Jack and said, "It wouldn't surprise me one little bit that you have your fingers in this somewhere. A case like this looks real good to the media. You'll be on the noon news, the six o'clock news and the eleven o'clock news. And your face will be the first one we see when we wake up in the morning to click on the TV. I want to know why and how you thought you had probable cause in the middle of the night or whenever the hell you went out to my client's house. Your Honor, I want an answer!" Nikki bellowed.

Throwing his arms in the air, the judge stood up. "Both of you, get out of my office and do your fighting somewhere else. Discuss it and settle it."

"But Your Honor . . ." Nikki pleaded.

The judge's face turned red and then purple.

"We're leaving, we're leaving," Jack said, cupping Nikki's elbow in the palm of his hand to usher her out the door.

"Take your hands off me, you . . . you . . . *prosecutor.*"

"Nik, wait."

Nikki spun around. "I'm going to bring you up on charges. Tell me now what your probable cause was . . . You didn't have one, did you? You son of a bitch!"

"Oohh, I love it when you get mad."

Nikki whirled around, Ruth McIntyre's perfume circling her like a fog. She got in his face and said, "Read my lips and kiss my ass!"

"There will be none of *that* in this office, ladies and gentlemen. Remove yourselves immediately," the judge's secretary bleated.

Nikki gave the old bat the evil eye. "You can kiss my ass, too, lady," Nikki shot back as she slammed the door behind her. *Great, that was just great. I think I just said goodbye to my law career.* The thought made her laugh. *I already did that when I joined the Sisterhood.* Her stomach stopped rumbling and the fluttering in her chest went away with the thought.

"Nik, wait up. C'mon, hold on here. Listen, we need to talk."

She kept on walking, trying to ignore him.

"Nik, listen to me. Don't go doing something stupid like filing charges. Goddamn it, I did have probable cause. I'm a damn good prosecutor because I have that gut instinct, that extra sense you need to be good in this job. I knew she was waiting for just the right moment. I knew, Nik. I swear to God, I did. I acted on my gut instinct. I was right, too. We both know it. She was looking at a possible life sentence. Hell, if I was in her position, I would have cut and run, too. She killed a man in cold blood. The whole world saw her do it. You want to burn my ass for that, go ahead. I'm going to find her. I will, Nik. If I find out you had anything to do with her taking off, I'll come after you. Whatever went on before won't matter. Now, let's go get a cup of coffee and talk like the educated lawyers we are."

Nikki smiled and offered up a single-digit salute by way of answer. Jack's eyes almost popped out of his head. Other lawyers striding up and down the hallway grinned as Nikki marched away.

*That was stupid, Nikki. You just gave him license to start watching you like a hawk. Stupid, stupid, stupid. Think. You need to think about what you just did and remedy the situation.*

And then he was beside her again. *Ah, God does work in mysterious ways.*

"We really do need to talk, Nik. Come on, let's grab some coffee."

She knew how to play the game. "Who was the redhead, Jack?"

"Is *that* what this is all about? You're jealous. I'll be damned," he said, smacking his forehead. "Okay, okay, I see now where that little tantrum came from." He looked down at his watch. "The sun will be over the yardarm soon, let's grab a brew at Gilligan's. It's public. Judge Olsen told both of us to talk this out. So, what do you say?"

*You dumb schmuck. Like I'm really going to fall for this. Whatever it takes to get you off my back.* "All right, Jack. One beer and that's it. I have to go on to the office and I need to get back to the farm to pick up my car. So, who was she?"

He answered the question with a question. "Are you seeing Mike Deverone?"

"I asked you first, Jack."

He shrugged.

"Fine. You keep your secrets and I'll keep mine. How's that?" She smiled.

"He's a nerd."

"Everything and everyone is in the eye of the beholder," Nik said sweetly. Actually, Mike is quite charming." *You aren't going to break my heart. I won't allow it.*

Jack huffed and puffed his way across the street. He held the door open. Music blasted outward. Cigarette smoke filled the bar area. Jack headed for the back and a quiet booth.

"Two Buds," he said to the waitress. "I've missed you," he said reaching for Nikki's hand. The combination of his good looks, his devastating smile, and his resonant voice were almost too much for her.

"Speaking of eyes, Nik, you looked frazzled. Is it the Lewellen case? C'mon, this is me. You can talk to me. Whatever we talk about here is personal, not case-related. Let's start over. How are you, Nik? I really missed you."

"I missed you, too." That was honest. She had missed him. A lot. "Where does this leave us, Jack? With Marie gone, if she's really gone, the case will stay open. Possibly forever. I guess we might as well say good-bye now."

"No, no, no, we'll find her. In a couple of hours her picture will be on the desk of every law officer across the country. Someone, someplace, will recognize her and call the police. That's a given. Possibly a month. Maybe even less."

"We aren't supposed to discuss the case, Jack. The probable cause bit, yes, but that's it." Nikki swigged from the bottle and set it down on the little square napkin.

"Are you going to file charges, Nik? Tell me now."

"You really pissed me off back there in the judge's office, Jack. But, to answer your question, no, probably not. I know a thing or two about gut instinct. I'm sorry to say I never suspected she would do this. You're right about her having help. Are you going to check out her relatives?"

"We're on it. I guess Myra is going to be upset losing all that money."

"Yes, she's very upset. She's still grieving over Barbara. All she could see was that that man killed a mother's child. We're discussing the case, Jack."

"It's hard not to. Let's talk about us."

"There is no *us,* Jack. There's just you and me. Separate people. We aren't a couple any longer."

"That's your fault, Nik. You never should have taken the case. If you hadn't been so damn bull-headed, we wouldn't be sitting here right now at each other's throats."

"It's not like the guy was innocent. He confessed and his DNA proved it. If it hadn't been for your boss blowing it, the guy would have gotten the death penalty. I asked you to pass on it, Jack, and you said no. If you hadn't been so power hungry to get your name in the papers and your face on the televison news, we wouldn't be sitting here. You're right about that." She drained her beer bottle and plopped it on the table. "Thanks for the beer. See you around."

Jack reached for her hand. "Listen, Nik. I'm hurting here. Can't we make peace? We had a good thing going before this damn case came up. We were the golden couple around town. Now there are days when I can't remember what you look like. Let's just say the hell with everything for the moment and go over to my apartment."

"Like a quick roll in the sack is going to change things. No thanks, Jack." Her stomach rolled itself into a tight knot when she saw an ugly look transform his features.

Nikki reached over to retrieve her purse and briefcase. She was so close to Jack's face she could see his five o'clock shadow. "You put a tail on me and I'll have your ass swinging from the flagpole outside the courthouse, so don't even think about it. I also reserve the right to file those charges we discussed earlier. Fuck up and you'll be begging me to defend you. Of course I'll say no. I don't need another loser of a case in my career. You know Jack, we could have cut a deal. Ten years, five off with good behavior. Your way, it was life and she pays the price for the guy killing her daughter. That's going to stick in my throat forever.

"By the way, the redhead was your sister. She dyed her hair last month. We met in the beauty shop." She smiled. "See ya, sweet cheeks," she said, tweaking his chin.

Jack waved his empty beer bottle at the waitress. While he waited, he whipped out his cell phone to call his assistant. "Listen to me, Harry, and don't say anything. I want you to put a tail on Nikki Quinn. I want a bug in her car and one in her apartment. I have the key. I know it's illegal, you asshole. Do it anyway. I want one in her office, too. As soon as possible. Don't screw it up, Harry."

Nikki walked into her law offices on G Street. She'd worked hard to build her firm and she was proud of it. She liked the idea of an all-woman law firm and she'd recruited the best of the best. They were winding down now for the day. Time to go home to their families, who would welcome them with open arms. All of them, she knew, would be taking home work.

The office manager paused and said, "Tough break, Nik. You couldn't have known, so don't go blaming yourself. If you need any of us, just call. By the way, the university called. I left the message and a bunch of others on your desk. The mail's there, too, along with a letter that came earlier by special messenger."

"Thanks. See you tomorrow."

Nikki walked into her office and sat down and kicked off her shoes. She eyed the mini-bar under the counter and decided another beer was in order. She scooted her swivel chair over to the bar and uncapped a beer. She slid the chair backward and then propped her feet on top of the desk. She rifled through the mail. Nothing urgent, nothing even remotely important. She sifted through the pink message slips. Like the mail, there was nothing urgent, nothing even remotely important except possibly the message from the university where she taught first-year law three days a week. The message read, *Call me up till 8:30 here at the office or home later.* It was signed by the Dean. She swigged from the bottle as she opened the gray envelope that had been delivered by a messenger.

Nikki took another long pull from the beer bottle before she ripped at the envelope. She frowned as she read it, wondering who she had to thank for it.

*Dear Miss Quinn,*
   *I want to thank you for everything you've done on my behalf. I know I let you down and I'm sorry. I wish it didn't have to be this*

*way, but I can't abandon my children and my husband. Please don't think too harshly of me.*

*I know the police will be looking for me but they'll never find us. Never in a million years. I've planned this for a long time. The only thing I wasn't sure of was the time and the place.*

*I know I have no right to ask this of you, but will you please do me one last favor. Tell the police no one helped me. No one else is involved. Even my husband and kids didn't know until it was the right moment to leave. I left the deed to the house in the cabinet over the sink. You can sell the house and whatever equity is in it, donate it to a victims' rights organization. Please do it in my daughter's name.*

*I don't know if you can explain this to Mrs. Rutledge or not. Please try. I know I can never pay her back and I won't even try. Just thank her for caring enough about me to want to help.*

*Maybe someday we'll meet again.*

*Marie Lewellen*

Nik walked over to the copy machine and slid Marie's letter underneath the cover. She carried the original and the copy back to her desk. She dialed Jack's cell phone number from memory. She didn't bother with niceties.

"I just received a letter from Marie Lewellen. It came by messenger earlier today. Come by *now* and pick it up. I'll have a copy hand delivered in the morning to Judge Olsen. Now, Jack. I'm getting ready to go back to the farm." She hung up before he had a chance to reply.

Her next call was to the Dean at the university. Her gut told her she wasn't going to like whatever he had to say. She identified herself and waited while he inquired about her well-being. "I'm sorry, Nicole, but the board feels you are too controversial right now. A leave of absence until possibly the next semester was the board's suggestion. At that time we will evaluate—"

"You're firing me, is that it?" she pressed.

"A leave of absence with pay is not firing you, Nicole. We do hope that Mrs. Rutledge's . . . the board feels . . ."

Nikki felt the fine hairs on the back of her neck stand up in anger. "You'll have my resignation first thing in the morning, Dean. I think it's safe to say Mrs. Rutledge's endowments will cease first thing in the morning. Have a nice evening, Dean. Like Myra said, everything comes with a price." She hung up and looked around the room.

"Hey, Barb! I'm calling your name! Can you hear me? I could use a friend right now."

*"I'm right here, Nik. The dark stuff hit the fan, huh?"*

"Yeah, and it's splattering in all directions. Can you . . . what I mean is, do you know what's going on, or do I have to tell you?"

*"I know. So you lost your teaching job. Big deal. Three days a week was three days too many. You were overworked anyway. You were on your way to burnout, girl. It's not like you need the money. What you and the others are doing is so much more important. Concentrate on that and you'll be okay."*

"Jack is on his way over. We had a parting of the ways and I feel . . . awful. You never liked him, did you, Barb?"

*"Not really. Maybe that's because I never really got to know him that well. He tries to put you down but you refuse to see it. Maybe I was looking at it all wrong. You are so much smarter than he is. He knows it and resents it. I think he's calculating as well as manipulative just like you are, Nik."*

"I already figured that out, Barb. I wouldn't put it past him to bug my office and my apartment. Shit, I didn't ask for my key back."

*"He's on his way. Ask him for it. I hear the elevator. See you back at the farm."*

"Yeah okay." *Am I nuts! Am I really talking to dead people? I'm breaking the laws I swore to uphold by the dozen. Yeah, I'm nuts.*

Jack Emery strode into her office and looked around. "Really nice digs, Nik. I know I say that every time I come here. Your rent must be half of what I earn in a year."

No matter what he said, she wasn't going to let him get to her. "Here, this is your copy. I keep the original. Check it over before you leave. This is the envelope it was delivered in. DBY Messenger Service on K Street. I don't know when they got it or how they got it. Now, I'd like my key back."

"Your key?" Jack hedged.

"Yeah, you know, the key to my apartment. I want it back and I want it back *now.*"

"I don't think I have it with me. Can I drop it off or mail it?"

"I don't think so, Jack. Let me see your key ring."

"No."

"What do you mean, no?"

"If I give you back the key that means it's over. I don't want it to be over. Give me a break here."

*"Get the damn key, Nik."*

"I want my key. If you don't give it to me, I'm going home and calling a locksmith. I know one that's open 24/7."

Jack licked at his lips. "Okay, okay." He fished in his pants for the keys and removed her key. He tossed it on the desk.

"Do you want a copy of both envelopes?"

"Yes."

"No problem."

"How about a beer?"

"Sorry, I'm on my way out. Perhaps another time. Thanks for coming by to pick this up. I knew you'd want to see it right away. I don't want you to accuse me later on of obstructing justice. By the way, the university fired me today."

To his credit, he looked shocked. "Jeez, I'm sorry, Nik. I really mean that."

Nikki bent down to put on her shoes. "I'll walk down with you." She was careful to lock the door.

Outside in the cool evening air, they parted company. Nikki walked one way and Jack walked the other way.

# Chapter Seven

Two days after Nikki's late night, tearful return to McLean, Myra Rutledge woke from a sound sleep and knew immediately something was wrong. Her motherly instinct was kicking in. She lay quietly a moment, listening. Moonlight filtered through the crack in the drawn draperies. That meant the weather was okay. She couldn't smell smoke. She swung her legs over the side of the bed and slipped into her robe.

She looked down at the overlarge digital numbers on the bedside clock: 4:20. The house was quiet. Charles, night owl that he was, was probably in what they were now calling the War Room. She tiptoed down the back staircase to see Nikki sitting at the table, her head in her hands, a coffee cup in front of her. And she was smoking, something she rarely if ever did these days.

"Nikki, what's wrong?" she whispered as she padded into the kitchen.

"Everything and nothing. Want a cigarette?"

The last thing Myra wanted was a cigarette. She reached for it, stuck it in her mouth and puffed as Nikki held the lighter to the tip. She coughed and sputtered but kept on puffing. "Talk to me, baby, tell me what's wrong. Just start anywhere," she said, the cigarette dangling from the corner of her mouth.

Nikki laughed. Myra was game for anything. "Let me get you some coffee. Maybe I'd better make some more. I've been sitting here since two o'clock just thinking."

Her eyes watering from the cigarette smoke, Myra transferred the cigarette to the opposite side of her mouth. Smoke spiraled upward. "I'm a good listener, dear. Are you having second thoughts about what we're doing?"

Nikki hitched the belt of her bathrobe higher and then yanked it tight. "In a way, but it's not what you think. It bothers me that Jack came out here and saw the truck and all the cars. That's for starters. At the moment he doesn't have a clue, an inkling of any kind as to what we're doing. He's sharp, though. He's a thinker. No grass grows under his feet. We had this . . . discussion. It wasn't a fight. I wish it had been a fight. I made him give me back the key to my apartment. I had this crazy feeling he might try to bug it. Don't ask me where that thought came from, Myra. I had the locks changed in case he had a duplicate key made." She plucked at a yellowing leaf on the African violet sitting on the windowsill. Her index finger worked the soil to see if it was dry. It was. She held it under the faucet, wiped off the bottom and set it back on the windowsill.

"I think I was blind where he was concerned. He's not who I thought he was, who I wanted him to be. He's power hungry, Myra. He loves being on the tube and in the papers. He is so pissed that Marie split. And rightly so. He won't give up where she's concerned. He's convinced I had something to do with it. Knowing him like I do, I know he has a tail on me. I know he's going to bug my office, my apartment and probably my car. I know this, Myra, because he used to tell me about all the times he's done it before. Just because we slept together and were planning on getting engaged won't make one bit of difference. Can you just see the headlines? D.A. arrests lover and he has tears dripping down his cheeks. Yeah, he'd do that." She reached for a cup in the cabinet. The minute the coffee stopped perking, she poured a cup for Myra.

"By the way, then the dean fired me. He didn't say, 'you're fired' but that's what it meant. He wanted me to resign so I obliged him and the board."

"Well, I fixed his wagon. I called him and told him the endowment was now null and void. Let him scurry around somewhere else for his money. He shouldn't have done that to you. I won't tolerate anyone taking advantage of my girl."

Myra puffed furiously on the cigarette, clouds of smoke circling the kitchen. "What *do* you get out of these things?" she demanded

"All kinds of health problems. Look, I'm throwing them away," Nikki said, tossing the cigarettes in the trash container under the sink.

Nikki sat down at the table, her hands cupping the mug full of fresh coffee. "I have to tell you something. You know me better than anyone else in the world. You're the mother I never had. You took me in when I was a little girl and raised me like your own daughter. Do you see a flaw in me? You know, did you ever . . . think maybe I had a screw loose?"

"Good heavens, no. Why are you asking me such a thing?"

"Because . . . because . . . do you believe in spirits, dead people coming back and . . . helping, talking to you."

"Oh, I see, this farm is finally getting to you, is that it? Dear, there are all kinds of spirits in this old place. They're floating all around. I've learned to pay them no mind. They're just restless and they did live here. If anything, they've given me a sense of security because I know they're watching out for me. But to answer your other question, no they do not talk to me and no I haven't really seen them. I feel their presence sometimes. It's not a bad thing, dear."

Nikki bit down on her lip. She'd almost confided in Myra about her little talks with Barbara. She was glad now she'd kept quiet. She sipped from the cup she was holding. She nodded. "Is everything on schedule, Myra?"

"As Charles says, we are on target. Kathryn and Yoko will be ready to leave for San Francisco as soon as Charles gets his cycle confirmations. Julia is . . . where she needs to be. She'll be doing surgery on her two patients at seven o'clock. She'll stay there for three days and then fly back here where they will do what needs to be done at which point she will then fly back to check on her patients, remove the sutures and then fly on to Los Angeles. Isabelle is now working out of the old summer pantry. She's ready to leave on vacation the minute we give her the go-ahead. Alexis is in town replenishing her . . . supplies. She'll fly out of Washington the minute everything is settled."

"Shouldn't I be doing something? I'm pretty much at loose ends, Myra. I turned my caseload over to my partners a few weeks ago. I'm not teaching now. I need something to do."

"Charles would dearly love it if you would help him. He's dying to show off all he's done to someone who can appreciate his expertise. I would never admit this to Charles or anyone else, but that War Room absolutely terrifies me. All those computers, all that knowledge stored on those little squares. The different programs, the lights, the bells and whistles." She shook her head, her arms flapping every which way.

"Does everyone have a laptop?"

Myra nodded. "Top of the line, according to Charles. He managed somehow to get what he calls a secure line. It's a line that no

one can bug. That means listen in on, dear. I believe they have
them in all the big government buildings. It's in case the girls have
to call in. From a pay phone, of course. Although Charles did give
them some kind of new cell phones. He held a class yesterday for
two hours teaching them how to use it. It was all Greek to me."

"After I shower, I'll volunteer my services. Are you wishing your
case was first, Myra?"

"I have to be realistic, dear. The man's embassy returned him to
China. There are billions of people in China. We could never touch
him over there."

"That's what you think. Myra, the man comes from an influential
family. If Charles hasn't already done it, he can get on the information highway and pull him up, in I'd say no less than thirty minutes.
I always wanted to see China," Nikki smiled.

"Are you saying we won't have to wait for him to return here at
some point in time?"

"That's what I'm saying, Myra."

"They never let you out of those Chinese prisons," Myra said.

"First you have to be caught and be in a prison," Nikki said smugly.
"That won't happen. Yoko speaks Chinese. Fluently. Kathryn speaks
Chinese and seven other languages. She told me she and her husband used to listen to the Berlitz tapes while on the road. She could
brush up and be as fluent as Yoko when your time comes. She's also
a brown belt. So is Yoko. Alexis can make us all look oriental. The
possibilities are endless. Now, you have something to think about
and plan while we're on the road or involved in a case." She gave her
a quick hug. "I'm going to take my shower now."

Myra beamed, her eyes sparkling. "Nikki, Jack is so unworthy
of you."

"Tell that to my heart, Myra. From lovers to adversaries." She
shrugged.

"You always tell me everything happens for a reason, Nikki."

Nikki carried her cup to the sink. "Myra, is there any way, any way
at all, that Jack Emery can find Marie Lewellen and her family?"

"Absolutely none, dear. He will have to get his notoriety from
some other case."

"And they are going to earn a living . . . how?"

"Marie is going to make quilts. She does lovely work. Handmade
quilts are outrageously expensive, as you know. Mr. Lewellen is going to make Shaker furniture and sell it on the Internet. He is so
detail-oriented. He does magnificent work."

Nikki burst out laughing. "And you're going to buy it all up, is that it?"

"Only in the beginning until they get established. I'll donate them all to the church bazaar at Christmastime," Myra smiled.

"I love you, Myra Rutledge," Nikki called over her shoulder as she made her way upstairs.

"And I love you, too, dear," Myra called after her.

Ten days later, the eighteen-wheeler gobbled up the miles on the interstate as Kathryn Lucas and Yoko Akia sat in companionable silence, the Belgian Malinois nestled between them. They spoke from time to time about the highway, the miles to a gallon the rig got, the scenery and the different loads of merchandise she had transported over the years.

They'd been on the road for two days and still hadn't discussed what had transpired back in Virginia or what would transpire once they got to California.

"We're going to stop at the next road stop, Yoko. Fish some money out of that shoebox. I'll need to fill up and it's time to eat. Remember now, don't do anything to call attention to yourself. This is a straight, legitimate run but we still don't want to give anyone anything to remember."

"I understand, Kathryn. Three hundred dollars should be sufficient," she said, reaching for the Ferragamo shoebox. She snapped the rubber band back into place and set the box back on the floor. She settled her baseball cap, a gift from Kathryn, more firmly on her head. She looked like a child of thirteen when in fact she was thirty-six.

"Are you going to keep driving, Kathryn? It must be very lonely for you with no one to talk to. I understand you talk to Murphy but he does not answer you back."

"It is lonely. I've been thinking about a lot of things but I'm so in debt I have to keep doing this. If I live to be a hundred, I'm not sure I can ever get caught up. Alan's medical bills were in the hundreds of thousands of dollars. If I don't drive, I don't know what I'd do. I can't see myself sitting in some engineering office working on something I probably wouldn't like. I've been on the road and in the open too long. They'd probably fire me after the first week, if I lasted that long."

Yoko stared out the window. "What state are we in again?"

"Kansas. We'll be bypassing Oakley soon. There's a decent stop ahead and the food is pretty good. They don't have rice, though, Yoko, and they aren't big on fresh vegetables."

"It is all right, Kathryn. When in Rome . . ." she giggled.

"You were so worried about being away the other day. How did you manage the time with the nursery? Who's going to take care of it?"

"A family friend. My husband is in California. I hope I do not run into him. He is a cinematographer. A very good one. I, too, am fond of the camera but the nursery pays the bills. I like working with the earth, with flowers and vegetables. I told my husband a fib. No, it was an outright lie. I said I had family matters to take care of and he would see me when I finished my business. When I thought about it, I realized it was not a lie. One day it will be my turn to avenge my mother but in order to do that I must be patient and help those who go before me. My husband is very modern in his thinking. He wants me to have my life, my space. We talked about this very much. Many times. It is I who worry. I will not let you down."

"We got off to a rocky start that first day. I'm sorry." Kathryn reached across to pat Yoko's arm.

"I understand. We were all jittery, not knowing what to expect."

"What we did, what we more or less expected, did it turn out the way you wanted? I guess that's what I'm trying to say." Kathryn said.

"I think so. I think each of us wanted our case to be first. I am content to wait my turn. I see now how things will work. Charles appears to have all the right connections. He must have been a very powerful man when he was in service to the Queen. I'm happy that you were chosen first, Kathryn. You have carried too many things too long on your shoulders."

"But you don't approve of the punishment." It was more of a question than a statement.

"I've had time to think about it and sleep on it. I now agree. However, I think the others are wrong about the men only going after you because the circumstances just happened to be right that night. I think those men have done this many times before. I think they feel confident enough, macho enough, to believe they won't get caught. And they haven't been caught. Until now. I think I will be proved right."

Kathryn concentrated on the overhead signs on the interstate. "That doesn't make me feel any better, Yoko. Nothing will make me feel better until those bastards get what they deserve."

"It will happen. We must stay calm, centered. You know that from your martial arts teachings. I like this truck," she said suddenly.

"I can teach you to drive it when this is all over if you like," Kathryn smiled.

"My legs are far too short. I am content to ride . . . lookout."

"Shotgun," Kathryn laughed. Out of the corner of her eye she could see Yoko scratching Murphy behind his ears. The big dog was in seventh heaven with all the attention he was receiving.

"Do you think your dog is starting to like me, Kathryn?"

"Yep. Show Yoko how much you like her, Murphy." The Malinois wiggled around, placed his front paws on her lap, and barked for her to lower her head so he could lick her chin. "Okay, you're his bud now. It's comforting to know there's someone, even if it's an animal, who will protect you with their life. If I tell you something, Yoko, will you promise never to tell anyone? You have to swear to me."

Yoko looked across at Kathryn, noticed the grim set of her jaw, the white knuckles on the steering wheel, the stiff set of her shoulders. "I swear," she said solemnly.

"I'm afraid. Every time I get in this truck, I'm afraid. I'm afraid to fall asleep for fear someone will break in and attack me. I'm afraid to go to strange places. I'm afraid of everything. I tried to put up a good front for Alan, but he knew. He did everything he could humanly do in his condition to help me but it wasn't enough. I tried to be so strong and so tough but it was all an act. I bluster, I say outrageous things just to get me over the bad moments."

"I know that. We Chinese are an intuitive lot, you know."

"So I've heard. I'm turning off here. This place is called Sam Slick's Truck Stop. There is no Sam but there is a Samantha. Everyone calls her Sam. She owns the joint. Nice lady. A little hard around the edges but she's good people. Good food, too. She likes to deck out in diamonds and spandex. Beats the hell out of me how she's never been robbed. Course she could be lying by saying they're diamonds when they're really zircons, but who cares. She says she likes to sparkle for the drivers. You'll like her, she's a hoot. The best part, though, is she's got clean showers and bathrooms. That counts when you're on the road. I'll gas up and meet you in the shower, okay?"

"Okay, Kathryn."

An hour and a half later, Kathryn slid into the booth across from Yoko. "What looks good today?"

"Actually everything *sounds* good." She pointed to the chalk-board over the cash register.

"Kathryn, long time no see," a pretty waitress with rough, red hands said.

"Hi Penny. Yes, it's been a while. How's everything? Did you get married?"

"No," the waitress sighed. "One of these days. Sam's out back. She'll be real happy to see you. Now, what can I get you?"

"I'll have the fried chicken, mashed potatoes, carrots, French dressing on my salad and cherry pie for dessert. Coffee of course, and I need an order to go for my dog. Three hamburger steaks, double order of carrots, and a cherry pie. Two bottles of water and fill our thermoses."

"Miss, what will you have?"

"I'll have the carrots and string beans. Cherry pie, apple pie and chocolate cake. Ice cream on all three. Coffee, too," Yoko said.

"Whoa, little lady, that's some dinner. Did you ever hear of the three food groups?"

"Yes, but I do not care for them. Thank you, my order stands."

Kathryn was finishing her pie when she felt a poke to her shoulder. "Move over, *sister.* Hey, hey, what's the matter? You turned white as a ghost. It's me, Sam. Sorry, kid, I didn't mean to spook you."

"You didn't, Sam. I guess my mind was somewhere else. Sam, this is Yoko. She's riding as far as San Fran with me. It's good to see you."

Sam Slick was as flashy as her neon establishment. Today she wore her waist-long hair piled high on her head with little ringlets cascading around her ears and down her back. Diamonds winked in her ears. Not just one but three to each lobe. Alan always said she put her makeup on with a trowel. He was probably right. She had a perfect smile and beautiful teeth that glistened when she talked.

Sam wiggled inside the lemon-yellow spandex dress that was two sizes too small. "We were just talking about you not long ago, Kathryn. Haven't seen you in a while and then one of the boys told me about Alan. I'm real sorry, kid. I didn't know. I would have sent flowers but none of us knew where . . . where you were when it hap-pened. The boys took up a collection. Yeah, yeah, they did. They wanted to, Kathryn. All the girls kicked in, too. You okay, kid?"

"No. It's hard, Sam. Alan was part of me. Now I have a dog. It's not the same."

"Of course it isn't the same. I felt like that when Beau passed on. Life didn't have any meaning for a long time, but time has a way of taking care of everything. I know you don't believe that right now, but in time you will. Let me get that collection for you. I've been keeping it in the safe all this time."

"I see what you mean about her being a nice lady," Yoko said.

"Salt of the earth. Did you see those diamonds on her hands?"

"I felt like putting my sunglasses on," Yoko giggled.

"Here you go, kid," Sam said, holding out a shoebox that said Pappagalo on the side. "We collected over ten grand. You're not going to bawl and embarrass me, are you, Kathryn? If you start howling then I'm going to howl, and I don't feel like gluing on these eyelashes again much less applying my makeup all over again."

Kathryn struggled for the words but her tongue felt too thick in her mouth. "I didn't have enough money for flowers and I had to put his funeral on tick. Will you thank everyone for me?"

"No. You just get on that CB and thank them yourself. Listen to me, kid, don't ever be too proud to ask for help. You should have called me."

Tears burned Kathryn's eyes. "I wish I had called you. No one came to the funeral except me and a local trucker named Carl Manning. Maybe it was better that way. Thanks, Sam."

"My pleasure, kid. Drive with the angels. You hear."

"I hear ya, Sam."

"Grab the food, Yoko, while I pay the bill. Leave the waitress twenty bucks. She has to hustle here and she's trying to put two kids through college."

Kathryn paid the bill, fed Murphy, and then walked him.

They were back on the highway in less than thirty minutes.

Fifty-two hours later, with catnaps of an hour or so along the way, Kathryn pulled the rig alongside the loading dock of the Home Depot. While her cargo was being unloaded she used the CB to call the dispatcher at the wholesale produce mart. "Vernon, this is Kathryn Lucas. Listen, I'm sorry but I can't take that load of carrots to Denver for you. My husband passed away and I need to get away for a few days. I'm going to park the rig and get a flight to someplace where I don't know anyone. Four, five days, I'm not sure. I can take some lettuce that way if you want when I get back. If you don't have anything for me on my return, I'll just head on home on empty. I appreciate your condolences, Vernon. Thanks. I'll call you the minute I get off the plane."

"Now what?"

"Now we head for Los Angeles and the motel to wait for the others. Call Myra and tell her we're right on schedule. Find out if everyone else will be on time. I really need to get some sleep. I can't wait to fill the tub and take a good long bubble bath. We have to find a laundromat once we check in. Sometimes motels have a facility but just as often they don't. I suppose we could buy some clothes. We certainly have enough money to do that."

"I can take care of all that while you sleep, Kathryn. I will call Myra now."

"Be careful what you say. Just generalities. She'll get the drift. We can't be too careful."

"Myra, it is Yoko. How are you? We're fine. A little tired. And the others? That's nice to hear. I hope you're well. The weather is very nice. I'll call again when we both have more time. Good-bye.

"She said everything is whirring. I have to assume she meant everything is in motion and we're all on schedule. It's just a matter of days now, Kathryn. Tell me something, if you could have anything you wanted right now, what would you wish for?" Yoko asked.

"A little cottage somewhere near the water. Maybe a lake or the ocean. A couple of acres so I had some privacy and Murphy could run. A house with a front porch with rocking chairs. A nice kitchen you could eat in. Modern appliances. A pretty bathroom with flowered wallpaper. A walk-in closet. I'd like one of those canopy beds with white lace. I'd like one of those big televisions and a chair that would hold both Murphy and me while we watch it.

"I saw some dishes once in a catalog that had tiny little bluebells on them. They were so delicate and so pretty. I'd like to eat off dishes like that instead of Styrofoam. I want big, fluffy pink towels with my initials on them so I know they belong to me. I'd like some bookshelves with lots and lots of books to read on cold winter nights. A fireplace, of course. I'd want a stack of cherrywood because it smells nice when it burns. I want to learn to cook and bake. I love looking at the pictures in cookbooks."

Kathryn laughed ruefully. "Since I'll be around eighty when I get out of debt, I doubt I'll ever get a house like that. It's okay to dream, though. I know how Alexis must have felt when she had to sell off her house to pay her legal bills. She told me she owes over two hundred grand in legal bills. I'm right up there with her."

"I think it's a wonderful dream, Kathryn. I hope it happens for you someday."

"I hope so, too. If it doesn't, my life won't be ruined. I'm going to get on the CB now and thank all my friends for the . . . you know. Go to sleep, Yoko. You look as tired as I feel."

"That's a very good idea, Kathryn."

Kathryn brushed at her eyes as she reached for the CB. "Hey you guys, this is Big Sis. Anyone out there?"

# Chapter Eight

*March 2000*

The room Myra called the sunroom was a beautiful room. It was an addition she'd added to the old farmhouse the year Barbara and Nikki turned thirteen. The year when sleep-overs, scout meetings, and parties took up both days of the weekends.

The sunroom was always both girl's favorite room in the entire house. They did their homework at back-to-back desks listening to loud music while the television blared in the corner. Back then there had been a litter box in one corner and a dog bed in another corner. More often than not, Sophie and Bennie could be found snuggled together in the tufted dog bed. Both were gone now, dying of old age. Irreplaceable, Myra had elected to forego animals in her life because it was too painful when they passed on.

The room was alive with luscious green plants and tall, bushy ficus trees that somehow had managed to survive her two-year hiatus in the nether world. Charles had seen to everything, making sure he fed the plants, trimmed them back and watered them faithfully because he knew how much Myra loved the room.

He knew his beloved Myra was troubled when she lowered herself into one of the his-and-hers chairs she'd bought for them when the girls moved out. More often than not they dined off trays while they either watched or listened to television.

Life until just recently had been placid, worrisome, and boring.

"I think we should get married, Charles," Myra blurted.

Charles lowered himself into his chair and kicked up the footrest. "That's probably the best idea you ever had, Myra. Name the date and I'll be there. Do you want to talk about it or is this just something that came to you in your dreams?"

"I do dream about you, darling. All the time. No, I've been think-ing about marriage a lot since we began our little project. The main reason is, I love you. I loved you the minute I spotted you standing at the foot of Big Ben. I took your picture, remember? Then we kept meeting up at different places. Husbands and wives can't be forced to testify against each other."

"That's because I was following you and the others. I was smitten the minute I saw you. I've always loved Americans. I can't say I loved your parents, though. They wanted no part of me. So, you are wor-ried about this project."

"Anxious might be a better way of phrasing it. My parents were not a romantic couple. They were afraid you would coerce me into staying in England. That's why they whisked me back home. The moment they found out I was pregnant they somehow managed to get Andrew Rutledge to make an honest woman of me. I regret that so deeply, Charles. I wish I had been more defiant. Andrew was a kind man, but so much older. He didn't have a fun bone in his stodgy body. I felt terrible when he passed on. I tried to find you, to tell you we had a daughter but you were gone. I grieved for you night and day.

"I still, to this day, remember the moment the call came from your embassy asking all those questions. And then your people came to interview me and to check out our security at the candy plant. They said you would arrive in twelve hours if I agreed to hire you on and never breathe a word of it to anyone. I was so speechless I could only nod. Those twelve hours until you walked through the door were the most anxious hours of my life. You just smiled at me and all those empty years were gone."

"I never stopped loving you, Myra." He reached for her hand and squeezed it.

"We should have told Barbara. She grew up and died never knowing you were her father. I regret that. We should have told her, Charles."

"No. She adored Andrew. You can't rip a child's world out from under them. I think in time she grew to love me as a substitute father. That was good enough for me. We've had a wonderful life, Myra. I have no complaints."

"Charles, don't you think it strange that Barbara's beau hasn't been in touch with us? The last time I saw him was at her funeral."

"Ben did call, Myra, many times during that first year, but you were so wrapped up in your grief you would just nod when I told you. Ben Gerrity is a fine young man. He moved to New York shortly after . . . after the funeral. He works for Goldman Sachs in the city and is doing well. In fact, he's getting married in June to a lovely young girl who is a physician's assistant to an OBGYN doctor. They're going to live in Bronxville in an old Tudor house."

"How do you know all this, Charles?" Myra asked in amazement.

Charles smiled. "I made it my business to find out. It wasn't that hard. I knew you would eventually get around to asking me and I wanted to have the answers for you."

"Whatever would I do without you, Charles?"

"For starters, you'd have to learn to cook. You'd muddle through, Myra."

"You'll be leaving in the morning. Isabelle left on a four o'clock flight. I'll be all alone here worrying myself to death."

"Nikki will be here, Myra. I gave her enough to do to keep her busy for weeks. She's such a quick study. You tell her once and she grasps it immediately. By the time this first case is over, she will have complete dossiers and files on each case. She's worried about Jack Emery. I have to admit I have some doubts myself where he is concerned. I think it was a stroke of genius on your part, Myra, when you had Isabelle draw up plans for remodeling the bathrooms upstairs. You even took it upon yourself to order four bathtubs, four vanities, four toilets and four shower inserts, not to mention the toilet seats, and store them in the garage. That covers us as far as Jack seeing Kathryn's truck parked here. However, my darling, you goofed up when you said the driver was a man. If he had the presence of mind to run a check on the license plate, he'll know it was a woman. Unless the plate and truck are registered in Alan's name." He slapped at his forehead. "How could I have let that get past me? How, Myra?"

"A senior moment?" Myra quipped. "Nikki's heart is breaking, Charles, and I feel responsible. If it wasn't for Marie Lewellen, Jack might have put the ring on her finger by now."

"You can't think like that, Myra, nor can you blame yourself. It's better she finds out now how power hungry Jack Emery is and to what lengths he'll go to achieve that power he craves. Sex," Charles said, looking up at the ceiling, "isn't everything."

"How long do you think he'll keep at it before he gives up on Marie Lewellen, Charles?"

"People like Jack never give up. The Lewellens are safe where they are in the Amish country. In a month's time they'll adapt. It's as good as it gets, Myra."

"I'm going to miss you. What should I do while you're all gone? If I just sit here and think, I'll go out of my mind."

"You could act on what Yoko told you on the phone last night about Kathryn and her little dream house. Or, you can see what you can do about buying back Alexis's house for her. On the other hand, my dear, you could do both. Vienna or Fairfax would be a nice area for Kathryn. You might want to think about possibly going a little further out to Culpepper. More land out that way. I'm not sure about water. If necessary you could build her a pond and put some ducks in it."

"That's an absolutely brilliant idea, Charles. Do you think I should arrange some surveillance for Mr. Emery?"

Charles threw back his head and laughed, a deep belly laugh that made Myra smile. "I already took care of that. It never ceases to amaze me, Myra. You think like I do. Just when I think I one-upped you, you come up with the same idea a short while later. The reports will be coming in over the computer. Nikki is aware of it."

"Why did Nikki go back to town this evening? Did she say anything to you, Charles?"

"Nothing, other than there were some loose ends at the office. I think she wanted to check for bugs. She said she's going to be staying at the farm for a while. I know that makes you happy."

"Oh, it does. I understood why she had to move back to town. The commute is long and often she has to be in court very early. Then there was Jack. I hate to see her paying that sky-high rent, but she said it's necessary. I wonder if Jack knows or is aware of Nikki's financial situation."

"When people are in love, they tend to share such things, Myra. I think it's safe to assume he's well aware of Nikki's holdings. Just like I'm aware of his. The man's got dick, Myra. He's maxed out on his credit cards and has a hard time making his lease payments on his Lexus. Nikki told me a while back that he wanted to move in so they could share the rent. She said no."

"Thank God," Myra sighed. She covered her mouth in a delicate yawn. She hoped Charles wouldn't insist on watching one of his favorite western movies.

Charles looked at his watch. "I think we should head off to bed, Myra. I have an early morning flight. I'm issuing an invitation here, Myra."

"And I'm accepting it," Myra twinkled.

\* \* \*

Isabelle Flanders adjusted her floppy-brimmed straw hat and dark glasses as she stepped from the taxi. She paid and tipped the driver. She waited another moment until a bellboy loaded her baggage onto a cart to take indoors.

A headache hammered away at the base of her skull and before long she was going to have a full-blown migraine. If not a migraine, then one of the hateful visions that had plagued her since the car accident. She didn't know which she hated more.

At the registration desk she handed the desk clerk Kathryn Lucas's Visa card. She scrawled Kathryn's name across the bottom of the reservation form and waited for her key. She mumbled a muffled "thank you" when the desk clerk slid the key along the marble counter.

She turned to follow the young man and her luggage to her private cottage. She was grateful that the walk was a short one. Later, after the migraine or the vision, she would check out her surroundings. For now she needed water and some aspirin. She tipped the young man and waited for him to leave.

"This is a swinging place, miss. We have five tennis courts, every water sport you can think of, and our nightly entertainment is the best on the island. The Seahorse Pub is where everyone meets in the evening unless they want to go to town. We have a mini-bus if you don't want to walk up and down the hills. The health club is new. The guests like to dance under the stars on the beach terrace. If you need anything, just call the front desk. Enjoy your stay, Miss Lucas."

"Yes, thank you," Isabelle said, handing him a twenty dollar bill. For sure he would remember Kathryn Lucas as a good tipper.

The moment the door closed behind the young man, Isabelle ripped off the sunglasses and straw hat. She rummaged in her purse for her aspirin bottle and gulped down four of them with a swig of water from the mini-bar. She walked out onto the lanai and sat down under the shade of an umbrella. She closed her eyes and waited. Either the headache would come on with force or the vision would appear behind her closed lids.

Why couldn't she be normal like everyone else? *Because Rosemary Wexler ruined your life, that's why.* She could hardly wait till it was her turn so she could rip Rosemary's face to shreds.

It came then in the form of jagged streaks of bright light and then the grainy, gray forms she didn't recognize that were people. This time she saw a car and something that looked like a black marble. The gray form was sticking the marble under the bumper of a

BMW. And then it was over. She rubbed at the corners of her eyes with the knuckle of her index finger. For some reason her eyes always teared after a vision.

The first time it happened, she'd gone to a doctor thinking she'd torn her retina or perhaps something worse. The eye doctor had sent her to have her arteries tested, saying possibly a piece of plaque might have broken off. The test had shown nothing wrong, at which point the doctor told her not to worry, her eyes were fine. When she'd gone back a second, a third and then a fourth time, the doctor had lost patience with her and referred her to another doctor who basically said the same thing. There was nothing wrong with her eyes.

The day she'd ruled out all medical reasons, she'd gone to the library and researched all things paranormal. She saw things but she never knew what they meant. She never recognized the places or the gray, grainy people that appeared before her. Until today. She'd seen the BMW clearly. What did it mean?

With nothing on her hands but time, Isabelle headed for the shower. It was such a relief to take off the heavy, red wig.

An hour later, dressed in shorts, T-shirt and sandals, her own hair piled high on her head, the straw hat on top, Isabelle fixed herself a stiff drink and carried it out to the lanai.

As she sipped at the scotch and soda, she wondered if she would be able to enjoy herself on this brief vacation. It had been six years since she'd gone on a vacation and even then the vacation had only been a four-day-long weekend with a man she thought she would one day marry. After the accident he'd disappeared, the way her business and bank account had disappeared. A businessman in town, he didn't want to be tainted with the same brush. "Screw you, Steve Whitmore!" she muttered. "And screw all the rest of you who believed Rosemary Wexler's line of bullshit. My day is coming!"

Isabelle downed the remains of her drink and eyed the mini-bar through the sliding glass doors. Why not? She was on vacation. She could use a little glow in her life, even if it came from alcohol.

"Shit! Damn it, I was supposed to call Myra." Her movements were frantic as she fumbled through her purse for the cell phone Charles had given her. She screwed her face into a grimace as she tried to remember Charles's instructions. She finally got it on the third try. "Hi," she said.

"Well hi yourself," was Myra's response.

"I should have called sooner but it's incredibly hot here and I wanted to take a shower. I had . . . one of those . . . you know."

"And?"

"I saw something I never saw before. A detail. In the past, every-thing was always vague, unidentifiable. This time I saw a man doing something with a marble to a BMW. I don't know what it means, since I don't know anyone who has a BMW. I can't seem to function after . . . afterward."

"I think you do know someone who has a BMW. I want you to think about it when we hang up. Sit back and relax. Eventually it will come to you. I assume, then, you had no problems with your flight or check-in?"

"None at all. It's very hot here. Oh, I said that, didn't I?"

"Yes. Everything is fine here. Enjoy your vacation . . . Kathryn."

Isabelle walked over to the mini-bar and reached for one of the small bottles of Dewars. She replenished her glass and headed back to the lanai.

She leaned back and closed her eyes. Whom did she know with a BMW? No one. BR or, before Rosemary, she knew several clients who tooled around town in BMWs. Somehow she didn't think that was what Myra meant. Then what did she mean? She brought a mental picture of the parked cars in Myra's oversized, circular driveway to the forefront of her mind. Pricey cars. The truck. The square black car, what was it. A BMW. Whose? The Jag belonged to Alexis and was leased. The Bentley was Julia's. The Benz belonged to Yoko and her husband. The Honda Civic was hers. Who did that leave? Nikki! Nikki drove a BMW. Okay, who was the man and what was he doing with a black marble?

Maybe it wasn't a black marble at all. Maybe it just looked like a black marble. As hard as she tried, nothing else would surface. Maybe after a few more drinks she'd be relaxed enough that she might remember something else.

Dusk settled quickly and before she knew it, the world outside her villa turned midnight black. She looked around as little lights sprang to life on the lanai, casting everything in a dim yellowish light that was not unpleasing.

She probably should think about ordering something from the kitchen. She'd only had a bagel at the airport, but that was over twelve hours ago. Maybe some popcorn shrimp, a garden salad, a slice of cake and then she could go to sleep. In the morning she could think about BMWs, black marbles, and Rosemary.

\*    \*    \*

Back in Virginia, Myra paced up and down her bedroom as she tried to figure out what Isabelle's vision really meant. She longed for Charles, who would undoubtedly have the answer. What did black marbles have to do with Nikki's car? Was someone putting them in her gas tank? Someone! *My foot, someone. More than likely that someone was Jack Emery.* Would he do something that stupid and hope Nikki would call him for a ride or ask him to pick her up? Myra shook her head. That scenario was too ridiculous for words.

She wished now that she had paid more attention to all the spy shows Charles was so addicted to, particularly the reruns of *I Spy* and *Mission Impossible*. That had been Charles's world for so long. A wry smile tugged at the corners of her mouth. He was certainly in his element now with everything he'd conjured up.

Myra looked at the little clock on her nightstand. Nikki would probably still be awake. Should she call her or shouldn't she? If anything happened to Nikki, she would never forgive herself. She didn't stop to think. She picked up the phone and punched out the numbers to Nikki's unlisted number. She would be so relieved when Nikki moved back to the farm tomorrow.

"Hello, darling, how are you? I just called to say good night. Did you finish everything you wanted to get done? I would like it very much if you'd do me a favor, Nikki. Ever since that ugly storm my car has been acting up. I was wondering if you'd lease a car and drive it out here tomorrow. It doesn't matter what kind of car you get. Either Charles or I will drive you back to the city to get your own car. By the way, dear, do you remember my friend, the one who 'sees' things? She called earlier and said she had a vision. I don't believe in things like that, do you? I feel just plain old silly even mentioning it. She always makes me nervous when she brings things like that up. Sleep tight, dear. I appreciate you doing this for me."

Myra stared down at the phone. Was she being silly? Would Nikki pick up on her subtle warning? Of course she would, Nikki was smart. She sat down on the edge of the bed. She thought about the conversation she'd just had with Nikki. It sounded like something out of a bad spy novel. And yet, Charles had seemed more than a little worried about Jack Emery. His words were, it's better to be safe than sorry.

Now that she was here alone in her bedroom, the house silent, she could give way to her fears with no one the wiser. She wondered what she would look like in an orange jumpsuit with shackles on her wrists and ankles. She flinched at the thought. On visiting days,

Nikki would cry and Charles would wring his hands. She'd probably cry herself and say something noble like, if I had it to do over again, I'd still do it.

Charles said everything he'd done was foolproof. Nikki backed him up. And yet, things had a way of going wrong at the last moment. A dog could upset a foolproof plan, a stranger could appear out of nowhere and screw things up. The human element was one thing impossible to foresee.

If she kept this up, she was going to go out of her mind. She needed to do something and she needed to do it now. What? She looked around as though searching for her answer. She saw it in the pile of comforters on the chaise longue in the corner of the room. She didn't stop to think. She gathered them up and in the hall she tossed them to the foot of the steps. She peered over the bannister to see if they had fallen on top of one another. They had. A second later she was sliding down the staircase, whooping in glee. She hit bottom none the worse for wear. She might do it again later on or in the morning. She smacked her hands together in satisfaction.

She rubbed at her rump as she made her way into the living room. Earlier, she'd closed the heavy draperies. Now all she had to do was close the pocket doors leading into the dining room and she could enter the War Room. Charles had scared the bejesus out of her by saying there were high-powered binoculars that allowed a person to see almost a mile away. Then he'd gone on to tell her about the night vision goggles. "Keep the damn drapes and doors closed, Myra," were his exact words.

She certainly was getting an education. It was exhilarating and scary at the same time.

The panel closed silently. Myra walked around the room, marveling at the high-tech world that was now part of the old farmhouse. She looked up at one wall and saw Chris Matthews talking to Mike Barnacle on MSNBC. She looked across the room to see Larry King talking to a psychic named John Edward.

She walked up the two steps that led to the platform where the bank of computers rested under the big screen closed-circuit monitor. She counted down, three, four, five, six. All had little envelopes twirling about signifying that there was incoming e-mail. They were probably from Charles's people. That's how she thought of them, Charles's people. Without those people working in the background, she wouldn't be standing here now, nor would she be obstructing justice and breaking the law.

Myra sat down at the round table and thought about King

Arthur. "We're sort of like that," she muttered. Her hands started to shake so she sat on them as she watched Larry King and John Edward. He was so young to be a psychic, but then Isabelle was young, too. Isabelle just saw things and didn't know what they meant. John Edward seemed to know what everything meant. She wondered what would happen if she called in to the show. Damn, why not?

She was out of the War Room in a flash and in the kitchen dialing the number of the show. She waited while she was put on hold. Her hands started twitching again so she tilted the phone on her shoulder and ear and sat on her hands. She almost fainted when she heard Larry King say, "Go ahead, McLean, Virginia."

Go ahead. What did that mean? Talk. Yes, she was supposed to say something. "Good evening Mr. King and Mr. Edward. I was wondering if you could tell anything by just my voice. You know, pick up on what's going on in my life. I'm not sure I believe in things like this but I like to keep an open mind."

"Can you tell anything by talking to this woman, John?" King asked.

"I see a high-impact hit-and-run accident. Did this happen in China? I see Chinese lettering of some kind. I see turmoil and a lot of activity surrounding you. I also see danger. You have to be careful. You like chocolate eclairs. I see you eating three at one time. I see you surrounded by motorcycles. Does that have any special meaning to you?"

Myra slammed down the phone so hard it bounced off the kitchen counter. She put her head between her legs until her head cleared and she could breathe normally. She was off the chair a second later, opening the refrigerator. She reached for Charles's vodka and took a healthy gulp. Then she took a second one. She debated about a third swallow and put the bottle back on the top shelf.

If she told Charles, he would say she was on the phone long enough for someone to analyze her voice. "Oh God, oh God, oh God." Well, she wouldn't tell Charles. Maybe she should tell Nikki. God, no! She could ask her tomorrow if Jack Emery ever watched Larry King. Probably not on a Friday night. Young, good-looking, power-hungry men like Jack Emery didn't sit home on Friday night watching Larry King. Did they? She would have to be careful when she quizzed Nikki in the morning.

There was no way she was going to be able to sleep now. Charles could always buy another bottle of vodka. Right now she needed it

# Chapter Nine

Kathryn Lucas looked around at the sleazy surroundings of the motel room she shared with Yoko. It was so depressing she wanted to bolt outside to where the air was clean and fresh. Alexis, Julia and Charles had registered earlier and were three doors down from her room. She sat down and sipped at the cold coffee in the Styrofoam cup she'd gotten earlier in the coffee shop. The harried waitress at the register hadn't bothered to even look at her when she paid for the coffee and a tea for Yoko.

Sometime during the night, Charles had attached a decal to both sides of the truck. A green and yellow sign that said in bold hunter green letters, TSOJ Manufacturing. Pictures of different types of scales dotted the long banner. Kathryn found herself giggling at what the sign represented. The scales of justice. On the sliding door in the back, he'd added another sign in bright red letters that said, How's My Driving? Underneath was a toll-free number to call should anyone have a complaint. The truck also now sported a Colorado license plate.

Just an hour ago, Charles had said in his best spy voice, "All systems are a go." She would have preferred him to say, "Time to rock and roll, kids." She blinked at the thought. That would have been movie dialogue. This was the *real thing*. She shivered inside her lightweight jacket.

"How much longer, Kathryn?" Yoko asked.

"Not long. Alexis is making the others up. She's going to do me first and then I'm off to see Dr. Clark Wagstaff to have him check my receding gums. From there I'm going to see the CPA Samuel La Fond. Then it's on to Sidney Lee to buy some insurance. I should be back here no later than eleven-thirty. The run doesn't kick off till one o'clock. We're okay time-wise."

"Are you sure, Kathryn, this is a wise thing you're doing by going to see those three men?"

Kathryn shrugged. "Wise or not, I'm doing it. I want to look into their eyes. I might have one bad moment when Wagstaff sticks his fingers in my mouth, but I'll think of more pleasant things while he's doing that. Just knowing that tomorrow he will be minus his balls will give me a rosy glow."

It was Yoko's turn to shrug. "Don't forget your street map."

There was no knock on the door, no indication anyone was near. Kathryn looked up to see Alexis opening a huge travel case. "You're first, Kathryn. Drag that chair into the bathroom where the light is better. Why do all motels think their customers like orange and brown drapes and spreads?" she grumbled as she opened pots and jars.

Twenty minutes later she stood back to view her handiwork. She clapped her hands in approval. "You look like an older version of Britney Spears, Kathryn."

Kathryn looked in the mirror. Alexis was right. She laughed aloud.

"Hey, I could have made you look like Madeleine Albright or Janet Reno. Just don't stand under any bright lights. This will hold up for about ten hours. We'll need to do a patch job when we get to Lone Pine. Change into that yellow suit and you're good to go, girl. "Yoko, let's get started on your boob job. So, what size do you want to be?"

"I want breasts like grapefruits," Yoko said smartly.

"You're too small-boned. How about big oranges?"

"Big oranges are good," Yoko giggled.

"Then let's get started."

Minutes later, Kathryn cleared her throat. "What do you think?"

"My God, Kathryn, you look beautiful," Alexis said in awe. "That suit fits you like a glove. Nice shape, girl. I like those shoes, too. Ah, a Chanel bag. I like that, too. You should get dressed up more often. Here are the keys to my rental car," she said, tossing the keys. Kathryn reached up and caught them in mid-air.

"Thank Myra. She bought everything. I always liked yellow. It's . . . never mind. I'll see you when I see you. I have the map, Yoko. Stop worrying. Good luck with the boob job."

Being the first appointment of the day guaranteed Kathryn an early departure to keep her other two appointments on time. She looked around the waiting room that was just like all dentists' waiting rooms. The paintings on the wall were imitation Chagal but not unpleasing to the eye. The magazines were crisp and clean, the plants thick and luxurious. The burgundy leather chairs were actually comfortable, the lighting just right.

She zipped through the form attached to a clipboard and scribbled a name at the bottom. She handed it to the receptionist just as a dental assistant called her name.

"Dr. Wagstaff will see you now, Miss Lowenstein." Kathryn followed the young woman down the hallway to a room with a large number three attached to the door. "Doctor is reviewing your chart. It will be just a few minutes."

She was young. They were always young. Either the doctor favored young blood or young, fresh-out-of-school girls didn't demand high salaries. She settled herself in the chair, allowed the sweet young thing to attach a paper bib around her neck. She crossed her ankles and stared at the tips of her Bruno Magli shoes.

She knew he was in the room even though the door had opened silently. She had one brief moment of blind panic when he came to stand next to the chair. His scent was all too familiar, so familiar she wanted to bolt out of the chair. She gripped the arms so tight her knuckles grew white.

"A little tense, are we, Miss Lowenstein? I don't bite. That was a joke. You were supposed to laugh, Miss Lowenstein. Do you mind if I call you Monica?"

Kathryn shook her head as she stared up at him. He was handsome, there was no doubt about that. And he had perfect teeth that he liked to show off. *All the better to bite with, you son of a bitch.* She stared up into his eyes, wondering what he was thinking. She saw absolutely no recognition. She smiled.

Out of the corner of her eye she watched him pull on latex gloves. To protect himself from her. She almost lost it then. He was afraid of her mouth but he hadn't been afraid to stick his dick in her without a condom. Hatred bubbled within.

"Do you have a fear of dentists, Monica?"

Kathryn struggled to take a deep breath. "Yes."

"I'll make this as painless as possible. I promise," he said in a reassuring voice. He flashed his pearly whites for her benefit. Kathryn almost gagged.

*I promise you pain like you can't imagine,* Kathryn thought to herself.

"Did I miss something here? One minute you're petrified and the next minute you're smiling. Share with me."

"My mother always said to think about something pleasant and wonderful in the dentist's chair. I was trying to do that."

"I see." Clearly he didn't see at all. "Open wide and say ahhhh." Kathryn obliged.

"I don't see a problem, Monica," Wagstaff said, poking and picking at her gums and tooth line. "I would recommend using a water pic if you aren't already using one, and flossing regularly. Your gums look sound and healthy to me. I'd like to see you in a year." He stepped back and allowed his assistant to tilt the chair into its upright position.

The doctor stripped off his gloves and handed them to his assistant, but not before he patted her rear end. Kathryn watched as she swished her way to the waste container, a smile on her face.

As she was ripping at the paper bib she noticed a framed newspaper article on the wall. She stared at it for long seconds. Dr. Wagstaff astride his Indian, his feet planted firmly on the ground, staring straight into the camera. She pointed to the picture. "Do you ride, Doctor?"

"A bit. I organized a bike run for a local group here to raise money for underprivileged children. I'm proud to say we raised close to fifty thousand dollars. A lot of children benefitted from that run with dental and medical care. As a matter of fact, this afternoon I'm doing a benefit ride to aid a battered women's group. Do you ride?"

Kathryn flipped her Britney Spears hairdo and said, "Goodness no. I don't even ride a bicycle."

"Now that I see you standing up, you remind me of someone."

Kathryn waved her hand. "People say that to me all the time. Just this morning someone told me I look like Britney Spears's older sister," Kathryn said, forcing a laugh.

Wagstaff shrugged. "See my receptionist and we can make an appointment for you in, let's say, ten months or you can call us around that time. It's up to you."

"That's fine. Thanks. I feel a lot better knowing my gums aren't receding."

"It happens to the best of us," the doctor said over his shoulder as he walked out of the room.

"Isn't he wonderful?" the young assistant gushed. "He's always doing something for someone. He's very civic-minded. He usually makes the newspapers once a month at the very least. It was nice meeting you, Miss Lowenstein."

"Likewise," Kathryn said as she opened her wallet to pay for the visit. She raised her eyes at the hundred-and-fifty-dollar office visit. She plunked down three fifty dollar bills and waited for her receipt. "I'll call when it's time for an appointment. I travel a lot and I'm not sure where I'll be in ten months." She stuck the receipt into the pocket of her yellow jacket and left the office.

Outside in the fresh, spring air, Kathryn took deep gulping breaths until she felt calm enough to head for the parking lot and Alexis's rental car, where she shed the yellow jacket in favor of a green one. She replaced the Britney Spears wig with an Orphan Annie one. Next stop, Samuel La Fond, CPA.

According to Charles's map, La Fond had a suite of offices two blocks west. She looked at her watch. She might be a tad early, but so what.

Kathryn stepped into the CPA's offices and fought with herself not to turn around and leave. On display, between the coffee table and two dark blue chairs, was an Indian motorcycle with a sign on it that said, DO NOT TOUCH. DO NOT CLIMB ON THIS MOTORCYCLE. The walls were peppered with framed pictures and newspaper articles attesting to Samuel La Fond's prowess on cycles. The only magazines on the table were biker magazines and biker catalogs. She wondered if he would set his pickled balls on one of the shelves when they arrived in the mail. She felt chagrined to see that there wasn't a lifesize wax figure of Samuel La Fond. She asked the receptionist.

"Mr. La Fond thought that would be a bit much. Mr. La Fond is free now. Walk through the door on the right."

He was a big man. Real big. He lumbered when he got up from behind his desk to walk around it to shake her hand. He'd put on a good twelve pounds, maybe fifteen, since that night in the parking lot of the Starlite Cafe. He had big hands. Those same hands had squeezed her breasts so hard the bruises stayed with her a full month.

"I need a good accountant for my business. A friend recommended you. I didn't bring anything with me on this trip but if you are taking on new clients, I would be happy to schedule a second appointment. I have an S Corporation and my corporate year ends the end of September. We have plenty of time, the way I see it."

"What type of business are you in, Miss Walley?"

"Bottle caps," Kathryn said, looking around at the pictures of La

Fond in various poses on different motorcycles. The room was like a shrine. To himself.

"Bottle caps?" La Fond echoed.

"Bottle caps. All bottles need caps. It started as a hobby. You know, collecting all kinds of caps. Then one day I got this idea and voilà! The company was born. We grossed twenty-three million last year and we're still in the embryo stage."

La Fond sat up straighter in his chair, his eyes greedy. "I can always find the time to take on a budding enterprise. Why don't we schedule you for, let's see," he said scanning his appointment book, "a month from today. How does ten-thirty sound?"

"That sounds just fine." She ran her fingers through her Orphan Annie wig and smiled. *A month from now, you bastard, you won't even remember this office exists. You'll be too sore to even look at those pictures on the wall.* She was up and off her chair with her hand on the doorknob before he could plough his way across the room. She noticed for the first time that his belly hung over his belt. There was no way she was shaking hands with this grotesque man. She walked through the doorway. "Is there a charge for this visit?"

"No. I'll bill you when you come in the next time. Have my secretary write out an appointment card for you. Actually, my secretary is my wife. I don't have to pay her a salary!" He laughed to show how smart he thought that was.

"Really," Kathryn said as she eyeballed the woman behind the desk. Myra would know to the penny what the woman had paid for her outfit. Straight off Rodeo Drive, if she was any judge. *No shortage of money here,* she thought. She stared at the woman's cleavage as she accepted the appointment card she handed her.

Two down and one to go.

In the car, she removed the green jacket and slipped into a long burnt orange lightweight coat. She looked around the parking lot to see if anyone was watching before she peeled off the Orphan Annie wig and plopped on a Tina Turner job. She adjusted the spiky, strawlike hair in the rearview mirror. She actually looked good in it. She hummed the words to "Proud Mary" as she turned on the ignition. Before she drove out of the parking lot, she scanned the map in her lap.

She had to backtrack and then head north for one mile, where she was supposed to make a left at the third traffic light. She closed her eyes, memorized the route and the landmarks. "Okay, Mr. Sidney Lee, you're next."

Thirty five minutes later she was seated across from Sidney Lee.

It was hard to tell what he was, other than a fast-talking insurance salesman. Swanky offices with rich paneling, good furniture, Berber carpeting, trophies out the kazoo and a clear polished desk. She couldn't make up her mind what nationality he was. He could have passed for Greek, Italian, or maybe even Jewish. But there was a cast to his eyes that said he had some kind of oriental blood in him. He went by the name Lee instead of Sid or Sidney. Strange.

"So, Miss Darnell, my secretary, tells me you want to buy some insurance. Well, you came to the right place. What exactly do you have in mind?"

"Well, Mr. Lee, the past five years have been extremely lucrative for my partner and myself. My accountants tell me I need to buy some Keyman insurance for both of us. He suggested ten million each to protect us, should anything happen down the road. We each want to take . . . oh, excuse me, my phone is ringing."

Her heart beating trip-hammer fast, Kathryn realized something somewhere had gone awry. Her hello was cautious. She listened.

"Kathryn, Sidney Lee is not going on the ride. He canceled out this morning at eight-fifteen. He didn't give a reason." Kathryn continued to listen to Charles's instructions, her heart fluttering in her chest. She turned away so Sidney Lee couldn't see her frightened expression.

"Really, Shelia. I'm at Mr. Lee's office now. Yes, I can do that. If you can hold on a minute, I'll ask him. Mr. Lee, by any chance can you find the time in the next ninety minutes to meet with my partner and myself at the Beverly Hills Hotel? We really want to sign off on these policies today, since Shelia is leaving tonight for England. We can pay the whole year's premium right up front and you can send the paperwork to our office later on. Do you see a problem?"

Lee's face contorted, making him look more oriental. "Ninety minutes isn't much time. Today doesn't seem to be my day. I had to cancel a motorcycle benefit run for charity today." Kathryn watched him, knowing greed would win out in the end. She felt like cheering when he nodded.

"Yes, Mr. Lee can make it." She frowned as she listened to Charles telling her he'd reserved a villa under the name of Shelia Star, supposedly her partner's name. "Villa number eleven. Tell him you can do business on the patio if he balks at being in a room with two women, which I don't think he will, but just in case. Now listen carefully to the directions in case he wants to follow you. Try to avoid that scenario." She listened, her trucker's mind filing away the directions. "I'll see you in a bit. Yes, I'll tell him."

Kathryn fought the urge to spit on the piece of scum standing in front of her. "I have a stop to make before I head back to the hotel. I'll meet you there. We're in villa eleven. We can sit on the patio and have drinks and lunch if you have the time. I hope that's satisfactory. I really have to run."

She carried his stunned expression with her all the way down in the elevator and out to the car. *Now what the hell am I supposed to do? Which disguise do I get into now?* She drove slowly, her heart slamming back and forth inside her chest. What were they going to do at the Beverly Hills Hotel? Charles said everyone would be there. Did that include Charles, too? Who was going to register?

The first glitch.

They were waiting for her when she knocked on the door. Her feet literally left the ground as Julia pulled her inside. In a million years she never would have recognized any of them, especially Charles.

"Time is your enemy, ladies. Alexis is going to be your business partner, Shelia Star. Julia and Yoko will wait in the bedroom until he's under the drug. I can't stay here with you. You're on your own."

"He's going to remember me, Charles. I sat across from him. If he goes to the police, he can describe—"

"—a bad Tina Turner wannabe. This is not a catastrophe. It's a little glitch and we've taken care of it. Admirably, if I do say so," Charles preened. "I'll see you in Lone Pine in, let's say seven hours or so, depending on traffic.

"Julia, slip this into his drink," Charles said, handing over a small vial he extracted from his leather jacket. "This will knock him out for eight to twelve hours. You only need one to two drops."

"This is Rohypnol! It's illegal to use this in the United States. Where did you get this, Charles?" Julia demanded.

"The black market is a wonderful thing. You're worried about illegalities! Get over it. Good luck." Charles walked out through the door onto the patio.

The women looked at one another just as a knock sounded on the door. Julia and Yoko ran to the bedroom and closed the door. Kathryn opened the door and ushered in the insurance man.

"I suggest we get right to it, Mr. Lee. You don't have to explain the policies, we're both familiar with them. Our accountants explained them to us in great detail. We'll just sign the forms and write you out a check. Here, have a nice cold bottle of iced tea," Kathryn said, holding out a bottle of Snapple.

"I don't like tea," Lee said, rummaging in his briefcase for the forms he wanted.

"Coke or Pepsi?" Kathryn asked.

"I don't like sweet drinks."

Alexis sucked on her bottom lip. "Are you saying you don't want to . . . to toast us for buying all this insurance with you? That's not very businesslike. How often does this kind of deal fall into your lap? I like to socialize with the people I do business with. I was really looking forward to drinks and a nice leisurely lunch. I know this is a rush for you, but time is money in our business."

"By the way, what *is* your business? I'm sorry. It's just that I promised my fiancée I would take her to a polo match. She's never been to one. I'm running late as it is. I'll have some bottled water if you feel a toast is in order. This is where you sign off on each of these forms. You know at some point you'll both have to take a physical, but don't worry about that. I know a doctor who will make sure you both pass."

"I don't know why, but I thought you were a married man with a bunch of kids. Most insurance men are married. At least the ones I know," Kathryn said, reaching inside the mini-bar for a bottle of Evian water. She turned around and opened the bottle of Rohypnol and added four drops before she put the cap back on the bottle. She was unscrewing it for his benefit when she handed the bottle to Lee. She handed Alexis a Coke and she kept the Snapple. "I thought I told you what our business was back in the office. We make tea bags. You know, those little paper things that have tea in them. We make the paper and the tag that hangs out of your tea cup."

"I thought Lipton made those."

"See, that's what everyone thinks. We're the brains and they get all the credit. Where should I sign? Oh, I see, right under Shelia's name. Shelia, honey, write this nice man a check so he can go on to his polo match. You didn't say, do you have children, Mr. Lee?"

"Four. Two boys and two girls. They live with their mother." Lee reached for the check, looked at it and almost swooned. He slipped it into a zippered compartment in his briefcase.

"Drink up," Alexis said.

Both women watched as Lee took a healthy swallow of the water in the bottle.

"Shoot!" Alexis said. "We didn't make a toast. Let's see, I think we should make a toast to Mr. Lee and a long profitable business association." She brought the Coke bottle to her lips and watched as

Lee tried to bring the bottle to his own lips. He took a long gulp before he slid to the floor.

"Okay, we're in business!" Kathryn shouted. "Batten down. Close the drapes and slide those dead bolts home, but make sure you hang out the Do Not Disturb sign. Julia, he didn't drink all the water. What if he doesn't have enough in him? I put in four drops, thinking we'd be lucky if he drank a quarter of it."

"I'll put a little on his tongue. Get the shower curtain and all the towels you can find. Strip him down, girls, while I get ready."

This was her moment. The day she'd waited for for seven long years. Kathryn stood on the sidelines as Alexis and Yoko hustled. She saw them spread the shower curtain and a thick, white towel on the coffee table. She watched as they pulled off his shoes, his trousers and his boxer shorts and then hefted him onto the coffee table.

Julia pulled a paper surgical mask across her face. She pulled on *two* pairs of latex gloves. She saw the others watching her. "Just in case of a nick. I don't want to kill him, considering my condition."

Kathryn ripped at the Tina Turner wig and threw it across the room. "The table's too low, Julia."

Julia dropped to her knees. She fixed her gaze on Kathryn. "This isn't exactly brain surgery. I can do it on my knees. Now, how do you want this done? The way it would be done in a hospital or do you want it quick and dirty?"

"Quick and dirty," Kathryn said clearly. Alexis's thumb shot upward. Yoko gave her new breasts a boost and nodded.

"You got it. I'll talk my way through it so you know what's happening." Julia reached for her scalpel. "I'm lifting his penis so I can cut into the scrotum. I am going to deliver it through the scrotum sac. You might not want to watch as this can be extremely bloody even though I'm going to clamp it off. I'm going to tie off the arteries with silk sutures. Then I'm going to tie a square knot around the cord. Just so you know, inside the cord is where the blood vessels are and the epididymis. I'm tying it off. I'm going to staple the skin to bring it back together. This might be a good time to rinse out that Snapple bottle, Kathryn, and fill it with formaldehyde. It's in my bag."

Kathryn's hands shook and then steadied when Julia dropped what looked like two balls into the bottle. "Screw the lid on tight," Julia said.

Five minutes later, Sidney Lee, insurance broker, was bandaged and being dressed.

"No more testosterone or erections for you, Mr. Sidney Lee," Julia said as she ripped off the surgical mask and stripped off the latex gloves.

"It was so . . . quick."

"Here today and gone tomorrow," Alexis said.

"I told you it wasn't brain surgery. I could have done it with my eyes closed. I want to do that to my husband so bad I can taste the feeling. Okay, we need to sweep this place clean. Everyone put on a pair of latex gloves and go over this entire place and clean anything you might have touched. The toilet handle, the refrigerator, the doorknobs. Keep the gloves on until we get in the car. Yoko, take the check out of his briefcase along with the insurance forms. Stuff them in my medical bag. Bundle up the bloody towels and shower curtain and put them in a pillowcase. Leave a hundred dollar bill on the dresser to pay for the towels, shower curtain and pillowcase. Leave another ten dollars for the drinks. Wipe the bills clean. It might be a good idea to wash them first. Kathryn, get your wig and put it on."

"What . . . what should I do with . . . this?" Kathryn asked, holding up the Snapple bottle.

"Stick it in your coat pocket for now. Mark it somehow so you know who they belong to."

"I don't need to mark it," Kathryn said.

"Okay, we're outta here," Alexis said, taking one last look around the villa to see if they had forgotten anything. "Everyone, just stop for a minute. Think carefully. Did you touch anything you forgot to clean? My fingerprints are on file. Yours are too, Kathryn. Julia, how about you?"

"Mine are on file, too. Yoko?"

"Yes, mine are also. I will go around one more time to be sure. The knob on the outside door needs to be wiped clean," she said breathlessly.

"Good thinking," Kathryn said, clapping her on the back. "Two out the back door, Yoko and I go out the front. We'll meet you at the motel."

"Do not look at him again, Kathryn. It will serve no purpose."

"How did—"

"I know. Come, we must hurry. We want to look normal so we should smile and talk as we make our way to the car."

"So, you're liking your new boobs, huh?"

"Yes, I do."

"You know, Julia could give you a *real* set if you want, I bet. You could surprise your husband for his birthday or something."

"I will think on the matter. It is not out of the question."

Kathryn laughed all the way to the car, Sidney Lee's nuts bobbing up and down inside the Snapple bottle.

Myra was out the kitchen door the minute she heard Nikki's car crunch to a stop.

"Myra, what the hell is going on? You scared me half to death last night with that phone call," Nikki said, climbing out of the car.

"I know, I know. Isabelle called and she had this . . . this vison. She saw someone bending over a car sticking a black marble on it. It was a BMW. You drive a BMW. I was too befuddled last night to think clearly, but now I've had time to think, I think someone planted a . . . a bug in your car. That's why I didn't want you to drive it. I hope I'm just being paranoid." She looked upward. "It's going to pour any minute now. Come along, dear."

Nikki tossed her purse and briefcase onto one of the kitchen chairs. "Do you have any fresh coffee? I just rolled out of bed, leased the car and here I am. I never feel alive until I've had two cups of coffee. He wouldn't dare. Jack wouldn't do that to me. Yes, he would," she said, her shoulders slumping.

Myra set a cup of coffee in front of her. "Isabelle always said her visions were never defined but this time she said she clearly saw the letters BMW. It might mean something and again it might not. You need to have a mechanic check out your car, Nikki."

"And if I do find out there's a bug in it, how can I prove Jack did it? I can't. I'll call a mechanic I know when I finish my coffee. Anything new?"

Myra sat down with a thump. "I think that depends on what you mean by new." She recounted the evening's events up until the moment she fell asleep on the sofa. "Does Jack watch the Larry King show? I rather thought Friday nights he would be out either with his friends or on a date with you. Does he, Nikki?" Myra asked, wringing her hands as she paced the kitchen.

"Sometimes he watches the show. Even if he was home, I doubt he would have stayed tuned once he realized the show was about the paranormal. He doesn't believe in stuff like that. The answer is, I don't know."

Myra continued to pace. "It's eleven o'clock here, so that means it's eight in California. Kathryn will be getting ready to visit those . . .

those men. I imagine we'll hear something from Charles via e-mail in the next few hours. There seems to be a lot of e-mail waiting. The envelopes were twirling all over the place last night. I didn't want to touch anything. You know how Charles is with his electronic gadgetry."

Nikki nodded as she tipped her chair back and reached for the phone. She squeezed her eyes shut as she tried to recall the number for Tony's Auto Body shop.

"Tony, it's Nikki Quinn. Listen, I have a tremendous favor to ask of you. No, no, you don't owe me anything because of your sister Angela. She paid the bill. I'm perfectly willing to pay you for your time. I'm working on this case and I have reason to believe someone bugged my car. It's parked on the street outside my apartment building. I keep a spare key under the right fender in a magnet box. Can you go there now and check it out? You can. Thanks. Now listen, I want you to write this down. Jack Emery is the person I want you to deliver it to if you do find something. I'll give you his address. Assuming you find something, when you give it to him make sure he understands it's from me. I owe you, Tony. You'll call me right away if you find something?"

"Right away, Miss Quinn."

Her eyes miserable, Nikki got up to put her cup in the sink. "It should take less than a half hour till Tony calls back. I'm going to scoot upstairs and take a quick shower."

Her own eyes miserable, Myra said, "I'll sit by the phone, dear."

# Chapter Ten

Sweat dripped down Jack Emery's body as he ran at five miles per hour on the treadmill in his apartment. He was breathing hard, his arms swinging at his sides. Ten more minutes and he would have run ten full miles on the machine, a gift from Nikki on his last birthday. He picked up his pace and did the last ten minutes at six miles per hour, the machine quivering under his fast-paced run.

*Six minutes flat,* he thought in satisfaction when he yanked at the safety cord and hopped off. He wiped the perspiration running down his face with the sweatband on his wrist and headed for the shower. The doorbell rang just as he turned on the hot water. He gave his boxers a hitch and marched out to the door. He looked through the peephole and frowned. The guy looked familiar but he couldn't immediately place his face. He yanked open the door.

"Are you Jack Emery?"

Jack pointed to his name over the doorbell. "Yeah."

"Then I guess this is for you. Nikki Quinn said I should hand deliver it to you. Have a nice day."

Jack looked at the electronic device in his hand. *Son of a bitch!* He slammed the door shut and marched back into the bathroom. For sure his relationship with Nikki was over. He cursed again, using words he hadn't used since his days on the street back in the Bronx.

In the shower he lathered up and let the hot, steamy water beat on his naked body. He stared into the steamy mirror as he dried off. If Nikki found the bug, that meant she was searching for it. Which in turn had to mean she had something to hide. His gut told him she was up to her eyeballs in Marie Lewellen's disappearance. And rich-as-sin Myra Rutledge was probably right there with her, aiding and abetting. "You fucking rich people think you can get away with anything," he muttered as he stomped his way into the bedroom to get dressed.

Now he had to go to the office so he could get to the bottom of Nikki's involvement. He had to satisfy himself one way or the other where she was concerned. The ironic thing was, Nikki would have done the same thing if she'd been in his position, even though she wouldn't admit it.

He was pulling on his socks when the phone rang. He debated a moment before he threw himself across the bed and picked up the phone from the nightstand. "Emery here," he barked.

"By any chance do you mean asshole Emery?" Nikki asked coldly. "You bugged my goddamn car, Jack. I want to know why."

Jack clenched his teeth so hard he thought he heard his jaw crack. "Because you're up to your neck in Lewellen's disappearance, that's why, and we both know it. Don't take that as an admission of guilt, Nik. I'm going to find her. Then I'm going to prove you and Myra are responsible. Yeah, old Myra said the words but she doesn't care about losing the mil. All she wanted to do that day was to get me the hell out of her house. Do you two think I just fell off the watermelon truck?"

"I'm going to fry your ass for this, Jack."

Jack looked around his messy apartment, trying to compare it to Nikki's bright airy apartment that was neat as a pin. It even smelled clean and good, like Nikki herself. His apartment was shabby, dreary and messy with beer bottles, pizza cartons, dirty socks and smelly sneakers all over the place. He closed his eyes. "Not if I fry yours first. Is that what you called to tell me?"

"Myra asked me to file a lawsuit against your department. She said you were supposed to be guarding Marie Lewellen and you let her get away. She's suing for the full million and she wants another million for the angst and fear she's going through. I'll file the suit on Monday. You want to settle now?"

"Up yours."

"Better tell your boss. I'll hand deliver the subpoena. Hey, look at it this way, you bastard, you'll get your picture in the paper. Don't call me, I'll call you."

Jack slammed the phone back into the cradle, his face murderous. She'd do it, too. Christ, now what was he supposed to do?

In less than thirty minutes he was storming into his office, the same murderous look still riding his features. He sat down at the computer and started to bang at the keys.

The scrap of paper torn from his notebook was alongside the

computer. He typed in the license plate number of the eighteen-wheeler parked at Myra Rutledge's house. They could have spirited the Lewellens away in the truck in the middle of the storm and no one would have been the wiser.

*Alan Stephen Lucas. Born August 3, 1958. Address, P.O. Box 206, Vienna, Virginia.* He stared down at the social security number and wrote it on a yellow pad of paper. He tapped in more numbers using the department code to allow him access to social security files. He blinked and then knuckled his eyes. *Deceased.* The guy was dead! He cleared the screen and typed in the number again. Alan Stephen Lucas was just as dead as he was a minute ago.

Did the guy sell the truck? Was it part of his estate? Why was someone still driving the truck and using Lucas's license plates? He scanned the screen to see the date of death. Not quite five weeks ago. Time enough to take care of details like selling the truck or changing the plates. Lucas wasn't old, so that had to mean there was a widow someplace. Then again, maybe the guy was divorced.

Jack yanked at his desk drawer and pulled out a well-thumbed booklet with access codes to the different government agencies. He typed in Bureau of Vital Statistics and then the name Alan Stephen Lucas and waited while the screen processed his request to be faxed a copy of Lucas's death certificate. He cursed ripely when he realized he would have to wait for Monday for the fax. He typed the words in capital letters, RUSH, TOP PRIORITY.

Did truckers belong to unions? He didn't know. He tapped and punched for the next hour until he came up with Local 233 in Roanoke, Virginia. Even if he sent an e-mail he'd probably have to wait until Monday for a response. Instead he copied down the telephone number and called it. He waited through eleven rings before a gruff voice came on the line and said, "Yeah, what's your poison?"

Must be trucker lingo. Jack identified himself and said, "I'm trying to locate Alan Lucas. Do you know how I can reach him or his wife?"

"Alan died a while back. I don't know where his wife is. She's probably on the road somewhere. She's the one that drives the rig. Alan was disabled. Why do you want him?"

Jack ignored the question and asked one of his own. "Do you know how I can reach his wife?"

"Do I sound like a private secretary, mister? Send her a letter."

"Yeah, thanks for your help." Wiseass.

It wasn't such a ridiculous idea. He cleared the screen, brought up Word, and typed a message saying it was imperative Kathryn get in touch with him as soon as possible. He filed the message in his personal file folder but not before he printed it out. He scribbled the address on the official stationery, ran it through the postage meter and dropped it in the mail basket.

He flexed his fingers. He was on to something. He could feel it. His nose twitched like a rabbit's. "Let's try the Bentley next," he muttered.

Jack stripped off his jacket and rolled up his sleeves. What the hell, with Nikki temporarily out of the picture, he didn't have anything better to do on a Saturday afternoon.

Winston Bugle frowned as he hung up the phone. He didn't have any use for cops or district attorneys. He reached for the CB and said, "This is Bugle Beagle out here. Anyone listening? I need to get a message to Big Sis. All you ears pay attention now, you hear. Tell her some D.A. called from the District asking questions. Saw on the I.D. he was calling from D.C. Keep trying Big Sis until she responds. Have her call me. Over an' out."

Myra made no pretense of not listening to Nikki's conversation with Jack Emery. The moment she hung up the phone she said, "Was that wise, Nikki? Won't that just fuel things with Jack?"

"It's called CYA. Covering your ass. I know Jack. From time to time he has to be reined in. I told you he's sharp. He's one of the best and for that I can't fault him. He has that old prosecutor instinct. I respect that. He really does hate injustice. He hates defense attorneys, of which I am one. He says they catch the bad guys and people like me make sure they walk away clean. We had a lot of fights about it. He'll shave a corner here or there to get the job done. His instinct has always been right on the money. He knows in his gut we had something to do with Marie's disappearance. He just can't prove it. Yet.

"I'll bet you fifty dollars, if I call him at the office, he'll answer. The minute he hung up from me he hightailed it there. He'll stay there all day, through the night and all day tomorrow if he's on to something. All I did was throw a bone he now has to deal with. It was just to throw him off stride a little. The man has a single-minded purpose in life. Shit, Myra, I can't even hold that against him. He came off the streets in New York. He worked his way through college and law school. No one helped him. He's where he is because he earned his way.

"Yes, he's power hungry. He likes being on the news and he likes getting his picture taken with the mayor and the police commissioner. So do a lot of other guys. He just made it happen for himself. He's pretty much going by the book and we're the ones that threw the book out."

"That was a sterling testimonial, Nikki. That tells me you are still very much in love with Jack Emery."

"I'll get over it."

"What do you think he'll do next, dear?"

Nikki threw her hands in the air. "My guess would be the first thing he'll do is change his underwear. The word lawsuit against the office is a really dirty word. He's going to have to call the D.A., the mayor and then the police commissioner. Then he's going to go to the office and run those license plates if he did take them down. Jack has a mind like a steel trap. There is one good thing about Jack in regard to his career and his profession, though. He keeps everything to himself, you know, close to his vest. Part of it is that wild ambition of his and it's also part of the thoroughness of him. What that means, Myra, is he gets all his ducks in a row first and then he pounces."

Myra sat down with a thump. She longed for Charles as she struggled for the right words. "Dear, does that mean we'll have to . . . *take him out?*"

Nikki doubled over laughing at the expression on Myra's face. She sobered almost instantly. "It just might come to that, Myra."


"Last minute check, sisters," Alexis said as she jammed her canvas bags in the trunk of her car. "Yoko, you're driving my car and I'm riding with Kathryn. That's in keeping with what Kathryn told Miz Slick, that you were just going as far as San Francisco."

"Is everything wiped clean?" Julia asked.

Yoko adjusted the blue bandanna wrapped around her forehead, allowing her long silky hair to cascade down her back. "I wiped everything twice," she said, peeling off the latex gloves. "With alcohol from Julia's bag," she added as an afterthought.

"We all checked out using the automatic room check-out. That's all taken care of. Yoko, did you clean off the remote controls?"

"Yes, I did, Kathryn. We're leaving the rooms cleaner than they were when we checked in."

Kathryn looked at the Dag watch on her wrist. It did everything but talk to her. "Time to rock and roll, sisters." Yoko giggled. "Stay close behind me and whatever you do, don't speed or call attention to yourself. We're driving straight through, so there won't be any stops. Anyone have to use the bathroom?"

"No, Mother," Julia grinned.

"Let's go. We're only forty-five minutes behind schedule. Jeez, wait a minute! Did someone remember to go to Home Depot to pick up the folding table? We do need an operating table."

"That was my job. I picked it up on my way in. It's in the trunk. I took it out of the box, so my fingerprints are all over it. If we leave it somewhere, remind me to wipe it clean," Julia said.

"I'll remember, Julia," Yoko said. She slid into the car. The moment she put the key in the ignition, she let out a yelp. "This is a stick shift! I do not know how to drive with gears."

"Oh shit!" Alexis said. "It was the only one left. Okay, okay, crash five-minute course. See this, it's in the shape of an H. Middle is neutral. Low, straight up is second, down to neutral, top of the H is reverse and then down again to third which is high and you cruise in high. You need to use both feet. At the same time, Yoko. You ease up on the clutch, feed a little gas and shift, low to second to third. Each time you have to use the clutch. For each gear, Yoko. You got that? Now, if you hit a hill, you have to be careful or you'll slide backward. Julia, you drive behind her in case that happens. That way she'll only slide into you. Try it, Yoko, once around the parking lot. If you get stuck, drive in first. We'll keep an eye on you."

"I'd say this is a glitch. That's two so far. Three, if you actually count the surgery," Kathryn said grimly. She watched with the others as the Ford Taurus bucked and chugged forward, then backward and came to a dead stop a foot from them. The car bucked and stalled.

"I think I got it. I'm ready. I can do this, Kathryn."

"I know you can, kiddo. Think wagon train, sisters," Kathryn said, hoisting herself up into the cab. She started to sing, "Rolling, rolling, rolling . . ."

They were ninety minutes out of Los Angeles when Kathryn's personal cell phone rang.

"You can't answer it, Kathryn. You're supposed to be in Bermuda," Alexis said.

"I know. It's a Nextel. It takes messages. When it stops ringing, I'll walk you through the process to retrieve the message."

"I have the same phone. I know how to do it. It's Sam Slick."

Alexis said, raising her eyebrows. "She said Bugle Beagle wants you to call him. Some district attorney wants to talk to you ASAP. She said you have his number. The call is out to all truckers to give you the message. She said if you need her to call any time of the day or night. That's it," Alexis said, hitting the power button to turn off the cell phone.

"Glitch number four. Call Myra on the cell phone Charles gave you. Repeat the conversation verbatim. I'm sure the D.A. is the one that came to the house. He ran a check on the license plate. I knew it. I had a bad feeling the day he came to Myra's house. Easy, Murphy, easy. It's okay," she said to the big dog who had picked up on the anxiousness in her voice.

Five minutes later, Alexis looked across at Kathryn as she absent-mindedly scratched Murphy's head. The big dog did everything but purr. "Nikki answered and she said to stick to the plan and to call the D.A. when you get back from Bermuda. I think Isabelle's flight gets in around eleven Monday morning. I'd say call him around twelve-thirty. Time for you to pick up the truck and your load of produce."

"Is this glitch four or is it five?"

"Four with a hangnail. It's okay, Kathryn. I like this dog of yours. The truth is, I like everyone involved in this little venture. Yoko is growing on me. I saw Julia smile and once she actually laughed out loud. That has to be hard with a death sentence hanging over your head. Nikki is the one I feel sorry for. Isabelle is so sweet and so very tired. Myra and Charles are just loves. You're okay, too, Kathryn. Being in prison had to be a piece of cake compared to what you lived through."

"What was it like, Alexis?"

"It was bad. The worst thing of all was when the doors clanged shut. The word clang is so perfect. Every damn time they shut, I wanted to jump out of my skin. I never close doors where I live now. Even the bathroom door stays open. I don't know if I'll ever get over that feeling. Everything smelled like Clorox. The food was inedible. The bed was hard as a rock. Roaches were everywhere. Everything was on a schedule. I made a lot of friends after I learned how to play the game. The whole time I was in there I didn't have one visitor, nor did I get one piece of mail. Most days I didn't know what day it was unless someone told me.

"The worst thing, though, was the nightmares. I lived with the trial and the outcome every day since I was convicted. I spent a year in prison so those slimeballs could cheat old people and fatten up their bank accounts. One of them even has a yacht now. I swear it's as big as an ocean liner.

"My real name is Ann Marie Wilkinson, not Alexis Thorne, and I damn well want it back. I was born with it and it belongs to me." Tears rolled down her cheeks. Murphy reared up and licked them away.

"We'll get your name back. Don't you worry about that," Kathryn said, with such vehemence Alexis bolted upright. "And I'm going to see to it that you get the ocean liner, providing you take me and Murphy on a cruise."

"You sound like my champion, Kathryn. Thank you for that."

"We're all in this together."

"You know what I think, Kathryn. I think we make one kick-ass team. I sure as hell wouldn't want to go up against us. Would you? Are you anxious about tonight?"

"A little. I was pretty calm when Julia did her number back there in the motel. He should be waking up just about the time we get to Lone Pine."

"What'd you do with his nuts?"

"They're swishing around back there in Alan's old lunchbox. It's in the back by his wheelchair."

Alexis burst out laughing. "How did you feel, Kathryn?"

"Angry. Bitter. Numb. It was all so surreal. I knew it was happening and I knew I was watching and being a part of it but only half of me was there. The other half of me was back there in the parking lot of the Starlite Cafe where it happened. He was the one that sodomized me. If his nuts hadn't been in that Snapple bottle, I would have jammed that bottle up his butt."

"Spoken like a true woman. One down, two to go. By midnight or thereabouts, you will be vindicated. Don't for one minute think you're going to magically find closure, Kathryn, because it ain't gonna happen. People always say they're looking for closure for this or that. It doesn't happen. You can't erase the memory. It will always be with you. The best you can hope for is some kind of vindication," Alexis said as she settled herself more comfortably in the seat. "Just knowing there are three men out there walking around without their balls is going to please me no end."

"Yeah, me, too. Do you suppose they'll walk differently, kind of duck-like?"

Alexis went off into a peal of laughter. "They won't have to worry about which side to put *them* on anymore. I heard Tom Jones the singer used to pad his pants onstage so people would think he had a big set. I wonder if that was true."

Kathryn laughed until her sides hurt.

An hour later, Alexis said, "Kathryn, do you see what I see?"

"It's the bikers. Oh, God, there's Charles in the lead. What should I do? Pass them or stay behind?" Kathryn dithered. "Shit, they're straightening out, that means they want me to pass them. Don't look at them, Alexis."

"Hey chickee baby," one of the bikers shouted as Kathryn pressed down on the gas pedal.

Alexis hung her head out the window and looked at Charles as Kathryn roared past the trail of motorcycles. "Yo dude!" she shouted. Charles waved, a wicked grin on his face.

"You had to do that, didn't you?"

"Yeah," Alexis laughed. I've been called a lot of things in my time but no one ever called me chickee baby before. They must have stopped for food or something. They had at least a fifty-minute head start on us. Before you can ask, I think there's thirty-seven of them. That's counting Charles."

"How far from ground zero?"

"Three hours, maybe a little less."

"I'm counting the minutes," Alexis said as she snuggled with Murphy.

Jack Emery rubbed at his tired eyes before he picked up the stack of papers he'd printed out. They could just be papers or they could be something else. He leaned back in his swivel chair as he scanned the sheets in his hand. Why would women in their late 30s and early 40s be playing bridge with an old lady like Myra Rutledge? Just by scanning the sheets he'd say they were more likely to belong to the same gym as Nikki. But they were at Myra's.

A prominent plastic surgeon married to a United States senator might conceivably travel in the same circles as mega-rich Myra Rutledge. He'd seen the power couple's picture in the paper at least once a week but never with Myra Rutledge. The name Isabelle Flanders tickled his brain but he couldn't remember where he'd heard it before. Alexis Thorne and Yoko Akia. And of course Nikki. Myra said Nikki wasn't there the day he'd walked through the ruptured gates. He frowned. Were the others in the house that day? If they were, he hadn't seen them. But that didn't have to mean anything. They could have been in the sunroom or the dining room. So what? People like Myra Rutledge played cards in the middle of the day and served little finger sandwiches to the cardplayers.

Unlike his mother, who cleaned houses for a living to support his three sisters and two younger brothers while he was growing up. She was always home to make dinner and then left again to clean offices at night. She didn't know the first thing about playing cards. She probably didn't know how to make little finger sandwiches either. He thought about the hundred bucks a week he kicked in along with his siblings to pay for her care in a nursing home. He didn't begrudge the money because he loved his mother. He just wished she would get better but he knew no one recovered from Alzheimers disease. His eyes burned when he remembered his last visit to the nursing home. For one minute she'd recognized him and called him Jackie. A second later she asked him if he was a doctor.

No, his mother didn't know people like Myra Rutledge.

He wondered now if he should have told Nikki about his mother. Why hadn't he? Why did he let her think he didn't know how to manage money, that he was a playboy D.A.? Why did he trade in his old reliable Honda for the Lexus and was now sucking wind because the lease payments were strangling him? Why did he do half the things he'd done where Nikki was concerned? Had he in some cockamamie way been trying to compete with the life she had with Myra Rutledge? Did he think a boy from the Bronx couldn't measure up? Yeah, yeah, that's exactly what he thought.

He looked at his watch. If he drove like hell, he could make the nursing home before they got his mother ready for bed. Maybe she'd call him Jackie again tonight. Maybe.

Jack made it to Winchester just in time before lockdown. He waved to the charge nurse and beelined down the hall to his mother's room. He stood in the doorway watching her for a full minute before he said, "Hi, Mom!"

"Is your mother here, young man? I don't see her."

"I guess she left," Jack said perching on the side of the bed. "Would you like some company?"

"I always like company. Where is your mother?"

"She's close by. She won't mind if I stay and talk with you for a little bit."

"I think I'm a mother. Do you know if I am, young man?"

"I think you're probably the best mother in the whole world. I'm

Jack. Do you remember me? Think, Mom. Jesus, I miss you. I try to get out here as often as I can but I can't always make it. I just want you to know I try."

"Are you going to cry, Jackie? It hurts me to see you cry, honey. No one is here so if you want to cry it's okay. I won't tell anyone."

Jack dropped to his knees. He almost swooned when his mother stroked his hair and started to hum under her breath, "Hush little baby . . ." He blubbered like a baby and didn't know why.

Jack moved away and reached for his mother's hands. "Mom, listen to me. If someone killed Betty Ann, what would you do?"

"Who's Betty Ann?"

"Your daughter, Mom. My sister. What would you do if someone killed her?"

"If I was Betty Ann's mother, I would kill them. What would you do, young man?"

"I tried to stop her, Mom, but I wasn't quick enough. I was going to send her to jail for the rest of her life but she skipped out on me. I have to find her."

The woman sitting in the chair grappled with what he was saying. Jack watched as she struggled to find words to respond. "Mothers are . . . they love . . . they protect their young with their lives. Are you sure I'm a mother? Do you need someone to protect you, young man? I think I can do that. Tell me what you want me to do."

Jack leaned over and kissed her cheek. "Just say good night Jackie. The nurse is here to get you ready for bed."

"Good night, Jackie."

"I'll see you next week, Mom."

"If I see your mom I'll tell her I saw you. What's your name again?"

"Jack Emery. Good night, Mom."

Outside in the hall he heard his mother say, "That young man lost his mother. It's so sad."

Outside in the warm spring night, Jack sat down on an iron bench in the little courtyard by the main entrance. He bit down hard on his lip, his shoulders shaking. He didn't see the tall thin man walk through the doorway, nor was he aware of him when he made his exit a half hour later. He did see the man talking on his cell phone when he passed his car on his way to the Lexus that was parked three aisles away.

\* \* \*

In the kitchen at the farmhouse in McLean, Myra Rutledge listened to the voice on the other end of the phone, her jaw dropping as she absorbed what the private detective was telling her. She hung up the phone and looked around for Nikki. She called out.

"I'm upstairs, Myra. Do you want me to come down?"

"If you don't mind, dear. I have something to tell you."

"I hope it's something good," Nikki said coming down the steps.

"It's sad, Nikki. Sit down and I'll tell you. It's about Jack Emery."

Nikki's face turned white. "Did something happen to him?"

"No, no, nothing like that." *She still loves him,* Myra thought.

"That was the private detective Charles hired to . . . a . . . tail Jack."

"What?"

"It seemed like the right thing to do at the time, dear. I think you'll be glad when I tell you what I just found out."

"This better be good, Myra."

# Chapter Eleven

Kathryn slowed the truck to a mere crawl as she instructed Alexis to look for a side road that Charles had marked on the map in red pencil. "We should be coming up to it any minute now. We've passed all the landmarks he told us to watch for. What does it say on the margin, Alexis?"

"You're to drive one and one-half miles down the road and park once you turn off. He said there is a huge outcropping of rocks on the left side. Once you pass that, there's a clearing and you can stash the truck and the girls can park. He said no one uses this road anymore."

Kathryn sighed. "How *does* he know all this? The man absolutely boggles my mind. No wonder he was tops in his field. If you stop to think about it Alexis, we wouldn't be here doing what we're doing if it wasn't for him."

Alexis waved her hands in the air. "He does that click, click, click thing with the maps on the computer. He can bring a dot on a map into full view and you can see the bushes and practically count the blades of grass. Who cares? I see the rocks, Kathryn. There it is, slow down. Turn on your blinker. Jeez, don't miss it. Can you turn this baby in there? Looks kind of narrow to me. Watch it."

Kathryn rolled her eyes. "Shut up, Alexis. I can do this. There, see, I did it. The others are following. I wonder if anyone is behind Julia. What if they see all three of us turning in here? For a secluded road, all of a sudden three vehicles turn off. That could rouse some suspicion."

"I don't think it's secluded. I think it's a bear habitat," Alexis grinned. "We aren't going to worry about this, Kathryn."

Kathryn parked the rig and opened the door. "No, we're not going to worry about this. Julia, was there much traffic behind you? Did anyone see us turning off here?"

"There was a pickup pretty far back. Why?"

Murphy nudged Kathryn's leg. "You stay right here with me. Go on, you can lift your leg on that tree. Right back here, Murph. I gotta go myself."

Alexis pointed. "I see four thick bushes. Take your pick. Here," she said, handing Kathryn a wad of tissues from her shoulder bag.

"The last time I peed in the bushes I was six years old. My mother told me to pretend I was picking flowers," Kathryn giggled. "Alexis said this is bear country, so we do it one at a time. Or were you putting me on?"

"I was. Go pee."

A light rain started to fall just as Alexis said, "Showtime, ladies!"

The women waited until Murphy bounded into the back of the truck before they boosted themselves up and inside. Kathryn lowered the back gate just as Yoko turned on six crank operated flashlights that Charles had ordered from the Sharper Image catalog. Guaranteed to provide light forever.

Kathryn stood to the side, Murphy next to her as the women stripped off their wigs and shed their clothes. Julia was so pretty in a wholesome way with her thick chestnut hair and light dusting of freckles. In one way she looked plain and in another way she looked elegant. In college she was probably called preppy. When she smiled, which was rare, her whole face lit up. Kathryn smiled at her assessment of the doctor.

"Julia . . . I . . . want to say something to you. 'Thank you' doesn't seem like enough. We," she said, waving her hand to indicate the others, "are just along for the ride, in a manner of speaking. It's your knowledge, your expertise, that is accomplishing what we set out to do. When it's your turn, I just want you to know I'll do whatever it takes to do whatever it is you want. That's a given. That's all I wanted to say."

Julia walked over to Kathryn and hugged her. "I know that, Kathryn. Now, let's get dressed. I can hardly wait to get on that Night Train again. You know, I just might buy myself one of those when we get back home."

Alexis dug into her magic sack of disguises. She handed out black push-up bras and skimpy bikinis. "It's part of a set," she said. "One goes with the other. So you give up your flowery underwear for one day, Kathryn, what's the big deal. Leathers for you, Yoko and you, Julia. Mine are over here. Dolly Parton wigs for everyone.

Bandannas for everyone. They'll help secure the wigs because they're heavy. Who wants to be a redhead?"

"Me," Julia said.

"I want the white one," Kathryn said.

"The sable brown one is mine," Yoko said.

"I always wanted to be a blonde," Alexis giggled. "A black biker chick with blonde ringlets. Just call me chickee baby." She pirouetted around the truck in her underwear for the benefit of the others. They clapped and whistled their approval.

Murphy howled when Alexis plopped the blonde wig on her head.

Kathryn, with Julia's help, set up the folding table. Yoko perched on the end to wait for Alexis to open her magic box of cosmetics. "Mata Hari, I think, Yoko. I'm going to give you a tattoo on the right side of your neck. I have the stuff that will take it off, so don't panic. I'm thinking since you're oriental, you might want a small dragon. One that's belching fire." She wiggled her eyebrows like Groucho Marx. "You okay with a dragon?"

"Absolutely."

Alexis's brush flew across Yoko's face. She dipped and swirled, patted and blew on the irridescent powder. "You want the ring in your nose or your eyebrow?"

"For real?" Yoko said, drawing back.

"No. But it will look like it's real. I know what I'm doing."

"I think I'll take the eyebrow."

"Done," Alexis said, fastening a small silver hoop to Yoko's thick eyebrows. "You're starting to look real good, kid." Alexis stepped back to view her handiwork. "Let's plump up those boobs. They're starting to melt. Somebody spit on this decal and paste it on her neck. In the meantime, pick out your own decals. I suggest you put them on the top of your boobs."

"I don't see anything symbolic," Kathryn grumbled as she flipped through the artificial tattoos. "I want one that says something. I'm going with the teddy bear."

"I'll take the rose," Julia said.

"What about you, Alexis?"

I'm going with Peace and Love," Alexis said.

"Wow!" Julia and Kathryn said in unison. Yoko shook her rump as she sashayed around the inside of the truck. They watched as she pulled on her jeans and the leathers. The boots had steel tips with flowers painted on the sides. The vest with the silver hob knobs was the last thing she put on. Her breasts spilled out the top, her cleavage deep and seductive. The dragon wiggled on her neck each time she took a deep breath.

Julia slid onto the table. "Alexis, you might want to put on a pair of latex gloves," she said quietly.

Alexis bent over until she was eye level with Julia. "I'm not afraid of you, Julia. I don't need the gloves. We aren't exactly exchanging body fluids here. Now sit still so I can make you more beautiful than you already are." She waited while Julia knuckled her eyes. "Okay, now, I'm going to make you look like Anna Nicole Smith, that blonde bimbo that married that really rich old man." She was as good as her word. Fifteen minutes later, Julia slid off the table. "Ta da!" she said, jiggling to unheard runway music.

"Fantastic!" Kathryn giggled.

"Okay, Barbarella, you're next."

Kathryn hopped up on the table. "Do it!" she said dramatically.

Alexis's brush swirled and dipped again, up and down, across and then back up. In the blink of an eye, Kathryn sported outrageous false eyelashes that were curly enough to hold a pencil. "This is the most petulant mouth I've ever seen in my life," she said, staring into the mirror Alexis held up. "I love it! I didn't think it was possible to look this *slutty.*"

"We look like tramps," Yoko said, peering at Julia.

"Yoo hoo!" Alexis said. They turned around and gasped in awe. Who was this long-legged creature in the leopardskin jumpsuit that was unzipped to the waist?

"Holy shit!" Kathryn said.

"Holy shit is right," Julia said.

Yoko was totally speechless as Alexis fastened her leathers and then slipped into the black leather vest. Her boots were covered in leopardskin and had three inch heels. She looked to be six feet tall. Murphy growled as he sniffed her feet.

"What time is it?" Julia asked.

"Ten minutes of eight," Kathryn said, staring down at her watch. "Yeah, yeah, it's time to roll out our transportation. I didn't see any road lights so that means it's gonna be dark. Just stay behind me once we get to the main road. We don't have far to go, so nothing should go awry. Oh, shit, it's pouring rain."

Alexis dived into her sack of goodies and came up with four black ponchos. Don't thank me, thank Charles," she said, tossing one to each of them.

Kathryn pulled hers on. "Come on Murphy, time to settle you down for the night." Inside the cab, Kathryn shooed Murphy to the back where a bed was set up. "Here's your baby," she said, handing the dog a battered, bald Raggedy Ann doll. "Here's a new fresh chewie and your ball. Your treat is by the water bowl. Your food is in your dish. You guard this truck with your life. We'll be back in a little while. I know you understand everything I'm saying, Murph. This is important. Don't bark."

The big dog licked her hand before he stretched out on the single mattress.

"Did you guys lock the cars? Of course you did. Just let me lock up here and we can be on our way. Why the hell did it have to rain? We're going to be leaving tire marks all over the damn place," Kathryn muttered as she straddled the '67 Electra Glide. She pressed the button and the machine came to life. She felt Yoko settle herself behind her just as Alexis's '93 Softail's engine turned over. She waited a moment for the sound of the FXSTB Night Train to come alive.

The night was pitch black as Kathryn led the group out to the main road. She looked both ways before she peeled out onto the macadam, Alexis and Julia behind her. She could feel Yoko's death grip around her waist. Hysteria bubbled up to her throat. *We must look like something out of a scary Halloween movie,* she thought as she crawled along the highway.

The minute she saw the blaze of neon lighting ahead she felt all the tenseness leave her body. She swerved into the parking lot of the Lone Pine Retreat, tooled around to the back and cut the engine. The others parked next to her.

"The temperature's dropping," Julia said.

"Is that important?" Alexis asked anxiously.

"No. I was just making conversation."

"Listen up, we wear these ponchos till we get inside. We hang them up and then we *strut,* ladies, to the bar. Strut. We do not sashay, we do not slink, we do not walk, we strut. No fancy drinks. Hard liquor. Scotch. That's what biker chicks drink. I read that in one of Charles's magazines. We are on the prowl, so look obvious. We're easy but make them work for it. You ready?"

Three ponchos bobbed up and down as the quartet ran for the main entrance.

It was like a million other bars, steamy, smoky and sleazy. It was just one big room with tables positioned around the bar. They were greeted with whistles, hoots and explicit suggestions. They waved and smiled as they swung their legs over the bar stools.

"What's your pleasure, ladies?" the bartender leered.

"Scotch on the rocks. A double," Kathryn said.

"I'll have the same," Alexis said.

"Make that three," Julia said.

"Four," Yoko squeaked.

Kathryn had to stand up to fish in her jeans' pocket for money. She half-turned so that the group at the long table could get a better view of her right breast and the tattoo. She slapped a fifty dollar bill down on the bar.

Julia reached for her drink and downed it in two swallows. She thumped the glass down on the bar and swivelled around, her long legs stretched out in front of her. She looked pointedly at the men sitting at the table. "That's some impressive machinery out front. We're on our way to the Harley-Davidson show. Would any of you be interested in buying an FXSTB Night Train? Sugar here is selling her '93 Softail, too."

"I might be interested in the Night Train," Charles said, getting up from the table and walking over to the bar. "Is it outside?"

"Sure is, honey. Be glad to show it to you after we get something to eat. We've been riding all day."

"Why don't you ladies join us. I placed our order but I don't see a problem adding four more steaks. Hey guys, swing four more chairs over here."

"Well sure, we'd love to join you. We got nothing better to do and we want to wait out the rain. Y'all staying around here or what?"

"We're camping in the Alabama Hills," Charles said.

"You guys on a run?" Alexis asked.

"Yeah," someone shouted from the far end of the table.

"We did it for victims of violent crimes," someone else shouted. "You *ladies* want to kick in some bucks?"

"Sure," they said in unison as each one of them handed over a hundred dollar bill.

The men sat up a little straighter when Charles scooped up the money and thanked them.

"So, where are y'all from?" Kathryn drawled.

"L.A." someone said. "How about you?"

"Oregon," Yoko said.

"So what do y'all do, do y'all work or do you just . . . ride around?" Kathryn asked as she maneuvered herself to the far end of the table to get as far away from Wagstaff as she could.

"Both," Dr. Clark Wagstaff said. Julia sat down next to him. "So what do you do?" she purred. "Claudia Abbott," she said, holding out her hand.

"Clark Wagstaff." He pumped her hand for a full thirty seconds. "I'm an oral surgeon. How about you?" Wagstaff asked as he eyed the tattoo on top of her left breast.

"I paint murals inside churches," Julia said. "The bikes are just a weekend hobby."

"What about your friends? By the way, I might be interested in the Night Train. I'd like to take a look at it later."

"Well sure, that's okay by me. Goes to the highest bidder. Candy down there at the end of the table makes muffins. Best muffins in the state of Oregon. Stella, over there, has her own bike shop in Portland. Makes money hand over fist. Mei Ling is a massage therapist. When she walks on your back you'd swear you died and went to heaven. She knows *exactly* how to please a man. So, what's good to eat in this dump? This is a dump, you know. Excuse me, I want to talk to that gentleman over there about my Night Train."

Julia wiggled her way over to where Charles was sitting. He looked at her with open admiration. "It's hard to believe you ride a Night Train," he said.

"You wouldn't believe the teacher I had. How's it going?" she asked under her breath.

"Another hour and they'll all be rolling on the floor. They're all heavy drinkers except our two. They pretty much have their wits about them," Charles said, *sotto voce.*

"The food should be coming out any minute now."

"I didn't order yet," Julia said.

"I took the liberty of ordering ahead of time. Steaks, baked potatoes and salad.

"I'd like to make a toast to all of you for taking the time to make this run for such a worthy cause. Bottoms up, gentlemen," he said. "To charity and the fine people who donate unselfishly of their time and money."

"Hear! Hear!" the men shouted raucously.

"And now for the winner of the restored, one-of-a-kind Indian. Did you all put your names in this shoebox?" Charles asked, pointing to the middle of the table. Heads bobbed up and down. "Good. Why don't we have one of these little ladies pick the winning name?" Charles pointed to Alexis, who stood up and leaned over the table. The two men across from her gasped when she daintily held up the little square of paper.

"Bobby Tufts, you are the winner of the Indian! This calls for a toast! To Bobby Tufts, may he ride in glory on his new Indian!"

"Man, did I really win? Me! Did you hear that, guys? I never won anything in my life. Man, this is so great. Wait till my wife hears about this. A toast, guys! To this kind, generous man. What's your name again?" he asked drunkenly.

"Alistair Fitzsimmons," Charles said regally. "You're right, this is one of those bottoms-up toasts. To Bobby Tufts!"

"Now, Mr. Tufts, where do you want the bike shipped?"

Bobby Tufts pulled a card out of his shirt pocket and handed it over. "My home address is on the bottom of the card."

"I see you're a loan officer at the Wells Fargo bank. Now I know where to go if I want a loan." Tufts doubled over laughing.

The food arrived, thick T-bone steaks, fat, loaded potatoes and a delicious-looking garden salad.

Two hours went by before Julia stood up and said, "I'm going to see if it's still raining. I think it's time for us to move on. Thanks for the dinner and drinks, Mr. Fitzsimmons. Do you want to look at the bike now or did you change your mind? Dr. Wagstaff over there said he wanted to look at it, too."

Alexis stood up and flexed her shoulders. "Hey, you guys, are any of you going to the Testicle Festival in Montana this year? If so, we'll see you there!" she said brightly.

"Yeah, yeah, we're all going," Bobby Tufts said.

"See ya. Nice meeting all of you," Kathryn said.

"Hey, Sam, come take a look at this lady's bike," Wagstaff said to Sam La Fond, who was staggering to his feet.

Kathryn and Alexis both grabbed three full bottles of beer off the table as they followed Julia and Yoko outside. Kathryn shoved her bottles into Yoko's hands so she could unscrew the bottle of Rohypnol that was in her pocket. In the darkness with the rain pelting them, she had no idea how much went into the beer bottles.

"That's a beauty, all right. Bet you want a pretty penny for it, eh?"

"A lot of pretty pennies. We're staying at the inn tonight but plan to leave around seven. We're heading north. If you want to come by early and take a look at it in the daylight, feel free. What about you, Dr. Wagstaff?" Julia said, holding out a bottle of beer to him. He gulped at it. Yoko held out a second bottle to Sam La Fond. Charles pretended to drink from his.

"Where's the car we're supposed to transport them in?" Kathryn hissed.

"The Ford Mustang parked next to the pickup truck. The key is in the ignition. I'll be by in the morning. I have to see about getting my guests back safe and sound to the campground now. I'm very interested," he said loudly, for the benefit of the others.

"I'm not interested," Wagstaff said, slipping to the ground.

"I think your friend is drunk," Alexis said. "Aren't you going to pick him up?"

"Why should I?" La Fond asked belligerently.

"It's raining. He could drown."

"What's it to you?"

"Absolutely nothing," Yoko said. "Just out of curiosity, Mr. La Fond, how many women did you and your buddy rape on these rides?"

"Lots and lots and lots," he mumbled as he fell on top of his friend.

"I told you, Kathryn," Yoko said gently. "Hurry, we have to get them in the car before someone comes out."

"He won't remember the question when he wakes up, Kathryn," Julia said just as gently.

It was better than a precision drill as the four women grabbed Wagstaff's legs and arms and dumped him unceremoniously onto the back seat. They did the same thing with La Fond. When he rolled onto the ground, Yoko shrugged. "Oh well."

"Looks like we're set to go. Yoko, wait till we pull out and you stay on our trail. Let's go," Kathryn said, straddling the cycle. She peeled out onto the road, the others right behind her.

Kathryn slowed to a bare crawl when she noticed oncoming headlights. She didn't pick up speed until the lights were out of sight. She swerved onto the rough road and tore down it at full throttle, the rain pouring down her back. She was soaked to the skin when she opened the tailgate to yank down the ramp. She was back on the Electra Glide and roaring up the plank a minute later, Alexis and Julia right behind her.

"Leave the headlights on, Yoko, until we get them inside. Same deal, sisters, feet and arms. No need to be gentle," Kathryn said.

"Listen, I have to take Murphy out. I'll be with you in a minute."

Yoko held out a napkin-wrapped package. "Take your time," she said. "I gathered up some of the steak bones for Murphy to chew on. Do you wish to give it to him? There's quite a bit of meat on them. Those men did not eat much. It was such a waste of food. I remember the days when I had only scraps to eat."

"That was sweet of you, Yoko. Thanks. Hopefully, it will keep him occupied. He's going to know there are strangers in the back. I don't know how he'll react. He might bark his head off and there's no way I can control that."

"So what. Dogs bark all the time. This," Yoko said waving her arms at the trees, "is pretty far out. We are soaked, Kathryn. We need to get out of our wet clothes."

Kathryn unlocked the cab and climbed up. Murphy licked her face and then snatched the napkin-wrapped bundle out of her hands. "Yoko, thanks for . . . you know."

"Yes, I know. You are welcome, Kathryn."

Fifteen minutes later, both men were inside the truck and the tailgate was closed and locked down. "First things first," Julia said. "We need to get out of these wet clothes and into dry ones. Stand still for a moment while I look around. "The sheets are in place, the entire floor is covered. That's good. The table is up, there's a clean sheet on it. We have a dozen towels. The lights are on. That's good. I can see perfectly. Gloves, everyone. Who goes first?" she asked, tying her surgical mask behind her head.

The women looked at one another. "La Fond didn't drink as much of the beer as Wagstaff did," Alexis volunteered. "You better do him first. Put a drop on his tongue, just to be sure."

Julia held up her gloved hands. "It's up to you three to boost him up to the table. Yoko, take both his feet, Kathryn and Alexis, grab him under his arms. There you go. Take off his pants. On second thought, just pull them down." She picked up the scalpel. She looked up over the mask. "Hospital procedure or quick and dirty?"

"Just do the Q&D," Alexis said.

Kathryn leaned against the wall of the truck, her eyes on Julia's hands. How deft and sure she was. She said it wasn't brain surgery, but still, without her skill, this wouldn't be happening. She blinked. It was happening. She was seeing it with her own eyes. She almost jumped out of her skin when she heard La Fond's jewels drop into a small pickle jar. Even from this distance she could read the Mt. Olive label. Two down and one to go.

"That's a very nice, neat bandage. Will it come loose?" Yoko queried.

"Probably. When they start rummaging for the missing goods, they could dislodge it. Depends on how frantic they get. Okay, this guy's done! Next!"

While the women lifted La Fond off the table, Julia stripped off her gloves and pulled on two new pair. She waited, her hands in the air until Wagstaff was on the table. Yoko yanked at his pants until she had them down around his ankles.

Kathryn sucked in her breath when Julia picked up the scalpel. Ten minutes later, Wagstaff's nuts plunked into a mayonnaise jar.

She slid to the floor of the truck and put her head between her knees.

"What are we supposed to do now? My brain's frozen. I can't think. What?" Kathryn shouted. "Somebody tell me."

"Hey, take it easy, Kathryn. We're taking them in the two cars back to their campground. We put them in their tents and split. Charles will be there to point out which tents belong to them. It's okay that you forgot. We have it under control. Now, let's move. If we fold up the legs of the table and lower it to the floor, we can slide it down the ramp and we won't have to carry them so far. We can drive the cars right up to the opening," Alexis said.

Kathryn shook her head to clear it. "Has Murphy been barking all this time?"

"Yes," Yoko said.

"Julia and I are driving. C'mon, Kathryn, look alive here."

"I'm alive. Let's do it."

Charles waved the light from a small flashlight to show them he was waiting. They drove the cars as far as they could before they climbed out. It took fifteen minutes before the men were settled in their sleeping bags. Yoko bent over and zipped them up. She smiled at Kathryn.

"Get out of here now," Charles said.

"What about the Mustang?" Julia asked.

"I'll drive it deep into the bushes. Did you wipe it clean?"

"I did," Yoko said.

"We're outta here," Alexis said, climbing into the driver's seat of the car.

"Wait a minute," Kathryn said. She unzipped the flap of the tent and stuck her head in. "In the words of President Bill Clinton, gentlemen, I feeeel your painnnn."

Charles clapped his hand over his mouth to keep from laughing as Kathryn sprinted for the car.

Back at their home base, Kathryn yanked at the tailgate. "Cleanup time! Somebody is watching over us. All this rain has to do is keep up for another couple of hours, and it looks like it will, and it will wash away our tracks."

They did what they had to do. The motorcycles were stashed in the back, the wheels on the tarp Kathryn had spread earlier. The sheets, towels, bloody gauze pads and gloves were shoved into heavy-duty trash bags. The table would be dumped as soon as they found a suitable trash container, the trash bag somewhere in San Francisco.

The mayonnaise and pickle jars were placed with the Snapple bottle in the lunchbox. Kathryn handed it to Julia.

The women stood outside the truck, the rain beating down on them. Their arms stretched out till they formed a tight little circle. No one said a word.

Kathryn climbed into the truck. She waved. "I'll see you all in five days."

The CB was in Kathryn's hand the minute she crossed the state line into Kansas. "This is Big Sis. You there, Bugle Beagle?"

"I'm here, Sis. Where you been? Had a call out to you."

"I know, Bugle, but stuff started caving in on me and I had to split for a while. Went off to Bermuda for some down time. What's up, Bugle? The messages sounded urgent."

A bird swooped down and flew across the windshield. Murphy let out an ear-splitting bark and lunged at the window. "Shhh, boy, it was just a bird. Sorry, Bugle."

"The guy said he was a district attorney in the District. You know my feelings on the law and how they hound you guys. Said it was important and you should call right away. I didn't tell him squat. You better give him a call. What'd you do with the dog when you went to Bermuda?"

*Dog. Oh shit. Screwup number five, or was it six?* Bile rose up to her throat. "I left him with a friend in San Francisco. Why?"

"No reason. I like dogs. You said he was the best thing that happened to you after Al died. Listen, drive with the angels and I'll keep in touch. You carrying lettuce or squash?"

"Romaine lettuce. I got two extra boxes if you want some."

"Nah. I hate rabbit food. I'm a steak and potatoes man. Take care, Sis."

"You, too, Bugle. Over and out."

She reached over behind Murphy and dialed Myra's number on the special cell phone. "Hi," she said in a shaky voice. "I just crossed the line into Kansas and called the dispatcher in Roanoke because the D.A. back there has been trying to get in touch with me. We had a nice talk. He wanted to know what I did with Murphy when I went to Bermuda. Imagine that."

"Why don't I put Charles on the phone, Kathryn?"

"That sounds good."

"Kathryn, it's so nice to talk to you again. Mike Daniels drove from Sacramento to San Francisco to pick up your dog. He lives at

3055 Fifth Avenue in Sacramento. He dropped him off at the airport when you landed."

"Thanks. See you in a few days." Kathryn clicked off the power and then clicked it back on. She dialed the number Jack Emery had given Bugle. She punched in the extension and waited.

"Jack Emery here."

"Mr. Emery, this is Kathryn Lucas. I understand you've been trying to reach me. I just got your message."

"You just got it! I thought you truckers lived on your CBs."

Kathryn took a deep breath and let it out slowly. "Some do, some don't. I don't. The reason I just got your message was I just returned from Bermuda. I needed some time to . . . think. I know you had no way of knowing this, but my husband just passed away recently. I needed to get away. What is it you want from me, Mr. Emery?"

"Did you make a delivery to Myra Rutledge and did you stay overnight and sleep in your truck while it was parked at her estate?"

"Why are you asking me these questions? Technically you're the police. I didn't do anything wrong. Hell, the woman hasn't even paid for the stuff I dropped off."

"What did you drop off?"

"First I think you better tell me why you want to know."

"I'm the one asking the questions, Ms. Lucas."

"And I'm the one that isn't answering. If there's nothing else, Mr. Emery, I'm going to hang up. I need to pay attention to the road. By the way, I'm in Kansas."

"When do you expect to hit Virginia?"

"Three days, four at the most. I have to drop off some lettuce in North Carolina."

"I'd like you to stop by my offices when you get here."

"Again, Mr. Emery, why? Look, if those bathroom fixtures are defective it has nothing to do with me. I just pick up and deliver. You're making this sound like I need a lawyer. If I do, I'll give you her name now and you can take this all up with her. I might be picking up a load of pine straw in North Carolina so I can't say for sure where I'll be. She'll know how to get in touch with me."

"Okay, what's her name? You did say her, didn't you?"

"Nicole Quinn. Her office is on G Street. If there's nothing else, I have to sign off here." Kathryn allowed a smile to tug at the corners of her mouth when she heard him curse under his breath. She broke the connection and tossed the cell phone on the seat next to

Murphy. He nudged it until it was behind him. He stretched out, his tennis ball between his paws.

Kathryn yanked at the baseball cap that said Lucas Trucking, settling it more firmly on her head. She adjusted her sunglasses and concentrated on the road in front of her as she tried to imagine what Clark Wagstaff, Sam La Fond and Sid Lee were doing. Murphy slept on the seat next to her.

Jack Emery stared at the phone on his desk. His heart pounded in his chest when he bellowed for his assistant. "Harry, get on the horn with Judge Olsen. I want a court order to impound Kathryn Lucas's truck. The minute she crosses the state line into Virginia, I want that truck snatched. I don't give a shit what's inside it. And while you're at it, put out an all-points on her. Pick it up yourself and get it to me as soon as you can. Why are you still sitting there? When I tell you to move your ass, I mean move your ass. Now, goddamn it!"

Jack leaned back in his chair staring at nothing, his eyes glazed. A sick feeling settled in the pit of his stomach. He reached for the phone and managed to send the papers on his desk flying in all directions. He bent down to pick them up. He stacked them any old way on his desk and then blinked at what he was seeing.

"Hey, Conrad, come here a minute," he called to another A.D.A. "Does the name Isabelle Flanders ring a bell with you? I know I heard that name somewhere. Take a look at this picture. It's kind of grainy because it's a fax. Does she look familiar to you?"

"Yeah. Yeah, she made the news a few years back when she killed a whole family driving in a hurry somewhere. Your girlfriend defended her. Lost the case. I think she was an architect. Why?"

"Just a detail that has to do with something I'm working on," Jack responded, sticking to his credo of not divulging details to those around him. It wasn't that he tried to hog the glory like Nik always accused him of doing. He was simply thorough, preferring to stack his bricks in a neat column so they wouldn't tumble down and make him look like a fool.

The sick feeling was getting worse. He reached for the phone and for a second time, ignored it. "Conrad, call Judge Olsen's office and tell him I need another court order for Myra Rutledge's house. Get Harry on the phone and tell him not to come back here unless he has both of them in his hands."

"Why am I doing your shit work, Emery?"

"Because I told you to do it and I have seniority. Just fucking do it, Conrad."

This time when he reached for the phone, he actually dialed the number he wanted. Nik's cell phone number.

"Nik, it's Jack," he said the minute Nikki said hello.

"Listen to me, Nik. I'm on my way out to the farm. I have a court order, so don't try to evade me. We need to talk. I have the court order," he lied, "but I don't want to come out there as Jack Emery, D.A. I want to come out and talk to you as Jack Emery, your friend. We were friends, Nik. I'll be there in an hour and a half."

"All right, Jack."

Jack beelined for the men's room, where he lost his lunch.

# Chapter Twelve

Charles and Myra watched as Nikki walked out to the long drive-way. By craning their necks they could see Jack Emery's car at the gate. Myra reached for Charles's hand. "This isn't good, is it, dear?"

"No, it isn't good. The really bizarre part of Mr. Emery's case is, Nikki really didn't have anything to do with spiriting Marie and her family to safety. I just don't know at the moment how it is all going to play out. It looks to me like he's studying the High Voltage sign attached to the gate. I'm sure he's wondering if it's real or not."

Myra leaned over and pressed her face against the window. "I think he is studying it, Charles. I think it was a stroke of genius to screw that sign on the gate. It gives one pause for thought. Are we, you know, going to . . . *take him out?*" Myra asked nervously. "That could stir up a whole can of worms, Charles."

"I know. I'm thinking, Myra. I wish I knew what they were saying to each other."

"Let's make a cake, Charles," Myra said, pulling him away from the window. "One of those seven-layer chocolate ones with pudding between the layers and real thick frosting all around. Nikki's going to need something sweet after this little talk she's having with Jack. She loves him so much. Love can be blind at times. I'll turn on the oven."

Outside their line of vision, Nikki walked up to what Myra called the walk-through gate and out to Jack's car. She opened the door and climbed in. She sighed, wishing she could lean over and kiss him. She realized she could if she wanted to. Instead, she said, "I really don't want to love you anymore, Jack. However, I think I'm one of those people who only love once. Don't look at me like that, Jack."

Jack pointed to the High Voltage sign. "Isn't that new? Why does

Myra Rutledge need a sign like that?" Nikki shrugged. "Listen, Nik, I need to talk to you. Jack and Nik, okay? Not prosecutor and lawyer. Can we do that?"

"We can try, Jack." She shivered inside her light sweater. Jack pulled her closer and put his arm around her shoulders. She knew she should move away, but she didn't because his arms felt so good. A flood of memories washed through her.

"This is what I have, Nik. I'm going to lay it all out for you. There's a strange group of women who come out here. You defended Isabelle Flanders and lost her case. Nobody could have won that one, so you shouldn't condemn yourself. Then there's the doctor married to the senator. Very high profile couple. She's not operating anymore, for some strange reason. Tops in her field, too. Guess she's going to fill up her days by playing cards with Myra. The Chinese girl and the tall, leggy black girl just don't fit the scene. Do you know what I mean? They're more your age and yet they come out here to do whatever it is they do. Myra couldn't seem to get her card games straight."

Nikki forced a laugh. "Sometimes they play Fish. It's more the companionship than the card playing. Myra needs to be around younger people. Are you saying you think all these women helped me spirit Marie Lewellen away? That is so outrageous, so off the top, I can't even give it credence. I had nothing to do with it, Jack. I swear to you on Barbara. What's it going to take to convince you?"

"I don't know. My gut is telling me I have to pay attention. I'm trying to do that. I want to see all the stuff Lucas delivered. She said she slept in the truck the night of the storm. I have some trouble with that. Why didn't Myra invite her to stay in the house? That would have been the decent thing to do. She lied to me about the driver, too. She referred to the driver as him. Not her. Him. She was very specific about him and his dog."

"I can't answer that, Jack. I wasn't here when she talked to you. I knew the driver was a woman because Myra said it was a woman. I remember thinking she must be pretty strong to drive a big rig like that." She shrugged. "A slip of the tongue. Whatever. Myra thinks women should stay home and knit and do good deeds. That's fine if you don't have to work for a living. Obviously the driver has to work for a living in order to eat and pay her bills."

Jack stared off into space. "I have an all-points out on her and the truck. The minute she crosses the state line we're hauling her in. We'll impound the truck and sweep it clean."

Nikki shrugged again. "I guess you have to do what you have to do. It's not going to get you anywhere, Jack, because she had nothing to do with it. You're grasping at straws here to make yourself look good."

"Is that what you *really* think, Nik? It happened on my watch. My boss is on my ass. You're threatening to sue the department. You know for every action there is a reaction. You're the one who told me that."

"I'll represent Ms. Lucas if you kick up a fuss, Jack. All this ugly stuff will come out. That probable cause crap isn't going to hold up and you know it. Myra is *very* influential. She knows everyone worth knowing. Senator Webster will come down on you like a ton of bricks if you even mention his wife and Myra in the same breath. She lost a million dollars, Jack. Yeah, I know you think she has money to burn, but she doesn't. She donates to every worthy cause there is. She'll hire some thousand-buck-an-hour attorney and he'll smash you to a pulp before you can say, I'll see you in court."

"Is that supposed to scare me, Nik?"

"No, of course not. I'm just telling you what you're up against if you take on Myra. That's your plan, isn't it? I know the way you operate, Jack. You're working this on your own because, as you said, you like to get everything airtight before you spring your trap. You really should share all this with your boss before you end up making a mess of things. Keep your friends close, your enemies even closer. That kind of thing, right?"

Jack's stomach worked itself into a knot. "Let's check out those bathroom fixtures."

"Why not," Nikki said, getting out of the car. "Be sure to bring that court order. Myra will want to see it."

Jack plucked it off the dashboard and handed it to Nikki. "Okay, this says you can search the garage, the barn and the house. Let's go. Oh, one more thing, when you haul the truck driver in, I want to be there. I'll do it pro bono. I mean it, Jack, don't question her until and unless I'm present."

Jack snorted. "How do you even know she'll want you to represent her? If she has nothing to hide, why does she need a lawyer?"

"To protect her from you. Besides, I am her attorney. She came to see me once but I couldn't help her."

"What did she want you to do for her?"

Nikki swatted him with the court order. "That's attorney-client privilege. You know better than to even ask. Go ahead, I'll wait here. The stuff is in the garage. There's a crowbar in there if you want to open the boxes."

When Jack joined her twenty minutes later, she said, "four bath-tubs, one misty green, one powder blue, garden tub in daffodil yel-low and one in shell pink. Matching shower enclosures. Toilets same color with matching toilet seats. Two double sinks, one single and one with three basins. The vanities have to be built. Did I for-get anything?"

"Yeah, the blueprints."

"Myra can show you those. I wish you'd stop being such an ass-hole."

Jack stomped ahead of her. "Let's go see those blueprints. Of all the architects in town and the surrounding area, why did Myra pick Flanders? She has a shitty reputation."

"You'll have to ask Myra yourself, Jack. Bathroom remodeling is not my forte. Aren't you going to check the barn?"

"When I'm ready," Jack snapped. Nikki opened the screen door that squeaked just the way a screen door is supposed to squeak.

"Oooh, what smells so good? Are you making a chocolate cake, Myra?"

"Yes, dear. Just for you. Hello, Jack, how are you?" Myra asked cooly.

"Fine, thank you." He nodded in Charles's direction. "I'd like to see the blueprints for the bathrooms." His tone was just as cool as Myra's.

"Charles, take Jack to the summer pantry. Isabelle is working there because I didn't have any other available space for her. Do not *touch* anything.

"Would you rather have stuffed peppers or pork chops for din-ner, dear?"

"Stuffed peppers. How about pickled red beets and the wilted lettuce with lots of bacon in it. Lots and lots of mashed potatoes."

"I think Charles can manage that. I wish I was half the cook he is."

"Satisfied?" Nikki asked sourly when Jack followed Charles into the kitchen. "Now what? If you want to check the rest of the house, go to it. He has a court order, Myra. That means he can do what-ever he damn pleases. That includes going through your drawers."

"I-don't-think-so!" Myra said, rearing up on her chair. "You try doing that, young man, and I'll call the police commissioner per-sonally. And the mayor."

Jack wagged his finger under Nikki's nose. "You really are a trou-blemaker. I'm not going through your drawers, Myra. However, I will open your closets and look inside. Don't worry, I won't *touch* anything."

"Don't expect us to help you. Go to it, Sherlock," Nikki said.

Jack returned to the kitchen thirty minutes later, his face bleak with disappointment.

"I guess I'll see you to the gate. Ooops, you gotta do the barn, don't you."

"Yes, I have to do the barn," Jack said, slamming his way through the open doorway. Nikki followed him.

"Don't spook the horses and don't—"

"—*touch* anything." Jack whirled around, his face full of disgust and anger. "What is it with you rich people?" He looked down at his hands. "Do you think us poor commoners have some kind of disease on our hands? That we aren't good enough to touch your precious belongings? I'm doing my goddamn job, is what I'm doing. If you don't like it, screw you."

"Jack, I didn't mean . . . Jack . . ."

When he returned, his face was still full of disgust. "You better walk me to the gate and let me out so I don't *touch* anything. Right now I'm wondering how the hell I ever fell in love with you."

"Jack . . ."

"Get out of my way, Nik. Don't worry, I'll have someone call you when we bring Kathryn Lucas in for questioning."

"I'm . . . sorry, Jack."

"Sorry is just a word. Now get the hell out of my way."

Tears streaming down her cheeks, Nikki turned away.

Fifty-six hours later, Kathryn saw and heard the siren at the same moment the Malinois slammed his body against the door. "Easy, Murph, easy. I see them." She slowed the rig and pulled to the shoulder a quarter of a mile down the road. In the side-view mirror she saw the cop exit his squad car. She watched as he leaned against the door. A second police car came out of nowhere and pulled in front of her. The second cop got out of his car and started to walk toward her just as the first cop swung around to the passenger side of the rig. Murphy, his hair on end, lunged at the door.

The CB squawked. "Hey, out there, this is Cornball, looks like Big Sis hit a spot of trouble. Sis, need any help?"

Kathryn picked up the CB. "Don't know yet, Cornball. Stay on my six and let's play it out. I'm riding empty this leg and heading home."

"Gotcha, Sis. Blue Rider is a quarter of a mile up and slowing down. Give us two blasts and we'll close in."

"You got it, Cornball. I'll leave the power on so you can hear." She leaned out the window but didn't say anything. Murphy was in her lap, his head next to hers.

"Are you Kathryn Lucas?"

"I am."

"We're impounding this truck. Follow the first car. I'll be behind you."

"Do you have a warrant?"

"No, ma'am, but there is one at headquarters. The district attorney said you would come in willingly."

"All right, but only if my lawyer is present. If you can't arrange that, I'm not moving this truck. Call it in and let me know the answer." Kathryn moved back from the window. Murphy continued to growl at the officer standing below him.

Kathryn risked a glance in the rearview mirror. Her eyebrows shot upward. She started to laugh when she saw the caravan of eighteen-wheelers spread out across the road. She looked forward and saw the same bridge a tenth of a mile up the road.

Ah, the power of the open road. Alan always said trucking was a noble profession because on any given day the drivers could bring the entire country to its knees simply by not turning on the engines. For one brief moment she felt almost invincible.

His hand on his holster, the first cop bellowed, "What the hell is going on here?" His voice sounded jittery to Kathryn's ears. She smiled.

The second cop looked back over his shoulder and then forward. Kathryn could see the sweat bead up on his forehead. The first cop looked up at Kathryn and said, "Get on that CB of yours and tell those truckers to disperse now."

Kathryn picked up the CB and said, "This is Big Sis. Listen up. These two fine officers standing next to my truck told me to get on this CB and tell you to *dissss-perse* now. She listened, the grin staying on her face as the truckers, one by one, professed to have serious engine problems.

"Officer, they seem to be having difficulty with their engines."

"Tell them to call the goddamn auto club!"

"This is Big Sis again, boys. These fine officers want you to call the auto club." She listened, her face going pink.

She leaned out the window. "I don't think you want to know what they said. They want to know if you have the number of the auto club. So, is my lawyer going to be there or not?"

"Yeah."

"Then why didn't you say so?" She reached for the CB. "Cornball, this is Big Sis. I'm okay. I'm going to follow the cops. They're impounding my truck and taking me to the district attorney's office. I'm going willingly. That's just for the record, okay. Thanks for your help."

"Any time, Sis."

As each truck roared past her, it gave two sharp blasts that she returned in kind. Murphy howled his outrage at these goings-on.

"I know exactly what you did, so don't try it again," the first cop said.

"Officer," Kathryn said sweetly, "those truckers would have sat there indefinitely. Even the National Guard couldn't have *disssspersed* them."

"Oh yeah?" the first cop blustered.

"Yeah," Kathryn shot back.


They sat opposite one another, glaring. Nikki felt the urge to cry just the way she'd cried when Jack was at the farm. The phone rang.

"Emery here," Jack growled. "Okay." He looked away and said, "They're bringing her up now."

Nikki remained silent, her face miserable.

Jack eyed the Belgian Malinois standing at Kathryn's side. "Have a seat. This won't take long. Your attorney has given us forty-five minutes to sweep your truck and then you can pick it up. I want a sworn statement from you and then you're free to go." Kathryn looked at Nikki who nodded.

"Before you ask me anything, Mr. Emery, I want it on the record that I'm willing to take a lie-detector test. Any time, any place."

"Write that down, Jack," Nikki said cooly.

"I wrote it down. If I think it's necessary, I'll notify you."

"In writing," Nikki said.

Jack lowered his head. "Do you know Marie Lewellen or any member of her family?"

"No."

"Were you ever introduced to her or to any member of her family? Did you ever see Marie Lewellen and her family?"

"No and no."

"Did you, on the night of January twenty-first, take Marie Lewellen and her family somewhere in your truck?"

"No."

"Did anyone other than yourself drive your truck on the night of January twenty-first?"

"No."

"Why were you at Myra Rutledge's estate on the night of January twenty-first?"

"I delivered bathroom fixtures. The storm got worse as I was unloading and I was tired. I asked Mrs. Rutledge if it was okay to sleep in my truck on the property and she said yes. She said I could sleep in the house but I had the dog and I knew he wouldn't be comfortable in a strange place."

"Were there other cars there when you arrived?"

"I don't know. It was already dark. I didn't pay attention."

"When you left the next day were there other cars there?"

"Yes."

"One last question. Do you know where Marie Lewellen and her family are? Did you, perhaps, overhear people discussing her disappearance or hear other people say where she might be?"

"No to both your questions."

"Is that your sworn statement then?"

"Yes, that's my sworn statement."

Jack pressed the Print button and waited for the form to slide out of the printer. "Read through it, let your attorney see it and if everything is in order, sign your name at the bottom."

Kathryn read through her statement and handed it to Nikki, who read it thoroughly. "It's okay to sign it, Kathryn."

"Can I go?"

"That was some stunt you pulled out there on the interstate," Jack said cooly, his eyes on Nikki.

Kathryn remained silent.

"What stunt?" Nikki asked.

"Her trucker friends blocked the interstate. They sandwiched the two police officers into a square. Said they had engine trouble."

"Anything's possible," Nikki said. "How much longer, Jack?"

Jack looked at his watch. "They should be finishing up right now. As soon as the sweep team calls and tells me everything is okay, you're free to go. Until that call comes in, you stay right here."

The call came in five minutes later. Both women watched Jack as he listened to the voice on the other end of the phone. He hung up and threw his pencil across the room. "They said," he enunciated each word carefully, "the truck was clean as a whistle."

"I always vacuum it out after a run. I just dropped off a load of pine straw in North Carolina. No one wants to have you haul a load of produce in a dirty truck. In addition to that, I'm a neat, tidy person. Make whatever you want out of that, Mr. Emery. Is this the end of it?"

"It's the end of it, isn't it Jack?" Nikki said coldly.

"For now," Jack said.

"Let's get some lunch, Kathryn. I know a nice outdoor café where Murphy can sit with us. It's nice out today, so eating outside will be a treat. I'll drive you to the impound lot when we're finished."

Neither woman said good-bye.

At the café, seated under a red-and-white-striped umbrella, Nikki leaned forward. Her eyes sparkled when she said, "Tell me everything and don't leave out a word."

Kathryn talked nonstop for fifteen minutes. "When it was over, we drove away."

"Was it worth it, Kathryn? Do you feel vindicated?"

"Oh, yes, Nikki. I'm glad Yoko asked Sid Lee about the others. If she hadn't, I think I would have always wondered. What they did to me, they did to a lot of women. They won't do it ever again, though. I don't suppose anyone heard anything, you know, on the news or in the papers?"

"Not that I know of," Nikki said. "I don't think it's the kind of thing that will make the news unless they go public. Although, you never know. I can't swear to it but I'll bet you a dollar Charles is tuned into the *L.A. Times*. By the way, you did good back there."

"You know, I really would have taken a polygraph test if they wanted to give it."

"Just the fact that you said you were willing was enough for Jack. Those tests cost money and he really couldn't justify it to his boss. Drink up, Kathryn," Nikki said, holding her wineglass aloft.

They smiled at each other, each busy with her own thoughts.

"Nikki, do you know if Julia . . ."

"She did it yesterday. She sent them Federal Express from New York. Alexis fixed her up and she drove up there, mailed them and then drove back. She sent them for a ten o'clock delivery. It's two o'clock here on the East Coast and eleven on the West Coast.. I think they're probably gazing at their jewels as we speak and wondering how it all went wrong."

Kathryn smiled and held her glass upward. "To the Sisterhood! Long may they reign!"


On a balmy spring day just as the first spring flowers bloomed, the Sisterhood met for the second time at Myra Rutledge's McLean estate.

This time, however, the sisters were more vocal with one another, asking about each other's lives and talking about the weather, social events and recipes. The mood was relaxed, not frightening like the first time. Nor was it exhilarating like they thought it would be. It was comfortable, each woman at ease and content in her own skin, knowing now their capabilities and using them to the fullest.

Myra banged her gavel on the round table. "The second meeting of the Sisterhood will now come to order. Are all present and accounted for?"

"Aye," came the reply.

"Then let's get down to business. In the matter of Kathryn Lucas, was the project successful? Do we have any unfinished business in regard to the project?"

"I think Jack Emery goes under the heading of unfinished business. At the present, I think it's better to let sleeping dogs lie. If the dog should wake and bark, then we can decide what we want to do. I do have one thought where he is concerned. At some point, he's going to remember the tunnels are under the house. Or, if he doesn't remember on his own, someone might tell him about them. He knows Barbara and I used to play in them when we were children. He knows that because I told him several years ago. I apologize."

"There's no need to apologize, dear. Six months ago, Charles had the part of the tunnel under the house closed off. Now it looks like the only entrance is from the barn. We used distressed wood and blew cobwebs all over the place. It doesn't look like anyone has been down there for years and years. That particular branch of the tunnel leads to the Danberry farm. There are no blueprints other than those that belong to this family. I know the Danberry's have a set of prints but they're just for their branch of the tunnels. If Mr. Emery's nose starts to twitch, we'll deal with it then."

Myra looked around the table at the faces she now knew and

adored. "I repeat, was the Kathryn Lucas project successful? How say you all?"

"Aye," came the reply.

"Kathryn, do you feel avenged?"

"Yes, I do. Thanks to all of you."

Myra banged the gavel a second time.

"The Kathryn Lucas project is now closed and sealed. We will never speak of it again. Do we all agree?"

"Aye," came the reply.

Myra banged her gavel a third time. "It's time to choose our next case. Yoko, do the honors, please."

Yoko leaned over the table and reached into the shoebox. She withdrew a folded slip of paper and handed it to Myra.

"Sisters, our next case is Alexis Thorne!"

# Epilogue

*Three days later*

"There's something about an early morning breakfast on a terrace that is so special it defies words," Julia Webster said. "Look and listen to all the birds. See how pretty all the flowers are in the yard and here on the terrace. I just love beautiful things. I don't mean material things, I mean nature things. Did I tell you all, I ordered a Night Train? My hus . . . the man I'm married to, said it was the stupidest thing I've ever done in my life. I corrected that statement and told him no, the stupidest thing I ever did was to marry him."

"Atta girl, Julia," Kathryn said. Julia beamed.

"What's for breakfast?" Alexis queried.

"Fresh melon, freshly squeezed orange juice and *beignets* A new shop opened in town and the baker is from New Orleans. Charles went to fetch us some. Oh, I hear his car now. We must remember to thank him, sisters. He does love doing things for us." Myra sighed happily and smiled as Charles opened the small iron gate leading to the terrace.

"Everyone close their eyes! I have a surprise for all of you!" Charles walked over to the table and placed the box of *beignets* in the center of the table. He then placed a copy of *The Tattler* in front of each woman, keeping one for himself. "You can open your eyes now!"

"Oh myyyy Goddd!" the women said as one.

"As you can see, this sleazy tabloid only mentions the men as Gentleman One, Two and Three. For privacy reasons, of course. The doctor all three men consulted had an assistant who spilled the story to *The Tattler* for fifty thousand dollars. She no longer works for the doctor, saying fifty big ones was a lot better than seven bucks an hour. That's a direct quote, by the way.

"She said, and this is another direct quote, One, Two and Three brought their . . . ah . . . bags with them and wanted to know if there was a way to . . . ah . . . reattach them. The contents, not the bags," Charles guffawed. "They were told modern medicine hadn't made any inroads in that department. The assistant also said the men were prominent businessmen, cycle enthusiasts, and two of them were married and one divorced.

"The men told the physician that it happened on a motorcycle run for a charity benefit. All three of the men think some women on their way to a Harley-Davidson show drugged their drinks and did the dirty deed while they were knocked out. One of them re-calls hearing a dog bark all night long. As the paper was going to press, no police reports had been filed.

"By the way, the assistant moved to New York the day she re-ceived and cashed her check. She is now represented by the William Morris Agency."

"Oh my goodness," Myra said.

"Hot damn!" Alexis said.

"No one said anything about my stitches. I do the best stitches in the business," Julia grumbled. "And you were all worried they might bleed to death. When I sew 'em up, they're sewed up."

"This is so exciting," Yoko babbled. We did *that!*" she said, point-ing to the paper in front of her.

"Yes, we did," Nikki smiled.

Both of Kathryn's fists shot in the air. "This is the first time I'm actually glad that modern medicine is lagging behind."

Isabelle burst out laughing and couldn't stop. Charles thumped her on the back. "I'm sorry," she continued to laugh. "I can just pic-ture them walking into that doctor's office with their nuts in those jars."

"No, no, Isabelle, I sent them in Ziploc bags in padded en-velopes," Julia said.

"Like when you get goldfish at a pet store! Kathryn, you are truly vindicated," Isabelle said, going off into peals of laughter again.

Charles opened the box on the table. *"Beignets,* anyone?"

# PAYBACK

# Prologue

Myra Rutledge, heiress to a Fortune 500 candy company, looked around her state-of-the-art kitchen, at the pots bubbling on the stove, at the table set for two. Even though it was late afternoon, the sun danced through the stained glass ornaments hanging on the kitchen window creating rainbows on the white walls all around her. The girls—that's how she thought of Barbara and Nikki—had made the colorful ornaments for her as gifts one year at summer camp.

She'd adopted Nikki at a young age, but she and Barbara couldn't have been more alike than if they'd come out of her womb at the same time. Barbara was gone now, killed by a hit and run driver in the District by a man with diplomatic immunity.

Myra tried her best not to let maudlin thoughts overcome her, but sometimes, like now, at the end of the day, she thought about her two girls and the dangerous path she'd embarked on. She needed to fortify herself against such thoughts because she knew they weren't going to go away on their own. A snifter of brandy helped a little. She poured generously, eyes watering at the first massive gulp. She always gulped brandy even though she knew it should be sipped. She took another mighty gulp as she looked at the clock. The girls of the Sisterhood would be arriving before nightfall, to prepare for their second mission. The thought warmed her more than the brandy did. They were like daughters now, and she loved them all.

She was worried a little about Alexis, though. She'd mentioned her worry to her live-in companion, Charles, the way she mentioned everything that bothered her, and he'd agreed that perhaps Alexis *wasn't quite* ready for her mission. If not, they'd open the shoe box, fall back and regroup. It wouldn't be a problem. With Charles at the helm, it would all go smoothly.

There was another problem, though, outside of the Sisterhood. Assistant District Attorney Jack Emery, Nikki's fiancé. Ex-fiancé to be more precise.

Myra set the glass down on the table and massaged her temples.

*"You're at it again, eh, Mom?"*

Myra's head jerked upright as she looked around. One of the stained glass ornaments, a red tulip hanging in the window, was jiggling on its little hook. "Barbara? My dear, sweet girl, I was sitting here thinking about you and Nikki when you were little. I miss you so."

*"I know, Mom, but I'm always close by. I'm looking at you right now. Don't worry so much. Things will work out. Trust Nikki."*

"But Jack . . . Jack could ruin everything."

*"Nikki won't allow it, Mom. I think what you're doing is super. That first mission of Kathryn's was really kick ass. Thanks, Mom. I know you're doing it for me, and I can't wait till it's your turn. I'll be with you every step of the way."*

Myra looked down into her brandy glass. Was she really talking to her dead daughter? Was her dead daughter actually communicating with her? Or was it the brandy? She finished it off, not wanting to let go of her daughter's voice.

*"Easy on the sauce, Mom. I'd hate to take away a vision of my mom dancing on the table. I know how rowdy you can get. I'm teasing, Mom."*

"I know, dear. I'm feeling a little light-headed right now just talking to you. I wish . . . Oh, Barbara, I wish so many things."

*"Don't, Mom. You can't un-ring the bell. I just want you to know how proud I am of what you and the girls are doing. Sometimes . . . sometimes you simply have to take charge and make things come out right. Kathryn is a new person these days. You're right about, Alexis, too. She isn't ready, but Mom, let her be the one to tell you she isn't ready. Don't make the decision for her. And, Mom, just keep doing what you're doing."*

"Oh, I will, dear, I will. I just thank God I have the money to fund this venture. And to think I don't even like candy."

*"I hear Charles coming. I'm going upstairs to spend some time with Willie. I love you, Mom."*

Myra smiled at the mention of Barbara's tattered teddy bear. "When Nikki moved back here to the farm she started to sleep with Willie so he wouldn't miss you so much."

*"I know, Mom. Trust Nikki. And, don't worry about Jack. Nik has it under control. Love you, Mom."*

Myra was up and off the chair in the blink of an eye. She ran over to the kitchen window to touch the stained glass ornament that was now still. Her hand flew to her mouth to stifle a sob.

She felt Charles's hand on her shoulder. She turned around to bury her head in his broad chest. "She was here, Charles. We talked."

Charles Martin, ex-MI6 operative who had devoted most of his life to Her Majesty, eyed the brandy bottle and the empty glass. "I'm glad, Myra. I'll finish up here. Why don't you check the bedrooms to be sure everything is ready for the girls. Did you buy something special for Kathryn's dog, Murphy?"

"Yes, Charles, I did, a chew toy and a box of jumbo biscuits. He's a wonderful animal, isn't he?"

"Yes, Myra, he is."

"I love you, Charles. I wish . . . I wish . . . never mind. Barbara said . . . it's all right, Charles. I'm not dotty. Isn't that a term you Brits use?"

"I'm an American now, dear. I say nutsy cuckoo like the rest of you. You are my dear, sweet Myra and I love you with all my heart. Scoot!"

Myra smiled. She adored flirting with the love of her life. "I'm going. I might have overcooked that mess on the stove, Charles."

"I'm throwing it all out, Myra, and starting over. It's all right, dear. You have other wonderful talents." He twirled the dish towel and then playfully swatted her backside.

Myra laughed all the way down the hall and was still laughing as she climbed the steps to the second floor.

# Chapter One

Alexis Thorn frowned as she looked around her small apartment. There was nothing about the tiny place to suggest permanency of any kind. There were no knickknacks, no green plants, no family pictures. It was a place to sleep, a place to come home to at the end of the day, nothing more. How could it be anything else when her name wasn't even Alexis Thorn? Alexis Thorn was an alias. She'd taken a new name with the help of her lawyer, Nicole Quinn, when she got out of prison for a crime she didn't commit. She didn't want to think about why she was living in this run-down apartment but she had to think about it, like it or not.

Without Nicole Quinn she didn't know where she'd be. Nikki had gotten her a job as a personal shopper to some of Virginia's older, wealthy residents. It was a far cry from being a high-powered securities broker in her other life, that was for sure. Nikki had helped her with a new identity, too. Who in their right mind would hire a jailbird? No one, that's who. These days she was Alexis Thorn and she liked it but someday when the time was right, she'd go back to being her real self.

Today, in just minutes, she had to climb into her little Mini Cooper and head out to McLean, Virginia. There at Nicole's adopted mother's palatial estate, she would join the other members of the Sisterhood. She'd joined a year ago, again, with Nicole Quinn's help. The Sisterhood wasn't just any organization. Myra Rutledge had formed the organization after her daughter was run down and killed by a diplomat's son. With the aid of Nikki's legal expertise, Myra formed the Sisterhood to help women get the justice and the revenge they deserved, even if it meant going outside the law to get it.

The Sisterhood consisted of six women, seven if you counted

Myra, all recruited by Nikki. They'd gone on one mission so far and it had been successful. At the end of that successful mission, they'd drawn names to see whose case would be next. Alexis's name—not her real name of course—had been drawn from the cardboard shoe box.

But she wasn't ready yet to seek the justice she deserved. She needed more time to wallow in her misery, and to build up her strength and resilience. She didn't know why that was, it just was. She would have to tell the sisters they needed to choose someone else for the second mission. She knew in her gut she was still too fragile, too broken with her thirteen-month stint in the federal pen. She tugged at her lavender dress, straightening it over her slim hips. The dress was one she'd chosen from her pitiful wardrobe and was a knock-off to boot. It went well with her brown skin and dark hair. She'd chosen the dress because she thought she looked best in pastels. The days were long gone when she didn't think twice about buying high-end designer clothes. Everything from her past was gone. Every damn thing she cared about. Even her dog.

Alexis started to shake when she tried to imagine what the other sisters would say when she told them she wasn't ready for her mission. Kathryn, the most verbal, and the toughest of them all, in her opinion, would narrow her eyes and tell her to grow up and get with the program. Isabelle, who saw things other people didn't see, meaning, of course, that she was psychic, would shrug and close her eyes, maybe in the hope of conjuring up the reason for Alexis's pass on the mission. Julia, a retired plastic surgeon, who had contracted AIDS from her philandering husband, the senator, would stare at her as if she were a speck under a microscope. She'd say, "You need to make those bastards pay for what they did to you and get on with your life because you *have* a life to get on with." Yoko would nod and say she understood whether she did or not. Nikki would use logic to try to convince her to take the bull by the horns, and Myra, sweet, gentle woman that she was, would smile wanly and say, "Honey, if you aren't ready then you aren't ready and we'll choose one of the other sisters." At which point she'd feel like a fool and probably start to cry. The others would look at her with disgust and she'd cry harder. They might even become so disgusted with her they'd try to drum her out of the Sisterhood.

She'd done so well with Kathryn's mission. It couldn't have succeeded without her expertise. She could take nothing and transform it into something wonderful and exciting. She was a master with a makeup brush and she knew it. Costume design was something she loved doing. Nikki said she was a master at that, too. She'd been so proud when Nikki had said that. All the sisters had complimented her. Life after prison. She owed this new life to Nikki and the sisters. And she was happy. So, what the hell was her problem?

Alexis eyed her suitcase by the front door, and then let her gaze go to what the sisters called her Red Bag of tricks, complete with everything she needed to alter a person's being. Makeup, spirit gum, latex, costumes, wigs, glasses. She had the talent to take an ordinary person and transform him or her into a movie star. Where she'd come by this particular talent, she had no idea. Everything in the Red Bag had been updated or replenished by Myra.

Alexis looked at her watch. Time to get on the road. The Sisterhood's hosts, Myra Rutledge and Charles Martin, didn't like to be kept waiting. She smiled when she thought of Charles, Myra's right hand man, and the one who planned each mission. Charles was an ex-British MI6 operative who had once worked for the queen on the other side of the pond until he'd been compromised. In the spook world, according to Charles, the bad guys had found out who he was and steps had to be taken to keep him safe. Now he worked and lived with and for Myra. Charles always said being a super spy for Her Majesty had equipped him to head up the Sisterhood. On top of all his other accomplishments, Charles was a gourmet cook. Alexis felt her mouth start to water at some of the wonderful meals he'd cooked for all of them. Today, she hoped, would be something just as wonderful.

Suitcase in one hand, the Red Bag of tricks in the other, Alexis still somehow managed to lock the flimsy door of her apartment. She didn't look back because there was nothing to see except a bunch of shabby, secondhand furniture. She hadn't seen the need to buy new furniture, preferring to bank all her money until she was sure where she was going with her life. A new life, a new name without the stink of ex-con attached to it. What more could a girl want?

Alexis tossed her suitcase into the back of the Mini Cooper, then climbed behind the wheel. Before she turned the key in the ignition, Alexis looked around the ratty-looking neighborhood and the building she lived in. They should just demolish the entire three blocks. Once she'd lived in a pretty little house with window boxes and flowers on her front porch. She had furniture that she saved for, beautiful linens, fine dishes and crystal. And she'd had a dog she'd loved dearly. It was all gone now, sold to pay her legal fees.

She'd been told that one of the officers who arrested her had taken her dog.

If anyone should be ready for revenge, it was she. She knew in her heart of hearts, deep in her gut, that the two partners who framed her for their own crime did it because she was a black securities broker. She'd been careful not to play the race card in her defense. Now, she wished she had. Maybe her problem was she couldn't come up with a suitable revenge that would make her whole again. Nothing she could come up with was bad enough, horrible enough, ugly enough to make her whole. Death was the only thing she could come up with but that wasn't an option. She had no desire to go to prison again.

Ever.

The engine of the Mini Cooper turned over and Alexis drove down the road to the highway. Another glance at her watch told her she had just enough time to make it to McLean. A smile tugged at the corners of her mouth. It would be good to see the sisters again.

As she drove away, Alexis noticed for the first time that spring had really arrived. The trees were dressed in their fledgling greenery and here and there she could see flower buds. Spring. A new beginning. She crossed her fingers the way she had when she was a child. Maybe this spring would be a new beginning for her.

As the miles ticked by, Alexis settled herself more comfortably in the driver's seat. She felt better already.

Myra Rutledge, Charles at her side, stood under the portico and watched as the cars inched their way through the open gates. Her smile rivaled the sun. "They're here, Charles! Every single one of them. I was so afraid they might have second thoughts. They look wonderful, don't they? I love the way they poke one another and make each other laugh. I am so relieved that they all get along just like real flesh and blood sisters."

Charles beamed. "Love, they are beyond wonderful. Julia looks particularly good, don't you think?"

"For now, she's in remission, but yes, she looks wonderful, just awfully thin. Look how they're all smiling, Charles. That means they're glad to be here. Turn off the power to the gate. We don't want any intruders today." Myra's voice dropped to a whisper when she said, "Nikki didn't say anything about . . ."

"No, Nikki didn't mention Assistant District Attorney Jack Emery at all. I didn't want to open any old wounds by asking. They broke off their personal relationship and Nikki is touchy on the subject of Jack Emery."

"A district attorney prowling around here with binoculars makes me worry, Charles. I know Nikki is still in love with him. I also know Jack Emery is not going to give up. He suspects that we were responsible for Marie Llewellyn's disappearance, a case that had nothing to do with the Sisterhood. He told Nikki so. That's why the two of them are estranged. They were on opposite sides of that case. He's trying to . . . to . . . get the goods on us, Charles."

Charles patted Myra's hand. "Not to worry, my dear. That will never happen. I want you to trust me."

Myra stared into Charles's bright blue eyes. God, how she loved this man, her daughter's father. "I do, Charles. I do. Now, let's welcome our new little family.

"Girls! Girls! Welcome back to Pinewood! Charles prepared lunch for all of us and we'll have it on the patio. Oh, how I've missed you," she said, opening her arms wide to gather all the young women close.

Murphy, Kathryn's dog, barked sharply for attention. Myra laughed. "You, too, Murphy. Charles fixed you a special treat." The big shepherd literally purred at her words.

# Chapter Two

"Listen to them, Charles!" Myra said, pointing to the ceiling. "They sound so happy. This old place is alive again. I love to hear them laughing and poking fun at one another. And, did you see Murphy? I love the way he cozies up to you because he knows what a good cook you are." She paused, and a frown replaced her smile. "Things are going to work out for Alexis, aren't they?" she asked.

Charles Martin stared at the love of his life and smiled as he expertly turned over the shrimp fritters in the frying pan. Alexis's favorite food was shrimp fritters and since they were here to plot out her mission, it was only natural for him to cook her favorite food. On more than one occasion he'd boasted, shyly of course, that he'd personally prepared beef Wellington for the queen. He always followed up that statement by saying, *of course, that was in my other life.* "We'll just have to wait and see. Let her tell us. We'll take it from there." He hugged her.

"There's a glow about you today, my dear. You look like spring itself in your flowered dress. And"—he leered—"you smell heavenly!"

Myra patted Charles's hand. "Thank you, dear. Charles, how can I be so happy when we do . . . when we . . ."

"Make things come out right for our friends?" Charles said, finishing her question. "We committed ourselves, Myra, to right old wrongs, to settle old scores and to fight for those who fell through the cracks while the law was looking the other way. Let's not worry about the dark side today. You're happy, I'm happy, the girls are happy, and we're about to embark on our second mission. As they say in the business, 'I got it covered, lady.'"

Myra burst out laughing as she started to set the table. She looked down at Murphy, who was watching Charles's every move. "It's time for lunch, Murphy, fetch the girls."

Murphy raced to the bottom of the magnificent spiral staircase and barked, then raced back to the kitchen. Myra patted his big head and smiled. "He's a wonderful animal, isn't he, Charles?" Not bothering to wait for a response she said, "I feel so much better knowing he's with Kathryn when she drives that big rig of hers cross-country."

"Darling, you're jittery. Calm down. I hear them coming down the steps. For all our sakes, I want you to look and sound positive."

Myra held her regal gray head even higher. "Whatever you say, *Sir* Charles!" She smiled, referring to his knighthood. Charles grimaced. He hated discussing anything about his old life.

Charles beamed when the women swooped into the kitchen jabbering a mile a minute.

Myra hugged them one at a time before they all sat down.

"Shrimp fritters! My favorite soul food," Alexis said.

Yoko reached to the middle of the table and said, "The tulips are real! They are so beautiful! My own at the nursery are just starting to bud."

Isabelle shaded her eyes with her hand and said solemnly, "I *see* acres and acres of tulips and they're all purple . . . I see . . ."

Kathryn turned in her seat and swatted Isabelle. "Then, oh mighty seer, you must be in Holland, you jerk!" Everyone laughed at Kathryn's reference to Isabelle's clairvoyant capabilities, which were iffy at best.

"Spring is my favorite time of year," Nikki said as she shook out her linen napkin. "The tulips are gorgeous. Are they the ones Barbara and I planted when we were little?"

Myra squared her shoulders, her eyes bright at the mention of her dead daughter. "No, dear, those are long gone. These are a new variety. Charles and I planted them last year. The colors are remarkable so that means the seed catalog didn't lie. The golden yellows are my favorite. Barbara loved the shell pink ones and those are just starting to bloom."

Julia, her eyes as bright as Myra's, said, "I don't know about the rest of you but I am so glad to be here. I feel . . . I feel like I've come home. I don't mean to sound maudlin or anything but I feel like you're all my family. So, let's make a toast to the Sisterhood."

"Hear! Hear!" Charles said, raising an exquisite crystal pitcher of sweet tea. He poured it into matching goblets before he took his seat at the table. As one, the women raised their glasses. Charles did the honors and said, "To all of us. To the Sisterhood and their lone brother!"

Myra was the first to burst out laughing. "That's my Charles," she said fondly. "Now, girls, let's devour this wonderful luncheon Charles has so lovingly prepared so we can get to work and do what we do best: going after the scoundrels who have turned your worlds upside down, so we can give you back your lives."

Midway through the meal, Murphy reared up next to Kathryn and let out a bloodcurdling howl. The women looked at one another in alarm. Kathryn got up and went to the kitchen door and opened it. Murphy raced outside, the hair on the back of his neck straight up. Nikki got up and followed Kathryn. "Easy girl, easy," Kathryn said, placing a hand on Nikki's arm. "It might be a squirrel or a rabbit. It doesn't have to mean it's Jack Emery out there spying on us."

"Yes, it does, Kathryn. He's been stalking me when I go into the city. I never see him but I know he's there. He's on a mission now just the way we are. He's got himself convinced we all helped to spirit Marie Llewellyn away after she killed the man who murdered her only daughter. He's never going to give up, that's why he's such a good district attorney. I hate to say this but he's better at tracking than a herd of bloodhounds. He's out there somewhere watching and waiting. I'd stake my life on it."

"Then I guess it's time we did something about Assistant District Attorney Jack Emery," Kathryn said flatly. "Come back to the table, Nikki, we can't let Charles's dessert go to waste."

Myra's voice was hushed when she asked Nikki, "Is it . . . ?"

"Jack? Yes, I think so, Myra. I think he's been stalking me. I also think he's got some of his people watching the rest of you, too. I don't know where he's getting the manpower unless he's calling in favors from his friends and they're doing it pro bono. D.A.'s do that all the time. Let's face it, he's got us staked out. We have to find a way to work around that or else we have to . . . do something drastic where he's concerned."

Dessert suddenly lost its appeal. Charles cleared the table and the women got up to help him. Kathryn went back outside. They could hear her whistling for Murphy.

Myra's back stiffened as she walked over to the kitchen door. "I hate it that people are spying on us. I'm going to call the K-9 Kennel in town and have them bring guard dogs out here to patrol the grounds at night. They do that, you know. They bring them late in the afternoon and the dogs patrol all night. Their handlers pick them up in the morning. I read about it in the Sunday section of the paper a while back. A lot of companies are doing that these days because they don't want to risk their employees getting shot during a robbery. That's not to mean they don't care about the dogs, they do. The dogs wear Kevlar vests and it's very difficult to shoot at a moving target."

"I think it's a good idea," Charles said, turning on the dishwasher. "Myra, take the girls to the war room and I'll make the call. I'll join you shortly. I'll have Murphy stand guard when I get ready to join you."

Myra led the way through the house to the library where she stepped in front of a solid row of bookshelves. She counted down the various carvings on the intricate molding that ran the length of the bookshelves. At the same moment her fingers touched the lowest carving, the wall moved slowly and silently to reveal a large room with wall to wall computers that blinked and flashed as well. A mind-boggling, eye-level, closed-circuit television screen was focused on the security gates. Each wall seemed to be made up of television screens. MSNBC was playing on the south wall, CNN on the north wall and the FOX news channel was playing on the east wall. Fans could be heard whirring softly. There were no windows.

They'd all been here before in the command center and knew that Charles had installed a modern day ventilation system. He had also installed a cutting-edge, solar powered electrical system. If the weather took a turn for the worse, there was enough stored power to last a month.

The women waited for Myra to secure the door before they took their seats at a large round table surrounded by deep comfortable chairs. The only thing on the table was a Keds shoe box and a stack of bright yellow folders at Myra's place.

When Myra joined them the women made small talk as they waited for Charles to join them. No one, it seemed, was interested in going to the Cherry Blossom Festival in Washington over the weekend. Nor were they interested in inspecting the new drainage and sprinkling system Myra said she had installed last month. They were saved from further mundane conversation when the door slid open and Charles entered the room.

"Six K-9's will arrive for duty at five this afternoon. All right, ladies, we're ready to discuss business. If anyone has a question or a problem, aside from the problem of Jack Emery, let's hear it now before we get down to work."

Alexis took a deep breath and raised her hand. "I'm not ready," she said. "I thought I was but I'm not. I've done nothing but think about this the whole past month and I can't come up with a suitable punishment for the people who framed me and sent me to prison. Well, that's not exactly true, I did come up with something but it's death. I don't want any of us to be responsible for a murder. So, I want to give up my mission, for now, to one of you."

Kathryn tugged at the sleeve of her flannel shirt. "Alexis, are you sure? I felt the same way when my mission was called first. Don't you want to talk to us about it? Maybe we can come up with something."

"Yes, I'm sure. I want to be the one to come up with a punishment. I was the one who sat in a federal prison for thirteen months. I haven't come to terms with it yet. Please, can we pick someone else?"

Myra looked at Charles and then let her gaze sweep around the table. "Raise your hand if you agree to cancel out Alexis and move forward with a new mission." Seven hands, including Myra's, shot in the air. Charles raised his hand at the last second.

"It's unanimous, then. Obviously, these are not needed now," Myra said, indicating the yellow folders that contained all the information the Sisterhood would need for Alexis's mission. "We'll need some additional time to plot out a new mission once we choose a new sister. Can you all return here in, say, three days? You're welcome to stay if you like. Perhaps I'm getting ahead of myself. Let's choose a name first," Myra said.

Everyone watched as Charles scribbled names on small pieces of paper, put them in the shoe box, then shook it vigorously. Isabelle did the honors and picked a slip of paper. She handed it to Myra.

Myra smiled as she read the name. "Julia Webster!"

Julia's clenched hand shot in the air. "Unlike Alexis, I am soooo ready! However, I wonder if I might request a two part mission. The one has nothing to do with the other but the reason I'm asking for this favor is . . . when . . . if I'm no longer here, you might want to consider replacing me with the person I want helped." Julia bit down on her lip, her eyes filling with tears. "Welcome her to the Sisterhood . . ."

Kathryn, who was tough as nails and meaner than a snake, slid her chair closer to Julia to put her arms around her. "I'm for whatever you want, Julia, and you're going to be with us for a long time. Tell us what you want."

Julia cleared her throat and spoke sharply and clearly. "I want my husband to suffer. I want him disgraced and destroyed for what he did to me. I want his face plastered all over the front pages of the newspapers. I want his colleagues to look at him with disdain and disgust. I want him destitute. I don't care if he has to live on the street and sleep in a cardboard box.

"The second part of my mission deals with a colleague of mine. She's an oncologist and has to deal with people who can't get the medical care they need because their HMO refuses to authorize the proper treatment. There is one HMO in particular that a good majority of her patients belong to, actually three HMOs under one umbrella and owned by the same family. My friend's name is Sara Lang and we've known each other since college. We roomed together. In many ways she's like a sister. She's at the end of her rope and talking about giving up on her profession. I just want to tell you about one patient of hers. It was a little nine-year-old girl with leukemia. Sara found a bone marrow donor for . . . for . . . Emily. The HMO wouldn't pay for it. The family, the grandparents, were broke. There was no place left to borrow. No place for them to go for help. Emily died last week. They all die! All her patients who have that crappy HMO die. Do you hear me, they fucking die!

"Now let me tell you about the family that owns the three HMOs. They have billions of dollars. That's billions with a B. It's a woman, her husband and her son who run the company. They're worse than those Enron and WorldCom people who cheated all their employees out of their pensions. They know every politician in Washington on a first name basis and that includes my husband. They throw parties, donate to causes if it gets their name mentioned or their picture in the paper. They are on every party list in town. I want them punished. I want it so bad, but if we can't do a two-part mission then I want to give up my personal mission with my husband. I'll just . . . kill him myself. What do I have to lose?"

Exhausted, Julia fell back in her chair.

The silence in the room was broken only by the whirring of the overhead fan. When Charles cleared his throat the sound was so loud, all the women jumped.

"I personally don't see a problem if the others agree. However, I'll need more than three days to pull all that together. Can we meet back here one week from today? If I manage to get everything together sooner, you'll be notified. Now, who wants to leave and who wants to stay?"

Kathryn elected to leave to do a run to New Jersey with a load of Florida oranges and grapefruits, promising to keep her cell phone on the entire time. Julia said she would go home, gather all pertinent papers and return, assuring everyone her husband wouldn't even know she was gone. Yoko had a husband and couldn't stay. That left Isabelle, Nikki, and Alexis who would stay and help Charles.

Outside in the bright spring afternoon, Myra gathered Julia in her arms. She felt so thin, so fragile. "We'll make it all come out right, dear. I wish I had known, I would have helped."

"Those bastard companies have to be made to pay. Maybe it will make the other HMOs sit up and take notice. I don't want to see Sara give up her career. She's one of those rare doctors who cares about her patients. She uses all her own money to help. She lives in a hovel if you can believe that. She's just too tired to fight anymore, Myra."

"It's now our problem, Julia. We'll take care of it. Hurry back but drive carefully."

"Myra?"

"Yes."

"He doesn't deserve to live. But I don't know if I really have the guts to kill him."

"Shhh. We'll take care of Senator Webster." Myra bent down and picked a bright red tulip from the border along the walkway. She handed it to Julia who smiled.

Myra waved as the women climbed into their vehicles and drove away. Murphy barked from the passenger seat as Kathryn's big rig sailed through the gates.

Myra stood where she was for a long time, her eyes scanning the dense foliage that surrounded the house. Somewhere out there, Jack Emery was watching her. She could sense it, feel it. She shivered, not with cold but with fear.

# Chapter Three

It was a balmy sixty-nine degrees outside; the women had been chattering about sunning themselves later if time permitted. Charles held up his hand for everyone to quiet down. He found the instant silence gratifying.

Today, a stack of green folders sat in front of Myra. "I think we can dispense with the formalities and get right to business," Myra said as she handed out the folders with Julia's case outlined in detail.

"What you have in front of you is the life history of Senator Mitchell Webster as we know it. Unfortunately, there really isn't all that much information so I'm hoping Julia can fill in the blank spots. Julia?"

Julia quickly scanned the loose sheets of paper and appeared stunned at what she was reading. "I don't see anything here about Mitch's childhood." Julia laughed bitterly at her own words. "His childhood, his background, was created by the very high-powered marketing firm, Johnson and Powell. You do stuff like that in the political game. I guess it's more glamorous."

"That particular firm certainly falls into the big league. I've heard of them," Charles said. "Julia, you need to explain exactly what the firm created in regard to your husband. Tell us everything you know even if it doesn't seem important."

"You mean besides creating a monster?" Julia shook her head. "I don't know where to start. It was so long ago. I was just starting medical school in New York when I first met Mitch. He could've sold me the moon and stars I was so awe-struck by him. I was twenty-two. He was thirty-four, an older man. I was flattered that he even talked to me, even more flattered when he asked me out for coffee. The rest, as they say, is history."

"He was a junior senator. What was he doing on a Manhattan college campus?" Nikki asked.

"He was giving a speech. I was just one of hundreds who skipped class that day to listen to him. Being a junior senator, he felt the need to distinguish himself from all the other junior senators as well as the senior senators. He liked to be noticed. He needed a *cause*, something that would get him singled out by the media, his peers, it didn't matter who or what it was, just as long as he got noticed.

"In the mid-eighties, the hot topic was abortion. That was Mitchell's ticket. Women's rights and abortion. He couldn't have picked better causes. Both were hot button issues. He was young, incredibly handsome. Women gravitated toward him. I was one of those liberated, pro-choice flunkies who hung on to every word he said. When he was in the paper, I read about it. Hell, I even clipped the articles and started keeping a scrapbook. When I learned he was giving a speech at Columbia, I was ecstatic."

Charles looked at Julia, a frown building on his face. "What was so horrible about his past that made him feel he had to reinvent himself? Was he afraid of something? Or maybe someone?"

"It's a long story," Julia said.

"We're not going anywhere, dear. We've got all the time in the world," Myra said in a soothing voice.

"I know, it's just that *I* don't have all the time in the world."

"I think you should start at the beginning, dear, just like we did when we were preparing to take care of Kathryn's problem. Charles, please turn the recorder on."

Julia licked at her dry lips and took a sip of water before she started her story.

"It was in the fall, around the first of November, the first time I met Mitchell. We met a few times after that, just going for coffee, that kind of thing. He appeared to like me because he called quite often and we'd talk. I had this really weird feeling that he had checked up on me and knew my family was wealthy. He never mentioned it, though. Each time I would try to find out about his background, he'd change the subject and say things like, 'What you see is what you get' or 'I'm an open book.' His evasiveness bothered me so I did a check on him myself. Nothing jumped out at me right away. He wasn't close to the people he left behind. And, no, I never did meet any of Mitch's family."

"Never?" Myra said.

Julia shook her head. "In a way it really didn't seem important. I was in medical school, Mitch was in Washington 'running the country' as he put it. We were lucky we could meet up twice a month. I knew there was something wrong but I didn't want to pry. Remember, I was in love. I was also young and impressionable.

"Anyway, I managed to get a little background on Mitch, just enough to scare me out of my wits. If what I found out was true, Mitch should be in prison. He'd been involved with a young girl who was later found dead. Mitch then disappeared, according to what I was able to find out. I thought there had to be a mistake and there were two Mitchell Websters. You don't get to be a senator without a thorough background check. I convinced myself Mitchell was who he said he was. I let it go. Years later when DNA became well known and used, it turned out Mitch hadn't killed her after all.

"Mitch and I got married a year later and moved here. I put his name on all my bank accounts and brokerage accounts. We were happy. At least I was. I never, ever, dreamed he was . . . seeing other women. I suspect now that he was an alley cat from the beginning. I was so busy . . . he was so busy . . . We had our weekends. That's what our marriage was for many, many years. Weekends. Then even those dropped away because Mitch was always going somewhere. He moved up, sat on more prestigious committees and became very high profile. I was busy with my patients. We still had sex once in a while, but the last three years of our marriage became strained. Mitch started staying away for days at a time, but he was mysterious about it. He said everything he did was on a need-to-know basis and he couldn't talk about it. I'm sad to say I believed him.

"When I had my physical I found out I was HIV positive. I was so numb with shock I didn't know what to do. I went to the Hay-Adams and checked in for a week to try to get myself together. I took three more blood tests, all with the same result. The only way I could have contracted HIV was through Mitch. I checked and double-checked each and every one of my surgeries. None of my patients had HIV. I had no mishaps in the operating room. Mitch gave it to me." She paused and looked around the table. Nobody moved a muscle. Everyone was looking at her, waiting for what she would say next. She took a sip of water and got her emotions under control.

"And now I want my pound of flesh. If you could rip his skin off at the same time, I'll accept that, too. I'm sure he doesn't even suspect that he's infected. If they don't do a full-blown AIDS check, HIV can go unnoticed. He would never believe he could contact such a violent disease. He simply wouldn't allow it."

Charles spoke first. "What kind of background did the firm create for Mitchell?"

"Everything that's public knowledge. His parents died, he had foster parents who put him through college. I think he has a sister somewhere who he pays to stay out of his life. I heard him on the phone one time but I never put it together until much later. At this point, I'm not even sure I heard what I heard. I'm not sure about anything anymore," Julia said sadly. "I guess my point is, no one in the media came up with anything on his background; his phony background. I find it strange."

Charles handed a box of tissues to Myra who then handed it to Julia. She wiped her eyes. "Was I an idiot or what? I can't believe I was so naive." She looked at the other women. She saw nothing in their expressions except sympathy and a new hatred for the man she was married to.

"So, where do we start?" Nikki asked Charles. "I know you still have connections at the White House, but are they secure?"

"Yes, but I don't think I'll need to use them just yet. We have several options. It's up to Julia to decide."

Julia looked around the table at her friends. "I want the bastard to suffer, and I want it to happen gradually. Mitchell believes he is invincible. It's going to take a lot more than a threat from me to bring him to his knees. He's a master at covering his ass. That means no matter what I come up with, he will have a pat answer. He'll turn the whole thing around and accuse me of having an affair. He'll say it often enough that he will believe it. Whatever you do, do not forget how powerful he is. His friends are even more powerful."

The group of women nodded. "What about his past? You said his entire background was phony. Can we actually prove it?" Charles asked Julia.

Julia laughed, a bitter sound. "Yes, and no. The problem is getting the right people to listen, and believe me, Mitch has spent most of his adult life on the Hill. He has lots of friends in Washington. Friends who owe him favors. Some of those friends are on the . . . scummy side. Mitch won't hesitate to call all his favors in if he thinks I'm going after him," Julia said.

"Tell me about his past. The real story," Charles insisted. "The story he doesn't want his adoring public to hear."

Julia nodded. "You'll probably find this hard to believe, but Mitch has no idea I know about his past."

"How did you find out and manage to keep it from him? I don't know if I would be able to keep quiet about my husband's past; if I knew he did something terrible I'd want to confront him," Nikki said.

"I lost count of the times I wanted to confront him but something always held me back. I'm afraid of him. He has a lot to lose and he wouldn't think twice about . . . letting me ruin his life. I want to think I was supposed to save this information to use at the right time. Now is the right time. The world is in bad enough shape without people like Mitchell Webster controlling it."

"Go on," Myra urged. "I want to hear what that horrible man has gotten away with. And to think I would have voted for him if I'd lived in Pennsylvania."

Julia smiled wryly. "He sucked you in too? Don't feel bad, Myra, it's what he does best. He's sucked in the whole state of Pennsylvania with that phony background he made up. He lied. He had sex with a girl who was later murdered.

"For starters, we all now know Mitchell is HIV positive. That in itself would blow his image all to hell but not enough to ruin his career because he'd find a way around it. He could say he was infected when he donated blood. He would come out the victor, I have no doubt. So that alone isn't enough to damage him permanently. And I want my vengeance to be permanent. I don't want to see the bastard resurface five years later. He may not even have five years." Julia paused. "I may not have five years left myself. I do have enough time to see that Mitch gets what's coming to him. All I need is your help in planning his destruction." She looked at Charles with hope in her eyes.

"You already have our support. What we need to do right now is decide in what order we're going to start dropping tidbits of information to the public," Charles said. "First, I think we should start by revealing his phony past anonymously to a few of the tabloids. Those vultures run with everything. Let Mitch go to war with them. Give him a few weeks to lie low, let the dust settle. Then, we move on to the next wave."

"Which is?" Julia questioned.

Charles spoke up. "You realize you will be in the public eye with him, don't you? Next, I think you should reveal that you suspect Mitchell is being unfaithful. But let it out accidentally. Better yet, let one of your friends do it for you. Would Sara, the oncologist, help you out here? We want your image to be that of a heartbroken wife who stands by her man." He heard several groans. "Scratch that thought. I'll come up with something better."

"I'm sure Sara will help. I will be more than happy to play the scorned wife. You know, there was a time when I first learned about Mitch's cheating, that I *was* heartbroken. After the fifth or sixth time, I didn't care anymore. I had my career, I was happy with that. If Mitch needed me at his side for some political function, I was there. I wonder how many times his colleagues were laughing at me behind my back. I guarantee Mitchell's cronies knew he was a cheating bastard." Tears formed in Julia's eyes. "You know what bothers me more than anything?"

"What, dear?" Myra asked, sensing Julia needed an older woman, a mother image, to listen and empathize with her now.

"Being laughed at. It enrages me to think about all the women he's had affairs with. I'm sure some of those women are the wives of his good old 'Capitol Hill buddies.' I wonder what those good old Capitol Hill buddies would do if they suddenly learned Mitch had affairs with their wives."

"I think I can find out everything you want to know. I, too, have friends on *the Hill*. We could use the information later if we need to. It couldn't hurt to have Senator Webster's cronies by the . . . short hairs," Charles said bluntly.

"Yes. I can give you names of some of the wives I've suspected over the years. Linda Cromwell for one. Her husband is Senator Cromwell from Delaware. She called the house several times when Mitchell didn't think I was home. I picked up the extension and listened to their phone conversation once. They weren't talking about politics."

Myra flinched. "And I thought Mrs. Cromwell was such a prim and proper lady. Very schoolmarmish. I saw her on *Face the Nation* the other day with some other senators' wives. They've formed a committee of some sort," Myra said. "I might be wrong but I think it had something to do with pediatric AIDS."

Julia nodded. "You're not wrong, Myra. The wives scheduled a fund-raising dinner for next week, five thousand dollars a plate. The proceeds will go to their newly established foundation. I can offer my help if you think it's a good idea."

Nikki beamed. "I think it's a wonderful idea but let's not decide just yet. If the senator's world starts falling apart, he's going to place blame on the person he's closest to. That person is you, Julia."

Julia nodded. "Yes, I suppose you're right. There is something else. After Mitchell and I were married I insisted his name go on all my accounts. Damn, I already told you that. I'm sorry. I'm starting to stress out about this. I haven't seen any bank statements for months. I don't know if that means anything, but he does have access to my money. What does that have to do with anything, anyway?"

Charles bit down on his lower lip. He didn't like the sound of this and it showed. "I want you to close out your accounts immediately. For your sake, Julia, I hope there is something left to close out. Can you do it without Mitchell finding out? You didn't do anything with your trusts did you?"

Julia swallowed hard and shook her head.

"That's good, at least you have money coming in. We might want to take a look at those trusts later on."

"I don't foresee a problem. The accounts don't require both signatures. I can do it first thing tomorrow."

"Good." Charles said. "The rest of us will be acting behind the scenes as much as possible. Tonight when you get home, act as if nothing has happened. Don't say or do anything that you wouldn't normally do."

"What about my leave of absence from the hospital? I went to Nicole's office to have her review my new contract with the hospital a while ago and to ask her advice. At that time I was still trying to figure out a way to stay on, perhaps as a consultant. We both decided it was a good idea to just take a leave of absence for now and not renew the contract. I had Nikki draw up my resignation papers but I haven't turned them over to the hospital nor did I mention it to Mitchell because . . . Nikki advised me not to. And as you all know, that's how I learned of the sisterhood. Nikki seemed to think I was a good candidate. I don't want Mitch to suspect I'm not working. I am a doctor and he might wonder why I'm not going to the hospital. I can't keep going shopping every day, which is what I've been doing. Not that Mitch checks up on me but there is a first time for everything. Do any of you have any ideas?"

"Have you taken a leave of absence before?" Myra asked.

"I've taken time off when Mitchell was running for office. I went on the campaign trail with him for a few weeks. Other than that, no."

"Let me ask you this, does Mitchell confide in you? Would he tell you about Governor Cartwright asking him to be his running mate if he decides to run for the presidency? Those rumors are floating all over the District."

"He confides in me about certain things. Yes, I think he would tell me about that. I think it's just a rumor that Mitch started himself. He likes to gloat too much not to tell me. This is just my opinion but I've always thought he felt inferior to me. Don't ask me why.

He's been a senator for sixteen years now. I suppose it could be my money. I've thought for years he resented me because of it but it doesn't stop him from spending it. Yes, I think he would tell me about the nomination, just to rub my nose in it. It's just a rumor at this point. Isn't it?"

Charles held up the latest edition of a smarmy tabloid and pointed to the headline that said, "Webster on Crawford's short list." "Then you have your answer. Don't tell him you've taken a leave of absence until he tells you about Crawford. After he tells you, wait a few days, *then* tell him you'll take a leave of absence to help him with his campaign."

"I can do that. Yes, I think it will work. I have to go to the hospital and clear out a few things in my office. I'll take a day longer. Mitchell doesn't keep close tabs on me anyway. He's never had a reason to."

"Now, Julia, tell us what you know about Mitchell's past. Everyone, take notes. I've got the recorder on, but notes are an extra precaution. Just in case. One of you might pick up on something the rest of us miss," Charles said, pointing to the high-tech recorder that was no bigger than a cigarette lighter.

Julia took a deep breath. This was harder than she'd thought it would be. When she'd learned she was HIV positive, her world had come to a crashing halt. Getting even with the bastard she was married to was the only thing that kept her going. Now that it was time to get down and dirty, she wondered if she had enough guts to make it happen. She didn't want to place herself in the same category as Mitchell and his Capitol Hill cronies, but if she didn't stop him, he would keep lying, seducing women and spreading a disease that would be the death of everyone he touched.

"I'm ready," Julia said as the others prepared themselves to take notes.

"Just start out telling us what he told you. Then you can tell us how you found out he lied," Charles instructed.

Julia nodded. "I always knew Mitchell's 'public' family history. I never had a reason to question it until after we were married." Julia twisted her hair around her finger, a faraway look in her eyes.

"Sorry. I was . . . this is harder to talk about than I thought."

Myra smiled gently. "Take your time. We understand what you're going through, Julia. You're human. You are about to destroy a man you once loved," Myra said.

"We married in November, almost a year to the day after we met. I was in love and all was right with the world. However, when the holidays rolled around I asked Mitchell if we would be going to Virginia to spend the holidays with his family. I still hadn't met them and I thought they'd want to meet their daughter-in-law. Mitchell got angry and told me he was estranged from his family. He said when he was ready for me to meet them, he would see to it that I did. I pretended to understand. Some families don't get along. Two years went by and I still hadn't met Mitchell's family. By that time I knew whatever was wrong had to be something more than a family dispute."

"Two years is a long time to wait," Alexis said.

"Yes, two years is a long time but I was in medical school and didn't have a lot of free time, so I didn't give the matter too much thought. Mitchell was busy running for another term at the time, we were both wrapped up in our careers. Christmas rolled around again. I asked Mitch if he was going home for Christmas and he blew up. He threw a few plates as I remember. We were having dinner together for a change. I guess I thought it was the right time to ask about them. It wasn't. I realized then there would never be a right time to discuss Mitch's so-called adopted family. I let it go. For weeks I thought about hiring a private detective to track Mitch's parents down. Turns out the father drank himself to death and the mother had the same addiction and died shortly after. I found out what the real argument was all about. I debated a few months, thinking it wouldn't be in the best interest of my marriage to send someone digging into Mitch's past. Of course I got over that after I convinced myself Mitch gave me no other choice. He was being dishonest and I wanted to find out why." Julia paused for breath, then took a pen and started to scribble on a yellow legal pad.

"When I found out I was shocked. I couldn't believe how Mitch had fooled the voters. To this day I don't understand why a tabloid hasn't homed in on this information and made it public. They feed on stories like Mitchell's. If he does run with Cartwright, they'll turn him inside out. Mitch and his public relations experts, if you want to call them that, said Mitch was adopted by a well-to-do Virginia family when he was thirteen, after spending thirteen years in and out of foster homes. I guess that was supposed to make him appear more sympathetic to his voters. I was his wife. You would've thought he would at least tell me the truth."

"They say the wife is always the last to know," Nikki mumbled.

Julia agreed with a nod and continued. "Finally, I hired a private detective. One of the best in New York City. Mitchell had his career. Despite all of my concerns, I didn't want to cause trouble for him.

Of course what Mitchell didn't know wasn't going to hurt him. I was overly paranoid. I guess I thought whatever my detective discovered he'd go public with it. Which, fortunately for me, and for Mitchell, never happened." Julia looked at the women. She had their undivided attention.

"Mitchell's adoption story was a lie. He was never in a foster home until he was sixteen. Evidently it was hard to place him at that age. Mitchell lived with his mother until he went to live with the Websters."

"If he wasn't adopted, how could he use their name?" Myra asked.

"He had his name legally changed when he turned eighteen. The Websters took him in when he was sixteen, then sent him to college. He was like one of their own, but they never formally adopted him. And they were not well-to-do by any means. Mrs. Webster's name is Lavinia and she worked in a grocery store. Her husband, Carl, worked for the state. They were a hard-working couple. They never had children of their own. Mitchell filled that void for a while. Both of them died in a car accident in the early nineties. Voters do not like to be lied to."

"And you never confronted him with this information?" Charles asked her, his voice registering shocked surprise.

"Never," Julia said flatly.

"This detective told you all of this?" Nikki asked in a plaintive voice. She looked at Myra as she shook her head.

"Yes. I have the report in my office. I never brought it home for fear Mitchell would find it. I didn't want him to know what I'd done. I felt in some crazy way that I had betrayed my husband by checking up on him."

"I can't believe a man with the senator's power and position in the Senate hasn't been exposed for the phony he is. I would bet my last dime that Senator Webster spends big bucks to keep his past out of the papers," Nikki said as she looked at Julia. "If I were you I would get my finances in order. If you have anything left to get in order."

"Mitchell's life is about to fall apart, isn't it? And I'll be the one to bring it crashing down. He'll kill me if he ever finds out what I've done."

"Then we have to make certain your husband never finds out, don't we?" Myra said to the room at large. "It goes without saying, this conversation is never to leave this room."

"When do we start to leak this to the press?" Alexis asked. Relief at being out of the spotlight shone on her face.

"Shortly," Charles responded as he scribbled on his own yellow pad.

"Be warned about Mitchell. He wants to control everything and everybody around him. He told me once that he loved the power being in the Senate gave him. He said he had the power to screw up lives if he wanted. Then he laughed. He thinks it's all about him. And it is. If marrying Mitchell Webster is going to be the death of me, I'd at least like to know before I die that the son of a bitch suffered too," Julia said vehemently.

All the women in the group centered their attention on Julia. If any one of them had a right to revenge, it was Julia. She would die because her husband was unfaithful. Her death, whenever it came, would not be in vain. The Sisterhood would see to it that Senator Mitchell Webster suffered before his death. Nikki would see to it personally.

Charles looked at the group of women. "Nothing that was said in this room today should be repeated. Not to your husband, your best friend or even your dog. You never know who might be listening. We must be very careful. This time we're not dealing with a gang of bikers or insane neighbors. We are going to be up against the federal government in a sense and I for one know what they're capable of. You don't want to find out the hard way. Let's call it a day. I will see you back here day after tomorrow at seven A.M. Does anyone have any questions? Is there anything else you want to add, Julia?" His voice was so kind, Julia found herself smiling.

"Well, there is one other thing. For any of you who are *really* interested, Mitchell has the American flag tattooed on his ass."

Charles choked and looked away. Kathryn guffawed and slapped her leg. The other women just tittered.

Kathryn managed to stifle her laughter. "What about the rest of us, Charles? Are we going to sit by and watch you have all the fun?" Kathryn asked.

Charles fixed his gaze on Kathryn. "I'm surprised you asked, you have barely said a word this morning. Yes, I have something for all of you to do. You're not going to get off that easy." He smiled at her and wiggled his eyebrows at the same time. Yoko, Isabelle, and Alexis laughed.

"As we know, Alexis is a master at disguise, having learned the art in college and Little Theater work. If the need arises, and I'm not sure at this point if it will, you will do what you do best with your big

Red Bag." He watched as she slid her notes across the semicircular table in front of her.

Charles looked down at his own scribbled notes. He held up his hand. "I made some changes since we're going to be running a dual mission this time around. Tell me if it's going to be a problem."

"Do I stay or leave?" Alexis asked.

"You can leave, but remember, be back in forty-eight hours." Charles admonished.

"Yes, sir!" She saluted quietly before she walked out the door.

"Yoko, you will assist Kathryn. I'm quite comfortable saying you both are going to be quite busy. I have a contact at Governor Cartwright's mansion in Maryland. They are in charge of decorating the armory where Jefferson Cartwright plans to announce his running mate. It's a good guess it will be Senator Webster. They will want floral arrangements for all the tables as well as the stage where the podium rests. I'm thinking somewhere around five hundred arrangements. Can you handle this, Yoko? That means no delivery of oranges to New Jersey for Kathryn. We're going to need her rig."

A look of panic settled on Yoko's face. "How do I explain all of this to my husband?"

"I don't think you'll have to explain anything, Yoko, I rather imagine your husband will thank you for securing such a large flower order."

"I can do a lot of things, but arranging flowers isn't one of them," Kathryn grumbled good-naturedly.

"And you won't have to learn, my dear. As it stands, Yoko and several of you will have one van for deliveries. It wouldn't do for Yoko to borrow the van as he will need it. It would take all day just to load the flowers and drive them to Cartwright's headquarters. With your semi you can do it in one trip. You'll be helping to unload the flowers. Our friend Mr. Emery may be watching so it will all seem quite natural."

"How can you be so sure Yoko will get the flower order? What a silly question." Kathryn grimaced as she remembered how Charles had pulled strings and arranged her mission down to the last detail. When one had powerful friends in powerful places as Charles did, anything could be accomplished.

Charles's voice rang with confidence, leaving little doubt that he could do what he said he would do. "Leave the details to me. If I say it will happen, it will happen.

"Isabelle, you will be working here at Pinewood with Myra. Nikki will assist me here in the war room. At this point it may seem like a walk in the park but don't be fooled. We're about to destroy a man's political life as well as his personal life. We have to be extremely careful so that we don't destroy our own lives in the process."

When the war room door closed behind the women Charles sat down in Myra's chair and looked around. His insides started to kick up a fuss at what he was contemplating on behalf of the Sisterhood. This was so unlike Kathryn's mission. This mission could, if not conducted properly, land all of them in prison. During his long and distinguished career in Her Majesty's Secret Service he'd been comfortable with his role of super spy because everyone he worked with knew his or her job. Their very lives depended on one another. The women of the Sisterhood were in no way professionals but they were women and in his opinion, women had an edge with their intuitive senses. Not that he would ever admit that to anyone except perhaps Myra, the one true love of his life.

His mind raced in all directions. He had to sit and think quietly to find the best way to conduct this new dual mission with a minimum of risk for the women he now thought of as his family. He looked around at what Myra called his lair. Everything in this room was state-of-the-art, so high-tech no one but government agencies knew about it and here it was, sitting in a secret room in Pinewood. Of course this could never have happened without Myra's wealth. When she said money was no object, she meant money was no object. His stomach crunched at the millions he'd spent in outfitting this room and she hadn't blinked an eye. He knew she would spend every last cent of her vast fortune to avenge her daughter's death. *Their* daughter. He couldn't wait for the day it was Myra's turn to be vindicated. That mission would be a mission of love with the Sisterhood.

Charles looked down at his watch. He chewed on his lower lip, something he did when he worried, and he was worried about Jack Emery. Strong measures might have to be taken where Assistant District Attorney Emery was concerned. How that would affect Nikki was something he didn't even want to think about.

From his perch, high in an oak tree, Jack Emery trained his binoculars on the vehicles leaving the Pinewood compound. He watched as the women hugged one another before Dr. Julia Webster climbed behind the wheel of her brand new Mercedes. Even from this distance Jack thought she looked thinner than the last time he'd seen her. She also looked pale to his trained eye. He shrugged; women were forever dieting.

Kathryn Lucas, the truck driver, was next. The huge black dog hopped into the cab and settled himself while Kathryn talked to the Asian woman. They hugged, too. Lucas left first in the rig and then the Asian woman followed her. That left the tall, long-legged African-American beauty. He watched until the Mini Cooper sailed through the gates. He could hear the clank of the gate closing from his perch high in the tree. He had operatives waiting along the stretch of highway to follow the women to wherever they were going.

That left Nikki, the Flanders woman, Myra Rutledge and Charles Martin, Myra's majordomo.

When Jack was sure there would be no further outdoor activity, he climbed down from the tree, dropping to his haunches. Something was going on, he was sure of it. For one thing, two visits by all the women in two weeks was one visit too many. Then there was the addition of the six Doberman dogs that arrived at five o'clock every afternoon and stayed through the night. Yes, something was definitely going on.

Jack dusted off his jeans as he started toward his car. He was so damn tired. How much longer could he keep this up? He was lucky to get three hours sleep a night. He knew he was obsessed with this place, these women, and Nikki in particular. Long ago he'd learned to pay attention to his gut instincts and those gut instincts said these seven women were up to their pretty necks in something covert. And whatever it was, Myra Rutledge was bankrolling the project.

He knew that somehow, some way, Myra and the women had managed to spirit Marie Llewellyn, her husband and children to a place of safety. He'd prosecuted that woman for killing the man who had killed Myra's daughter. He hadn't wanted to do it but it was his job. The law was the law. He'd looked like a fool to his superiors when he couldn't figure out how Marie and her entire family dropped off the face of the earth on a wild, stormy night. To this day, there was not a single clue as to what happened. Nikki knew what happened, he was sure of it.

Jack opened the door of his car, climbed in and started the engine. His cell phone was in his hand a second later as he called his operatives for reports.

Damn, he was so tired he could hardly hold up his head. When he turned the power off on the cell phone he started to think about Nikki. He knew in his gut he was one of those guys who would only love once. Nikki was that love. He should never have given her that ultimatum. Ultimatums never worked. Someone always won and someone lost. Nikki had chosen Myra over him. It was the bitterest pill he'd ever had to swallow.

# Chapter Four

The war room buzzed with the hushed voices of the women seated at the table. Charles, busy on the computer, only half listened to their conversation. What he was doing right now was solidifying the plans for Julia's revenge. He was tired but exhilarated. He'd called in favors from other retired operatives who were only too glad to offer their expertise in their chosen field. He held up his hand and shouted to be heard over the fax machine that was spitting out paper at the rate of twenty-six pages a minute. Overhead the television monitors came to life.

Charles stood high above the floor on a specially built dais. The king of all he surveyed. When he had the women's attention, he pressed a button on the huge monitor next to where he stood. The scales of justice came into view; Lady Justice in all her glory lit up the room. As always, when the women saw Lady Justice they became subdued.

"First things first. I want to apologize for the late hour," Charles said, motioning to one of the clocks hanging on the wall. It was eleven o'clock in the evening, time for the late news. The sound was muted. He would turn up the volume in exactly ten minutes for the sound bite he wanted the sisters to hear. Now, though, he spoke quickly and concisely.

"Nikki has returned from Lynchburg. I thought it wise to send her on a scouting mission to make sure our facts are on the money. You'll all be given a copy of her report. I regret to say that Senator Webster is not responsible for Janet Bradshaw's death. Julia already told us that but I didn't want to leave anything to chance. Nikki and Julia both spoke with the young girl's mother. There is no point to going into detail. DNA doesn't lie. Senator Webster did have an affair with the young girl but he was not the father of the child she was carrying. Yes, the man is a philanderer. Yes, he has a shady background. But he did not kill anyone. I want to be sure we're all clear on the matter. Nikki was unsuccessful in locating any stray members of the senator's real family. What that means to all of us at the moment is the senator gave himself a make-believe background which in itself is not really a crime. What he did to Julia is the crime. We need to be clear on that.

"That leaves us with Julia's immediate problem. We cannot turn the senator over to the authorities for manufacturing a phony background. Millions of people do it every day. The fact that the man is a United States senator does, however, make a difference because that means the man duped the very people who put him into office. Will that matter? I doubt it.

"All we can do now is go after Senator Webster for what he's done to his wife. And to other women we don't know about at this point in time." Charles held up his hand for silence as he turned up the volume on the huge television set. "Listen!"

The evening news anchor looked gleeful when he said, "Just hours ago we received Governor Cartwright's short list for his running mate in the presidential race. Heading the list is Senator Mitchell Webster. What was up to this point an unsubstantiated rumor has now been confirmed. Channel Five tried to reach the senator for comment before airtime but we were unsuccessful." Charles turned the volume down.

"Well, that's never going to happen!" Julia shouted. In a lower tone, she said, "Is it, Charles?"

Myra reached across the table to pat Julia's hand. "No, dear, that is not going to happen."

Charles took up his usual position behind Myra's chair. "We have five days before Governor Cartwright's party where he will make his announcement. We have one foot in the door with the flowers. What that's going to get us is not quite clear yet but I am working on it. Julia will, of course, be there along with her husband. Our first leak to the tabloids will hit the paper the day before the event, the second, the day after the event when the senator is on a roll.

"Now, this is where it's really going to get interesting. The Monarch family, owners of the three HMOs we discussed previously, will be at the party. What that means is all three of them will be at their mansion in Manassas prior to the event. At the moment they're in their other mansion up in Peekskill. They're due to arrive in town tomorrow or the day after."

"Oh, Charles, hurry and tell them the best part," Myra said, excitement ringing in her voice.

Charles laughed, a robust sound. "Myra received an invitation to attend the party. If she had opened last week's mail last week, we would have known sooner. Now, what that means to the Sisterhood is this. You're all going to attend. We're creating new identities for all of you. You'll be considered heavy hitters with pockets full of money. The only thing politicians love more than themselves is people with money. Alexis, with her magnificent bag of tricks, will alter your appearance so you don't look like yourselves. Simply put, you'll be going in disguise. Myra has ordered exquisite fashions for all of you. And, as I said, Julia will be there on the arm of her husband."

Kathryn slapped the table with the palm of her hand. "Way to go, Charles!"

"Then what happens?" Nikki asked.

Charles waited a minute before he spoke. "Then we snatch them all!"

"Oh, girls, don't you just love the way that sounds?" Myra bubbled.

"Kidnaping is . . . it's . . ." Isabelle struggled for the proper word.

"Against the law? Well, of course it is. So was slicing off those guys' balls who raped me but we did it anyway. What's a little kidnaping charge?" Kathryn growled.

"Then what? Where? How? Details, Charles, details," Nikki said.

"All in good time. We have five days and I will need every bit of that time to fine-tune everything. As you all know, the devil is in the details."

Julia raised her hand. "What will we do with them when we . . . snatch them? Do you have even a vague idea of where we'll take them?"

"The revenge is yours, Julia. You and the others have to decide what their punishment is to be. I'm just your backup. I think you all might need the five days that are coming up. The one thing you can count on is that the location will be secure."

Charles walked back to his station. He returned with an armful of stapled bundles. "What this is," he said, handing each woman a document, "is the list of all the Monarch HMO subscribers. It's a bit mind-boggling at first, but go to the summary at the end where I've listed those claims that were denied, the deaths of the subscribers due to denial of claims, pending cases, closed cases. It's all broken down by age groups. The last page is Monarch's P&L sheet. You might want to keep those numbers front and center when you decide on the family's punishment."

Kathryn was the first one to bellow, "This is outrageous!"

"Scum of the earth," Nikki said.

"It's pitiful," Myra said.

"I didn't know it was this bad," Julia said.

"We should kill them all," Yoko said heatedly.

"Killing them is too good. They need to be punished and I do mean punished. They need to suffer," Alexis said angrily.

"I think we're ready to adjourn for the evening, girls. Let's head for the kitchen and some nice hot cocoa. Charles, would you care for some cocoa?"

"Not right now, Myra. I have hours of work ahead of me. We'll meet again in the morning at eight-thirty."

They were a somber group as they meandered around the kitchen getting in Myra's way as she tried to prepare the hot cocoa. When Nikki's cell phone chirped, their gaze whirled to the clock over the stove. They listened as Nikki clicked the on button.

"Hello," Nikki said quietly.

"Nik?"

"That's my name. What do *you* want? Do you know what time it is?"

"Of course I know what time it is, it's almost midnight. Guess your Tiddly Wink game is over for the night or are you guys having a sleepover? Kind of old for that kind of thing, aren't you, Nik? What'd you go to Lynchburg for? Never mind, I already know. When is everyone going to leave?"

"You sneak! You're spying on me, aren't you? I'm going to file a harassment charge against you, Jack. Don't call me again, either."

"Come on, Nik. You know you love me. I know what you're doing. Give it up before I have to arrest you."

"I'm not doing anything but playing cards. If you want to make an ass of yourself by trying to arrest me, go ahead. I'll fry your ass and I won't need any help doing it either. You'll be the one who gets arrested. You're out there, aren't you, you son of a bitch! I bet if I went outside and waved you'd see me, wouldn't you?"

"Why does Myra suddenly need six vicious Dobermans, Nik? What kind of gig are you women running out there at ye old farm, *Nik*?" His voice was so sarcastic Nikki shivered.

Nikki sucked in her breath. Her heart started to pound in her chest. "We aren't running any kind of gig out here and the reason

Myra got the Dobermans is to keep people like you off her property." Without waiting for a reply, Nikki clicked the off button.

The women clamored for an explanation at the angry look on Nikki's face. She stuttered and sputtered until she got every word of Jack's phone call out.

"So what you're saying is Jack is *on to us*," Julia said.

Nikki gulped her hot cocoa and then bellowed when she burned her throat. Her eyes watering, she gasped, "What it means is, he *thinks* he's on to us. Yeah, he's on to us."

Yoko, the gentlest, the quietest of all the women, started to pace around the kitchen table. "Then we have to . . . eliminate him, is that not right?"

Kathryn slapped Yoko on the back. "God, we're corrupting you, Yoko. What's gotten into you? You were a pacifist when we first met!"

Yoko squared her slim shoulders. "He's spying on us so he can send us to prison. I do not like that. That's what they do in countries where there is no democracy. And, he's broken Nikki's heart. Now he's threatening all of us. We have to do something!"

Myra spoke in a soothing voice. "Our plates are rather full right now, Yoko. I don't see how we can . . . perhaps we should invite Mr. Emery for tea."

"Mr Emery doesn't sound like a reasonable man, Myra," Alexis said. "We can't let him keep doing what he's doing, which is spying on us. Eventually, he's going to nail one of us. I'll kill myself before I let anyone send me back to prison."

"Shhh. You aren't going back to prison," Nikki said. "I'll take care of Mr. Emery. You know, Myra, inviting Jack for tea isn't such a bad idea."

"What will we do with him?" the new Yoko demanded.

"We could have those vicious dogs guard him," Julia volunteered. "Yes, I think that's a viable solution. But, that means Myra will have to make arrangements for the dogs twenty-four seven. Perhaps we should vote on it."

Nikki's mind raced. Did they dare snatch Jack? She looked around at the women. She saw panic and anger in their faces. Even Myra looked . . . disturbed. But tea? Yes, Myra would invite him for tea but would Jack take her up on the invitation? For some reason she didn't think so. Jack was out for blood. Still, it was worth a chance.

"Should we do it, dear?" Myra asked. "I think we should . . . what's that saying police officers use all the time? Oh, yes, chop him off at the knees. That's what we need to do. Should we tell Charles?"

"Absolutely we should tell Charles," Nikki shot back. "I'll do it now."

"More cocoa, girls?"

"No!" the women chorused.

"Then why don't we all smoke a cigarette. Does anyone have a cigarette?"

"No!" the women chorused.

One by one they trooped out of the kitchen, muttering a good night as they passed Myra's chair. Left alone with her thoughts, Myra's shoulders slumped. Her eyes filled with tears. Jack Emery couldn't be allowed to compromise what they were doing. He just couldn't.

Myra got up and reached into the cabinet over the sink for the bottle of brandy she kept handy for medicinal purposes. If ever there was a medicinal moment, this was it. She didn't bother with a glass but upended the bottle and took a hearty gulp. Her throat burned and her eyes started to water. She took another huge gulp before she corked the bottle and set it back in the cabinet. She tottered to her chair and plopped down. She started to cry. "Oh, Barbara, honey, I think I might be failing you. If Jack catches us, all this will be in vain. I only set this whole thing up to avenge your death. Now, it's more than that. I want to help the others, too. What a silly old woman I am to think I could make this all happen. Just a silly old woman."

*"Mom, there's nothing silly about it. Stop worrying."*

"Barbara, is that you? Darling girl, talk to me. Are you at peace? I think about you every day. I miss you so. The others have made my loss bearable, but now with Jack out there somewhere," Myra said, waving her arm in the general direction of the back door. "I don't know if we can hang on. Nikki's living here now, you know." Dear God, she was babbling to her daughter's ghost.

*"I know, Mom. I'm glad she's here with you. Trust her. She can handle Jack. I have to go, Mom. Nikki and Charles are coming back to the kitchen. I love you, Mom. Mom, lay off the sauce, OK?"*

"Where are you going, honey?"

*"Upstairs to cuddle with Willie for a little while."*

A wild *swoosh* of air circled Myra and then the kitchen was still.

Nikki stood in the doorway. She, too, felt the swoosh of air. She knew instantly that Barbara had paid a visit to her mother.

*"Talk to you later, Nik."*

Nikki knew when she went upstairs to bed that Barbara would be sitting in her old rocker with Willie in her lap. They'd talk like they did sometimes about everything and anything.

Charles stopped in his tracks. "Was that . . ."

"Yeah," Nikki whispered.

"Oh."

Myra looked up, her lips trembling, her eyes moist. "I think I'm going to go to bed. I had . . . What I mean is, I drank some brandy. Maybe it was a lot. Is everything all right?" she asked as an afterthought. "Oh, would you like me to make you both some hot cocoa?"

"Good God, no, Myra. You make terrible cocoa," Charles said.

The heiress to a Fortune 500 company sniffed as she got up from her chair to go upstairs. "So what if cooking isn't one of my strong points. I have other talents, don't I, Charles?" She giggled like a schoolgirl as she sashayed past Nikki who did her best to hide her smile. Charles's ears turned pink. Myra whirled around and almost fell. "Should I wait for you, dear?"

In spite of himself, Charles chuckled. "Is that an invitation, Myra?"

Myra drew herself up to her full height. "Damn straight it is, Charles."

This time, Nikki did laugh aloud. "Go!" she said. "Before she kills herself going up the steps."

Nikki sat for a long time at the kitchen table. She felt like the weight of the world was on her shoulders. What was she going to do about Jack? If they snatched him, the D.A.'s office would start to look for him. Appealing to his sense of decency was not an option. Jack was a bull dog with the instincts of a bloodhound. And he was angry with her. That alone was motivation enough for him to want to put the screws to her and the others. She wondered how much he really knew and how far he was willing to go to nail all of them.

Nikki fished her cell phone out of the pocket of her slacks, turned it on and dialed Jack's number. A cell phone ringing in the woods. How funny was that? She almost laughed when a vision of the ADA, sitting high in a tree, his binoculars trained on the house, appeared before her.

Jack picked up on the first ring. Nikki figured it was lonely in the woods. "So how's it going out there in the piney forest, Jack?"

"I'm not in the piney forest," Jack said.

"Liar! You're up in a tree spying on us. You aren't the only one with high-powered binoculars. We've got the night vision ones. You know the kind where everything looks green. You get yours at Radio Shack?"

"Smart ass! I'm home in my living room."

"Liar! I'm calling to invite you to tea tomorrow." When there was no response, Nikki said, "Well?"

"You must have me mixed up with someone who would be impressed with an invitation to Pinewood for tea. You know I hate tea."

"OK, coffee. What? You're afraid of me all of a sudden?"

"Hell, no, I'm not afraid of you. The woman hasn't been born who can scare me. I don't trust you or Myra. By the way, I've got a dossier on all those fine women visiting out there all the time. A real mixed bag, Nik. The bunch of you are up to something. I can smell it, and you know damn well I have excellent instincts."

Nikki sucked in her breath. Her hand holding the phone to her ear was shaking. "So, is that a no or a yes?"

"Like I'd allow myself to get within ten feet of you, counselor? Did I say I don't trust you?"

"Yeah. Yeah, you did say that. Ten feet, huh? I remember when we were molded to each other. You were my second skin if I remember correctly, but that was when you loved me, right?"

"Get off it, Nik. I'm not going down that road. Don't think you can sucker me in with an invitation to a tea party. I gotta go, time for bed."

Nikki snorted. "Be careful you don't fall out of your tree, there, Mr. ADA."

"You're a hateful woman, Nicole Quinn, and yet I still love you."

Nikki looked at the dead phone in her hand and started to cry. "And I still love you, too, Jack."

# Chapter Five

Charles served breakfast on the patio to a group of somber, sleepy-eyed women who also looked angry.

"Ladies, ladies, how can you look so glum on such a beautiful spring morning?" Charles asked as he held the wrought-iron chair for Myra who was all smiles this morning. His voice dropped to a whisper. "Voices carry," he said, waving his arms to the thick forest that surrounded Myra's estate. "Generalities, ladies."

Nikki looked toward the piney forest wondering if Jack was still out there. She couldn't help but wonder if Jack really did have some hightech equipment that would allow him to overhear their conversation. She struggled for something to say. "The patio flowers are so pretty this year, Myra." The others, taking their cue from her, concurred.

Myra was still smiling. "Lu Chow, the gardener, brought them over yesterday. They look like a veritable rainbow, don't you think? I'm thinking I should dispose of this overhead sun umbrella and get one of those retractable awnings. Yes, I've made up my mind. Isabelle, dear, can you design something so that it doesn't look new? You know, have it blend with this old farmhouse?"

"Of course. What color would you like?"

"Green and yellow. Outdoorsy, if you know what I mean."

And so the conversation went until the girls cleared the table and trooped back inside. Myra closed the patio doors and drew the blinds.

A whispered conversation followed as Charles instructed Julia to drive back to Georgetown. "It's imperative that you find out as much as you can from your husband. If possible, you can return here this evening or tomorrow. Once Crawford makes his formal announcement that your husband will be his running mate, the Secret Service will move in and you will be under a microscope."

Julia looked stricken. "I never thought of that, Charles. How . . . what . . . I'll be a liability to all of you if that happens."

"No, you won't dear. Charles will figure out something. This is your mission and nothing is going to stop us from carrying it out, not even the Secret Service. Now, do as Charles says, put a happy smile on your face and go home to talk to your husband."

"Today is Saturday. Mitch plays golf on Saturday. He might not be home. I see problems already."

Charles placed a comforting hand on Julia's arm. "There will only be problems if we don't act as a group. When you get to your car, use your private cell phone and call your husband. Be firm when you tell him you must talk with him today. I think he'll cancel any plans he might have to talk with you. He needs you now. And the press will be buzzing everywhere. I've taken the liberty of writing out some instructions for you. Peruse them when you make a stop at the hospital to pick up your shopping list of possible drugs we might need. You won't get another chance to go to the hospital again before we begin our mission." Seeing the panic in Julia's face, he said, "Julia, you can do this. I wouldn't ask you to do this if I didn't think you were up to it."

Julia drew a deep breath and squared her shoulders. In a jittery voice she said, "Of course I can do it. I won't let you down. I guess I should be going. I just need to get my bags." She looked around. "You know, in case anyone out there in the woods is watching us."

One by one the others volunteered to go with Julia. Charles just shook his head. "Trust me, Julia will be fine."

They all walked Julia to her shiny black Mercedes. They waved and laughed as Charles instructed. Julia waved back, a sickly smile plastered on her face.

During the drive to Georgetown, Julia gritted her teeth, repeating over and over, I can do this. I will do this. I have to do this. She reached down for her cell phone and hit the button on her speed dial that would connect her with her husband. She was stunned when she heard her husband's voice.

"Mitch, it's Julia. I'm on the way home and I need to talk to you. Please wait for me. I really don't care if you have a tee time or not, Mitch. I need to talk with you." She listened to her husband's litany of excuses. Suddenly she was sick of it all, sick to death of her husband and sick to death of knowing this was the man who was responsible for giving her a death sentence.

When he finally ran out of reasons why he couldn't wait for her, Julia said, "Listen to me very carefully, you son of a bitch. You need me. I do not need you. You either wait for me or I'll give an interview to the press and I won't be shy about mentioning what an alley cat you are. And you'll be attending Crawford's announcement party by yourself. How will that look, Senator? Now what's it going to be? And, Senator Webster, I want to know what you did with all that money you took out of my account, which by the way, I closed out yesterday. You *will* wait for me, Mitch."

Julia hit the end button and turned off her phone. Let him keep hitting his own speed button till his damn finger fell off. That was almost funny because she knew her number wasn't on his speed dial because he never called her. If and when he did call, it was one of his aides with a message. She struggled to remember the last time she'd had a phone conversation with her husband but in the end she gave up. What did it matter now?

In the parking lot of the Georgetown Hospital, Julia read Charles's instructions three times until she had them committed to memory. Her eyebrows shot up once and then twice at the impressive list. Charles was right, she'd never get another chance to do what he wanted after today. When she was sure she had everything clear in her head, Julia tore the list into little pieces and stuffed them in her pocket. Once inside the hospital she would throw the pieces in different trash containers.

Julia, brisk professional that she was, made no stops on her way to her old office. Inside, she ran Charles's shopping list over in her mind as she opened and filled her medical bag. Her task completed, she looked at the sorry-looking philodendron on her desk. She wondered why no one had watered it. Maybe, like herself, it was meant to die. Like hell.

Julia grabbed the plant and raced down the hall to the kitchen where she used a plastic fork to stir up the hard earth. Somewhere in one of the cabinets there was a bottle of plant food one of the nurses had brought in. Six drops to a plant was what she'd said. Julia watered the plant, soaking it thoroughly before she added the six drops of plant food. With a paper plate underneath the plant she made her way back to her office where she set the plant on the desk. With a pair of old surgical shears, she trimmed off the yellow leaves. The plant still looked sickly and half dead. Just like me, she thought. Julia remembered reading somewhere that you were supposed to talk to plants to make them thrive.

Julia muttered and mumbled as she looked through her desk to see if there was anything else she needed to take with her. At the last second, she opened the drawer and took out all of her prescription pads and jammed them into her medical bag.

Done.

Julia was just about to walk through the emergency door exit when she stopped and ran back to her office. She reached for the plant and smiled. "You still have six leaves, my friend. That's not a death sentence." She stopped in the kitchen and took the bottle of plant food and left a ten dollar bill with a note in its place. Now, she could leave this place. In her heart she said good-bye because she knew she'd never be coming back.

Fifteen minutes later, Julia entered her house in Georgetown carrying her plant. She set it on the kitchen counter, then turned to face her husband. Mitch Webster roared like a lion as he stormed about chastising her for making him wait when he had a golf date with the House Speaker.

"Ask me if I care, Mitch. I don't. Did you make coffee? I need a cup. Would you like one?"

"No, I don't want any coffee. What the hell's gotten into you, Julia? I just heard you took a leave of absence. Why?"

"I felt like it. Overwork, you know," Julia said as she scooped coffee into the plastic container. She turned to look at her husband with clinical interest. He was still a handsome man, tall and lean, exquisite tailoring, just the right tan to his face. He must use a sunlamp, she thought. His nails were manicured. She hadn't noticed that before, either. Just the right amount of gray at his temples to make him distinguished. Beautiful, dove gray eyes, thanks to artificial lenses. Capped teeth that had made some dentist happy. A good-looking man who shared her house, and a senator to boot. She wondered why she didn't feel anything.

"Congratulations, Mitch! You should have told me."

"They told me not to say anything. You knew I was on the short list. It was in all the papers. It's a whole new ball game now, Julia."

"You bet it is. Well, guess what, I don't want to play in that ball game, Mitch. The reason I wanted you to wait for this little talk was to tell you I want a divorce. I also want to know, down to the penny, what you did with all the money you took out of my account. Close your mouth, Mitch, you look like a hooked fish."

"What the hell's gotten into you, Julia? You can't divorce me. Not now. I'm going to be the next vice president of the United States."

Julia sniffed. "I hope you don't expect me to be impressed, Mitch, because I'm not. I have no desire to live in Washington's fishbowl. Being a senator's wife was bad enough. I'm surprised you're so willing to give up your senate seat. Being a vice president will be incredibly boring. All those funerals you have to attend. You'll have to give up your tomcatting ways because every move you make will come under scrutiny. Like I said, I want a divorce."

"Julia, Julia, Julia. I can't believe what I'm hearing. We're an old married couple. We're going to grow old together. That's what we promised each other when we got married. Look, I know we more or less lead separate lives these days but that's what this fast paced life is all about. You have your career. I never interfered with what you wanted to do when you wanted to do it. I tried not to make demands on you. I know how you hate politics. But for Christ's sake, Julia, this is the vice presidency. I could even be president some day."

"Don't grovel, Mitch. It's very unbecoming. You made a fool of me with all those women you chased around with. I know about them all. This whole town has been chittering about you for years." *I should tell him now that I have AIDS. Why am I so unwilling to say the words aloud? I should be sticking a knife in his gut for what he's done to me. Charles said this wasn't the time.*

Mitch's face lost some of its color. "I'm not going to deny it, Julia. But, I was discreet. It's your fault. You were never home. You never wanted to go anywhere or do anything. You turned into some old frump. And let's not forget how tired you always were and how many headaches you had. What was I supposed to do? You need to take your share of the blame for that, too."

"I'm not willing to take the blame for anything, Mitch. No one forced you to have affairs. They're going to vet you big time. How long do you think that make-believe background of yours is going to hold up? Voters don't like it when their politicians lie to them. You lied. You made up a phony background. You pretended to be something you're not. You'll be fodder for the press from now till the election in November. They're going to find out about all those women you had affairs with. Give it up now."

"Oh, I get it. You're right, Julia, sometimes I am stupid. You're having an affair yourself, aren't you? Who is it, one of the pretty doctors you hang out with? One of the guys who speaks your language that I'm too stupid to understand? That's it, isn't it? Well, they'll be vetting you right along with me. How's that going to look to your board of directors? Now, let's get serious here."

Julia poured herself a second cup of coffee. "Yes, let's get serious. I went to the bank yesterday. You've taken three quarters of a million dollars over the years from my account. Where did it go,

Mitch? What did you do with it? Like I said, I closed out the account and I'm going to close out the others, too. You can live on your salary and might I also remind you, this is my house, left to me by my father. I can kick your ass out of here any time I want to." She tapped her foot impatiently as she waited for her husband's reply."

"You told me the money was at my disposal. I used it for things. Golf memberships don't come cheap. Clothing isn't cheap. Cars aren't cheap. The cost of dining out is astronomical. I didn't *steal* your money, Julia. You insisted on putting my name on your accounts when we got married. You said what was yours was mine. I believed you. Are you saying you lied to me?"

He was right, she'd done just what he said. But she'd been in love back then and believed her husband loved her. "The well's gone dry. You'll have to live on your salary. I meant it when I said I wanted a divorce."

"Well, I don't want a divorce, and I will fight you. I want this nomination, Julia, and I want you at my side when I accept it."

Julia pretended to think on the matter. Charles would say she overplayed her hand and now she had to backpedal. "I'll tell you what, Mitch. I promise to rethink my feelings but on one condition. I want you to sit down at the table right now and list every single woman you slept with from the day we got married, and the dates and how long the affairs lasted. Just for the record, I am not nor have I ever had an affair. The FBI can vet me from now till the end of time and I will come out clean. Unlike you, I honored my marriage vows. Take it or leave it, you son of a bitch!"

"You want me to do what?" Mitch snarled.

"You heard me the first time." Julia whirled around and fished in one of the kitchen drawers for a pencil and a pad of paper. She tossed them on the table. "Get busy because I have to leave shortly. No list, no marriage."

"You miserable bitch!"

Something snapped in Julia. Her eyes narrowed to slits, venom dripping from her tongue as she let loose. "Listen to me, you bloodsucking son of a bitch, you make the list or I will contact that guy who comes on the FOX network at eight o'clock every night and tell him my story, and your story, and I won't leave a single thing out about our perfect marriage. I'll even tell him about your made up background and that girl Janet Bradshaw the police thought you killed way back when. So you see, you aren't as smart as you think you are. I found out and so will the FBI. Now, god-damn it, write!

"I'm going upstairs to pack. When I get back here, that list better be finished."

In the whole of his life Mitch Webster had never seen such hatred spew from anyone's eyes. He reached for the pencil with the dull point. He started to write. He needed to have the last word, though. "You're going to regret this, bitch!"

"What I regret is the day I married you."

Halfway up the stairs, Julia grasped the railing and sat down on the steps to calm herself. Who was that person back in the kitchen? Her eyes welled up. That was the real Julia Webster, the Julia Webster who could be dying. That's who the person was back in the kitchen.

When she felt strong enough, Julia got to her feet, her legs shaky. She made it the rest of the way up the steps and down the hall to her bedroom. She packed a bag quickly, wondering as she did so if she'd ever come back to this house. If she couldn't go back to the hospital and couldn't come back to this house, where would she go? To the cemetery, next to her father? The tears spilled over and dropped on her hands. She brushed at them impatiently. She still had time.

Julia carried her bag downstairs and set it down by the front door before she made her way to the kitchen. Mitchell was still writing. Julia poured more coffee into the cup she'd left sitting on the counter. She risked a covert glance at the list her husband was writing. Suddenly, she felt sick to her stomach. She had no idea the list would be so long. It would take her forever to weed through the names to find out which of the women had infected her husband with the AIDS virus. She couldn't help but wonder how many of the names on the list she would recognize, how many she knew personally and how many she'd operated on.

"One has to wonder how you had time to perform your senatorial duties, Mitch. That's starting to look like a very impressive list. Did I tell you I want addresses, too?"

"No, you didn't tell me that and no, I am not writing that down because I don't know. I always met them someplace. If your next question is did I ever bring them here, the answer is no."

Julia snatched the list and read through the names. She gasped. "You did . . . and her husband never found out! I guess you were discreet because you'd be dead if he did find out, Mitch. I'm leaving now," she said as she folded the two sheets of paper and put them in her purse.

"Where are you going? What if I need to get in touch with you? The party is less than a week away. The press is going to want to talk to you. I want an answer, Julia."

"It's none of your business where I'm going. Do I ask you where you're going when you leave the house? Have your people call my people. Isn't that what all you power politicians say to each other? I'll call you when I'm ready to call you."

"Then you aren't going to file for divorce?" There was such relief in Mitch's voice, Julia almost laughed. Squirm, you miserable bastard.

"I didn't say that. I said I would think about it. I'm thinking. When I'm done thinking, I'll let you know. Now, get the hell out of my way. I can't bear to look at you. You disgust me."

Julia was outside when she remembered the green plant. She opened the door and walked back to the kitchen. Mitch had the phone to his ear, shocked to see her. What woman was he bleeding to this time? She ignored him as she picked up the plant and left the kitchen.

Seated in her car, she stared across the driveway at Mitch's bright red, $165,000 Porsche. Two seats. She'd never even ridden in the car her money had paid for. What a fool she was.

For the next four hours, Julia followed the instructions Charles had laid out for her. She shopped, she filled prescriptions, she had a bite to eat and then she headed for a well-known steak house where she parked her car and got out. A dusty black Suburban pulled right next to her car. Julia blinked when she saw Kathryn behind the wheel. She grabbed her bags and the green plant and hoisted herself into the backseat. Murphy barked a greeting from the front seat.

"How ya doing, Miss Daisy?" Kathryn laughed.

"Just peachy. Were you followed?"

"Not that I could see. Were you?"

"If I was, they're good. I don't think so but that doesn't mean anything, as we both know. God, what are we going to do about that D.A.?"

Kathryn drove the Suburban the way she drove her eighteen-wheeler, with gusto. "I guess that's up to Charles. You don't want to know what I'd do to him if it was left up to me. He grilled me months ago when he thought he had the goods on us. The guy is relentless but Nikki had it covered. She's in a bad place, Julia. She still loves the guy but her duty is to the Sisterhood. Hey, how'd it go with the senator?"

Julia told her. "The worst part was, some of those women were friends of mine. There were some I even operated on. I must be naive. Kathryn, I had no idea there were so many unhappy married women who slept around. I'm thinking he picked married women knowing they wouldn't put the squeeze on him. Married women were safe."

Kathryn leaned on the horn to speed up a gray Taurus that was going too slow for her comfort. When she sailed past him she offered up her middle finger. Julia laughed and didn't know why.

"I know this is a stupid question but are you OK, Julia? What's with the green plant?"

"Yeah, I'm OK. My last checkup was better than I expected. I'm holding my own. The new drugs are terrific. I have some time yet, Kathryn. You don't know how badly I wanted to kill my husband a few hours ago. It was all I could do not to blurt it out. But, like a good little soldier, I held my tongue just the way Charles told me to. I have to find a way to let all those women Mitch had affairs with know they need to get tested but I want to do it anonymously. Charles can help me locate them. I'm having a hard time dealing with the fact that some of my friends slept with my husband and then went to lunch with me the next day."

"Yeah, I'd say that pretty much sucks. My God, Julia, why didn't you ever tell your husband?"

Julia stared out the window. "I had to get used to . . . to . . . I just had to deal with it first. In the beginning I had to check on every patient I'd operated on in the last year. That took some time. Once I was certain I didn't get infected from one of my patients, I knew it had to be Mitch. I made myself sick over it for a while. I was almost ready to confront him when I met up with Nikki a year or so ago. The rest is history.

"The plant was in my office. No one watered it, and it was dying but I found some plant food in the nurses' kitchen and doctored it up. I guess I felt it was like me, on its last legs. Maybe with some tender loving care, it will come back to life. It has five leaves on it, Kathryn, and one that might or might not fall off. I don't want it to die, that's the bottom line. I thought maybe Myra would let me keep it on the kitchen windowsill for the morning sun."

Kathryn listened to Julia's desperate-sounding voice. "I don't think that's a problem at all. Myra loves green plants."

"But I want to take care of it."

"I don't think that will be a problem either, Julia."

"Good. What did you all do today?"

"We all watched Charles bustle about. He did take a short nap and he was right back at it. We're to meet in the war room after dinner, which, by the way, is a full-blown turkey dinner, just like at Thanksgiving. Baked Alaska for dessert. Murphy is drooling already. For some reason I don't think you're supposed to give a dog turkey. I think I read that somewhere."

"I'm sure Myra will have something for Murphy."

"The dogs are there, Julia. The handler came by this morning and Myra and he talked for a long time. Isabelle is having a dog compound constructed for them for daytime use. They eat red meat. Murphy's nose is out of joint."

"Kathryn, are you worried about Jack Emery?"

"Yeah. So are the others. If we allow him to home in on us, we're going to do a nice long stretch in the federal slammer. Your husband is a goddamn senator."

Murphy started to bark.

Kathryn laughed. "This dog is starting to think of Pinewood as home. We're almost there, Julia. You look tired. No one will mind if you take a nap before dinner."

The gates swung open. Kathryn drove through and then waited a few seconds to make sure they closed behind her before she drove on.

Home sweet home.


"That dinner was scrumptious," Isabelle said as she pushed her chair back from the table. "I feel like going to sleep right now."

Charles stood up and winked at the women. "That, dear lady, is not an option. I cooked, you all clean up. Trust me, you will wake up rather quickly when you start to scour the pans. I'm off now. Join me when your kitchen duties are finished."

"That baked Alaska will stay on my hips for months," Nikki protested as she, too, started to help clear the table. She looked over at Julia who was staring at the green plant on the kitchen windowsill.

"It should have perked up by now," Julia muttered.

"By tomorrow it will be fine," Myra soothed. Kathryn had clued her in earlier about the plant. "Maybe the plant food was old. It may require repotting. Let's just wait till morning to see how it does, Julia. I've always found philodendrons to be extremely hardy."

"I thought I was hardy, too, and looked what's happening to me,"

Julia muttered a second time. "I'll scour the pans, you dry, Nikki. We have way too many dishes for the dishwasher as it is."

"No problem," Nikki said, reaching for a dish towel. "I'm not going to be joining you all in the war room. I'm going out to the woods to talk to Jack."

Myra's hand flew to her heart. "Dear, that definitely is not a good idea. Did you tell Charles?"

"Yes, I did tell Charles, Myra. I thought I'd take Murphy with me. He'll pick up Jack's scent and lead me right to him. I worked with Charles all afternoon so I know what's going on. I don't need to be there this evening."

"What if Jack isn't out there tonight? Then what?" Myra asked, her brow furrowed in worry. "And if he is, what are you going to say to him? What if he won't listen? We all deserve to know what you're planning."

"If I knew, Myra, I would tell you. I'm going to wing it. Jack's a wild card and I don't know how he'll react or what he'll do. He is on your property, Myra, and the property is posted, which means he's trespassing. He wouldn't give a little thing like a no trespassing sign a second thought. You can have him arrested because he's breaking the law. In fact, Myra, I want you to give me fifteen minutes and then I want you to call the local police. Murphy and I will guard him and send up a flare. I'd like to see him explain all of this to his superiors."

"But won't that . . . you know . . . *piss* him off even more?"

Nikki threw her arms around Myra. "I love you, Myra," she gurgled. "Yep, it's gonna piss him off big time. But he won't try it a second time. Not if he wants to keep his job. Use your clout, Myra."

Myra looked doubtful. "All right, dear, if you say so." She looked down at her watch. "Should we synchronize our watches?"

Nikki grinned. "Yep, that's a good idea, too. She looked at both her own and Myra's watch. We're within a minute of each other. Fifteen minutes. No, better make that twenty."

Myra's heart thumped in her chest as she watched Nikki run across the yard and out the gate, Murphy on her heels.

Julia, still busy at the sink, thought about the bag of drugs she'd brought with her at Charles's instructions. Sodium Pentothal had been on the list. She looked down at the last pot in the sink, and shrugged as she reached for a Brillo pad. This was no time for any of them to get squeamish.

\* \* \*

Charles eyed the women as they took their seats at the table. From his perch, high above them, he clicked the remote in his hand and Lady Justice appeared on the monitor. She was quickly replaced with a picture of three people staring into the camera.

Charles's voice was cold when he said, "Ladies, meet the Monarch family. The woman on the right is Elaine Monarch. The man on the left is her husband Derek Monarch and the young man in the middle is their son Ethan Monarch. I've compiled a dossier on all three of them and it's in front of you, but for now I want you to pay attention to the background I'm sharing with you. Elaine Monarch is the president of Monarch HMO. Derek is the vice president and Ethan is the secretary treasurer. They've been dickering with the idea of taking the company public but that hasn't happened nor do I see it happening because they want total control.

"Elaine . . ."

"Oh, my God, I gave that woman a face lift," Julia said, interrupting Charles.

Charles didn't miss a beat. He continued right on. "Yes, I know. She inherited a rather large sum of money fifteen years ago and that was used to set up these three HMOs. The stats are in your folder and you can peruse them later. Money flows into Monarch like a raging river and the family spends it at the speed of light. Fortunately, even with all their outrageous spending, they can't spend it all. The company is more than robust. There's over a billion of unspent money that is earning healthy interest every single day. But there is one thing that eludes the Monarchs. They want an Ambassadorship to some country. They don't care if the country is one no one has ever heard of. They'll do anything for that little prize. Just keep it in mind, ladies.

"Mrs. Monarch is a collector. Of everything. At the moment she's into the Ming Dynasty. She's paid out millions for her treasures. Two years ago she was into Japanese collectibles. I understand she has a real Samurai sword and several real robes. Again, she paid out millions for these things.

"The family has houses all over the world. They spend more time in Manassas than any other place because Elaine likes to be near the power brokers in Washington. It's that old ambassador devil she covets. Ideally, they'd like His and Hers ambassadorships. Mrs. Monarch hasn't quite been able to join that elite circle of women who are the real social power brokers. The family is more or less on the fringe, rather like a small band of groupies. They would do anything to land on the A List. It won't happen because just the word

HMO leaves a bad taste in everyone's mouth. The politicians accept their money, though, so that puts them way down on the B List. I have it on good authority the family will be at the fund-raising party next week. We have to make that work to our advantage."

"That means all four of our subjects will be under the same roof. Are we going to do a snatch and grab?" Alexis asked.

Charles smiled. "That's exactly what it means. Play close attention. Yoko and Kathryn will be delivering the plants and flowers to the armory. At the end of the evening the plants and flowers will again be loaded into Kathryn's truck and taken to different hospitals and nursing homes in the area.

"Myra, one of this administration's heaviest contributors and right up there at the top of the A List will mingle and approach the Monarch family. She'll stay glued to them, right up to the end when she'll complain about how stuffy it is inside and suggest a breath of fresh air and invite them to join her.

"Julia will be there with her husband, smiling, and doing everything she's supposed to do as the wife of the soon-to-be vice president. Beforehand she will tell him that they both need to get away, to try to patch up their marriage. The plan, as far as Mitchell Webster knows, is they will leave the following morning on Myra's Gulfstream. Their destination, the Caribbean."

Kathryn whooped her pleasure. "Charles, this is so perfect. Where are we taking them? What about Jack Emery?"

Charles held up both hands for silence. "One thing at a time. I haven't definitely decided on where Operation Revenge will take place. Possibly the Monarch home in Manassas, possibly here at Pinewood. I have a great many details to work out first.

"I'm not worried about the senator and Julia. The senator will do whatever Julia wants at this point in time. Before I can plan further, all of you have to tell me what your plan is for the senator and the Monarch family. What's your decision?" He didn't pause long enough for them to answer.

"Now, I know you're all worried about Assistant District Attorney Jack Emery. Myra has a call in to the governor as we speak. For those of you who don't know this, Myra and the governor are . . . I believe the correct term would be *tight*. The governor will take care of ADA Emery. I don't think I need to spell that out, do I? Of course not, you're all way ahead of me.

"Myra, it's time for you to make your call to the police. You have two minutes. It might be wise for you to stay in the kitchen until the police arrive." Myra nodded. A moment later the secret door to the main house moved and then she was gone.

"We're missing all the fun," Kathryn groused. "I'd pay to see that ADA's ass hauled off to jail."

Yoko tilted her head to the side. "No, you wouldn't, Kathryn, because then you would have to see Nikki's tears and know her heart is breaking. It's better that none of us see that."

Kathryn reached over and squeezed Yoko's slim hand. "You're right, of course. Sometimes I speak before I think."

"Sometimes?" the others squealed. "Sometimes?"

"OK, OK, my mouth is my downfall. Can we move on here?"

"Gladly," Charles said. "Eyes on the monitor please. What I'm going to show you first is some of the decadence of the Monarch family. Then I'm going to show you some still photographs of some of Monarch's subscribers and their families. When I'm finished, I think you'll find it quite easy to come up with a suitable punishment for the Monarch family."

Charles stepped down to the main floor and walked over to Julia's chair. "When I'm finished with the stills of the Monarch family I plan to show photos of the women your husband had affairs with. It's not very pretty, Julia, so if you want to join Myra in the kitchen, it will be fine with all of us. It's up to you."

Julia clenched her teeth so hard she thought her jaw would crack. Her voice was firm, however, when she said, "I'll stay, Charles. It's not like I haven't known about them."

"All right, ladies, here we go!"


Nikki, Murphy at her side, entered the piney forest where she'd played as a child with Myra's daughter Barbara. She knew every inch of the vast forest. Oh, how they'd run and scampered out here. One time they'd even pitched a tent. Scared out of their wits, they'd managed to make it through the night with sugar cookies and peanut butter and jelly sandwiches. It wasn't until later that they found out Myra had been less than a hundred yards away making sure they were safe. They'd ridden their ponies through the forest and had picnics almost every day during the summers they were home from school.

A lump formed in her throat at her memories. Barbara was gone now and Nikki missed her terribly.

How fragrant the forest was. She sniffed appreciatively. "Oh, Jack! Come out wherever you are! C'mon, Jack, don't make me search all night! I know you're up there in one of those trees spying on Myra and everyone in the house. Be a man and come down out of that tree! Don't make me come up there after you!" Nikki shouted. When there was no response, Nikki looked down at Murphy. "Go get him, Murph!" The huge shepherd raced off, Nikki right on his heels.

When Murphy skidded to a halt and started to growl, Nikki slowed down. She casually meandered over to a tree and flashed the beam of her flashlight upward. "It's supposed to rain tonight, Jack! Come on down and let's go into the house for some coffee. It's going to be a very cold spring rain. You know you're trespassing, right?"

Jack Emery cursed as he slid down the tree. "The stars are out so I doubt it's going to rain. The temperature is seventy. Trespassing? I didn't damage the tree. I was communing with nature. Isn't that what you're doing, Counselor? So, run me off. Or are you planning on calling the cops? Nice doggie," Jack said, attempting to pat Murphy on the head. The shepherd growled once, then again, before he lunged. Nikki pulled him back before his teeth could sink into Jack's arm.

Nikki's laugh sounded forced to her ears. "Do I look like I'm calling the cops? Go ahead, search me, I don't even have my cell phone with me. I came out here to tell you to get off Myra's property. She doesn't like it when people spy on her. You were spying on her, Jack. And guess what else, I don't like it either. You're really becoming a pain in my ass, ADA Emery."

"Then fess up and I'll get out of your hair," Jack said coldly.

"That ain't gonna happen, Jack, since only a fool would confess to something they didn't do. Get over that cockamamie notion you have that Myra did something illegal. I don't want to hear your theory that rich people are above the law."

"You're pretty cocky there, Counselor. Does it have anything to do with Myra's house guest, the one whose hubby's going to be the next veep? Poor choice. The guy's a dud."

"Be that as it may, it's none of your business who Myra entertains."

"Sure it is, Nik. That just shoots old Myra right up there on the Washington power pole."

"You're paranoid where Myra is concerned. You need to get over Marie Llewellyn. So you had her under house arrest. So she took off on you. She had help. It was a wild and stormy night. Stop blaming yourself and stop trying to pin her disappearance on Myra. In other words, get over it, Jack."

"Then why did you dump me? We were engaged, Nik. We were supposed to get married. You said you'd love me forever. When push came to shove, you chose Myra over me. There had to be a pretty strong reason for you to do something like that."

"Yeah. Like maybe Myra adopting me when my parents died? Like maybe Myra taking care of me, sending me to college and being a mother to me. Yeah, I'd say that's a pretty damn strong reason to side with her. It didn't have to be that way but you're so damn pig-headed you wouldn't listen to reason."

Jack pushed his billed camouflage cap farther back on his head. He was so damn weary. "You're blowing smoke, trying to divert me. It's not going to work, Nik."

Oh, isn't it? Nikki thought as she saw pinpoints of light in the distance. Her stomach started to crunch up at the thought of the police taking Jack off in handcuffs. Jack saw the lights at the same time and prepared to run, but Murphy had other ideas.

"Stop where you are and put your hands in the air," came the command. Nikki's hands shot in the air in the blink of an eye. Jack wasn't quite as fast but his hands did go up.

"You witch! You miserable, lying witch! You called the cops and tricked me! Jesus, what the hell *are* you women doing in that house? This is a new low even for you, Nik."

Nikki didn't respond, she was too choked up. She started off in the direction of the house. She knew if she looked back, she'd crumble into a million pieces. She started to run but Murphy beat her by a nose. She collapsed in Myra's arms.

"Are you all right, dear?"

Not "What happened, is he going to turn us in?" No, that wasn't Myra. Myra loved her and her first concern was her welfare. Whatever Jack did or said, she would deal with.

"I'm OK, Myra. They took him off in handcuffs. I didn't stick around to watch but I did hear the clink of the cuffs. He was madder than a wet rooster, I can tell you that. There was a little name-calling but nothing I can't handle. Myra, he isn't going to give up. We have to make some decisions."

Myra wrapped Nikki in her arms. "I've taken care of everything, dear. I called the governor. Word will filter down to the right people within the hour. Mr. Emery will not be bothering us any longer."

Nikki gasped. "You called the governor of Virginia because . . . because . . ."

"Because ADA Emery is becoming a thorn in our side. As you know, Tyson Jackson is a personal friend. He's been here to dinner more times than I can remember and I am the godmother of his first grandchild. One always calls upon one's friends when one is in trouble, although I didn't say I was in trouble. Tyson said he would take care of the matter, so we don't have to worry about Mr. Emery any longer. I took care of everything, dear, so don't worry."

Nikki slapped at her forehead. "Oh, God, Myra, that's where you're wrong. You don't know Jack. Having the governor intervening on your behalf will just convince him that we're up to something. I want you to believe me when I tell you Jack will quit his job and make this personal. He's like that, a dog with a bone. He never gives up until he gets a conviction. What we did tonight was piss him off to the nth degree. Now, he'll be out for blood. This is all my fault, Myra. I shouldn't have had you call the cops. I wish you had told me you were going to call the governor."

"Maybe I wasn't cut out for this spy game," Myra said as she led Nikki and Murphy into the house. "It's starting to rain, dear. We should roll up the awning on the terrace. Never mind, let it get wet, who cares?"

"Jack didn't believe me when I told him it was going to rain," Nikki said.

Myra whirled around. "Is that important, Nicole?"

In spite of herself, Nikki burst out laughing. "No, Myra, it isn't important. The damn awning isn't important either. Neither is Jack getting arrested."

"Would you like some hot cocoa, dear?"

"God, no, Myra. I'm going to bed."

"Good night, dear. Sleep tight," Myra said as she pecked Nikki on the cheek.

"You, too, Myra."


A hollow-eyed, unshaven Jack Emery marched into his office. No one looked at him. Maybe he smelled. He was angrier than he'd ever been in his life. One night in jail could do that to a person. He'd been released on his own recognizance and told to report to his superior, Chad Bartlett, stat, which meant immediately in D.A. speak. So, here he was. And there was District Attorney Chad Bartlett, clean-shaven, dewy-eyed and smelling like the prairie.

"Don't say a word, Emery, not one goddamn word. I got a call from the police commissioner last night. He actually woke me up. He said he got a call from the mayor. It seems the mayor got a call from the governor. You following me here, Jack?"

Jack winced. "Yes, sir."

"It seems that Ms. Myra Rutledge called her good friend Tyson Jackson over at the governor's mansion and said you were perched in a tree and trespassing and spying on her and her guests and she wanted you arrested and she didn't want it to happen again. And then this morning, my secretary handed me a copy of this police report that has your name on it. You better have a damn good explanation, son."

Jack licked at his dry lips. The inside of his mouth felt and smelled like his old sneakers. He cleared his throat. "I believe Myra Rutledge and a group of her friends are involved in illegal activities. I think they're the ones who spirited Marie Llewellyn . . ."

"Stop right there, Emery. The woman disappeared on your watch. You take responsibility for that. We've been over that, up and down that, and we even went over it crossways. Myra Rutledge had a rock solid alibi on that night. Don't go there again, Emery. This has something to do with your fiancée, according to your coworkers. If I even get a sniff of something going on where you and your colleagues are concerned, I'll personally throw the book at you. Miss Rutledge, her friends and her adopted daughter Nicole Quinn will be forever off-limits to you. All I need is one sniff, Jack, that you aren't following orders, and it's all over."

Jack's mind raced as he tried to calculate how much money he had in his account. Maybe he could draw on his 401K. "I need to apply for a thirty-day leave of absence, sir," he said stiffly.

"Denied. Is there anything else?"

"Sir, my mother is ill. She's in a nursing home. I need the time. If you can't see to granting the leave then I have to resign." His mother was ill and in a nursing home but his taking a month off wouldn't help her in any way. It could all be verified. *Liar, liar, pants on fire.* Whatever it takes, Emery, whatever it takes.

"All right, Jack, I'll give you the month with the understanding and the promise that you will not harass or cause Myra Rutledge one iota of trouble. Assign your pending cases to whomever you think is best equipped to handle them. Remember what I said, one sniff of anything improper and your ass is on the unemployment line."

"Yes, sir. Thank you, sir."

"Go home and take a bath, for God's sake. You're smelling up my office. And, Emery, Ms. Rutledge, fine woman that she is, will not press charges if you toe the line. Step over it and you're in the slammer. Go on, get out of here!"

An hour later, Jack Emery was back in his apartment, hunched over his computer. The small television he kept on the kitchen counter was turned on to CNN, his favorite news channel. He felt lower than a snake's belly as he mapped out his itinerary for the next thirty days. He'd used up all his favors with his friends so he was on his own. He knew in his gut if he made one misstep, his ass would go in a sling and he'd be out of a job. If he wasn't careful, he could be living on the street.

The headache pounding inside his skull was louder than a bongo drum. Where the hell should he start? With those women of course. He hadn't been lying to Nikki when he said he'd run profiles on every one of them. They were as complete as Lexis Nexis could make them. He turned when he heard the name Webster on the television. The doctor's husband, Senator Webster, was going to be Governor Crawford's running mate in the presidential election. Whoa!

Jack sat back in his swivel chair, his mind racing. If it was true, and CNN rarely got it wrong, why was Dr. Webster hanging out at Pinewood? Shouldn't she be at her husband's side, being interviewed over and over again? He put a large red question mark on Julia's folder. Then he added a second one for emphasis. She'd consulted Nikki Quinn's law firm but whatever went down there was considered privileged.

He moved on to Isabelle Flanders. He studied the report. At the height of her career she'd been involved in a terrible car accident killing an entire family. He remembered the case well. Her defense had been beyond weak, blaming her assistant for the accident. Till the end of the trial she'd professed her innocence. She'd lost everything, her home, her business, her reputation. She'd floundered for a while, working in a dress shop, a convenience store and other menial jobs. She'd consulted with Nikki's firm but again it was privileged.

Alexis Thorne wasn't really Alexis Thorne at all. She'd been convicted of securities fraud and sent to prison. She'd served her time, gotten out, and changed her name, presumably with Nikki's help since she, too, had consulted with Nikki's legal firm. Now she worked as a personal shopper to the rich and famous. Again, everything was privileged.

Kathryn Lucas. He flinched when he remembered how he'd had her and her eighteen-wheeler hauled into the compound. He'd grilled her, with Nikki representing her, but he'd gotten nothing from the woman. Dead husband. She worked with a ferocious dog, the same dog who'd held him at bay last night in the woods. He had no clue as to why a truck driver would consult Nikki's high-end law firm.

Yoko Akia had consulted Nikki, too, possibly for incorporation of her garden nursery. Nothing out of the ordinary had surfaced on his various searches for her or her husband. For all intents and purposes, both husband and wife were who and what they said they were.

Jack chewed on his lower lip. The one thing they all had in common was Nikki. There was no way that group of women would have found Myra Rutledge on their own. None of them had anything in common with Myra. It all came back to Nikki.

Jack got up to take some aspirin and to make coffee. One of these days, he thought, I really have to get some sleep. I can't keep going on pure adrenaline. He stared out his kitchen window as he tried to make sense of everything.

Nikki knew all the women, probably represented them all or, at the very least, counseled them. Myra had the money. Maybe she was helping the women on Nikki's advice. Myra was known for her philanthropy. But this time she was all over the map. Odd for Myra.

One thing he was certain of, the women didn't meet up at Pinewood to play cards. They met up to . . . to . . . do what? Jack had to admit he didn't have a clue. Then there was the business with the pack of Dobermans. Myra never felt the need to have guard dogs in the past. Why now all of a sudden? Why was everyone so bent out of shape because he was spying on them? What were they afraid he would see? He wrote the word SECRET in big red letters on top of Nikki's folder. All he had to do was find out what the secret was.

Jack slouched up against the kitchen counter while he waited for the coffee to finish dripping into the pot. He'd purposely made the coffee strong, so strong it looked like tar. For sure his eyeballs would pop to attention.

The secret! What the hell was the secret? Think, Emery. How in the hell was he going to find out what it was since Nikki chopped him off at the knees?

Jack carried his coffee back to his desk, shifted his mental gears to what he called his neutral zone, and let his mind take off. Everything went haywire with Nikki when Myra's daughter was killed. Good, good, Emery, great jumping-off spot. Nikki changed then and so did their relationship. Then came Marie Llewellyn's trial. He'd prosecuted her because that was his job. It didn't mean he didn't feel the woman's pain. He wasn't heartless. *Hell, if someone raped my daughter who knows what I would do. I was doing my goddamn job was what I was doing.* He scribbled furiously. The rape killer had gotten off scot-free thanks to a creative defense team. Then when the killer walked down the court steps, Marie Llewellyn pulled out a gun and shot him. Right in front of the whole world to see on their television sets.

Llewellyn had been arrested. Nik got pissed off. Myra posted a million dollars bail to get the woman placed under house arrest. There had been a rumor going around that Myra had called her old friend the governor to intercede on the bail, a rumor that Nik refused to confirm or deny. Nik asked him not to prosecute because she was going to defend Llewellyn. He'd refused. They had one fight after the other. Nik sided with Myra. Oh yeah, Nik sided with Myra. Myra again. Filthy rich Myra. Jack continued to scribble.

Ooops. Back up, Emery. According to Nik, Myra was the next thing to catatonic over the death of her daughter. Then, all of a sudden, Myra is full of piss and vinegar and wants Nik to defend Marie Llewellyn. Myra posts the outrageous bail. What's wrong with this picture, he wondered. He scribbled some more.

Then just before trial, Marie Llewellyn and her family disappear. For all intents and purposes, they simply walked out of the house, leaving everything behind. On one of the stormiest nights of the year. The children's toys, their bank books, food, their cars—everything was left behind. They weren't rich. In fact their savings account held a meager $751. Their checking account held $81.25. The family walked away with whatever they had in their pockets.

Because . . . because . . . They had help. He'd gone so far as to accuse Nik and Myra of spiriting the family away. Of course they'd denied any and all involvement. That's when things had really soured between himself and Nik.

Myra had flourished, though, while Nik just got more hateful. Then Nik moved back to the farm and the card games started. "Card games my ass," Jack muttered.

Jack spent the next ten minutes taping together sheets of paper that he then taped to his living room wall. With a red marker he proceeded to draw a map, enter notes and draw arrows all over the place. He mumbled as he swirled and twirled his marker until he was satisfied. He stared at the names on the right hand side of his map. Okayyyyy. The red marker scrawled across the page. More arrows followed.

Nikki and Myra. Myra and Nikki. The brains and the money. The money and the brains. What the hell were they into? Something serious, that's for sure. But what?

The red marker moved again. Doctor, florist, architect, securities broker turned personal shopper, truck driver, lawyer, rich woman. Then there was Charles. Just who the hell was he?

Truck. Medicine. Architect. Flowers. Legal. Money. Truck. Jack drew a big red circle around the word truck. An eighteen-wheeler. You could put two cars in one of those babies. Webster was a plastic surgeon. Maybe she gave the Llewellyn family a whole new look. How far-fetched was *that*? The red marker moved again and again. The truck could have been used to spirit the family away. Now *that* was not far-fetched.

Myra's money could have been used to give the family a new identity. Not far-fetched at all. Nikki was part of it. The brains.

But . . . That was all months and months ago. Why were the women still meeting at Pinewood? The same women. Why did Nikki take a leave of absence from her job and her teaching position?

It was a club. A goddamn fucking club of some kind where those seven women did . . . what did they do? Something outside the law? Something they needed Nikki to orchestrate while Myra paid the bills.

Jack went back to the kitchen to pour more coffee into his cup. It was still hot, still black, and it tasted like crap. He drank it anyway.

He was closing in, getting a handle on things. He could feel it. Nikki used to tease him about his gut instincts while he teased her about her woman's intuition. What a match they were. And now it was all gone.

Maybe he needed some expert help. Someone with clearer vision, someone who could be objective. Maybe his old friend Mark Lane in the J. Edgar Hoover Building. He thought about it for all of ten seconds before he reached for the phone but suddenly, he couldn't remember the number. That had to mean he hadn't called his buddy in a long time. He fumbled for his address book and dialed Mark's cell phone. The FBI agent picked up on the third ring. Jack identified himself and they talked pleasantries until Mark said, "I hope to hell you aren't calling me because you want me to get you some information from the FBI database."

"Nah. I want you to meet me for a drink. I have a story to tell you and I need your analytical input. Yeah, I'm paying. I invited you, didn't I? No, Nikki and I are on the outs. Actually, she dumped me. Yeah, yeah, I couldn't believe it either. She'll never find anyone half as good as me. Yeah, I'm saying that with a straight face. Seven o'clock at Mc Guire's. See ya, buddy."

Jack spent the next few hours going over his finances. If he sold his skis, his snowboard, his snorkeling gear, took cash advances on his credit cards that were almost to the max, plus what he could wrangle out of his 401K, he should be able to get through the month, pay his rent, his car payment, the minimum on his plastic and eat macaroni and cheese, and peanut butter and jelly, he might squeak by. But, just in case, he went online and applied for a new credit card and then filled out the forms to increase his credit line on his existing cards.

His mind going full blast, he headed for the shower. He emerged feeling almost like his old self. It was always this way when he was closing in on the tail end of a case.

With nothing else to occupy his time, Jack went back on the computer to do more searches on the women who played cards at Pinewood.

Two hours later, Jack walked back to the kitchen, this time for a beer. Alexis Thorne's case bothered him. Nothing in her background even alluded to the fact that she was dishonest. On the contrary. She'd protested her innocence, said she was set up, but she was convicted anyway. She was from a poor black family but she'd worked her way through college. She belonged to the drama club because she wanted to be an actress but didn't have the talent, so she'd gone into costume and makeup and learned all the tricks of the trade.

When she graduated from college she'd gone to work in a small brokerage firm where she was able make use of her education while still pursuing her drama hopes by volunteering her services for Little Theater. Her mentor, a guy named Cyril Therman, had bequeathed his "bag of tricks" to Alexis on his death bed. Or so said the only interview Alexis had ever given after being convicted of securities fraud. Some smart-ass lawyer must have told her a good human interest story would go a long way at her sentencing. It hadn't.

Jack went back to his map on the wall and wrote the words makeup, costumes, disguise. It sort of went with Dr. Webster's specialty, plastic surgery. Underneath he wrote the word "innocent" with a large question mark. His heart started to thump in his chest when he moved down to Isabelle Flanders's name. She, too, said she was innocent. Said one of her trusted employees was driving the car that killed a family.

Two women who claimed to be innocent of the crimes they were convicted of.

Well, what have we here? A lot of loose ends. Maybe Mark would see something he wasn't seeing. Maybe.

Seven o'clock couldn't come soon enough for him.


It was like every other bar in D.C. All mahogany, brass, and sawdust on the floor. A local watering hole for the young hipsters and government workers. The only problem was you couldn't hear yourself think, much less carry on a conversation. However, it was a good place to ogle the sleek young female lawyers with their tight suits and roving eyes. With no interest in ogling anyone, Jack had chosen seven o'clock to meet up with Mark because the five o'clock crowd was starting to leave and the evening customers hadn't arrived yet. He figured he had a forty-five minute window to tell Mark his story and get his feedback.

Like old buddies, they clapped each other on the back before they bellied up to the mahogany bar for their Buds and waited for a table to clear in the back of the bar. While they waited they dissected every female within eye range, a temporary distraction to pass the time. When a table cleared they beelined to it and yelled their order to a cute waitress who grinned at them. Her skimpy shorts, long legs and tight spandex top did not go unnoticed.

Jack blurted out his story as he played with the long-neck in his hands. When he finally wound down he said, "I need you to tell me if I'm nuts or if I've got something going on here."

Mark removed his glasses, pinched the bridge of his nose and then settled the wire rims more firmly before he spoke. "Man, you got something going on here. You took a fucking month off just to work on this! What if you can't nail it by the end of the month?"

Jack eyed the pudgy man sitting across from him. His dark brown eyes behind his wire rimmed glasses were starting to steam up with his excitement. It looked to Jack like Mark was losing his hair, too. Better not to mention something so personal. Damn, it had been a while since they'd seen each other. "I don't know, Mark. I just know I gotta do it. What's your spin on this?"

"Off the top of my head, and it's a wild guess on my part, I think you're looking at a bunch of female vigilantes. What's with that Charles character?"

Jack shrugged.

"Maybe he's the brains of the outfit. Excuse me but I think you're giving Nikki too much credit here and, besides, you want it to be her so you can get even with her. How'm I doing so far?"

"To what end? Who? What? Where?"

"How the hell do I know? You just told me the damn story. The only player I know is Nikki. Maybe that Llewellyn babe was their first shot. Hey, it worked, smart ass. She's gone and it was on your watch. Maybe they're gearing up for something else. The only thing of interest going on in this town right now is Senator Webster being picked to be Crawford's running mate. Both parties are sniping at each other. Nothing new there. No big time stuff out of the ordinary is going on at the Bureau. The world is a crazy place these days, Jack."

Their double burgers and sides of fries arrived along with two more long-necks. The friends wolfed down the burgers and ordered seconds. While they waited, Jack said, "What would you do if you were me?"

"Go home and get under the covers and don't come out till the end of the month. How the hell should I know what you should do? You're not going to leave it alone, are you?"

Jack shook his head.

"That's what I thought." Mark sighed. "OK, what do you want me to do?"

"You're pretty much a nine-to-five guy. Help me out at night. See what you can come up with on Charles Martin and Senator Webster. In the morning I'll drop off the files I've accumulated unless you want to go home with me and get them tonight. By the way, how's your love life?"

"In the dumps like yours. Don't go there, Jack. You're gonna owe me for this."

"Yeah, I know. Good burgers, eh?" Jack said, chomping down on his.

Between mouthfuls of food, Mark asked, "Just how rich is Myra Rutledge?"

"Fortune 500 company. Did I say she's personal friends of the governor? She called him last night to get me off the property. Don't you think that's a stretch?"

Mark belched, then apologized. "Depends on what she's involved in and what she's trying to hide. Everyone needs a big gun to call on when their ass is about to be nailed to the wall. It doesn't get any better than being on a first name basis with the governor of this fine state."

Jack leaned back in his chair. "You're my big gun, Mark."

"God help us both, Jack, if I'm the best you can do."

# Chapter Six

"Are you ready, girls?" Myra all but squealed, her face alight with excitement.

"We're ready, we're ready. Show us! Myra, stop torturing us," Isabelle shouted to be heard over the din of the others.

"All right, all right! Our outfits arrived just minutes ago. I couldn't wait to show them to you and Charles is slightly miffed that I pulled you all out of the command center. Fashions first! Who wants to go first?"

"Me! Please let it be me," Yoko said.

Myra smiled as she rummaged among the tissue paper in the huge white box that had arrived by courier. She withdrew an electric blue gown with a stand up collar and a generous slit that was thigh high. The gown was so severe it shrieked dollar signs. Yoko rolled her eyes in ecstasy. "I've never had anything so grand. Thank you, Myra."

"Kiddo, you are going to look like the empress of China. Was she beautiful?"

Yoko giggled. "No, but that is all right. I will accept the compliment."

Myra rummaged again among the tissue paper. "This is for you, Julia," she said, handing over a slim, gold leaf dress with a high neck and long sleeves.

"Oh, this is too gorgeous for words," Julia said. "I love the way the dress flares at the ankle. Matching shoes. I hope I don't have to do much walking."

"Not to worry, dear. We'll take your rubber soled shoes in the limousine when we have to . . . ah . . . burn rubber." She held out a scarlet dress to Kathryn who blinked.

"I'm going to feel naked, Myra. I never wore a strapless gown in my life. Are you sure it will stay up?"

Alexis giggled. "I'll make sure it stays up. It's gorgeous. Absolutely gorgeous."

Nikki's gown was black shot through with silver threads. Isabelle ooohed and aaahed over her white crepe gown with spaghetti straps and a flare at the knees. Alexis reached for her gown that was the color of sienna. It too was strapless.

"Show us yours, Myra. What color did you choose?" the women asked all at the same time.

"I chose dusty rose and my gown has a hip length sheer coat. Silver shoes and bag. I'm so glad you all like your dresses. It was so hard to choose."

"Who is the designer?" Kathryn asked, peering at the label.

"No one famous. Yet. I expect she will be after Saturday night, though. Be sure to tell the press your outfits were designed by Callie. That's the name she goes by. Her real name is Calista Cole. She's a client of Nikki's. I think we should be getting back to Charles. We certainly don't want him upset today of all days."

"No, we certainly don't want to do that because then he'll serve us wieners for dinner. I hate wieners. Isn't today the day . . . ?"

"The day Charles drops the first bombshell to the tabloids on Mitch. Yep," Julia said happily as she led the way down the steps and across the hall to the living room where Myra opened the secret door to what she called Charles's Lair.

The women filed into the war room and took their seats. Their thoughts, however, were back in Myra's bedroom with the Callie fashions they would all be wearing in a little over thirty-six hours. They came back to reality when Charles homed in on Julia. He didn't say anything but waited for her to speak, his eyes full of questions.

"I haven't actually spoken to Mitch, Charles. He's called numerous times and left messages. The last message he left said he is the definite choice although he and the governor are the only ones who know that. The official announcement and his acceptance will be made on Saturday evening. They always pretend no one knows but everyone inside the Beltway knows before it even happens. Some of his messages weren't too nice but then Mitch isn't very nice these days. I did leave one message saying I would be home this evening. I really don't want to go until tomorrow. The less time I have to spend with him, the better."

"Tomorrow will be fine, Julia. I don't want you to put any undue stress on yourself. Our first little tidbit will hit the airwaves around noon today. I already sent an anonymous E-mail to one of the tabloids. It goes without saying that the senator will be unavailable for comment. He'll call the charge scurrilous and say it was put out by the other side. A dirty tricks campaign. By next week it will be a free-for-all. Now, have you all come up with a plan of action?"

"We have, Charles, but we need to know the location before we can put it into play."

Charles pressed a button on his remote. A blueprint sprang into view. Charles clicked the remote again to enlarge the print on the screen. "This is the floor plan of the Monarch house in Manassas. I considered several choices but in the end this one won out. Because, just in case anyone sees the truck or the limo entering the estate, it will be OK. Everyone got invited back to the Monarch home for drinks after the party. There's nothing unusual about that at all.

"I've taken the liberty of arranging vacations for the help. All six of them, a housekeeper, cook, chauffeur, gardener and two maids will board Myra's Gulfstream for a fully paid three week vacation in the Caribbean. The Monarchs have always been more than generous with their servants so this will not raise any eyebrows. They will board the plane right after the Monarchs leave for the party, having been told by the new chauffeur that their employers are going to Europe for a month.

"I've engaged the services of several operatives whom I trust implicitly. They will open the house, clear the alarm system, deactivate the security gates outside and then put us in a lock-down mode until our mission is completed. Are there any questions?"

There was only one question, posed by Yoko. "What about Jack Emery?"

Nikki was about to reassure her when Charles quietly responded to the question. "ADA Emery has taken a thirty day leave of absence. He is under surveillance and will remain under surveillance for the next thirty days. If he goes anywhere near any of you, we'll know in an instant and in that instant we will be forced to make a decision. Do you all understand what I just said?"

Nikki looked everywhere but at Charles.

"Would you care to divulge your plans for the senator and the Monarchs?" Charles asked as though he was inquiring about the weather.

"Actually, Charles, we're winging this one. We want you and Myra to come back here after the party. That means you'll have to engage two limousines for Saturday night. I'll dismiss the driver who takes Mitch and myself by saying we're going with friends for drinks. No details."

"That's not a problem. You'll all have your secure cell phones and we will be available should you need us."

"Charles, would you mind bringing up that blueprint again and printing it out for us. There's a home theater in the house, isn't there?"

"Complete with popcorn machine. And a bowling alley and an indoor pool."

"What about computer equipment?" Nikki asked.

"They have it all, Nikki."

"A safe?" Alexis queried.

Charles smiled. "Several, as a matter of fact. One vault. I marked them with big red Xs on the original copy. If your next question is where do they keep their business records, the answer is in the floor safe in the laundry room. The Monarchs cart those records with them everywhere they go."

The women eyed Charles with baffled expressions.

"How do you know this?" Yoko squeaked.

Charles smiled. "Let's just say I know, and leave it at that."

"Which safe holds their personal bank records? I'm assuming you know that, too, right?" Isabelle asked.

Charles chuckled. "Of course I know the answer. The box spring in the guest bedroom on the second floor, the second room going down the hall, has been hollowed out in the center. The records are right there just waiting for you. The Monarchs seldom have guests while they're in Manassas so the maids aren't overly zealous in their cleaning duties."

Kathryn's eyes widened in awe. "And you know this . . . how? Never mind. I'm sorry I asked."

Charles smiled. He loved it when he could surprise the sisters. He reached across to the printer for the copies of the Monarchs' floor plans and passed them around the table. He was back at his computer station in a second. He turned the volume up on one of the television monitors.

The women looked upward and gasped.

"Can this be true?" someone named Jared on the FOX network asked a visiting guest.

The guest, a retired something-or-other, the way most of FOX's guests were, grimaced as he shrugged his shoulders. "I think this is Washington political spin. If you're asking me if Senator Webster is a philanderer, my answer is I have no way of knowing. You could ask him for a comment."

Charles risked a glance at Julia who was biting down on her lower lip, her hands clenched into fists on the table.

"The senator hasn't been available for comment. His aide said it was hogwash and just spin because his boss is on the short list."

A second retired something-or-other spoke up. "Where there's smoke there's fire. I would be interested in the women's comments. I understand one name is already public and up on Matt Drudge's Web site. Hey, we're talking about the veep nomination. The ghouls are out there. Both sides do the same thing. They have specialists who dig up dirt; we all know that."

Jared looked from one to the other of his retired guests. "What do you think something like this will do to his nomination?"

The first retiree spoke up, "Depends whether Webster comes out and makes a comment. It's usually best to be front and center and bite the bullet. If he waffles and the press comes up with proof, he's dead in the water."

The second retiree smirked. "All the senator needs to do is admit to a little dalliance, with his wife on his arm saying she knew and forgave him a long time ago."

Jared looked into the camera and said, "Thank you, gentlemen, I'm sorry to cut you short but we're heading into a hard break."

Charles turned down the volume on the television. "Any comments?"

Julia looked sick at what she'd just seen. "Mitch won't make a comment. He's too arrogant. He'll call it bullshit smut being dug up by the other side to embarrass him. Or, he might accuse me of leaking it all for my own personal reasons. One thing I know for certain, he will be absolutely livid. Ah, my phone is vibrating." Julia reached to her belt where her cell phone was clipped. "Yes, it's Mitchell. Obviously, I am not going to answer the phone."

"Having said that, I suggest we get down to work, girls," Alexis said. "Charles, are we going to the party under our own names or are we using aliases? Do we have invitations? Do we need to alter our appearance?"

"Yes, to everything. Aliases of course. I created copies of the invitation from Myra's original. And, yes, ladies, you all need to alter your appearance, not that you aren't beautiful as you are. Nothing drastic, slight changes so if anyone is asked to recall any of you, their description at best will be vague. Myra and I will be going as ourselves since we will be returning here after the party. We always go to these functions so we're not going to appear out of place. I'm going to leave you for a while to do whatever you have to do. I'll start dinner. Myra, keep your eye on the oven. Oh, one last thing. Julia, let me know when you leave. I want to make sure you're not followed and I want you kept safe. Promise me."

Julia felt a lump form in her throat. "I promise."

# Chapter Seven

Mark Lane cursed as he wedged his way into traffic, three cars behind the shiny black Mercedes. He didn't like a three-car lead; two was best if you didn't want to lose the person you were tailing. Since he had Dr. Webster's home address, he wasn't too worried that he might lose her in late Friday night traffic. Still, Jack would pitch a fit if he did lose the woman and she went somewhere else. Where the hell would she go in the pouring rain? Women didn't like to get their hair wet. Nah, she was going home. He called Jack who was somewhere on the same road he was, tailing the big rig with the two women who had left earlier.

Mark reached over to the passenger seat for his cell phone and worked his speed dial. "Where are you, kemosabe?"

"Sitting in traffic. Where are you?" came the response.

"Tailing the doctor. Do you believe this rain? I'd probably make better time if I got out and started to swim. She's three cars ahead of me. Don't worry, I'm not going to lose her. I have eyes like a hawk. Where's that rig going?"

"Alexandria would be my guess. The Asian girl buys in volume from that particular nursery. Why she's going there at this hour of the night is beyond me. Wouldn't surprise me one bit if she isn't doing the decorating at the armory for the shindig tomorrow. You can fit a lot of plants in back of one of those rigs."

"Listen, Jack, I have to hang up. It's raining harder and we're coming up to a few exits. If I can't see in this glop, I might miss her."

The wipers on Lane's Pathfinder worked furiously against the driving rain. Visibility was almost nil with a low fog starting to roll in. Mark cursed again until he saw the Mercedes inch to the right. Good, she was getting off the highway. He wasn't sure but he thought he left the fog behind. If there was one thing in life he hated, it was fog with a bunch of asshole Washington drivers.

He was behind her now and within minutes knew she was indeed headed to Georgetown. He followed her as far as Dumbarton, parked, got out and ran back to the street where the doctor lived. Mark pulled up the hood of his sweatshirt as he pretended to be on his way home. He passed the senator's driveway aware that the doctor was just sitting in her car with the lights off. What did that mean?

Mark continued walking to the corner, then doubled back. Ah, she was getting out of the car and walking toward the front door. He stepped behind a firethorn bush and tried to ignore the rain dripping down his neck. Looks like the senator is home, too, he thought as he peered through the leaves of the firethorn bush at a spiffy Porsche sitting right next to the Mercedes. These people paid more for their cars than he'd earn in five years, maybe seven. Shit!

He watched as Dr. Webster started toward the house. A sensor light came on and he could see her clearly. She looked tired and unhappy. She also didn't look like she was in a hurry to enter the house. As she drew closer he saw something else he wasn't expecting to see. He saw the doctor raise her hand and bless herself before she entered the house. Son of a bitch!

Mark raced back to where he'd parked his car on Dumbarton. He worked his speed dial a second time. Jack sounded tired when he responded.

"OK, buddy, our bird's in the nest. Listen, I have to tell you something. Our bird is scared out of her wits. I was *this* close to her, behind a bush. Her feet were dragging. She didn't want to go into that house. She also made the sign of the cross before she opened the door. I don't feel right leaving but I'm not supposed to be here. My section chief will string me up by my balls if he finds out. Should I go home now?"

"Yeah, go on home, Mark. I owe you. We're just observing. We can't interfere. For starters, I live in Virginia. Yeah, yeah, you fibbies supercede us dicks. But I don't want you getting your ass in a sling with your boss either. You sure we're covered for tomorrow night? I don't want to show up and get my ass bounced outta there."

"Section chief approved it. We got more than a dozen guys out with some kind of crud. The gig tomorrow night is considered a big shit detail. My boss hates these things and is grateful for your help. I don't know how grateful he'd be if he knew why you wanted to be at the armory tomorrow night. Tobias approved you and signed off on it. I have the papers right here in the car. We're supposed to show up at four-thirty. We're teamed together and working the parking lot. If it rains, we're screwed."

"It's not going to rain, Mark. The rain is supposed to clear out by morning. My girls are doing just what I thought they were doing, loading the truck with plants and flowers. I'm going home now myself. Make sure you're back at Myra's by eight o'clock tomorrow morning."

"Listen, Jack, I don't feel right about leaving. I'm worried about that woman but I guess you're right, we can't get involved." Mark made a right-hand turn and drove through a mini pond. "Jack, did you hear the news today?"

"Is somebody bombing us? If not, I don't want to hear it."

"Yeah, you do. They're saying Senator Webster had some extramarital affairs and the women are going to come forward to confirm it. I heard it on the FOX network this afternoon. How's that going to play out tomorrow night?"

"Jesus! Are you sure it's Senator Webster?"

"Yes, I'm sure. The senator wasn't available for comment. You have to wonder if Dr. Webster knows. Maybe she knows all about it and that's why she's spending so much time at Pinewood. Women consoling women. That kind of thing. Maybe that's why she wasn't anxious to go in the house. I bet she knows."

"We'll talk in the morning. I need to think about what you just told me. By the way, what did you find on Charles Martin?"

"Give me a break, Jack. I was going to work on that when I got home. My home computer is tied into the one at the office. You have me going in six different directions. I can tell you this, the guy didn't exist prior to his employment at the Rutledge candy company. I did get that far."

"What the hell does that mean, Mark?"

"It means your guy doesn't have a background. No trace of him up to the day he started to work as head of security at the Rutledge business. I'll check Interpol. I have a few contacts abroad. Listen, I'm home. We can talk in the morning."

"Wait a minute, Mark. Run a check on Myra, too, way back to when she was born, OK?"

"Sure, why was I stupid enough to think I need sleep."

Ten minutes later, Jack parked his car in the first parking space he could find. He needed to think about what Mark had just said. He racked his brain as he made his way to his apartment in the pouring rain to remember everything Nikki had ever said about Myra's live-in companion. The only thing he could come up with was Charles should be anointed for sainthood. He was a gourmet cook, he loved Myra and Nikki and he had loved Barbara, too. He ran security at the candy plant. He had all kinds of talents. He knew Myra when they were young. Myra had gone to England with her father, and they met and fell in love, and then something went awry. What went awry? Did Nik ever tell him? If she did, he couldn't remember.

Was Charles British? For some reason, he thought so. He'd been in his company twice to his knowledge. Did the man speak? Shit, he couldn't remember. He should know that. Yeah, yeah, he was British. Nik said he made Beef Wellington all the time but no one liked it but Charles. He liked to drink PIM's too, a British drink.

Screw it all, he was going to bed. Tomorrow was another day.

# Chapter Eight

Out of sorts, unsure what was bothering him, Mark Lane changed into dry clothes and took his place at the computer. He polished his glasses, cracked his knuckles and stared at the blank screen in front of him. All he could see was the fear on Dr. Julia Webster's face as she prepared to enter her house where Senator Webster awaited her.

Dr. Julia Webster wasn't his business or FBI business. All he'd done was help out an old college buddy who had a few screws loose.

Mark cracked his knuckles again. He was no longer a field agent due to a heart attack at the young age of thirty-two. These days he was a desk jockey who ran computer programs for the Bureau. He missed being in the field which was why he'd agreed to help Jack. What was a little clandestine surveillance? His field instincts were just as good as ever. He hadn't lost those with his surgery. Something was wrong in the Webster household. Maybe Jack wasn't as paranoid as he originally thought.

Mark looked at the time on the bottom window of his computer. Eleven o'clock.

At this hour of the night he could make it to Georgetown in ten minutes. To do what? Stand in the rain and play Peeping Tom?

"I'm going! No, I'm not going out in this rain! Hell, yes, I'm going."

Five minutes later, dressed in one of his FBI slickers, Mark was in the Pathfinder headed toward Georgetown. What he was going to do when he got there, he had no clue.

Julia tried to be quiet, hoping against hope that Mitch was upstairs in bed. Unlikely, since the house was lit up like a Christmas tree. He was probably glued to the television waiting for the eleven o'clock news. He probably had a good bit of liquor under his belt, too. She hated it when Mitch drank to excess because he was an ugly drunk.

In the kitchen, Julia opened the refrigerator and poured herself a glass of orange juice. She carried her glass over to the sink and stared out at the black, rainy night. All she could really see was the gas lamp with its sickly, yellow light shining downward.

She raised her eyes to see Mitch's reflection. He was standing in the doorway wearing the same suit he'd probably started the day with. His tie was askew, his power suit rumpled. In his hand he held a highball glass. Julia turned around but didn't say anything. She waited, her stomach in knots.

"Where the hell have you been, Julia? I called you a hundred times. We need to get on the same page here. Where were you?"

"What page is that, Mitch? I said I would be here to go to the party. Here I am."

"You couldn't wait, could you? You had to run screaming to those slimy reporters and spew your garbage."

Julia sipped at the orange juice. "I did not run screaming to any reporters nor did I spew any garbage. I would never do that to you. What you and I discussed in this house stays between us. I see no need to air our dirty laundry for the gossip mongers of this town. If you're looking to place blame, look somewhere else."

"And you expect me to believe you?" Mitch ranted.

"Yes, Mitch, I do." Julia sipped at the orange juice again. It tasted bitter.

"Well, I don't. No one else knew. You made me write out that goddamn list. Now I know why you wanted me to do that. You need to call those slimy people and retract what you said. This is going to kill me politically."

*Better to die politically than to die physically.* "You're delusional. I told you I didn't do it, therefore I cannot call and rescind. Look somewhere else. There are a lot of people who hate you in this town and we both know it."

Julia moved across the kitchen to turn on the small flat screen television on the kitchen counter. "Let's see what they have to say," she said quietly. *His eyes are getting mean. He's working up to something.*

They didn't have long to wait. The second sound bite of the night had to do with Senator Webster's supposed dalliance. Julia watched her husband out of the corner of her eye. She could see that Mitch had set his highball glass on the counter and was smacking his clenched fist into his open palm. The venom he was spewing scared her; then a long-legged model type flashed on the screen. She looked to be in her mid-twenties with a wealth of shimmering blonde hair and breasts that couldn't be real. Julia listened to the lie she was telling. For some reason it sounded more of a lie because of her pronounced southern twang. "I have not had any kind of relationship with that man, Senator Webster." Julia almost laughed aloud. Miss Connie McBride was the third name on Mitch's list of paramours. "I'm very flattered but unfortunately, it's just all a vicious lie. The right wing. Y'all know how that works in this town. Now, y'all aren't going to start following me around and hounding me, are you? Now, don't be calling me at all hours of the day and night, ya hear?" She winked seductively at the reporter interviewing her.

Julia's heartbeat quickened. If Connie McBride was third on Mitch's slut list, there was a good chance she was a recent affair, which could well mean she was infected with HIV. Her gaze returned to the television screen where the buxom, long-legged blonde was still pretending to be outraged at having her character besmirched even though she was flattered.

Senator Webster looked absolutely livid as he downed the last of the scotch in his glass in one mighty gulp.

Outside, the rain slashed against the kitchen window as a lightning bolt shot across the sky. An early spring storm, just like the storm going on in this kitchen, Julia thought crazily. Her voice was calm, and it surprised her, when she said, "Now, Mitch, if you can lie as good as that slut you have nothing to worry about. Just for the record, she didn't convince me and she looked guilty as hell. Let's not forget how flattered she is to be coupled with the distinguished senator from Pennsylvania. Those boobs aren't real either."

"Will you shut up. Why would she lie?"

"I can't believe you just said that. You wrote her goddamn name on the goddam list. She's lying, just the way you lie. Excuse me, lied. I have the list in my purse. She was number three on that list if you recall. It's going to snowball, Mitch."

"You did it to get even with me. I know you did and you stand there looking like some sick saint. What the hell's wrong with you anyway? You look like shit. You have bags and dark circles under your eyes and your hair is like straw. I hope to hell you have some good makeup and a decent dress that won't make you look like a scarecrow for tomorrow night. The cameras are going to be on you all night long."

Julia bit down on her tongue. *Wait and see how you look when this devil illness hits you, you bastard.* She turned to walk away, her shoulders slumped. Then her feet left the floor and Mitch had her under the armpits holding her in the air. "I want an answer, Julia. Why did you turn on me like this? For Christ's sake, they were just affairs, they didn't mean anything. Just about every man in this fucking town is having an affair and if it isn't with a woman it's with another man."

"Take your hands off me. If you don't, I'll call the police and file a domestic abuse report. You wouldn't want that now, would you? You disgust me. I'm not going to tell you again, put me down," Julia screamed.

"You want down, you bitch! I'll show you *down!*' Mitch released his vise-like grip on her, and Julia fell to the floor with such force she literally saw stars. Too stunned to do anything, she started to cry.

"That's it, cry. Bawl your head off. You ruined me. You damn well ruined me!"

"You ruined yourself, you ass. If you had kept your pants zipped, you wouldn't be in this position and I wouldn't be . . . I wouldn't . . ." Julia bit down on her lip. She'd almost blurted out her medical condition. She inched away when she saw Mitch's foot swing out but she wasn't quick enough. She screamed with pain when Mitch's wing tip got her smack in the rib cage.

Outside in the bushes by the kitchen window, Mark Lane took in the situation. He skirted a forsythia bush in bloom and leaped up onto the small stoop that led to the back door where he started to pound at the door. "FBI," he shouted to be heard over the driving rain.

Mitch whirled around, his eyes wild. "What in the damn hell is the FBI doing here?" Julia didn't answer, she just cowered in fear and pain against the sink. "You called in the fucking FBI?"

"No!" Julia whispered. "No, I didn't."

Outside in the pouring rain, Mark kicked at the door. "Open on the count of three or I'll knock this door down!"

Mitch walked over and opened the door. Agent Lane stepped into the kitchen and went immediately to where Julia was crouched in the corner, her face full of pain.

"Let's see some goddamn ID," Mitch blustered.

Mark dug in his shirt pocket and pulled out his credentials. He flashed them as he leaned over to Julia. He was stunned speechless when she said. "Charles sent you in the nick of time. Thank God.

Get me out of here before he kills me. Please, take me back to Myra's. I think he cracked my rib cage. Just get me out of here."

Charles. That had to mean this woman wanted him to take her back to Myra Rutledge's estate. She thought Charles Martin sent him. Shit, now he was into something right up to his neck. She was whispering again. "I didn't tell him. I almost did but I knew Charles would have a fit. Oh, God, Oh, God!"

*What the hell?* "Can you walk, Dr. Webster?"

"I think so. I'll crawl if I have to. Just get me back to Myra and Charles."

Mitch finally found his voice as Agent Lane half carried his wife toward the kitchen door. "Where the hell do you think you're going? I don't give a good rat's ass if you're FBI or not. What was your name again?"

Mark ignored him as he struggled to open the door. "You're going to get wet, Dr. Webster."

"I don't care." Julia shot a look at her husband. "Just take me to the hospital. I'll say I fell off a ladder."

Outside in the pouring rain, Mark found his voice. "I thought you said you wanted me to take you to Myra and Charles. Do you want to go to the hospital instead?"

"No, I just said that so he wouldn't call the FBI. I know you're not a real agent, you're one of Charles's operatives. I don't know how he does it. You arrived at just the right moment. If you told me your name, I can't remember it. I'm sorry. Can you get my medical bag out of the car and the satchel next to it? I need to take some Advil. I should have killed him but he took me by surprise."

*Shit! Shit! Shit! She wanted his name. Oh, Emery, I am going to fucking kill you when I get my hands on you.* "Tom. Tom Warwick," Mark said as he helped Julia into the Pathfinder. He set the medical bag on her lap and her other bag on the floor.

"I didn't want him to call the FBI because I know . . . Oh, God, I almost blew it and told him I was HIV and he was the one who gave it to me. But then you know all that already. I didn't tell, though, even when he kicked me. He still thinks he can save his career. Listen, I'm sorry you had to witness that scene back in my kitchen. Mitch was so angry, I thought he was going to kill me. Thank God for Charles and his . . . for you and for everyone helping me with this mission," Julia gasped.

*Mission? Oh, shit, oh, shit! What the hell is she talking about? First I'm going to torture you, then I'm going to kill you, Emery.* Mark made a noise in his throat that he hoped sounded sympathetic as his mind raced. On the other hand, Jack might kill him if he *didn't* ask questions. What the hell should he ask? He grappled with something to say. He finally came up with something brilliant. "So, how is all of the rest of it going?"

"We're on target. You know Charles. He is so brilliant he boggles my mind. Did you work with him when he was MI6? No one ever told us his real name. It probably has something to do with his work as a spy. I guess you know all that, too. I'm just talking to hear myself so I won't think about the pain I'm in."

*We're on target.* Well, hot damn? He wondered how he could find out what *the target* was. Maybe Jack would know. "No, sorry, he was before my time. But the man is a legend in his own time." Well, that was brilliant. There was so much saliva in his mouth, Mark thought he was going to drown in his own drool.

"You can say that again. God, this hurts. I should have taken some painkillers. It's OK, I have to be careful what kind of meds I take these days. We'd all be dead in the water without Charles. He pulls it all together."

"Yeah, yeah, he's that kind of guy. He knows how to . . . to . . . pull things together. A master." Another brilliant statement but the doctor was buying it.

Mark drove in silence as he racked his brain. How much to say? How much not to say? He wished he could call Jack for instructions.

"Dr. Webster, how long has your husband been . . . abusing you?"

"He's never abused me. Tonight was . . . was the first time. He blames me for leaking his affair with that young woman. His career is ruined. I don't know why he's going to go through with the announcement tomorrow night. We really didn't talk much before you arrived."

"Uh-huh," was all Mark could think of to say. He cautioned himself to say as little as possible so as not to arouse her suspicions. Damn, he could hardly wait to tell all this to Jack. "Are you still planning on going to the armory tomorrow evening? Will you be up to it?"

Julia shifted in her seat. She undid her seat belt and then rebuckled it. "I have to attend. I can't let the others down. We work as a team and they depend on me. Once my ribs are taped up, I'll be OK. No one will think twice about me going by myself. I'm a doctor. Doctors are always late. I always show up at these functions, not necessarily on my husband's arm. Most times I show up when the affair is almost over. That's because I hate all that political nonsense. Tomorrow night, though, the press will read whatever they want to read into my arrival. Charles will have it under control. Besides, Mitch is just part of the mission."

Mark's mouth filled with saliva again. *Holy shit! Part of the mission.* This time he didn't trust himself to even grunt. Finally, he managed to say, "We're almost there, Dr. Webster." This is where I get my ass handed to me on a platter. As soon as miracle worker Charles Martin got him in his crosshairs, he was dead in the water. He'd probably call the local authorities and charge him with impersonating an FBI agent. Hell, he was an FBI agent. If he wasn't so nervous, he would have laughed.

"Thank you, God," Julia said quietly. "Listen, Tom, you'll have to drop me at the gate. I'll walk through. If the dogs don't know you, they'll rip you to pieces. We have a twelve foot high fence to . . . to keep people out. The dogs patrol the fence. We . . . we had an intruder the other night but he was outside the fence. I'll be fine once I get inside. I don't know how to thank you. You saved my life tonight. I never thought . . . I didn't expect . . ."

Saved. He was saved. They weren't going to string him up by his thumbs. *I'm still going to kill you, Jack.* He hoped the exquisite relief he felt didn't show in his voice when he said, "Well, I certainly don't want to . . . you know, screw things up. If you're sure you'll be OK, I'll simply turn around and head for home."

"I'm sure. Thank you again, Tom."

Mark hopped out of the car and ran around to the side and opened the car door for Julia to climb out. When she couldn't do it, he reached in and lifted her out and set her on the ground. She felt so thin, so fragile. "Look, I can't leave you here like this. What about your bags?"

"Take a look at those dogs by the fence and say that again. Just toss the bags inside when I open the gate. Someone will come out and get them. I'm fine. I hope I can do something for you some day."

Mark watched as Julia keyed in a code and then walked through the gates when they opened. The Dobermans didn't bark but they didn't move either as Julia moved among them. The instant the gates closed, Mark was back in the Pathfinder. He backed up and then spun around and headed away from Pinewood, rain cascading all around him.

Ten miles down the road, Mark was finally able to take a deep breath. What in the hell had he just stepped into? It was a myth that FBI agents had nerves of steel. He was twanging from head to toe.

He wanted to call Jack so badly he could taste the feeling but he'd left his cell phone back in his apartment which meant he had to drive to Jack's apartment and wake him up. An evil grin stretched across his face at the pleasure that was going to give him. "Mix me up in your shit and you deserve whatever you get, old buddy," he mumbled.

Twenty minutes later Mark was banging on Jack's door. He kicked at it a few times in between knocks. When the door finally opened he looked at his friend who was dressed in white boxers sprinkled with red hearts. "Wow! Do you always look like this when you wake up?" Mark asked, referring to Jack's overlong hair that was standing on end, his unshaven face, hairy chest and skinny legs. "No wonder Nikki dumped you. You'd scare the devil in the morning."

"I should kill you right now but I don't know where my gun is. Do you know what time it is? Did the J Edgar Hoover building blow up or something? What? Speak." Jack growled menacingly as he eyeballed his friend.

Mark shoved Jack backward and headed for the kitchen where he opened the refrigerator and uncapped a Michelob. He took a long swig before he spoke. "The building is still standing, thank you very much. This is better. Sit down, Jack, because if you don't, I'm going to deck you. What the hell is this shit you got me mixed up in? I don't think you covered the half of it."

"I told you all I know and everything I suspect. What happened? Don't make me beat it out of you, Mark."

Mark repeated the night's events right up to the point where his tires spun on the gravel outside the gates of Pinewood. "I just left her there. I felt like shit doing that but I wasn't about to take on a pack of Dobermans and besides, she insisted."

"No one dies of broken ribs. I never liked Senator Webster. All he does is talk so he can show off his pricey porcelain. Never would have figured him for a wife beater. Are you sure Dr. Webster . . ."

"Jack, I'm sure. She thought Charles Martin sent me. Hey, I announced myself when I banged on their back door. The senator wanted to see ID and I flashed it. In case you haven't noticed, I am wearing my FBI windbreaker. You'd have to be blind to miss those big yellow letters but I was smart enough to give a phony name. Just call me Tom Warwick."

Jack hitched up his boxers and then scratched the stubble on his chin. "She actually used the word mission?"

"Several times as a matter of fact. She assumed I knew what was going on. I did my best to act like I knew. I never felt so clueless in my life. The woman is sick, Jack. I picked her up and she weighs nothing. I wanted to do something, say something, but I didn't know what to do. I thought about going back there before I came here to deck that bastard but common sense brought me here instead. She got infected from her husband who she has kept in the dark for some reason. From what she said and didn't say, the senator doesn't know he's HIV. Tell me this isn't some heavy duty stuff. How does all this fit together with what you've been saying and thinking, Jack?"

"It's the word, mission, that's boggling my mind. Maybe they're setting the senator up for something. They leak his infidelities to the press and boom, his nomination goes down the tubes. He's ruined. Then there's good old Charles. MI6, huh? See, now, that puts a whole other spin on things.

"Mission. MI6. Myra Rutledge's wealth. Seven women. All strangers to one another until they hired Nikki. Nikki is the catalyst. I guess you didn't hear from your friend at Interpol, huh?"

"I was kind of busy, Jack. I was going to work the computer but I couldn't get the doctor's face out of my mind, so I went back there. I'm going home now and going to bed. All right, all right, I'll send off an E-mail before I sack out. I can't go on adrenaline like you do. Thanks for the beer," Mark said, tossing the empty bottle to his friend who caught it by the long neck.

"Thanks, Mark. I'll see you at three-thirty. You did real good tonight. I owe you for this."

"Don't think I'm going to forget it either," Mark snapped as he let himself out of the apartment.

All the way back to his apartment he could only think about Dr. Julia Webster. He hoped she would be all right. Then he started to worry. Did the security monitors pick up his license plate when he was turning the car around? He wasn't sure but he thought he backed up far enough so that he was outside the ray of light over the keypad before he swung the Pathfinder down the drive and then out to the highway.

Maybe he wasn't going to sleep after all. Maybe he needed to call Ambrose Coxney instead of E-mailing him. No point in leaving a paper trail. He could always take a nap later on.

Mark let himself into his apartment. From long years of training, he stood in the open doorway and looked around trying to see if anyone had entered his apartment while he was gone. The peanut shell was still where he'd left it by the front door. The pencil was still lying across his keyboard, the eraser pointed toward the Back-space key. He nodded in satisfaction as he headed for his bedroom and his shower. When he returned to his spare bedroom turned office, he was wearing pajamas and slippers. His receding hair was slicked back and his wire rimmed glasses were polished. He reached for an apple and a box of crackers to fortify himself as he logged on to his computer. He needed a picture of Charles Martin to forward to Ambrose. He remembered seeing one on the Rut-ledge Candy Company Web site. It was taken when Charles Martin signed on as new chief of security at the factory years and years ago. With luck, Ambrose could match it up from his side of the pond to Martin's dossier when he was with MI6.

As his mouse clicked and clicked, Mark realized Jack was on to something serious.

Myra was about to turn off the kitchen light and follow Charles upstairs. The others had retired earlier, leaving them alone to share a late night cup of tea. Out of the corner of her eye, she could see movement on the monitor by the security gates. "Charles, someone is coming *through* the gate. Who is it, dear?" She ran to the door to peer out in the rain. "It's Julia! Quickly, Charles, something's wrong." Before Charles could get up from the table, Myra was run-ning outside and across the lawn to where Julia was staggering toward her. Myra caught her in her arms just as Charles arrived.

Charles reached out and scooped Julia up in his arms. She moaned in pain. Like Mark Lane, he was stunned at how little she weighed.

Inside, Myra ran to the laundry room for towels and blankets. She returned in time to hear Julia say, "He was so livid, he lifted me off the ground and started punching me. Then he put me down and kicked me in the ribs. Your operative arrived just in time and got me out of there. He wanted to take me to the hospital, but I told him to bring me here. Just tape me up, Charles. I took some Advil but I need some more. I don't want to mix my meds with painkillers. Even if I went to the hospital, all they would do is take an x-ray and I'd have to lie through my teeth. Mitch thinks I went to the hospital. I told him I would say I fell. At that point I would have said or done anything to get out of there. I think I'd like some brandy, Charles."

Myra moved out of Julia's eye range, her hand fluttering, panic written all over her face. She needed both hands to grasp the brandy bottle. In the end, she got more of the plum brandy on the counter than she did in the glass.

Charles worked quickly, taping her ribs, then sliding a soft T-shirt over her head. He held Julia in his arms as she sipped at the fiery liquid. Her eyes watered at the onslaught on her throat. Exhausted, she leaned back. "It feels so much better with the tape. It doesn't hurt to breathe. Stop worrying, Charles, I'm a doctor. I'll be fine. I wouldn't be so fine if your man hadn't showed up when he did. Mitch was . . . he was so . . . so violent. He saw the eleven o'clock news and that's when he turned on me."

Charles released his hold on Julia and walked deeper into the kitchen so Myra could dress Julia in warm clothing. He was as close to panic as he'd ever been in his life. What in the name of God was Julia talking about? What operative of his had intervened?

He galloped up the back stairway and ran down the hall to Nikki's room. He knocked and then entered. She was sound asleep. He shook her gently. "Shhh, it's me, Charles. I need to talk with you."

Nikki reared back and sat up, her eyes frightened. "What's wrong? Don't tell me something happened to Myra. Please, Charles, don't tell me that."

"No, no, it's not Myra. It's Julia." He quickly recounted what had just happened. "I don't know, Nikki. Maybe it was Jack. I don't think she's ever met him so how could she know? She's so fragile and she's in a lot of pain. I don't want to frighten her so I thought you and Myra could sit with her and get the whole story out of her. She's going to be devastated when she realizes the man who saved her isn't one of our people. The best we can hope for right now is she didn't give up anything. Hurry, Nikki, before she drops off to sleep. I need to know what we're up against."

Nikki bolted from the bed and raced downstairs, her heart pumping in fear.

"Julia, Julia, I am so sorry. Is there anything I can do?" Nikki asked, dropping to her knees beside the sofa where Julia was lying. Myra sat cross-legged on the floor, holding Julia's hand.

"I'm OK, Nikki. I'm going to be stiff and sore for a few days but I will make it tomorrow night. I just won't be going with Mitch." Her eyes drooped and then closed.

Nikki watched as Myra threw a light blanket over Julia. "What did she say?" Nikki whispered.

Myra motioned Nikki to follow her out to the kitchen where

Charles was waiting for them. His eyes were full of questions. Both women shrugged. "She's sleeping, Charles. I didn't have the heart to question her. Morning will be soon enough."

"No, Myra, morning won't be soon enough. We have to get on top of this right now. Otherwise, we have to postpone tomorrow night's activities."

"It's the middle of the night, dear. What can we possibly do other than wake up Julia?"

"Julia is bound to stir eventually. I want you both to sit with her. The moment she opens her eyes, question her. I'll be in the command center. What bothers me is that she never met Jack Emery. It could have been Jack who rescued her. Julia did say the man said he was from the FBI and very nice. She said the letters, FBI were on the back of his windbreaker."

Nikki turned off the stove and filled three cups with water and tea bags. Something tugged at her, something she should be remembering. She twirled the tea bag in her cup, frowning. FBI. Who did she know in the FBI. No one. Who did Jack know in the FBI? "Oh, my God! Mark Lane!" The agent had stopped by their table once when she and Jack were at McGuire's.

At Charles and Myra's startled looks, she explained. "Jack has a friend who's an agent at the FBI. I met him once. Nice guy. Kind of sad, though. He had a heart attack shortly after he joined the FBI. He was a field agent, a good one, too, according to Jack. After his recovery he became a computer programmer. Maybe Jack . . . I'm reaching here, Charles, but maybe Jack enlisted his help. I can tell Julia what he looks like. If it was Mark, we're in trouble."

"I'll see what I can come up with on Agent Lane. I might be able to get a picture. Do you know where he went to college or where his hometown is?" Charles asked.

"I don't know where he's from but he went to Duke University with Jack. It was a long time ago, Charles. I just have a foggy memory of it. I more or less homed in on the fact that a young guy like him had a heart attack. I'm sorry, Charles."

"No, no, that's perfectly understandable. The fact that you remembered at all is a tremendous help. Come to the command center if Julia wakes and tell me what she says."

Myra sipped at the herbal tea and eyed Nikki over the rim of her cup. "How . . . how serious is all this, Nikki?"

Nikki wished there was something she could say to drive the worry from Myra's eyes but there wasn't. "About as serious as it gets.

I guess it's time to do something about Jack before he involves someone else. I don't know if we have any other choice, Myra."

"I am so sorry, dear. I wish . . . oh, Lord, I wish so many things. If you want to . . ."

"Stop right there, Myra. I'm not going to back out of the Sisterhood because of Jack Emery. We just have to find a way to deal with him that will work to our advantage."

"Can he be bought? A bribe?"

"Don't even go there, Myra. The short answer is, no. Jack has an ego and that ego has been bruised by a bunch of women. It's not that he's against women or anything like that, but he goes by the book, it's black or white. There are no gray areas where Jack is concerned. He lives for the law. At least he did. In a million years he would never be able to deal with what we're doing. He wants us locked up and the key thrown away. And, don't forget, he's been called on the carpet, courtesy of the governor's call to the police commissioner on your behalf. Last but not least, he's bent out of shape because he thinks I chose you over him." Nikki threw her hands in the air to show what she thought of that particular statement.

Nikki eyed her adopted mother who looked exhausted. "Myra, go to bed. You haven't had any sleep yet. It's going to be a busy day and night. You need some rest. I've had a few hours sleep so I'll sit with Julia. I need to do some deep thinking. It's all doable, Myra, so don't be worried. If I need you, I'll call you."

"All right, dear. You're right about me needing some sleep. I'm sorry but I do worry. I feel so terrible about you and Jack. I wish . . . never mind, good night, dear. Be sure to call me if you need me."

"I promise. I'll check in on Charles in a bit." Nikki allowed herself to be hugged before she waved good night.

Nikki made fresh tea and carried it into the den where Julia was still sleeping on the sofa. She stared down at her friend and wondered how she herself would handle what Julia was going through if the situation was reversed. I'd probably be a raving lunatic, she thought. She sat down, mumbling a prayer for Julia that somehow, some way, a miracle would happen for her.

Nikki's mind raced as she sipped at her tea and struggled to come up with a solution to what was going on in her life. Eventually, because she was tired, she dozed off to be awakened hours later when she heard Julia whisper her name. "I need to use the bathroom, Nikki. Can you help me get up?"

Both women were back on the sofa minutes later. The clock on the mantel said it was four o'clock in the morning. "I'm all right, Nikki. I'm sore but that's to be expected. Can you get my cell phone out of my bag? I want to see if Mitch called."

Nikki rummaged in Julia's bag until she found the phone. She watched as Julia pressed a series of numbers to pick up her messages. A look of pure fury replaced the pain in her face as she suddenly threw the small phone across the room. "Typical, Mitch, threaten and intimidate when he doesn't get his way. He *demands* that I come home. Like that's really going to happen."

"Tell me what happened, Julia. Don't leave anything out. We need to get a handle on all of this before tonight." Nikki leaned back in her chair, her legs tucked beneath her. The scene could have passed for a girls' sleepover where telling secrets was the order of the day.

"The eleven o'clock news came on and this woman, Connie McBride, who was number three on Mitch's slut list, appeared. She denied having an affair with the distinguished senator from Pennsylvania but she was flattered nonetheless. Do you believe that? Maybe late twenties, married to a first term congressman. Long legs, artificial boobs, blonde. Beautiful. Any man would be attracted to her. Compared to her, I look like a down and out bag lady without even a cardboard box to sleep in.

"Mitch and I had words. Before I knew it, he grabbed me under the arms and lifted me off the floor. He's really strong. We were screaming at one another. I told him to put me down, and he just . . . he just dropped me. I literally saw stars. Then he kicked me. It would have been worse but I moved when I realized his intent. The pain really rocked me.

"I couldn't believe it when there was a knock on the kitchen door and the man said, open up, FBI, or something like that. I knew instantly that it wasn't the FBI but one of Charles's people. Mitch didn't know that, though. He asked for ID, and this guy Tom showed him his badge or whatever agents carry around. I was in so much pain I wasn't paying too much attention.

"Agent Warwick picked me up and I told him to take me to the hospital—that was just for Mitch's benefit. Just seconds before I whispered for him to bring me here and he said OK. He was so nice, Nikki. So concerned. I had the feeling it was all he could do not to punch Mitch out. He really did want to take me to the hospital."

Nikki's heart fluttered in her chest. "I want you to think very carefully, Julia. What exactly did the agent say and what did you say to him? Exactly, Julia."

A flicker of fear showed in Julia's eyes. She clutched the light blanket with both hands. "I did most of the talking. Agent Warwick . . . that's what he said his name was, was concentrating on his driving. The weather was terrible. I was babbling. I was so upset, Nikki. We talked about Charles. I kept saying I was so grateful Charles had sent him and he arrived at just the right moment. We talked about Charles being in Her Majesty's service. I said I didn't even know what his British name was. He said Charles was a legend in his own time but it was before his time. That kind of thing."

"Did you mention tonight's activities?" Nikki asked carefully.

"Yes. I talked about the mission, he seemed to understand and didn't ask any questions. Why, Nikki? You're starting to scare me."

"Tell me what he looked like. Did you have to give him directions out here?"

"No, he knew the way. He was plain-looking, sandy hair, receding a little. Young—and by young I mean maybe mid thirties. He was wearing an FBI windbreaker. The letters were big and yellow on the back. He wasn't fat but he was a little overweight for his height, which was about five-eleven or so. He was extremely competent and I felt safe with him. He seemed more concerned with my well-being than anything I said. I don't know, Nikki, I was in a lot of pain and gulping Advil. Say it, say I screwed up."

"You screwed up, Julia, but I probably would have done the same thing. The person you described is not anyone any of us knows. Charles did not send him. At first we thought it was Jack but Jack is tall and movie star handsome. I think the person who saved you is a friend of Jack's and his name is Mark Lane. I met him once when I was with Jack. You're right, he's a nice guy. The description you just gave me fits Mark. What happened when you got to the gates?"

Julia groaned, her head dropping to her hands. "I told him to let me out because of the dogs. He seemed . . . relieved. I don't know if this means anything but instead of turning around, he backed way down the road before he turned around. I thought that was strange but now when I think about it, I guess he didn't want the camera to pick up his license plate on the back. It was a Pathfinder. Nikki, I am so sorry. It was the jacket, the nick of time save. I have to tell Charles."

"You stay right there and rest and don't beat yourself up over this. Being forewarned will keep us from walking into an ambush. Charles is in the command center. He'll know what to do. The others are sleeping. I'll make us all some coffee."

Julia beat at the pillow with her clenched fists as tears rolled down her cheeks.

In the kitchen, Nikki zipped around running water, filling the pot, pouring in coffee grounds and getting out cream and sugar before she raced through the house to the secret war room.

"We're in the brown stuff, Charles. Julia didn't quite give it up but she said enough so that when Mark Lane goes back to Jack, he's going to know. She told him about you and Her Majesty and Lane said you were a legend in your own time even though you were before his time. Seems he knows about you or else he pretended. She pretty much hinted at the mission and used that exact word. She's devastated, Charles. What should we do? What *can* we do? I'm making coffee."

Nikki had never seen Charles ruffled but he was ruffled now. It frightened her.

"Coffee sounds good, Nikki. I'd like it black with a shot of brandy in it. Is Julia all right and is Myra sleeping?'

Nikki felt even more frightened with Charles's order for coffee. He always took heavy cream and four sugars. "OK on the coffee. Yes, Myra is sleeping and no, Julia is not all right. Considering the situation, I tend to think I might have reacted the same way she did."

"Yes, yes. I understand. I'm not blaming her. We just have to fall back and regroup. I need to . . . hurry with the coffee, Nikki."

Nikki trotted off. "I should kill you, Jack. At the very least, incapacitate you for a good long while," she muttered to herself as she prepared Charles's coffee. Her shoulders slumped when she returned yet again to the kitchen to prepare coffee for Julia and herself. Jack was an officer of the court, doing what he was supposed to do. She and the others were breaking the law. No matter how she sliced and diced it, the Sisterhood was in the wrong. Jack was in the right. In her heart of hearts, she couldn't blame him for listening to his instincts and acting on those instincts. The big question was, if things got down and dirty, would she be able to go along with her sisters to do something drastic to the man she loved. Or would she break all the rules and warn Jack. It was going to come to that; she could feel it in her bones. Which way would she turn? Right now, right this very moment, she didn't have an answer.

"Want some more Advil, Julia?" Nikki asked, setting the coffee cup down on the cocktail table. "Would you rather be alone or do you want to talk?" she asked gently.

Julia grimaced. "I think I already talked too much, Nikki. What did Charles say? How upset is he with me?"

"Julia, Charles understands. We all understand. He's working on it. Knowing Charles as well as I do, I think we're still on for this evening. There will be some changes but we're going to pull it off. Hey, we're women! We can do anything if we put our minds to it. Remember, there were some glitches during Kathryn's mission. We pulled it off and no one was the wiser."

Julia struggled to find a more comfortable sitting position. "Jack and his new partner know too much, Nikki."

"Yes, I know. They could do real damage to Charles and his new identity here in this country. If you want to know what my secret fear is, it's that Charles will tell his people on the other side of the pond and they will take care of Jack and Mark."

Julia clutched one of Myra's needlepoint pillows to her chest. Tears trickled down her drawn cheeks. "Oh, God, I didn't think of that, Nikki. Will they . . . will they . . ." Julia couldn't bring herself to finish what Nikki was thinking.

"I don't know. I think so. That covert spy stuff by both governments is serious stuff. We're babes in the woods compared to what those guys do. I suppose it's possible they could arrange *to talk* to Mark and Jack." Nikki shivered as she crossed her arms over her chest.

"The FBI and the Secret Service will be at the armory this evening. I'm surprised Mitch doesn't have an all points out on me. If he doesn't withdraw or tell the governor he doesn't want to be his running mate, I'm fair game from here on in. I'll be under a microscope."

"Charles is working on it, Julia. Right now, I'm concerned about you. Can you take a shower? I'll help you."

"It doesn't matter if I should or shouldn't. I'm going to do it. I got caught in the rain twice yesterday. You can help me wash my hair if you don't mind. Then you'll have to re-tape my ribs. I . . . I want to look as nice as I can this evening. Mitch said some ugly things to me that I will never forget. I guess he hasn't taken a good look at me lately. He was very cruel. I can't forgive him for that. You know, Nikki, I almost blurted it all out but I bit my tongue so hard I drew blood. I was married to that man for God's sake. Why didn't I ever do something? Why did I stay? What's wrong with me?"

Nikki held out her hands, dug her heels into the carpeting and pulled Julia to her feet. Together they made their way to the downstairs bathroom where Nikki got out towels, soap, and shampoo. "Hot, warm or cool?"

"Hot. I can adjust it after I stand under the steam." Julia stood still as Nikki helped her undress.

Nikki held her tears until Julia stepped into the shower. She wiped at her eyes on the sleeve of her pajamas. When it was time for her to make a decision where Jack and Mark were concerned, all she would have to do was remember this moment. Julia deserved her revenge.

Charles paced his domain as he waited for his secure cell phone to ring. After all these years he was in danger again. Like the CIA in Langley, MI6 never slept. What was taking so long? Why weren't they calling him back? He looked into his coffee cup and was surprised to see it empty. He had no clear recollection of finishing it. He started to pace again, the empty cup in his hands.

Dear God, what if MI6 insisted on moving him. Well, that simply wasn't an option. If that was their decision he might have to go over their head to Lizzie. The mere thought of having to do that gave him indigestion. He couldn't leave Myra and the girls. They needed him, depended on him. He could make *Lizzie* understand that. No, leaving his little family was not an option.

The phone rang. Charles clicked on the button knowing his conversation could not be heard by anyone in the world except the person he was talking to.

The voice on the other end of the line apologized for the short delay in not getting back to him sooner. "I'm sorry, Sir Malcolm, but I had to boot this up about nine levels to get you the person you need to speak with. Hold while I transfer this call."

Charles drummed his fingers on the desk in front of him. "Sir Malcolm, Rodney Abernathy here. I caught your call. I don't see a problem. We'll take care of it. Would you like to move on to a warmer climate?"

Charles felt light-headed with relief. He wouldn't have to go to Lizzie after all. "Not at all, Rodney. I just want to be reassured."

"Rest easy, Sir Malcolm. We fielded a call a short while ago from Interpol. One of your FBI agents imposed on a friendship to make inquiries. There are so many red flags on your file, the man went to his superior. Everything has been taken care of. Is there anything else I can help you with today, Sir Malcolm?"

"No. Thank you. I'll stay in touch should things change." Charles clicked off the phone. How strange to hear himself called Sir Malcolm. His birth name was Malcolm Sutcliff. Lizzie herself had given him his new name when he was sent to America and he'd grown over the years to believe he really was Charles Martin.

Charles felt his shoulders straighten. He had work to do. Lots of work. But first he needed a gallon of coffee to jump-start his adrenaline again. Good Lord, he must have become Americanized along the way. A relieved smile on his face, Charles decided it wasn't a bad thing.

Shortly before the noon hour, the foursome were ready to tee off when the director of the CIA felt his secure mobile phone vibrate inside his shirt pocket. His golfing buddies, the senior senator from Illinois, the Speaker of the House and the FBI's second in command groaned as one. The director clicked on his phone and walked away so his conversation couldn't be overheard. He listened, the expression on his face going from furious to livid to murderous. "Yes, I do recall a similar situation where you did what we requested with no repercussions. I'll see to it. You can assure Her Majesty your man is safe and there will be no need to move him to another location. Of course, I'll get back to you. I'll take care of it as soon as I hang up." The director waved off his friends and headed back to the clubhouse.

Inside his car, his chauffeur standing outside, the director made his first call. It wasn't *that* unusual for the director of the CIA to call the director of the FBI but it wasn't quite normal either. The two men exchanged guarded pleasantries before the CIA got down to business. "Now means now, Adam. They tell me on the other side of the pond that this is crucial. Can you hog-tie your man and his friend? I just want to be sure, Adam. The *lady* across the pond is in a pissy mood from what I gather. No sense in riling her up any further. The fact that the PM isn't involved shows how serious this is. I'll return the favor, Adam, should the occasion arise. Call me when you have something to report. I'm ten minutes late teeing off. Oh, you're on the ninth. I heard about that hole in one you got a few weeks back." The connection ended and the cell phone went back into the director's pocket. Ten minutes later, he said, "OK, boys, what are we betting today?"

A light misty rain was falling outside as Mark Lane tugged at his tie. He straightened the Windsor knot, looked at himself again to make sure he looked professional, checked his watch to make sure he had plenty of time to pick up Jack Emery. More than enough time. They'd be outside in the rain, and he'd probably catch a cold. One of those spring-summer colds that lingered for weeks. Just the thought depressed him.

Time to warm up the coffee in his cup. Maybe he should eat something. He knew he'd never get a chance to get even close to the buffet table with the delectable tidbits the governor would be serving at this particular bash. Been there, done that.

As Mark waited for the countdown on the microwave he realized he was not looking forward to the evening even though it meant he was "out in the field" so to speak.

A sharp knock startled him just as the microwave beeped signaling his coffee was ready. It must be Jack, so anxious he drove over here to cut down on driving time. Coffee cup in hand, he marched to the door and didn't bother to check the peephole to see who it was. He was about to offer up some kind of blistering comment until he saw the two men standing facing him. His mother hadn't raised any fools. He knew trouble when he saw it. The coffee cup in his hand started to shake.

"Agent Lane?" one of the men said.

Mark blinked as his right eye started to twitch. "Yes. What can I do for you?"

"For starters, you can invite us in unless you want your neighbors knowing your business," the second man said as he flashed his credentials.

Mark stepped aside to allow the two men to enter his apartment. Coffee sloshed out of his cup onto the floor. He ignored it and he used both hands to steady the cup.

"Going somewhere, Agent Lane?"

"The fact that you're standing here tells me probably not. I was going to the armory. I signed on for the extra detail. You can check with my boss."

"We already did, Agent Lane. You're right, you are not going to the armory. Where's your buddy, Jack Emery?"

"Probably home. I was supposed to pick him up."

"That's not going to happen either, Agent Lane. Call him and tell him something came up and he has to drive over here. In the spirit of cooperation. That's all you say, Agent Lane. You say another word and I'll shoot you on the spot."

Mark looked down at his shoes that he'd polished earlier to a high sheen. He could feel his back start to stiffen. "I think I want to know what this is all about. I don't work for you. What does Jack Emery have to do with anything?" *Stupid ass question.*

Mark's thoughts were faster than speeding bullets. He liked his job. No, he loved his job. He had good health benefits which he needed. He didn't need any black marks on his sheet. Still, how could he in good conscience turn Jack over to these guys, and that's exactly what he would be doing if he called him? Plus, Jack was on a thirty day leave without pay. Technically, that made him a civilian. *I knew I should have killed you, Jack.*

"We don't have to tell you squat, Agent Lane," the first man said quietly. Mark heard the menace in his voice. "Make the call."

Mark walked through the living room and down a short hall to his second bedroom that was a home office. He sloshed coffee all the way. He sat down on his swivel chair because he was scared out of his wits. He dialed Jack's number from memory. The second man reached over and pressed the speaker phone button. Jack's voice came across loud and exceptionally clear.

"If this is you, Agent Lane, telling me you changed your mind, I'll come over there and personally kick your ass all the way to New York. What?" he barked.

"Something came up, Jack. Drive over here. I'll be ready to . . . to leave when you get here."

"All right, all right. You fibbies are the pits, you know that. You're so disorganized I have to wonder how you get anything done. Plus today is Saturday, your day off."

"I didn't say it was work related, Jack. All I said was something came up."

The first man pressed a button and the call ended. Mark replaced the phone. He brought the cup to his lips, stunned to see he'd lost the contents. Shit, now he was going to get ants. He tried to take a deep breath and made a horrible sound in his throat. Neither man looked concerned.

"How long will it take Mr. Emery to get here?"

"Depending on traffic, maybe fifteen minutes. If he hits the right lights, ten minutes." Mark continued to hack and sputter. Both men walked back to the living room. Mark followed and sat down in his favorite chair. He'd seen pictures of the shields both these men carried but on a wide screen at a briefing. The instructor at the academy had said in any given year, maybe three such shields were issued by the president of the United States. One year, the instructor said, there had been four. One year, none. What that meant to the students was, if you ever come across someone carrying that particular shield you immediately stand down and turn over everything to the person carrying the shield. The instructor had droned on to say that MI6, Interpol and the Mossad had similar shields. All were compatible which meant the holders of the shields worked in harmony.

Mark thought about the call he'd made to his friend at Interpol. *Bastard. See if I ever do anything for you.*

The minutes ticked by. Mark finally got up and replenished his coffee. He drank it cold. All the while he wondered where his next assignment was going to be if they didn't fire or kill him. He didn't even want to think about what they'd do to Jack. He remembered his old instructor saying the guys with the special shields were meaner than cat shit, and worse than hired assassins. All the students, including himself, had laughed when he said they shoot first and take names later.

The knock on the door sounded impatient. Neither man said a word as Mark trudged forward.

"C'mon, c'mon, open up, Mark. Let's get this show on the road," Jack bellowed from his side of the door.

Mark opened the door and watched in horror as Jack was literally lifted off the floor and thrown across the room with such force he made a thumping sound when he landed on the sofa. He wondered giddily, how they'd managed to gauge the distance so he didn't crash through the glass topped coffee table. Then again, maybe it was just pure dumb luck.

Mark stared at his friend. He'd seen normal fear, abnormal fear and then the kind of fear he was seeing on Jack's face in his earlier years in the line of duty. *Oh, shit. This is where the rubber meets the road. Keep your mouth shut, buddy, and maybe, just maybe, we can get out of this with our skin intact.*

# Chapter Nine

Alexis hopped on the bed and clapped her hands for silence. "Yo! Listen up everyone and get in line. Who wants to be first?" She jumped off the bed, to land with a thud next to Yoko. She eyed the Asian with a practiced eye.

"Might I say I do admire those new boobs of yours. I think I can say I've never seen a four foot eight, eighty-five pound female with a set of thirty-six-inch knockers."

Yoko preened and then pranced around Alexis's bedroom. "My husband loves them. Thanks to Julia's colleague, I was able to have it done. No charge. How do you say, complimentary?"

"Wow!" Kathryn grinned. "Do they feel the same?"

Yoko giggled. "My husband says they do. He said he likes it that I am an experimental, progressive woman. Free!"

Julia felt the need to explain. "A colleague of mine has an intern who needed the practice. We did it after hours. I was in the clinic when they were done. Good job if I do say so myself."

It was just enough conversation to defuse the tension in the room before Alexis got down to work. Her famous Red Bag was voluminous and no one was permitted to touch the contents but Alexis herself. The others called her a magician because she could transfer any likeness to something totally different from when she started, with the aid of latex, spirit gum, makeup and costume.

"Who am I going to be this evening?" Yoko gurgled as she gave her new boobs an uplift bounce.

Alexis looked down at the chart Charles had given her prior to all of them retiring to her room to *get ready* for the evening's festivities. "It says here I am to make you three inches taller, pile your hair on your head for added height and transform you into a beautiful regal Chinese royal." She looked Yoko up and down. "I don't know if I can do that. Those boobs are going to throw me off. Besides, you're already beautiful." At Yoko's crestfallen look, she hastened to add, "I'm teasing, dipshit."

Alexis began taking things out of the oversized Red Bag, grateful for all the backstage training she'd had when she worked in Little Theater.

The gig was on.

As Alexis pinched and prodded, glued and pasted, her brushes and fingers moving like magic, the others chattered nonstop, mostly to Julia as they clustered around her, offering support.

Nikki looked up from her nest of pillows on the bed. "Are we all clear on every single detail?"

"Got it down pat, Nikki. Wait till you guys see the job Yoko and I did at that armory. It looks like a rainbow. One of the governor's people actually came out to thank us. Gave me a fifty buck tip and winked at me. Yoko got a hundred bucks. I haven't been able to figure that out," Kathryn groused.

"There's going to be a thousand people there this evening and that doesn't count the press," Isabelle said. "Charles said the expected donation was a thousand bucks each. He gave me our checks earlier to distribute. No grass is growing under the nominee's feet on this one. Announcement, pony up, and get the hell out of there. Whatever you do, girls, do not, I repeat, do not forget to bring your invitation. Charles did a masterful job of duplicating them."

"Ta-da!" Alexis said dramatically.

"Oh, myyyy, God!" the women squealed.

"You look like . . ." Kathryn struggled for words and was unable to come up with any. Murphy, who was on the bed with Nikki, reared back and howled.

"Let me save you the trouble and let's go with high priced Asian slut with family ties to the Ming family! The Monarch family will be dying to make my acquaintance." Yoko giggled as she strutted around the room in her underwear.

"I can go with that," Kathryn guffawed. "Girl, when you get that dress on you are going to turn every head in the armory."

The surgeon in Julia leaned over to inspect Yoko's face, trying to see what Alexis had accomplished without the aid of a scalpel. Her cheekbones were higher, her chin more defined. Her face was no longer round but elongated. The dark eyes were now a startling blue. Her nose that had been on the small side was now defined, the nostrils flaring dramatically. Her long, black, silky hair was swirled and coiled on top of her head and held in place with two ivory picks. "My dear, you would put Mata Hari to shame."

"Thank you, Julia. I have to practice walking now in these outrageous shoes. I hope I don't kill myself."

The hours ticked by while Alexis worked her magic on the others. "I deserve a medal for this! Now if you don't mind, I need to work on myself. Someone should call Myra and Charles to see if they approve."

"I'll do it," Nikki said as she pulled on a robe and left the room.

When the door closed behind Nikki, the women started chattering again and as usual the talk centered on men.

"That lets me out," Julia said as she relaxed under Alexis's spell. "Make me look like something other than a walking cadaver."

Alexis pretended to swat her the way the others pretended not to hear Julia's comment. "When I'm done with you, you are going to be one ravishing, kick ass broad. Now, pucker up and let me get to work. If you get tired or if you just want to get up and walk around, let me know and we can take a break. It's not going to take me long to work on myself. I'll look like a long-legged Diana Ross in ten minutes." No one doubted her for a minute.

Another hour wore on as Julia dozed off and on in her chair. The others kept looking at her, hoping she'd make it through the night. No one realized how quiet it was until Julia opened one eye and smiled. "Stop worrying about me. I can do this. If I couldn't, I wouldn't be here. I'll hold up my end. I know exactly what my role is and I won't let you down. You're all so kind to be so concerned. It's been years since anyone really cared about what happened to me. You're my family now. I'll do my share this evening. Ohhh, I can't wait to put on that gown. I can't remember the last time I got really dressed to the nines."

The women relaxed but the concern stayed in their eyes. They would all look out for her during the evening. That was a given.

"What's the latest on Jack Emery? Does anyone know?" Yoko asked.

Alexis stopped what she was doing and said, "Charles was like a scalded cat when the stuff hit the fan. Then he turned into a pussy cat so that tells me Myra's call to the governor took care of things."

Yoko moved to the center of the room in her spike heeled, platform shoes and said, "Men like Jack Emery do not give up. He will find a way. What is that saying Americans have? Yes, yes, he marches to his own drummer. He will find a way to intrude into our lives again. That means we must always be vigilant. Did I say that right, Kathryn?"

"Perfectly, kiddo. Before you know it, you're going to be as American as apple pie. Keep practicing in those shoes or you're going to fall flat on your ass. Maybe you should tape up your ankles or something."

"Can one of you hand me a secure cell phone? I want to call Mitch to tell him I'll be there by six-thirty."

Isabelle handed Julia the cell phone from her pocket. Julia dialed knowing Mitch wouldn't be able to trace the call. She crossed her fingers that he wouldn't answer so she could just leave a message. She wasn't that lucky, Mitch picked up on the first ring.

"Julia, is that you?"

"Yes, Mitch, it's me. I'm just calling . . ."

Mitch interrupted her before she could say anything else. "Jesus, Julia, I am so sorry about last night. I don't know what the hell got into me. Listen, honey, I'll make it up to you. I swear I will. I promise. Are you all right? Please say you forgive me. What the hell happened to that FBI guy? Did you smooth things over? They aren't going to show up and cause a scene tonight, are they?"

"No, Mitch, I'm not all right. You cracked my ribs. I'm all taped up. There are no plans in my immediate future to forgive you. I just called to tell you I'll be at the armory around six-thirty. Give or take a few minutes either way. I don't plan on staying long but I will make an appearance. As to the agent from the FBI, I don't know his plans as he didn't confide in me. Do the wise thing, Mitch, and back out now."

"Back away from the vice presidency of the United States? Are you out of your mind. I've lusted for this my whole life and you want me to withdraw my name. The answer is, no. Crawford is old, he could bite the dust in a year or so and I'll be ready to step into his shoes. Are you on painkillers to make you say such a thing?"

"Yeah, I'm on painkillers," Julia said, clicking off the phone.

Julia looked around the room. "OK, girls, my husband is fair game tonight! Anything goes."

"Oooh, I love it when you talk like that." Kathryn laughed.

"We're all going in different limos, right? That didn't change, did it?"

Kathryn shook her head. "Nope. We're each responsible for our own gear for this little caper. Murphy stays behind tonight. Charles and Myra are coming back here so they'll take care of him till we get home. I think we're ready to roll as soon as Alexis finishes up with Julia and does her Diana Ross thing."

"She's done," Alexis said softly. "Turn around Julia."

"Julia, you look . . . beautiful!" Yoko said, running over to the dresser for a hand mirror. "You will outshine every woman at the party." This last was said so sincerely, Julia smiled and allowed herself to be hugged . . . very gently.

"Just don"t go shaking your head too much or the hair strands will come loose. And, whatever you do, don't stand under any bright lights. Your gown is padded in all the right places. Try not to move around a lot. We'll all be within eye distance and earshot so if you want something just tug on your earlobe or something." Alexis dropped to her knees and reached for Julia's hands. "All I did was improve on something that was almost perfect to begin with. You're a beautiful woman, Julia. I want you to believe that."

"And miracles happen every day. I overheard Charles telling Myra there's a special place in Switzerland he wants to send you to. He said they work miracles for AIDS patients. Act surprised when he tells you, OK?" Kathryn whispered.

They all looked away at the hope in Julia's eyes.

"Mum's the word, girls. Dress up time!" Julia said. "We leave in exactly forty-five minutes." She pointed to her satchel and medical bag sitting next to five heavily loaded backpacks that contained the tools of their new trade. Alexis's Red Bag of tricks would be piled on top for Charles to carry down when the limousines arrived.

The wind knocked out of him, Jack stared up at the two men towering over him. They were his height, his weight. He could probably take on one of them but not two. His gaze swivelled to Mark who looked like he was going to get sick at any minute. It was a wise man who knew when to fold and walk away. No one ever said he was a wise man. "What in the damn hell . . ."

"Shut up, Emery. You talk when we say you can talk. One more peep out of you and you'll be swallowing your teeth. Agent Lane, tell this pissant who we are and where our authority comes from."

Mark wiped at the sweat forming on his brow. "Jack, each year of the presidency, according to the instructions at the FBI Academy, the president forms a small task force, for want of a better term. It usually consists of two, sometimes three men. They only answer to the president himself. They've got carte blanche. That means they

can snuff us out, walk away and nothing will ever happen to them.
Are you following me here, Jack?"

Jack nodded.

"When you asked me to help you, I thought it was some kind of
local stuff and I was just doing a favor for a friend. But this ain't
some kind of local stuff, Jack. These guys work with MI6, Interpol
and all that heavy duty spy stuff that goes on all over the world, stuff
we never get to hear about. Right now, I just want to forget I ever
knew you. I like my job and I want to keep it. You're bush league,
these guys are the big league."

Jack blinked but he didn't say anything as he struggled to an upright position. In his life he'd never seen colder or deadlier eyes.
What the fuck was going on? What did he stumble onto? More to
the point, where did Nikki and Myra fit into this whole damn scenario?

"You can talk now, Mr. Emery," one of the men said.

"That's Assistant District Attorney Emery to you . . . *sir*."

"That still makes you a pissant. Now, tell us what you've been up
to and why you're harassing those nice folks out there in Virginia."

Jack's mind raced. Common sense told him to opt for the truth.
He told them in as straightforward a manner as he could. "I'm in
law enforcement, I'm not paid to look the other way. Yes, I tres-
passed on Myra Rutledge's property. But it was on my own time. I
was trying to get enough evidence to do something about the Marie
Llewellyn case and in the course of my search, I discovered those
women who congregate out there are up to something else. I think
they're taking the law into their own hands. Vigilantes." He felt silly
as hell and he could see that the special gold shield guys weren't
buying his story.

"Mark has nothing to do with any of this," he went on. "I asked
him for a favor and he helped me out. You want to cut off my dick,
go ahead, but leave him out of it."

The men looked at one another. The first one shrugged. The
second one smirked as he hauled Jack to his feet. "We're going to
be on you like white on rice from here on in, Emery. You get within
a mile of those people at Pinewood and you'll never be seen or
heard from again. Remember, we answer to only one man. Right
now that man doesn't like you very much."

Jack saw the fist coming but couldn't duck in time. At some point
during the beating, he blacked out. When he finally came to, the
gold shields were gone and Mark was bending over him, his face

furious because he hadn't been able to help his friend. There was blood everywhere. He picked up the phone to call 911.

"No!" Jack croaked. "Help me up and out to my car. Then you can forget you ever met me."

"Jesus, Jack, what the hell did you stumble on to? Let me patch you up first. You should go to the hospital."

"No," Jack croaked again. "Get me some aspirin and a couple of shots of whiskey. Were you telling me the truth about those guys? The president really has a goon squad? Damn, what would the American people think if they knew that?"

"Jack, leave it alone for God's sake. Don't move till I get back."

In less than a minute, Mark dropped to the floor, and opened his first aid kit and cleaned up Jack's face the best he could. "How are your ribs? Listen, Jack, I didn't mean all that shit I was spouting before."

"Yes, you did. Don't apologize. They got me in the gut and my kidneys. I won't be able to have sex ever again. Where's the damn aspirin?"

"Here," Mark said, holding out the bottle. "I'll get the whiskey. I don't think you're supposed to take aspirin with whiskey, Jack."

"Sez who? Help me up."

"I can drive you home, Jack, and have a friend drop off your car tomorrow. Oh, shit, you aren't going home, are you?"

"No, Mark, I'm not going home. You don't need to know where I'm going. Look, I'm sorry I got you involved. I won't call you again. Take my number off your speed dial and don't bother to send me a Christmas card. I'll see you around."

Mark looked and felt like he was going to cry. "Listen, you crazy son of a bitch, you're going to get yourself killed. How am I supposed to live with that?"

"By pretending you never met me, that's how."

Agent Lane's eyes burned when the door closed behind his friend.

# Chapter Ten

It could have been the Academy Awards with the glittering outfits, limousines, and hoards of reporters instead of a political turnout. The only thing missing was the red carpet and Joan Rivers. A light rain was falling when the parade of limousines from Pinewood drew up to the armory. The time was ten minutes past six when Myra Rutledge and Charles Martin exited the lead limo. The chauffeur held a huge golf umbrella over them as they scurried to the entrance, their invitation in hand.

The others followed within fifteen minutes of each other. Julia was last to arrive. Her husband was waiting inside the doorway to guide her into the vast area filled with orchids and every flower and green plant known to man. Colorful balloons were tied to the rafters and to the backs of chairs to add to the festivities. There was even an ice sculpture of the American flag on the buffet table. Julia thought it matched the one on her husband's ass except his was in living color. She said so, sotto voce.

Having lived in Washington all her life she could pick out the Secret Service, the FBI and all the other security. She mentioned that, too. Tonight, though, they were equal. She, too, wore the tiny microphone on the sleeve of her gown. All she had to do was pretend she was touching her nose and speak into the gizmo on her wrist, just the way all the security spooks did. Even the little buttons in their ears were so high-tech they couldn't be detected. The sound was short of phenomenal, allowing them to hear a whisper from ten feet away.

Mitch ignored his wife's barbed comments. "Baby, you look sensational." He looked around at the other women in the room. He appeared stunned for a moment. His wife was the best-looking woman in the entire room. She seemed to have picked up several pounds and in all the right places.

"Don't call me baby, Mitch. Save that kind of talk for your bimbos. I heard on the way here that the press is set to leak more info on you in the *Post* tomorrow. Back out now before it's too late." Her voice was colder than ice. Mitch opted not to notice.

"That's all garbage. It's politics at their worst. But, if I ever find out it was you who is doing the leaking, you'll regret it."

"Is that a threat, Mitch? If so, you might want to retract those words right now. By the way, I'm leaving you. Excuse me, I have to circulate. That's why I'm here, isn't it? Don't even think about touching me or I might scream in pain with my cracked ribs. And, by the way, the leak in tomorrow's *Post* is about that phony background story you made up on your life because you were ashamed of your own family." She shivered inwardly knowing Mitch's eyes were boring into her back.

Julia started to gingerly make her way across the vast room only to see Isabelle and Alexis at her side to run interference as they jostled their way toward the buffet table.

"There's more security here than guests. I can spot those spooks a mile away," Julia murmured. "Have you seen the Monarch family?"

"Not yet," Isabelle said.

"Good God, Alexis, you really do look like Diana Ross, right down to that wild hair. From some of the looks you're getting, I think the guests think so, too," Julia said.

"Well, that makes my day. The flowers are beautiful. Where in the hell did Yoko get all those wild orchids? By the way, where is she?"

A roving waiter appeared with a tray balanced on one hand filled with plastic flutes of champagne. The women each accepted a glass and pretended to drink. No more than a few sips, Charles had warned. You need your wits about you tonight with all the security.

"Myra is to initiate contact with the Monarchs and then she'll introduce them to Yoko. That's when it's all going to come together. I saw Nikki a moment ago and I know she's on the lookout for Jack Emery. I hate parties like this," Alexis grumbled. "Ah, we made it to the buffet. Some big bucks went into this spread," she said, smacking her lips.

Music could be heard from a small combo. Typical "oldies" fare which meant warbling by Sinatra, Crosby and Como for the older crowd. The crowd with the open checkbooks. The acoustics were horrendous. Isabelle moved off to chase down Kathryn who was talking to a fat lobbyist ogling her bosom. Alexis guided Julia to a less congested area on the far side of the buffet.

"Here comes my husband," Julia told Alexis. "Stay as close as you can. Pretend you're eating or eat, just don't leave me alone with him."

"There you are, darling," Mitch said. "Come, I want you to meet Mrs. Crawford."

"Later, Mitch."

The senator clamped his lips shut but somehow managed to say the words, "Now, Julia."

Julia ignored him. "Oh, look, there's Myra Rutledge. Now Mitch, that's someone you want to meet. She has a war chest that just oozes money. Excuse me, I see our hospital administrator. I have to say hello. We have the whole evening ahead of us," she called over her shoulder as she moved away, Alexis behind her. The senator was left with no other recourse but to smile and reach for a plate.

"You did good, Julia. Your husband is sweating up a storm. I caught a glimpse of Governor Crawford and he does not look like a happy man. Do you suppose he's heard about the next leak?" Alexis whispered as they continued their trek through the crowds.

"Looks that way to me, too."

"Mrs. Crawford looks pretty young to me," Alexis said.

"They're all young," Julia said, sadness ringing in her voice. "They look good in photo ops. It's a trade-off. They like the prestige, the glamour of the White House and all the crap that goes with it. They lunch with their friends, grouse about their *old* husbands and have little flings on the side. They never think they'll get caught. The first Mrs. Crawford was a lovely woman, but she was plain, and she wouldn't allow them to *fix her up*. If I remember correctly, her home in Maryland was known for the rosebushes she planted. She was active in PTA. A Mom. She was a real mom until they used her up and the governor found the present Mrs. Crawford. Everyone in this room has a story and none of them are family reading."

Towering at six feet, the Diana Ross look-alike surveyed the crowd. "Kathryn looks stunning. Do you think she'll ever fall in love again? She took her husband's death so hard," Alexis said, hoping to wipe the sadness from Julia's eyes.

"I certainly hope so. She's too young to go through life alone. I can't see Yoko or the Monarchs. Help me out here, Alexis. Do you see them?"

Frank Sinatra was warbling about a summer wind as the women

finally approached Yoko who was chatting it up with a female con-gresswoman from Virginia. As they approached they could hear that the discussion was about orchids. Julia smiled at the congress-woman as Alexis steered Yoko out of earshot. "Have you seen those creeps?"

"If you mean the Monarchs, no. Myra was supposed to corner them and steer us in their direction. Maybe they decided not to at-tend. Is Julia all right?"

"Julia is holding up just fine but her husband is trying to put the squeeze on her. However, she isn't biting. She's one tough lady. The Monarchs are here, we just haven't seen them yet. You do-ing OK?"

"My feet are killing me. People keep staring at me."

"Suck up the pain, my friend, and people are looking at you be-cause you're a knock-out. Head for the buffet while I try to corner Myra and Charles. Have you seen Nikki?"

"A few minutes ago. She didn't say so but I think she's on the lookout for Jack Emery. Look, there she is! Over by the middle EXIT door."

"OK, see you later. Eat something, Yoko, you're going to need your strength for what's to come later."

"Is the food any good?" Yoko queried.

"No. Yes. I don't know. I ate a shrimp. Tasted like shrimp. I want to talk to Nikki. Don't look right now but I see Myra at three o'clock and she's talking to three people who can only be the Mon-archs. Give them ten minutes before you make contact, and don't forget to eat."

"Yes, Mama." Yoko giggled just as an announcement blasted through the armory via a man in a tuxedo with a microphone in hand on stage. The huge room quieted almost immediately as the governor of Maryland, the Democratic candidate for the presi-dency of the United States, hopped on stage followed by Mitchell Webster.

Nikki whirled around, a crumpled note in her hand. Should she stay or should she go outside? Her stomach tightened into a knot. Charles said everything had been taken care of, and yet, here was Jack sending her notes right under the eyes of the FBI, the Secret Service and God knew who else. The decision was taken out of her hands when she grew light-headed. She needed air, not this canned stuff she was breathing in great gulps. She elbowed the door and stepped outside, but didn't release her hold on the door. It was an

EXIT only door. If it closed, she'd have to walk all the way around to the front.

She saw him hobble toward her holding a lopsided umbrella. In the dim yellow light over the EXIT door she could clearly see Jack's battered, bloody face. Her heart thumped in her chest. He looked to be in excruciating pain. She wanted to run to him, to say something, but she couldn't move. He stopped two feet away.

"I just wanted you to see what they did to me. Take a good look, Nik. This is all your doing. They said they'd kill me if I didn't drop my investigation. Who are *they*? Well, dear Nikki, let me tell you who *they* are. The president's goon squad sicced on me by your very own Charles Martin and Myra. They probably will kill me. You live with that because no way in hell am I going to knowingly allow all of you to break the law. You used to be a lawyer. You swore to uphold the law like I did. Now you can go back in there with all your high powered rich friends. And when they do kill me, you damn well better not show up at my funeral."

Tears rolled down Nikki's cheeks. "Jack, wait . . ."

Jack stopped, the lopsided umbrella tilted so that it covered his knees. "Go to hell, Nicole and don't make any stops on the way down." He let go of the umbrella and it slid across the parking lot. He didn't seem to notice.

Nikki did her best to digest what she'd just seen and heard. She was in a far-away place when she felt a hand on her arm and a voice said, "Ma'am, these doors have to be closed at all times." The strong hand drew her back inside and she didn't protest. She no longer felt light-headed, just sick to her stomach. She had to find Charles and she had to find him right now.

She was startled to hear a loud voice from the stage followed by loud applause. That had to mean Senator Webster was still going to be Governor Crawford's running mate in the election in November. She swivelled in every direction to see where Myra and Charles were. How stupid she was. She moved her arm so that her wrist grazed her lips and said. "Charles, I need to see you *right now*. I'm by the middle EXIT door."

Nikki felt blind with rage when she recalled Jack's battered face, his lips split, top and bottom, his eyes swollen shut, blood oozing from all his cuts and bruises and the fact that he could barely walk. Rage was too kind of a word. What goons was he talking about? And what did he mean about someone coming back to kill him? *You swore to uphold the law like I did. And when they do kill me, you damn well better not show up at my funeral. Go to hell, Nicole, and don't make any stops on the way down.* No, no, that wasn't going to happen. She didn't sign on for anything like this.

Nikki looked away for a moment and when she looked back at the crowded room, Charles was less that a foot away from her. Right at that moment she hated the man, hated that they were all here, hated what was going to happen. She didn't know if she hated Myra and the others or not. Probably.

Charles held out his hand and Nikki shoved the crumpled note into his hand as she gave it a hard shake. "What did your . . . your goons do to Jack? He's half dead. He said they were going to kill him. He should be in a hospital. He was just doing his damn job, Charles. We could have worked around him, outwitted him. What did you do, Charles?"

"Nothing, Nikki. I made some calls. That's all I did. Let's move away from here so we can't be overheard. It was supposed to be a cease and desist, fear of God scare. I certainly didn't authorize any . . . any physical harm to his person."

"That's not good enough for me, Charles. You didn't see Jack, I did. For all I know he could have internal injuries. Look at my feet, Charles. Right now they are rooted to the floor. I'm staying right here until you come back to me with an answer that I can live with. Otherwise, I'm walking out of here and I'll never set foot in Pinewood again. I'll leave it up to you to explain to Myra and the others."

"Wait here, Nikki. This may take a little while. I'll find out what happened. Please, give me the chance to find out. Will you at least do that?"

"Yes. I'll wait right here."

A little while turned into forty-seven minutes. When Nikki saw him making his way toward her she could see the fury in his eyes. Her own eyes narrowed as she waited for an explanation.

"I'm sorry, Nikki. The orders were misconstrued by the president's men. What happened had nothing to do with . . . with our little . . . mission. Jack's pal, the FBI agent, somehow stumbled on to me. He called a fellow agent at Interpol who then notified MI6 that my new identity and location were about to be compromised. If that were to happen, I'd be whisked away in the blink of an eye and I'd never see Myra or any of you again. That's what this is all about and it has nothing to do with the Sisterhood. You're right, we can out-think and outwit Jack. Actually, I view it as a challenge."

It all rang true to Nikki's ears. She found herself nodding. "I want your personal word that Jack is safe from physical harm, Charles."

"You have it, Nikki. I know how much you love him." Nikki didn't bother to deny it this time around. "I can send over medical help if you like, to his apartment."

"Yes, do that, Charles," Nikki said flatly. "What's going on?"

"Myra is entertaining the Monarch family. They're hanging on her every word. When Myra said she could possibly arrange an ambassadorship, all three of them literally swooned. Myra was getting ready to introduce them to Yoko when you flashed me. Is there anything else, Nikki?"

Nikki shook her head before she made her way through the crowd of people, her thoughts not on the mission ahead of them but on Jack Emery.

# Chapter Eleven

Myra Rutledge wore a smile that made her face ache. This Monarch family was despicable and yet here she was talking to them and making them phony promises. All they did, the three of them, was feed off innocent people who bought into their HMOs so their families could be protected in case of illness. Three vultures waiting to pounce on the innocent.

She really had to stop smiling; her teeth were starting to ache. Her eyes left the little group for a few seconds as she tried to locate the girls. Where was Yoko? Ah, there she was, headed her way. A sigh escaped her lips.

Myra was resplendent in diamonds and designer wear, far above what Elaine Monarch strived to be. If she had to take a wild guess, the Monarchs' glittering attire probably cost somewhere in the neighborhood of fifty thousand, give or take a few thousand dollars, and they still looked tacky and artificial. She noticed early on that no one at the event made any effort to either shake their hands or even speak with them unless they initiated the contact. HMO was truly a dirty set of initials in this fair city.

Elaine Monarch reached for Myra's arm. "You do understand that my husband and I would be more than willing *to pay* for the ambassadorship. We don't even care what country it is."

Myra pretended horror. At least she could stop smiling for a few minutes. "No, dear lady. One does not pay for such a position. They pay you. One just accepts graciously when one is appointed. I have considerable influence and will certainly put in a kind word on your behalf. I don't see any harm in making a donation to some worthy cause if you're successful in being appointed." *Dear God, please don't let me gag.*

"You are so very kind, Mrs. Rutledge. Isn't she kind, Derek? We almost didn't come this evening but Ethan said we needed to show our support for the Democrats. Meeting you, Mrs. Rutledge, has been the highlight of the evening," Elaine continued to gush.

Myra had to smile again. "I so enjoyed hearing about your . . . ah, various collections. You did say you have many priceless antiquities of Ming origin, didn't you?'

The skinny dandy son named Ethan chirped up. "Mother has a fabulous collection and is constantly on the lookout for more. They're incredibly hard to come by as I'm sure you know. Are you a collector, Mrs. Rutledge?'

"Of many things, young man." She could tell by the look in Ethan's eyes that Yoko was close by. He did everything but drool, as did his pudgy, balding father. Elaine's head went a little higher, her see-through hair glistening in the artificial light.

Yoko's voice when she spoke was soft, cultured and *whispery*. "I wonder if I might have a quiet word with you, Mrs. Rutledge, before I leave?"

"But of course, my dear. Let me introduce you to this delightful little family. Elaine and Derek Monarch, and their son, Ethan. This is Su Li. She is a descendent of the Ming dynasty. Isn't that absolutely amazing? She probably knows everything there is to know about the treasures you've been collecting." Yoko gave a slight nod of her head, her hands folded demurely in front of her. Ethan looked like his eyes were going to pop right out of his head. His father was so busy undressing Yoko with his eyes he didn't notice the jealous glare in his wife's eyes. Myra felt pleased at what she was seeing. She decided to stoke the fire a little. "Su Li will be your competition for the ambassadorship, Mrs. Monarch. She really doesn't want it, though. We've been doing some arm twisting."

"My father is old-fashioned," Yoko explained. "He does not believe women belong in the political arena but I am a modern Chinese. It's just that my life is so very full right now that I have no time to take on such a prestigious position and do it justice. Still, if the powers that be offer it to me, I would want to do my duty and would probably accept the appointment," she said sweetly. Elaine Monarch scowled at these words.

Myra smiled again. "Su is being modest. She single-handedly runs her father's import-export business. Perhaps you've heard of it, Li Luc Imports."

Derek Monarch's eyebrows shot upward as did his son's. "Your father owns Li Luc Imports?"

"Yes," Yoko said quietly.

Obviously, Myra thought, the male members of the Monarch family were aware of Li Luc Imports's financial status. She could tell they were impressed by their greedy expressions. Elaine had no clue what anyone was talking about. Myra looked around, trying not to be obvious about it. The crowd of supporters was starting to thin out. The buffet table was a mess, the way buffet tables always were at the end of a party. The musicians were packing up their equipment. Where were the girls?

"The night's still young," Derek Monarch said as he looked down at his watch. We live in Manassas which isn't far from here. Would you ladies like to come up with us so we can show you our treasures and perhaps talk a little about that ambassadorship?"

Yoko tilted her head sideways. "I am so sorry but I cannot make it this evening. I am leaving for China early in the morning. It was a pleasure meeting you all." She bowed slightly.

Elaine's see-through hair waved in the breeze created by the various fans overhead. "So, does that mean you do or do not want to be appointed to the ambassadorship. Miss Li?"

Yoko lowered her gaze. "The appointment has not been offered to me as yet, Madam Monarch. Mrs. Rutledge, I understand, will have considerable input when it is time to make the final decision. She is aware of my position. Good night, everyone, it was a pleasure to meet you all."

"Can I escort you to your car?" Ethan asked.

"That would be very kind of you, Mr. Monarch." As they walked away, Myra could hear Yoko ask, "And what is it you do, sir?"

Myra eyed the offensive woman standing in front of her. She knew both husband and wife would kiss her feet if she asked them to. She held out her hand when she saw Isabelle waving across the room. Elaine Monarch looked like she wanted to cry. She poked her husband on the arm. He turned to Myra and said, "We'd be honored if you could see your way to joining us in a nightcap somewhere in the city, Mrs. Rutledge, if you aren't up to a trip to Manassas."

"There's nothing I would like more than that, Mr. Monarch. Unfortunately, I have house guests at home. Perhaps another time. If you're amenable, Mrs. Monarch, and if my schedule permits, we could do lunch next week. By then I should have more information on the ambassadorship."

The relief on Elaine's face was short of comic. "Derek, give Mrs. Rutledge one of your business cards. I'll wait for your call. I have the entire week free, dear lady."

*I just bet you do.* Myra's teeth were starting to ache again as she forced still another smile. It was a relief to shake hands and move away.

As Myra made her way to the front exit, stopping to chat with a federal judge here, a socialite there and a handful of other dignitaries she could hardly wait to get in the car and get home so she could take a shower. All she could think about was the obnoxious Monarch family and how they'd fleeced their subscribers to satisfy their own greed.

Outside, the rain came down in torrents as limo drivers jockeyed for position fearing their customers' wrath at not being by the door to greet them. Security was sloppy at best.

Charles appeared as if by magic holding a large black umbrella. Myra stepped under it. She squeezed Charles's arm. All around her people were muttering and some were cursing the weather, the security and the limo drivers. "I suggest we walk down the road to where our car waits. That's if you don't mind getting wet."

"You can keep me warm, darling." Myra's eyes twinkled. "Let's hurry, though, before those three vultures come anywhere close. As it is, I can't wait to take a shower."

"Were they that bad, Myra?"

"Worse, Charles. All I could think about was all the people who were denied coverage with deadly consequences. Can you imagine people like that coveting an ambassadorship?"

"Yes, dear, I can imagine it. Look, Myra, there's Kathryn with her truck backed up to the back of the armory. And, there's Yoko! They look like our girls. It's amazing how glamorous they can look one minute and the next they're just our girls."

Myra did her best to peer into the driving rain. She saw two figures running back and forth with flowers and plants in their hands. Whistles shrilled and blasted as the local police tried to direct traffic in the soggy night.

Twenty minutes passed before Charles looked down at his digital watch that glowed blue in the dark. "On the count of five, we should have total darkness. One, two, three, four, five!" Myra clutched his arm as the world turned totally dark. "Three minutes before our man drives the Monarch Town Car right up the ramp into Kathryn's truck. Another minute to discard the ramp and Kathryn will take off. The girls are right behind the rig in their individual limousines. No one will ever be the wiser. The only thing the security detail is concerned with at this moment is the governor."

"Darling, you are too clever. I'm not even going to ask you how you arranged all of this."

"We arranged the cars just as Yoko left. It wasn't easy with all the security, and a limousine is not the easiest vehicle to back up and turn around. I relied on the congestion, everyone's short temper and, of course, this pouring rain which worked to our advantage."

"What about Julia and her husband. Don't they have a security detail?"

"They *did* have a security detail. Julia pulled off what Kathryn would call the old switcheroo. The detail is following an eighty-year-old couple from Arlington. All of our people, as I speak, are on their way to Manassas. We can now go home knowing the Monarch family and Senator Webster are in capable hands." Charles looked at his watch again as he counted under his breath. "Three minutes and counting. The lamp posts will come to life and our caravan will be safely out of sight. I just love this rain, don't you, Myra?"

Myra giggled as she snuggled closer to Charles. "I do love the rain but I love you more. What are we going to do when we get home, Charles?"

Charles looked at Myra in the dim yellowish light of the limo. "Unfortunately, not what we would both like to do. We have a job to do."

Myra wiggled even closer, "Oh . . . poop!"

# Chapter Twelve

Jack Emery did his best to bellow, "Come in" to the person knocking on his door. It came out little better than a hoarse croak. He flopped back on the sofa, drained with the effort. *They* were probably coming back to finish the job they started. He wondered what it would feel like to die, to take his last breath, to see the world turn fuzzy and gray. Would he see the white light, the angels everyone talked about, when he drew his last breath?

He tried to open his eyes but finally gave up. "Just fucking do it and get it over with. I'm an easy target, I can't move. Well, what the hell are you waiting for? Look, my eyes are closed. Shoot me and get it over with."

"Jack, it's me, Mark. Look, I'm sorry the way all that crap went down back at my place. I came over to take you to the hospital. You need some help, buddy. For whatever it's worth, I'm on your side. I admit, back there, they scared the living crap out of me. Then I realized I can't stand still for that kind of thing just the way you can't. I'd rather quit. After I get you patched up, I'm calling my boss and whatever happens, happens. Worst case scenario, we open up our own security agency. I have some money saved. My dad will lend me the rest to get us up on our feet."

"Are you nuts! You're looking at a real loser here. Why in the hell would you want to tie yourself up with someone like me? Forget it. Go home. Forget you ever knew me. Let me lie here and die. Go on, get out of here, Mark."

Mark ignored the tortured words as he headed for the kitchen and the freezer. He took out a plastic bag of peas and shook them loose. Jack had to be the only single guy in the world who kept frozen peas in his freezer. He walked back to his friend and placed the package on his battered face. He then made his way to the bathroom and rummaged till he found a first aid kit. He was on his knees about to dress some of Jack's cuts when a knock sounded at the door. In a heartbeat, he was on his feet, his gun in his hand. "Come in." The sound of the hammer clicking back was so loud in the quiet room, Jack almost fainted.

A middle-aged woman dressed in a nurse's uniform and a swarthy man wearing a white lab coat and carrying a medical bag stepped into the room. They seemed oblivious to the drawn gun. "You won't need the gun, young man. We're here to help Mr. Emery and to offer . . . apologies." At least that's what Jack thought he said, his accent heavy and guttural.

"I don't think so," Mark said. "How do we know you aren't here to finish the job? No shots. No nothing. Turn around and leave. I'll take care of my friend."

"No. Your president sends his sincere regrets for this unfortunate turn of events. Allow us to help make it right," the guttural voice said.

Mark dropped to a crouch to shield Jack but not before he stiff-armed the nurse. "We don't need your help. I'll take care of my friend."

Jack would have cried if he could have made his tear ducts work. Loyalty was something he hadn't encountered in a long time. He continued to listen to his friend.

"You are to call this number," the guttural voice said, handing over a slip of paper.

"Yeah, like I'm really going to do that and lay down my gun, too. Take a hike, buddy. There's no way you're squirting anything into my friend's veins."

"Call the number, Mark, or hand me the phone and I'll do it," Jack said. "Tell them to back off toward the door."

"You heard the man," Mark said, brandishing the gun. Both white-coated figures moved backward while Jack dialed the number Mark read from the slip of paper in his free hand.

"United States White House."

Jack ended the call. "It was the White House. What now, Coach. I'm in a lot of pain, here, buddy."

"OK, open the bag and let's see what you got. You can examine him while I watch. No shots, no pills. Clean him up and dress the cuts. That's it. *Capice!*"

An hour later when Jack was done howling and kicking his feet, the doctor stepped backward. "Give him these every four hours for pain. It's Demerol. The word is written on the tablet. They're safe. I taped his ribs. He should see his own doctor as soon as he's comfortable doing so. If his condition changes, you can call me at this number," the doctor said, scribbling a cell phone number on the corner of a magazine on the coffee table. "The number is only good for twenty-four hours at which point it will be disconnected. The best thing for him right now is sleep. We can see ourselves out."

Mark stayed a safe distance behind the couple as they exited the apartment. He shot the dead bolt and the other two locks Jack had personally installed. He himself had the same kind of locks at his own apartment. No sense looking for more trouble.

"Guess they belong to the spook brigade," Jack mumbled. "Get me some whiskey, Mark. It's in the kitchen cabinet. I went to the armory, Mark."

"Tell me something I don't already know," Mark said, looking around the messy apartment. "You really should clean this place up, Jack. You could probably catch a disease just living here."

"Yeah, yeah, yeah. I kind of lost all heart when Nikki dumped me. I always kept it clean for her. The whiskey, Mark?"

Mark poured liberally and then had second thoughts so he watered down the Jim Beam. Jack swallowed it in two gulps.

Mark stuffed the gun he was still holding into the shoulder holster under his armpit. He perched on the end of the couch. "What do you want me to do, Jack?"

Jack knew he was about to fade out. "I don't know, Mark. You know as much as I do right now. Hell, man, you're FBI. If this was your case and there were no obstacles, what would you do? Treat it like it's the most important case on your desk and go on from there. You can use my computer. My password is . . . is . . . Nikki. Don't let me sleep too long, OK?"

"Yeah, sure, Jack."

Mark looked around. If there was one thing he couldn't stand, it was a mess. One of seven children, he'd been taught at an early age how to clean, cook, do laundry, and take care of himself. He started to work. First, he cleared out all the trash, empty pizza boxes, empty Chinese containers and stacks and stacks of beer bottles. The empty dishwasher yawned in his face. He loaded it and what didn't fit, he soaked in the double kitchen sink. He used the vacuum and Dust Buster and loaded the washing machine with a load of pitiful-looking towels. The dirty clothes strewn all over the floor went into an already overstuffed hamper.

Now, he could sit down at the computer where he tapped away for hours without taking a break. When he finally looked up he was surprised to see gray light seeping through the open blinds. It was still raining.

Mark checked on Jack and then went into the kitchen to make coffee and toast for himself. He massaged his neck and shoulders as his mind raced. The big question in his mind was what seven very diverse women had in common? Add one very important man named Charles Martin to the mix and what did he have?

One big mother of a mess was the answer.

Well, hell, he was a computer programmer for the FBI. Even the CIA and the DOJ borrowed him from time to time because he was beyond good. How modest he was, he thought. In the spook world he traveled in, you had to blow your own horn from time to time. He'd installed and programmed some of the most sophisticated computers in all three organizations. As such, he knew where the fire walls and back doors were, how to undo and patch up the fire walls so no one would notice if he accessed them. The big question was, did he really want to put his ass on the line for Jack Emery?

Coffee cup in hand, Mark made his way back to Jack's computer. He stopped a moment to stare down at his sleeping friend. The answer was yes.

# Chapter Thirteen

Julia Webster leaned back against the plush cushions of the limousine. She was exhausted but she'd done her part. The driver of the limousine she and Mitch were riding in would have Kathryn's rig in sight all the way to Manassas, Virginia. For now she just had to listen to her husband's tirade which was getting louder by the moment. It was typical Mitch. Place blame, cry poor poor me. If she wanted to, she could recite the litany verbatim.

"Where the hell are we going?" Mitch bellowed. "This isn't the way to Georgetown! Where's our detail? You really are stupid, Julia. We're in the wrong limousine! This is your fault. Where the hell are we going?" he bellowed a second time.

Julia yawned elaborately. "You're right, we're in the wrong limousine. Your detail is following some Republican couple to Arlington. Or maybe it's Alexandria. We're going to Manassas to have drinks with those horrid Monarch HMO people. I'd appreciate it if you'd lower your voice. You're giving me a headache."

Not about to give up, Mitch moved forward until he was next to the partition separating the driver from the passengers. "Turn this damn car around and take me home. To Georgetown. We changed our mind, we don't want to go to Manassas."

"Too late, sir," came the response. Isabelle took her eyes off the road for a minute to glare at her passenger. "Sit down and buckle your seat belt. If you force me to stop this car, you won't like the consequences."

"Are you threatening me?" Mitch shouted.

"Yes," Isabelle shouted in return.

"Do you know who I am, driver? I'm a United States senator! You just threatened a United States senator! I can have you thrown in jail for threatening me."

"Go for it, Senator!" Isabelle snapped.

Julia smiled to herself. Her eyes still closed, she sensed Mitch returning to his seat. She knew he was searching for his cell phone he'd laid on the seat earlier. She was now sitting on it. She smiled again.

"Well, we'll just see about this. Where's my cell phone, Julia?"

"I have no idea, Mitchell. Maybe you left it back at the armory."

"I brought it with me. Will you move, please. Maybe it slid across the seat."

Julia made a pretense of looking and patting the seat. "No, Mitchell, it isn't here."

"Then let me use yours. C'mon, c'mon. I think we're being hijacked here. Though who would be stupid enough to do something like that boggles my mind."

Julia handed over her evening purse. "There was no room for a cell phone so I left it in my car. Relax, Mitchell, and think about how you can snooker the Monarchs into doing some fund-raising for your campaign. The night's still young. We'll be back home by midnight."

"What was that crap before about leaving me? You said if I gave you that list you'd stand by me."

"I lied."

"Oh, no, it doesn't work that way. I need you, Julia. We're going to discuss this when we get back home."

"Whatever you say, Mitchell." Like that was really going to happen.

Fifteen minutes later the limousine slowed to a crawl.

Up ahead, Kathryn's eighteen-wheeler approached the security panel outside the Monarch estate. Kathryn glared into the electric eye and speaking box. She pressed a series of numbers on a portable keypad Charles had given her. The gates—some kind of thick wood mixed with heavy iron—swung open. The only thing missing was coiled razor wire. Kathryn pulled ahead and then waited until Isabelle's limousine cleared the gates before she pressed a second series of numbers. She waited another few minutes until she was certain the gates were closed and locked. She then pressed a third set of numbers that jammed the gates. Safe.

Nikki was in the passenger seat while Yoko was settled in the small area where Kathryn slept when she was on the road. In the back of the truck, the Monarch family huddled together inside their car in the dark. Alexis was their driver.

"Do you suppose the Monarchs think all this security makes

them important or do they have something inside they don't want anyone to see? They aren't the type to hide out. They like to be seen. It is impressive, though. I wonder how many of their subscribers had to die for them to get all of this," Nikki said.

"Too many," Kathryn said curtly. "Nikki, call Charles and tell him we're inside the gates."

The driveway that looked more like a two lane highway was lined with tall cypress trees that formed a canopy as the big truck lumbered around the snake-like road that was a mile long.

"I can't wait to see this place in the daylight. I read in one of the reports that the Monarchs pay their ground keepers two hundred thousand bucks a year! Do you believe that? This is way too decadent for me."

Kathryn drove the rig up to a concrete apron in front of an eight-car garage. She cut the engine, hopped out of the cab, and ran around to the back to unlock the huge door. She sucked in her breath when the huge metal door slid upward. Headlights glared in the darkness. With Nikki's help, she lowered the metal treads that would allow Alexis to back the Town Car out.

"You ready, Nikki?"

"Yep." Nikki pulled a nine-millimeter Glock out of the waistband of her slacks and brandished it about. "Open the door!" Kathryn obliged. Ethan Monarch was the first one out as he swung his arms ready to do battle. Kathryn brought up her elbow and smacked him square in the throat. He collapsed to his knees. He looked like he was praying as he gasped and sputtered.

Elaine Monarch was next. She looked frightened. "What do you want? We'll give you anything you want. Don't kill us. Please don't kill us."

Kathryn looked at Nikki and shrugged. She looked back at Elaine. "Clarify what you mean by, 'anything.'"

"Whatever you want," Derek said as he minced his way over to stand next to his wife.

"OK, we'll think about it. Let's go in the house. That goes for you, too, Junior," Kathryn said, giving the young man a none too gentle kick with her booted foot. "Don't even think about pressing the panic buttons on the alarm system. They've been disabled. I'll take it as an act of bad faith if you try. Move!"

"Who are you people?" Derek asked, his voice quivering with fright.

Nikki waved the Glock. The trio picked up their feet and practically scampered to a set of French doors. Nikki aimed the gun and shot off the lock. She blew imaginary smoke from the barrel of the gun. The trio moaned as they grasped at one another."

"Great shooting, girl!" Kathryn said. "Lights, people!"

Elaine scurried to a row of switches inside the door. Kathryn and Nikki both blinked. It wasn't a room, it was a cavern. They took a minute to look around in disbelief. Oriental and Aubusson rugs, inlaid marble, French parquet, stained glass skylights and windows, priceless paintings, brocade-covered furniture, spindly tables with spindly legs. Nikki looked upward at the vaulted ceiling that had cherubs and angels floating overhead. "What's this room?" Nikki asked, directing her question at Elaine.

Elaine looked like she was trying to decide if there was a right or wrong answer to the question. "It's just . . . a room. We don't use it."

"Then why do you have it?" Kathryn asked.

"To . . . to hold our treasures. We . . . we call it the French room. Everything in this room is priceless, one of a kind. Things a collector dreams about," Elaine responded. She appeared relieved that she'd apparently given the right answer.

"We sent your servants on a little vacation. The chauffeur and the garden crew, too. There's no one here but us," Nikki said as she continued looking around.

"Where is your home office? According to this," Kathryn said, pulling a folded sheet of paper out of her shirt pocket, "it's next to a suite of rooms on the second floor. Who wants to lead the way? And your home theater, where is that?" Derek pointed to the doorway on the left.

"Where's the safe?" Nikki asked.

"We don't have a safe," Derek bleated.

Kathryn waved the paper. "Rule number one. Don't lie to us. If you do, you will be punished," she singsonged. "Take us to the office. Lead the way, Junior. Mummy and Daddy, follow Junior."

Junior led the way through two more cavernous rooms—a Japanese room and a Chinese room. Kathryn and Nikki rolled their eyes at one another. The rooms were *stuffed* with treasures. "Does this remind you of a museum?" Nikki whispered.

"Yeah, one where the curator has really bad taste. Ah, we're here," Kathryn said, poking her head into the Monarchs' private office. She whistled at what she was seeing. Nikki simply gawked.

"Yo, Derek, what is all this?" Kathryn asked, waving her arms about. "Remember rule number one when you answer."

"Tell them, Derek," Elaine said, clutching her husband's arm.

"Don't tell them anything, Pop. This is a home invasion," Ethan squawked hoarsely. "You're going to pay for this," he squawked again.

Nikki waved her gun. "I-don't-think-so! Lookee here, we're the ones with the gun." Ethan clamped his lips shut.

"It's a duplicate of Monarch's home office," Derek said. "Everything is at my fingertips. Tell me why you're doing this."

"Really," Kathryn drawled. "This is Washington. You gotta keep up with the trends. I'm thinking this is a trendy operation. No more questions. Show my friend how everything ties together while your wife shows me where your home safe is. But before we do that, Junior, strip down and then sit down. Well, what are you waiting for, strip!"

"Oh, my Godddd!" Elaine dithered. Her eyes sparked momentarily as though she understood she would be next. "Is it really necessary to do this? We're cooperating with you. Why do you have to humiliate us?"

"Because we can," Kathryn said coldly. "Humiliation is the least of your worries."

Ethan stared defiantly at Nikki and the gun she was holding.

"Do you really want me to count to three?" Nikki aimed the gun and mouthed the numbers one through three. When Ethan made no move to undress, she fired at the point of his shoe. Shiny black patent leather and splinters of hardwood flew upward. And a waterfall of blood mixed with black nylon from his sock. Elaine stumbled. Kathryn didn't look back.

"Where the hell is the safe, Elaine? We've been walking for a long time here. You better not be stalling me," Kathryn hissed angrily.

"It's in the private wing of the house. We really don't use this section. It's for . . ."

"I know, housing your treasures. You should get one of those moving walkways."

"We looked into it but it didn't . . . seem feasible," Elaine whined. "This is the beginning of the private wing."

Kathryn looked around. More cavernous rooms, more priceless rugs and paintings. "OK, show me the safe and open it up."

Elaine Monarch moved toward a door in the center of what looked like a sitting room that held no less than seven ugly couches and eleven ugly armchairs. She opened the door, stepped through the opening and then opened another door. She stood to the side. Kathryn gaped at the heavy steel door. A vault similar to those used in banks. Her insides started to twitch. "Open it!"

"It can only be opened at three minutes past the hour. The time is precise." Elaine looked down at the diamond studded watch on her wrist and then at the digital clock mounted in the vault door. "We have five minutes to wait," she said nervously.

Five minutes later a tiny ping of sound could be heard from the mounted clock on the vault door. Elaine moved forward and punched in numbers. It took all her strength to turn the huge wheel but finally the door moved and then slid silently to the side on well oiled hinges. She pressed another switch that flooded the room with light.

The inside of the vault was possibly eight by ten feet in size with floor to ceiling shelves on all three walls. A small chair and metal table sat in the middle of the room. An overhead fan whirred to circulate the air. Probably so the money lining the shelves wouldn't dry out, Kathryn thought inanely.

She turned to her hostess and said, "I really don't have time to count all this but how much money is on those shelves? Remember rule number one."

"Twenty-five million dollars," Elaine mumbled.

"And the jewelry? That is jewelry in those velvet boxes, right?"

"Around sixteen million," Elaine mumbled again.

"All right, let's just leave this door open for now. Is there a short-cut back to your offices?"

"Yes."

"Then hit it, lady. Don't mess with me again. Why did you take me on the scenic route instead of the shortcut?"

"Why should I help you? You're going to kill us, aren't you? You people have no mercy."

Kathryn chewed on her lower lip. "No, we don't. Have mercy, that is. Come on, pick up those stilettos and let's move. We wasted enough time with your scenic tour." Elaine teetered on her spike heels but did as Kathryn ordered. Both women were breathless when they entered the Monarch home office.

Both senior and junior Monarch were stark naked. It wasn't a pretty sight. "You're next, Mom," Nikki said, waving the gun. Elaine started to cry. "Don't make me help you." Elaine complied. A naked Elaine was not some kind of pretty. "OK, sit down," Nikki said, indicating three small chairs on casters as she pulled a roll of duct tape out of her back-pack and tossed it to Kathryn.

"Oh, God, why are you doing this to us? I opened the safe. Take the money and leave us alone." Elaine sobbed.

Nikki shoved her gun into the belt of her slacks the moment

Kathryn secured the little family to the swivel chairs. Cell phone in hand, she called Charles but not before Kathryn whispered in her ear. "All our chicks in the area are secure. Tell me what to do." Nikki scribbled furiously. "Got it. I'll get back to you," she told Charles.

"Turn them around so they can see the monitor." Kathryn turned the chairs and waited.

"I'm only going to ask you these questions once. If you stall me, give me the wrong answers, you will feel"—she pointed to the cattle prod Kathryn was holding upright—"some severe pain. How do I access the business account?"

Derek blurted the information, his eyes never leaving the cattle prod. Ethan glared defiantly. Elaine continued to sob.

The question and answer routine went on for twenty minutes. When Nikki had all the information she needed she nodded to Kathryn.

A picture of a small blonde girl flashed on the screen. It was followed by pictures of a middle-aged man and then an elderly lady in a white shawl. Picture after picture appeared on the screen. The Monarch family looked at each picture not understanding what they were seeing but they didn't ask any questions.

Then a series of pictures, possibly a hundred or so, appeared on the screen. They were all small children from newborns to children five or six years of age. All looked listless, their arms dangling at their sides. They looked like tiny robots.

Thirty minutes later, Nikki finally stopped popping pictures. She held up a thick stack of photos six inches thick. "Do you know who those people are?" she demanded.

"How could we possibly know that?" Elaine cried. "Just take the money and leave us alone. What are you doing? What do you want from us?"

"We're going to give all your money away. To people like those you just saw on the screen. And, to these," Nikki said, wagging the stack of photos in their direction. "Those people are your subscribers. You denied their claims. Most of them died because they couldn't get the care they needed. The children were all born with Erb's Palsy because their mothers were sent to a doctor Monarch approved of. When they were born, there was no doctor in attendance, the families tried to sue Monarch. Once again, you greedy people ordered arbitration by retired judges who were on your payroll. Needless to say, the verdicts were always on Monarch's side because those judges didn't want to lose the income you provided.

Someone has to pay for that. We find you guilty as charged so you are going to pay. We're going to bankrupt all three of your Monarch HMOs. And we're going to ruin all the people who have helped you launder that money sitting in the vault in your personal quarters. When we're done with you, we're going after the doctor, his staff and all those bloodsucking judges on your payroll."

Elaine continued to wail. Senior and Junior glared. They were getting good at it.

"Now, give me your personal bank information and that also includes all your off-shore accounts. Come on now, don't be shy. Kathryn you might want to . . . ah . . . prod them a little to move things along."

Kathryn yanked at the charged up cattle prod and gave Junior and Senior a none too gentle prod. They screamed in pain just as a knock sounded on the door. Elaine stomped her bare feet and tried to shout something but the duct tape Kathryn quickly put on muffled the sound.

"Oh, gee whiz, company," Nikki said as she busily clicked the keys in front of her. She nodded to Kathryn who obediently trotted across the room to open the door. Julia waltzed through, followed by her husband. Kathryn slammed and locked the door.

Mitch Webster looked around the room, the color draining from his face.

Julia walked over to the duct-taped family members, leaned over and said, "I'm a doctor. Are you all right?" Her tone clearly indicated she didn't care one way or the other. She dipped her hand into one of the pockets of her wrap and brought out a bouquet of hypodermic syringes. "You name it and I got it," she said cheerfully.

"Julia! What the hell is going on here? Who are these people?"

"Well that one and that one," Julia said, pointing to Nikki and Kathryn, "are my friends. These three are scum of the earth. Strip down, Mitch!" Julia looked at Kathryn and said, "I don't smell it, do you?" Kathryn shrugged, not understanding the question. Julia laughed. "Testosterone! I think it evaporated." She turned her attention back to her husband, the bouquet of syringes still in her hand. "Strip or you get one of each!"

"Are you crazy?"

The charged up cattle prod snapped outward and Mitch doubled over. Kathryn struck a second and third time. Mitch took off his clothes. Kathryn clucked her tongue. "You bad boys never seem to learn."

A knock sounded on the door.

"Oh, gee whiz, more company," Nikki gurgled as she sent blizzards of numbers flying across the screen.

Kathryn tossed the roll of duct tape to Julia who shoved her husband onto the last chair in the office. "My goodness, where *are* my manners? I'd like you all to meet my philandering husband, Senator Mitchell Webster. Mitch, these lovely naked people are the Monarchs of the infamous Monarch HMOs. We're giving away all their money and making restitution to their subscribers. Actually, what we're doing is bankrupting them and their company."

Mitch opened his mouth to snarl something but Julia slapped a strip of tape over his mouth.

The door flew inward as Kathryn backed up. Two black clad figures brandishing swords danced into the room. Only their eyes were visible in the black hoods. Yoko advanced, brandishing a wicked-looking sword as she yelled, *"Eyow!"* she followed up with a high pirouette. A puff of smoke exploded from her hand before a steel star sailed through the air to land between Ethan Monarch's legs. Urine squirted high in the air.

Not to be outdone, Alexis whooped, whirled and dipped as she, too, delivered puffs of smoke and loud bloodcurdling shouts.

"Ninjas!" Derek Monarch moaned pitifully, his eyes on the star between his son's legs.

Elaine screamed at the top of her lungs.

Derek looked down at his privates and then at the swords in the hands of the black clad figures. Mitch tried to cross his legs. "Just think of us as a bunch of party animals, Mitch." Then Julia laughed. And laughed.

"By the way, we're all together," Nikki called from her computer station. "It's time to divvy up," she called out cheerfully. She pointed to Kathryn. "Do you have any special causes?"

"Let me think. Can I pick anyone I want?"

Nikki nodded.

"Let's donate twenty thousand to Green-peace. Another twenty thousand to the Sierra Club. Two million to the ASPCA. Twenty million to Emily Sanchez's family." Kathryn turned to the Monarchs. "Monarch said the bone marrow Emily needed was unnecessary. Emily died. Nah, make that twenty-five million. I heard the Cartoon Network is in financial trouble. Let's give them a hundred thousand. Murphy loves watching cartoons."

Nikki directed her next comment to Derek Monarch. "We're sending a year's premiums back to all your subscribers and advising them to sign on with a PPO opposed to an HMO. All existing claims will be paid *in full.* We're also ignoring the deductibles."

It was Julia's turn. She looked at the robust bottom line on Nikki's chart. "Ten million to the Haggerty family. Mr. and Mrs. Haggerty used up all their savings and are currently in the welfare system because you denied the coverage that would have made him whole. Greed is a terrible thing."

Derek Monarch started to drool when he realized what was happening. Ethan slumped in his chair as his millions were allocated to worthy recipients. Elaine wept noisily, so noisily Kathryn pointed the cattle prod at her perky silicone breasts. She shut up instantly and then hiccupped.

"You raided this company for your own personal greed," Nikki said. "We simply can't allow that. We find you three, guilty as charged! Damn, I already said that, didn't I? Well, that's what we're doing."

"Oh, dear, Mitch wants to say something," Julia said, walking over to her husband. She yanked at the strip of duct tape.

"I don't know these people. If they did what they did then they deserve this but what the hell am I doing here? I hate HMOs. It's the Republicans who love those HMOs. I'm a goddamn Democrat. I demand you let me loose immediately."

"Demand all you want, Mitch. We're going to deal with you later. Make another peep and the Ninjas can have you. Do I make myself clear?"

"Are we having fun yet?" Kathryn chortled.

"I didn't know any of this," Elaine Monarch sobbed. "I didn't know those people died. How could you do such a thing, Derek?"

"Shut up, Elaine. Where did you think the money came from for . . . all of this?"

"Your salary. That's what you told me. Oh, God, Oh, God!" She sobbed.

"Ooops, more company," Nikki said when a knock was heard at the door. The two Ninjas stepped aside as Julia ran to open it.

"Refreshments!" Isabelle trilled as she trundled in a huge dolly laden with food.

Nikki stepped away from the computer to stand in front of the four bound figures strapped to the chairs. "OK, the fun's over. Do any of you four have even one compassionate bone in your bodies? How could you knowingly withhold crucial medical care to those who need it the most? How? Do you have any idea how many deaths and crippling illnesses are lying on your personal doorstep?" She didn't expect an answer and she didn't get one.

"As of Monday morning, Monarch's doors are closed. Every account that has your name or a family member's name on it is now carrying a zero balance. We've only made a dent in what we plan to do to right all the wrongs you three made in the name of your greed. It's going to take us weeks to notify and make restitution to all those you've damaged but it will be done. You are now going to sign off on some quit claim deeds to all the different properties you own. Everything is going to be sold and given to the people you bilked. All your cars, your boats, that fancy Gulfstream plane will go on the auction block. The whole ball of wax. But first the three of you are going to sign this power of attorney allowing me to dispose of your assets and the company's assets. Kathryn, untie their writing hands then bind them back up."

"Why am I here?" Mitch bellowed. "I'm a goddamn United States senator! I demand you release me immediately. You better not be thinking about murdering anyone!"

Isabelle, who was spreading caviar on crackers and handing them out with glasses of champagne, looked at Julia and said, "This might be a good time to tell your husband why he's here."

"I think you're right. Take the tape off one of his hands so he can read my medical report."

Kathryn, her hands shaking, undid the tape and handed him Julia's diagnosis. She stepped back to watch the senator.

"What the hell is this? It says you . . . it says you have AIDS! I knew it! I knew you were screwing around! You bitch!"

"Oh, God! Oh, God! Did you touch me?" Elaine Monarch squealed in fright.

Julia closed her eyes and would have dropped to the floor but Nikki caught her. Kathryn handed the senator a second medical report. An evil grin stretched across her face. "Read it and weep, Senator!"

"You gave me AIDS! I'll kill you for this."

Isabelle was in his face in the blink of an eye. "Look at the dates, Senator. *You* gave AIDS to your wife. You're the one. And you infected everyone you came in contact with. That's why your wife wanted the list of women you slept with. You have AIDS, Senator Webster."

"You're lying! You're all crazy! I didn't have a blood test," the senator blustered.

"You gave blood, you just don't remember. I took a blood sample while you were sleeping. I am a doctor, you know. I had you tested. I'm more than willing to leak *that* to the *Post,*"Julia said.

Mitch continued to bluster. "I don't believe you. I feel fine. I'm healthy as a horse. You're lying!"

"I felt fine, too, in the beginning. The drugs will work for a while and then they won't work anymore. Your immune system may be stronger than mine. You have it, Mitch, make no mistake about it."

"I'll throw all of your asses in jail the minute I get out of here. I am not without influence."

"You aren't getting out of here, Senator," Isabelle said. "Caviar, anyone?"

"What the hell does that mean? Kidnapping is against the law. You can't kidnap a United States senator. This scum," he said, jerking his head in the Monarchs' direction, "yeah, but not me."

"Oh, well!" Kathryn said.

Nikki looked down at the stack of quit claim deeds in her hand. "Now, let's tackle those trusts you think you're getting away with. I'm going to need all of your signatures quite a few more times. Shame on you for not mentioning the trusts. I think you were just so agitated you simply forgot."

The women moved toward the door, Isabelle pushing the dolly ahead of her. She closed the door behind her. They all walked down to the end of the hallway.

"We did it! We actually did it! Julia, honey, are you OK?" Alexis asked.

"I'm fine. Did you see his face? I will take that look of disbelief with me forever."

Alexis and Yoko ripped off their black masks. "Now what?" Alexis demanded.

"Charles said we have to dismantle all the computers," Nikki said. "He won't care if we smash them up. We have to sanitize this place. Charles is working on something for the *Post* and it will hit sometime this week. By then, the four of them will be so far away no one in the world will be able to find them."

"What about all these treasures, the paintings, what's going to happen to them?" Alexis asked.

"They go with the house. Mr. Monarch signed off on everything. Everything will be sold. Charles has it all arranged. Private collectors, you know. We have to take all the money and the jewelry out oᶜ the vault and take it to McLean."

'Alexis, you and Yoko take Junior and Senior out to Kathryn's rig. Stick them in the car and use the handcuffs to shackle them to the door handle. Mrs. Monarch gets the passenger seat in front. The senator can bounce around inside the back of the truck for all I care. Tape his hands behind his back and his ankles as well," Nikki said.

Kathryn led Julia over to a brocaded sofa and helped her to stretch out. "Take a nap, Julia. We'll wake you when it's time to leave." Kathryn kissed her cheek and touched her hair with gentle fingers. Julia closed her eyes and was asleep within minutes.

As one, the sisters wiped at their eyes. "Time is money, ladies, let's get to it," Nikki said.

They worked feverishly as they trundled the dolly back and forth to the eighteen-wheeler. It was up to Nikki to sanitize the residence which she did with the air of a professional.

Two hours later, the Monarch mansion was swept clean. Kathryn took a crowbar from the back of her truck and proceeded to smash every machine in the Monarchs' office. The women clapped with enthusiasm. Then they high-fived each other.

Nikki looked around the office. "Charles would be so pleased."

"Did we get everything?" Kathryn asked.

"I went over it twice," Nikki said. "I cleaned out all the other safes on Charles's map and just threw everything in those garbage bags." She held out her hands encased in surgical gloves.

"I'll carry Julia. She's still sleeping. I'll put her in the backseat of the car they arrived in. You're driving her, Nikki. Isabelle will be with Alexis, Yoko and myself. Can you handle it?" Kathryn said.

"Not a problem" Nikki replied. "Be careful, Kathryn, you're carrying some strange cargo this trip. You're going to Baltimore Washington Airport where Charles's people will take over. I'll see you back in McLean."

"See ya!" Kathryn said as she picked up Julia and cradled her to her chest. Her eyes sparkled with unshed tears as she carried her friend out of the house to the car for her ride back to McLean.

"Kathryn, be careful, OK?"

"You know it."

# Chapter Fourteen

Jack Emery looked down at the bottom of his computer monitor to see the date and the time. Then he fingered his battered face. It was healing much too slowly to suit him. He still wasn't comfortable with the temporary caps on his front teeth. He felt like he had a mouth full of mush that made him lisp when he spoke.

He felt beaten, worn down. Ten long days since he'd been beaten to a pulp. He probably would have starved to death if it hadn't been for Mark and take-out restaurants that delivered. The outside world no longer beckoned. He liked sitting on his chocolate colored sofa watching stupid shows on television and swigging beer from long-neck bottles until he fell asleep. He'd only been out twice, to go to the dentist and to pick up prescriptions.

Jack had no idea what was going on in the outside world. Ten days' worth of newspapers was piled high on his kitchen counter along with ten days' worth of mail. He hadn't turned on a newscast in the same length of time. He knew his old-fashioned answering machine either wasn't working or the little tape was full. He knew this because two red lights glowed on the square black box. One red blinking light meant there were messages, two blinking lights meant the tape was full. It simply did not matter in the scheme of things.

Jack clicked off the computer before he shuffled out to the kitchen and opened the refrigerator. He was stunned to see an array of food filling the shelves. Fresh orange juice, a new container of milk, a new twelve-pack of Bud, apples, cheese, a loaf of bread, lean-looking bacon, a dozen eggs. Cold cuts from a deli in individual plastic bags, hot dogs, some ground beef, cottage cheese, yogurt and salad greens. Mark must have been here during the night. Obviously, he'd tidied up while he was here, too.

Good old Mark. He felt bad that he'd sucked his friend into the mess he'd gotten himself into. He didn't deserve a friend like Mark. Mark agreed. Jack found himself grinning at the thought.

He knew he had to get off his ass and join the world again. Some world where the bad guys got away with what they were doing and the good guys got the living shit beat out of them. There was something wrong with this picture. Something really wrong.

Jack headed back toward the chocolate colored sofa. Nikki had helped him pick it out, and the day it was delivered, they'd christened it by making love all night long. He looked over at the matching recliner where he liked to tilt back to read the paper. He eyed the sofa but opted for the recliner. His biggest problem right now was what to have for dinner. Maybe chips and salsa or maybe some of the pre-cooked pudding he'd seen in the refrigerator. Both would require little chewing.

Jack propped up his feet and swigged from the Bud. He should go back to work. Back to the grind where he tried to put away the bad guys so some smart-ass defense attorney could lie through his teeth to get his client off so he could do the same damn thing all over again. Where the hell was the justice he'd believed in all his life? Where? He felt like crying but big guys didn't cry. That was a crock. Everything was a crock of crap.

Jack adjusted the volume on the TV set. He watched ten minutes of Montel Williams interviewing defiant, pregnant teenagers before he switched channels. Judge Sophie was railing against some guy who had stiffed his landlord. He switched channels again to a rerun of *Law and Order* where the good guys made things right in sixty minutes. Another crock. He finally pressed the mute button and reached down into the magazine basket to pull out last month's issue of *Field and Stream.* Maybe he needed to go fishing so he could commune with nature and think about his life. He didn't even know where his fishing pole was. He dropped the magazine back into the basket.

He thought about Nikki because when he came to this point in his daily thinking, memories of her surfaced no matter how hard he tried to block them out. Where was she? What was she doing? The image of her stunned expression when she saw him outside the armory would stay with him to his dying day. He knew then she hadn't known about the beating he suffered. She might not have been privy to the actual details but his gut told him she knew something bad was going to happen. Otherwise . . . why did a doctor and nurse show up so conveniently?

He went back to thinking about what he was going to have for dinner when he heard noise coming from his small foyer. He moved fast, quicker than he'd moved in the last ten days, to the sofa and his gun that was between the cushions. It was in his hand in the blink of an eye, the hammer pulled back. He waited, his heart pounding in his chest.

"It's me, Jack!" Mark called. "Man, it's pouring cats and dogs out there. It took me an hour to get here but I did stop at Mozellie's for some spaghetti and meatballs."

Jack clicked the hammer back into position before he pushed the gun down between the cushions.

"You gotta stop doing this, Mark. I'm not some charity case on your conscience. Tell me how much I owe you so I can square off with you."

"What's a little food between friends? Sorry I haven't been able to get over here more during your waking hours. You were out like a light when I stopped by last night. You look a little better today." All this was said as the FBI agent took out cartons and plastic silverware from the shopping bag that oozed the scent of garlic and parmesan cheese and set everything up on the oversized coffee table. Napkins, little packets of salt, pepper, and a plastic container of grated cheese followed. Mark trotted off to get two fresh bottles of beer. He uncapped both of them. "Dig in, buddy, because this is the best spaghetti and meatballs in the state of Virginia."

As they gobbled their food, they talked baseball and fly fishing. When they were done, Mark tossed everything into the shopping bag along with the empty beer bottles and carried them out to the trash chute in the hallway. The apartment still smelled like garlic and cheese.

The FBI agent and the ADA eyeballed each other from their respective positions. Mark took the initiative and spoke first. "Are you ready to hear about what's going on in the outside world?"

Jack swigged from his bottle. He shrugged. "Not unless it directly affects me. I'm about ready to go back to work. I have a meeting with my boss in two days. Figure if I wear dark glasses, don't smile and try to walk normally, I can pull it off. The truth is, Mark, the job has lost its luster. If it doesn't go well then I'll start looking for a job in the private sector where the pay is a hell of a lot better plus you get a sign-on bonus. How're you doing, buddy?"

"I gave my notice last week. I told you but I guess you don't remember. You were pretty high on pain pills that night. After that visit from those . . . those *shields*, I started looking at things a lot differently. I just couldn't get back into the swing of it. Then they farmed me out to the DOJ and somehow, I screwed up the program. They chewed my ass out and it was the last straw. These last few days I've been busy *correcting* some of the programs I wrote and installed for the Bureau."

"What's that mean?" Jack asked.

"What that means, buddy, is I can access all those programs and no one would ever be the wiser. Same goes for Department of Justice. My codes, my own private back doors, my own fire walls, that kind of thing."

"You sly devil!" Jack said in awe. "Does that mean you're going *private?*"

"What it really means is, *we're* going private. Wait till you hear this. I put up a quickie Web site about ten days ago. I called it the Justice Agency and added a little blurb about righting wrongs, etcetera, etcetera. I applied for grants all over the place under that name and within two days I got a hundred-thousand-dollar-grant from some spinoff of that Monarch HMO setup. Of course you haven't been reading the papers or listening to the news so you might not know about that. I got the check today. Just like that—a hundred grand. Say something, Jack."

Jack hoisted himself up to a better sitting position. He winced, pain flashing across his face. "Are you telling me Monarch went belly up? If that's the case, how'd you get money out of them?"

"No, no, they didn't go belly up. If you'd read the papers you'd know all about this. It happened a day or so after that armory shindig, after those shields paid us a visit. It was on the front page, above the fold, for about four days. Monarch was private so they could do whatever they wanted. They returned premiums, paid off people whose claims were originally denied. They even printed a list in the paper of the recipients along with apologies. A legal firm in D.C. handled the payouts."

"Which firm?" Jack asked, although he already knew the answer. His hands started to shake.

"Nikki's firm, Jack. Man, think of all those billable hours. Damn, that was a plum for her. There's more. The Monarchs dropped off the face of the earth. No one is looking for them, if that's your next question. And, why should they? They disbanded, got religion, whatever, and decided to right the wrongs the company was responsible for. I have to file reports but that's no big deal. We can keep tabs on Nikki and her firm as well as the others and no one will be the wiser. With my expertise I can hack into her computers anytime I want. Win win, Jack. End of story."

"Why do I feel there's more?" Jack asked uneasily. Dropped off the face of the earth. *Just the way Marie Llewellyn dropped off the face of the earth.*

"Because there is more. Senator Webster and his wife disappeared at the same time. Somehow or other, according to the press, the doctor and the senator got into the wrong limousine and no one has seen them since that night at the armory. The weather was a bitch that night and the senator's detail ended up guarding some elderly Republican couple instead of the Websters. There were some pretty red faces come Sunday morning. The Bureau is on it. Mrs. Webster is gone, too. Seems she had earlier resigned her position at the hospital citing family obligations. As far as I know, no one, and that includes the Bureau, is linking the two together. All five of them literally dropped off the face of the earth. Doesn't say much for the Secret Service, now does it?"

Jack rubbed at the stubble on his bruised and battered face. "I'll be damned."

"So are you in with me or not?"

"That hundred grand isn't going to last very long, Mark."

"Oh, did I forget to tell you, the grant runs for ten years? Ten years, Jack. It will pay us a modest salary, pay the rent on an office plus utilities. We can share an apartment in the beginning to cut down on our personal rent. We're bound to get some clients if we advertise. We can do this, Jack. I can freelance on the side. You gotta resign, though. Can you do that?"

Could he? "Yeah, I can do that. That means we . . ."

"Yeah, that's what it means, Jack. If we go private we don't have to answer to our bosses and we can play detective all day and all night, twenty-four-seven. And remember this, the mightiest weapon of all is the written word. All we have to do is find some gung ho seasoned reporter who will listen to us, and wait to print the story we give him. When we have a story to give him, that is. I even think I know the right guy, Bob Lyon. They call him The Lion."

"I'm going home now. I suggest your start reading those newspapers on your kitchen counter and then prepare your resignation letter. You OK?"

"I think I just crossed the threshold to wellness. I expect my recovery to be short of immediate. Should I thank you, kiss your feet, what?"

Mark laughed. "Buy dinner tomorrow night. That means you go out and pick it up. We're gonna get them, Jack."

"Yeah, Mark, we're gonna get *them*." If they don't get us first.


Less than twenty-five miles away, Myra and Charles walked out into the velvet darkness, crystal goblets of wine in hand. They sat down next to one another. Myra reached for his hand and squeezed it before she placed her head on his shoulder.

"It's a beautiful night, isn't it, Charles? It's so quiet. Even the Dobermans are quiet."

"That's because it's midnight," Charles said.

"So it is. We should make a toast, Charles."

"Not yet, dear."

Myra sat up and placed her wine on a rattan table next to the swing she and Charles were sitting in. "Charles, we never speak about . . . about your grief where Barbara is concerned. It's always me wailing. Do you . . . ?"

"No, Myra, I don't. I know you aren't going to understand this and sometimes I don't understand it myself but I just can't . . . I don't know how . . . it's all locked up deep inside me."

Myra patted Charles's hand. "I understand. I didn't think it would ever be possible to love another human being the way I loved Barbara. It's not the same yet it is the same. I think I would lie down and die if anything happened to *our girls*. I pray every night for Julia. I pray for all of them. I hope at some point they can all find happiness. I want so much for all of them. I want Alexis to be able to take her birth name back at some point. I want them all to be whole.

"I wish, Charles, that we could find a way to bring Nikki and Jack together. They were meant for each other. Oh, look, Charles, a shooting star! Quick, make a wish!"

Charles squeezed his eyes shut as did Myra.

*"That was me, Mom. How'd you like that?"*

Myra's eyes flew open.

Charles bolted off his chair, his eyes wild.

*"Whatcha think, Charles? Was that nifty or what?"*

"Darling, time to go in, it's getting late."

Myra laughed, the sound ringing across the lawn. "That was the most spectacular shooting star I've ever seen."

"Beyond spectacular," Charles said.

# Chapter Fifteen

The gorgeous, orange ball in the sky slowly dipped beyond the horizon as the sisters leaned on the railing to watch it disappear.

They were dining by candlelight on the terrace this evening. Even though the table, the retractable, bright colored awning, and the crocks of brilliant flowers were cheerful, the mood was somber. There was no sparkling repartee, no poking one another in fun, no jostling. Even Murphy was subdued, lying on the top step of the stairs that led to the lawn that was greener than any golf course.

The table was set for six instead of the usual eight place settings. The French doors opened as Charles pushed a heavily laden serving cart onto the terrace. He tried to be cheerful when he rattled off the food he would be serving he knew no one was going to eat. He could have served dry shoe leather with ketchup and no one would have noticed or complained. He felt sick to his stomach and there was a knot in his throat as he ladled out food onto the fine china.

Charles watched as the women stirred and mashed and then stirred some more. He was right, no one was eating. Murphy looked up and then ignored what was going on.

"It was a beautiful day today, wasn't it, girls?" Myra said. The others nodded.

Myra tried again. "You all look so beautiful in your summer finery. I do love flower patterned dresses. I think they just make a person feel good." The others nodded.

Myra tried one more time. "Let's all have some cigarettes and beer."

"Now you're talking, Myra," Kathryn said as she got up and beelined for the kitchen. When she came back with a twelve-pack of

Corona beer she said, "With a few of these under our belts we'll be able to handle . . . maybe we'll be able . . . shit, never mind."

"I hate beer," Yoko said, as she squeezed lime on the rim of the bottle then upended it. "Where are the cigarettes? I never smoked before."

"And you won't be smoking after tonight either. This is a special occasion. Actually, it's beyond special," Kathryn said fiercely. "Just puff and blow the smoke."

A lot of coughing and sputtering went on to Charles's amusement as he fired up his pipe and leaned back in the springy chair he was sitting on. He didn't know when he'd ever felt this sad, this melancholy. The truth was, he wanted to cry for what was about to happen.

The cicadas sang their song and the night birds chimed in. The old oaks overhead whispered their own song. A faint quarter moon could be seen riding high in a sky sprinkled with millions of stars. The night was deliciously warm but no one seemed to notice.

"I'll have another one of these," Yoko said. "Beer is nothing like tea. I think I like it. Is it mandatory to smoke cigarettes when you drink beer?"

"Yeah, it is," Kathryn said, clapping her on the back. "Drink up. We have another hour to wait."

Twenty-four bottles of beer and two packs of cigarettes later, the women jumped as one when they saw headlights at the security gates. Murphy reared up and then leaped down the steps, raced across the lawn and howled a greeting to Alexis and Julia. Alexis stopped long enough to open the door for Murphy to climb in before she barreled up the drive to come to a screeching halt.

The occupants clustered into a tight knot on the terrace as they watched the two women follow Murphy. Alexis moved off to the side of the little group to watch the reaction of her sisters.

It was Julia Webster but it wasn't Julia Webster. The woman standing in front of them appeared to be in her late sixties with stooped shoulders, snow white hair and bright blue eyes. She was dressed for traveling in a cream colored suit. Wire rim glasses perched on her nose. She smiled and she was suddenly Julia Webster again. "What do you think? Even I didn't recognize myself when Alexis got through with me. Can I have a beer? I'll take a cigarette, too. By the way, I am now Penelope Tremaine. I have a driver's license, a Visa card, a Master Card, an American Express card and a passport to attest to my new identity, thanks to Charles."

Yoko stumbled all over herself and then giggled as she rushed into the house for more beer and cigarettes. She handed them over with a flourish. "Down the hatch!"

"Don't mind her, she's tipsy," Kathryn said.

"It's a nice memory to take with me." Julia smiled. "Listen, do all of you mind if I take a walk through the house one last time. Alone."

Heads bobbed up and down. Julia moved off, gliding across the terrace and through the open French doors.

Nikki chewed on her lower lip. Kathryn puffed furiously on a cigarette dangling from her lips. Yoko cried openly as Isabelle blew her nose. Myra clung to Charles's arm, her whole body shaking. Charles stared off into the distance as Murphy prowled the terrace from end to end.

"Is she going to be all right or not?" Kathryn growled.

"I don't know, Kathryn. I can't lie to you. The treatment is experimental. It's the only chance she has. We'll know in time."

"She doesn't have time, Charles," Nikki whispered.

"Yes, she does. How much, I can't say. She'll fly through the night and when she arrives in Switzerland, she'll be met by the best team of doctors and nurses in the world. Thanks to Her Majesty. Listen to me now. Even if it kills you, I want smiles. I want cheerful words. I want happiness. I want Julia to leave here with that memory. Do you understand?"

"The car is here, I can see the headlights," Isabelle said.

The sisters turned to see Julia outlined in the doorway. She, too, had seen the headlights. She backed her way into the kitchen. More attuned to Julia than the others, Kathryn dropped her beer and ran into the kitchen to see Julia looking at the plant on the windowsill. She sucked in her breath.

"You better not cry, Julia, or all that shit on your face is going to melt. The plant's alive. We saved it, and look, it's going to get a new leaf any day now. We gave it life, Julia. You and me."

"Don't let it die, Kathryn. Please."

"I promise. When you get back that plant is going to be as healthy as you will be. That's a Kathryn Lucas promise."

"That's good enough for me. Charles said we could call one another. You'll keep me posted on the plant."

"I will."

"I have to go now. I didn't think this was going to be so hard. What am I going to do without all of you?"

"You're going to be pretty busy, Julia. Go on now so we can all bawl our eyes out." Julia hugged her. Kathryn turned and kissed her on the cheek. "Go on, beat it." She stood at the kitchen window and watched as Julia said her good-byes. She held up until Murphy trotted over to Julia and put his huge paws on her shoulders to balance himself. He nuzzled her neck and growled deep in his throat. Kathryn dropped to her knees, her hands covering her mouth so she wouldn't howl as loud as Murphy.

And then Julia was gone.

# Epilogue

Midnight. The witching hour.

Charles took center stage. The others waited for him to speak. They all pretended not to notice how gruff and hoarse his voice was. "I'm optimistic where Julia is concerned. She's going to the right place for her now. Having said that, I suggest we leave Julia's chair empty for now. We're going to take a brief hiatus after we choose the next mission. Does anyone have anything to say before we begin?"

"I do," Nikki said, standing up. "Since you all left it up to me to decide who should get what of the Monarch monies, I made a decision. I awarded a $1.2 million-grant to the Justice Agency. A hundred thousand dollars a year. It's a brand spanking new agency headed up by ex-FBI agent Mark Lane and ex-ADA Jack Emery. If they file all the reports the way they're supposed to, we can keep tabs on them as they are keeping tabs on us. Win win, ladies."

"Bravo, Nikki!" Isabelle said. "I see it now, we're at loggerheads and it's male versus female. We're winning! They're no match for us." Yoko threw a pencil at her.

"It's been a month since . . . since the Monarchs and the senator were spirited away. Is there any news? Are you going to tell us where they are and how they're doing? Did you really send them off wearing loin cloths and . . . whatever that thing was Mrs. Monarch was wearing?" Kathryn asked.

Charles allowed himself a brief smile. "That thing was a muu-muu. I like to think of them as our guests. They are in Africa working on a farm. They get paid twenty-five cents a week. A week, not a day. When they arrived in Africa, they were whisked away to a clinic where all four of them were hypnotized and sent on their way. They believe they belong on the farm and have no recall about their lives here in the States. They will be evaluated from time to time. Their health will be seen to. I understand their appetites are hearty. Their futures have been taken care of. Any other questions?"

"In that case," Myra said, "let's get on with it." She reached for the shoe box and moved it in front of Nikki. "Choose a name, dear."

Nikki drew in a deep breath and reached for the square of white paper with a printed name on it. She unfolded it, opened it and announced: "Myra."

Myra slumped back in her seat as the others leaped off their chairs to gather around to congratulate her. She was teary eyed as she hugged the women who had become like daughters to her. "Is it really my turn?"

"You bet your sweet bippie it is," Kathryn said.

*"Nice going, Nik."*

Nikki turned around so she was facing the wall. "Is it OK, Barb?"

*"More than OK. See ya upstairs. Willie's waiting for me."*

Myra looked up at Nikki and smiled. "It's my turn, Nikki. At last."

Nikki nodded. "We'll do our best to make it come out right, Myra."

"I know that, dear. I know that."